TEXAS PRIDE

JEANNE WILLIAMS

FROM BESTSELLING AUTHOR
AND AWARD-WINNING MEMBER
OF THE WESTERN WRITERS OF
AMERICA COMES THE SWEEPING
SAGA OF A GREAT TEXAS FAMILY
THROUGH THREE GENERATIONS.
RICH IN HISTORICAL DETAIL,
JEANNE WILLIAMS'S NOVEL BLAZES
WITH THE HOPES AND THE PASSIONS,
THE JOYS AND THE HEARTBREAKS
OF A PROUD PIONEER LAND
AND THE COURAGEOUS PEOPLE
WHO FORGED ITS DESTINY
AND THEIR OWN!

Other Avon Books by
Jeanne Williams

THE CAVE DREAMERS
THE HEAVEN SWORD
SO MANY KINGDOMS

Coming Soon

A LADY BOUGHT WITH RIFLES

TEXAS PRIDE

JEANNE WILLIAMS

AVON
PUBLISHERS OF BARD, CAMELOT, DISCUS AND FLARE BOOKS

TEXAS PRIDE is an original publication of Avon Books. This work has never before appeared in book form. This work is a novel. Any similarity to actual persons or events is purely coincidental.

AVON BOOKS
A division of
The Hearst Corporation
1790 Broadway
New York, New York 10019

First Avon Printing: January 1987

AVON TRADEMARK REG. U.S. PAT. OFF. AND IN OTHER COUNTRIES, MARCA REGISTRADA, HECHO EN U.S.A.

Printed in the U.S.A.

K–R 10 9 8 7 6 5 4 3 2 1

For June and John
With love and admiration

Author's Note

This book began on a moonlit November night on a lease near Brownwood. John and June Wylie and Pete Williams were drilling a well there, and my good friends, John and June, brought me out to see it and to spend the night. As we sat by a fire and coyotes gossiped in the distance, John and June began talking about their families. Some of the stories I'd heard before, but as they reminisced, it struck me suddenly that between them, their families had been involved with oil from its beginnings in West Virginia and Pennsylvania, had been at many of the fabled booms, had drilled in Mexico, and to this day, although John and Pete have other careers, they drill on weekends and on vacations. In fact, it was from making coffee and tortillas while they poor-boyed a well near McCamey almost twenty years ago that I came to write a book for young adults about the oil patch, but I had never thought about using oil as the background for an adult novel until that night of memories at the rig.

The human stories were what beguiled me: June's great-grandmother orphaned during the Civil War, trudging with her younger brother all the way from Georgia to Texas; a Texas Ranger great-uncle who'd raised his motherless son in Ranger camps; a grandfather who got rich wildcatting and then sunk everything in the deepest cable tool hole ever drilled, went broke, and died within the year, some say of cirrhosis, some of a broken heart.

Later, John's mother, Irene Wylie of Albany, Texas, told me about her first home being a lean-to built against a lease shack and about what life was like in Ranger during the big boom. Her husband lost most of his right-hand fingers in the bull-wheel cable, but he continued to work in the fields.

This book would never have been, except for these friends. I owe John and June special thanks for reading the manuscript for accuracy. The characters are fictitious, of course, but several of them sprang from "what-ifs" I wove around my friends' forbears, and many incidents are true, though taken from experiences of numbers of people. My brother, Lewis Kreie, worked as a roughneck for a while, and I have also drawn on his recollections.

The world of my first heroine has little in common with that of her daughter and grandson, except for human loves and fears. The following books I found most useful, and believe they would also interest anyone with an appetite for more reading about those exciting days when the world changed with dizzying speed as new uses were discovered for oil, notably as fuel for engines:

Voices from the Derrick Floor by Paul F. Lambert and Kenny A. Franks (University of Oklahoma Press, Norman, Oklahoma, 1984) is a fascinating collection of first-person accounts transcribed from an oral history project. *Voices from the Oil Fields* by Mody C. Boatright and William A. Owens (University of Nebraska Press, Lincoln, Nebraska, 1982) are longer memoirs by drillers, roughnecks, tankies, shooters, and boom-town prostitutes. *Early Texas Oil* by Walter Rundell, Jr. (Texas A&M University, 1977) has fascinating photos of workers, rigs, blowouts, and boom towns, accompanied by a lively but accurate text. *The Greatest Gamblers* by Ruth Sheldon Knowles (University of Oklahoma Press, 1978) profiles the adventures of a number of famous wildcatters. *Folklore of the Oil Industry* by Mody C. Boatright (Southern Methodist University, Dallas, Texas, 1963) has tales of doodlebugs and seers, fabled oil-field workers, and songs and verse. *Early Day Oil Tales of Mexico* by Charles W. Hamilton (Gulf Publishing Company, Houston, Texas, 1966) is a gripping account of a young geologist's risky duties in the rich Golden Lane during the Mexican Revolution.

Of many sources, these were the most helpful and interesting, but the knowledge and assistance of June, John, and Pete have been indispensable.

Jeanne Williams
Cave Creek Canyon, Arizona
January 20, 1985

TEXAS
PRIDE

Book One _____

VINNIE

I _____

When they reached the Red River, twelve-year-old Vinnie McCready kilted up her skirts frayed from roads that stretched back to West Virginia, took her younger brother's hand, and splashed with him through mud and water. When they scrambled up the bank behind the Prichards' wagon, she hugged him and said, "We're in Texas, honey! Now we're in Texas."

Thos's yellow hair was plastered to his sunburned forehead. As he knuckled at sweat trickling into his blue McCready eyes, he stared from pines and red earth in Arkansas to pines and red earth in Texas.

"It looks just the same."

"Well, it's not," she insisted. "Texas is our home now, Thos. Of course, it's still a ways to Uncle Kirby's."

A mighty long way. Through pine-forested hills with mounds where Mr. Prichard thought Indians had buried their dead, into the broad, fertile Red River Valley where, as in the conquered Southland they had passed through, many fields were unworked and weed-grown but some new cotton showed green against the black loam. Through Dallas, a city of several thousand on the forks of the Trinity, where the Confederacy had headquartered its Commissary and Quartermaster departments for the trans-Mississippi armies and where there'd been a camp for Union prisoners. The center of trade for all the region, Dallas swarmed with Southerners whose home states had been so devastated by the war and Reconstruction that they'd come west to start fresh.

Two days across the Grand Prairie, Fort Worth was sadly different. A smithy, a cobbler's, and a few stores faced the unfinished limestone courthouse while the officers' quarters of the onetime dragoon outpost stood abandoned on the northeast side of the square. To the west stretched rolling plains, almost treeless except for those marking the Clear Fork and West Fork rivers, which united here to form the Trinity.

The Prichards were staying in Fort Worth with relatives who made up part of the twenty or so families that held on there in spite of fear of Indian raids. Aging and in poor health, the Prichards, who'd been neighbors of the McCreadys' in West Virginia and whose wagon the children had followed all that long way, offered to keep them, but Vinnie knew that was charity.

"We've got to get on to Uncle Kirby's," she said. "They don't have young'uns old enough to help, so we can be real useful."

And have a home again, with their own kin.

The Prichards found them a ride with a farmer driving to Waco, gave them all the food they could spare, and wished them well. As they rumbled along, Amos Blakely, a burly young man with a limp from a Yankee bullet, boasted that he had just sold a good wheat crop to the mill and that next year he'd grow more.

"Damn scalawags and carpetbaggers have it their way right now, what with that 'ironclad oath' a man has to take before he can vote, and there's Yankee soldiers, lots of 'em black, lording it over us because we're still under military rule. But we'll just tend our crops and wait. We'll get Texas back and young folks like you will help." He halted the wagon and stared at a cloud of dust. "Now what in all that's wonderful is that?"

The three in the wagon heard the lowing of cattle long before they saw them, heard muffled trampling increase till it reverberated through the earth.

"Cattle headin' north," said Amos. "But where they think they'll sell 'em beats me. Missouri's scared to death of Texas fever, and Kansas, Nebraska, Colorado, and even Illinois and Kentucky have laws against bringing in Texas cattle. Too bad, because those feisty old longhorns are about the only thing besides trouble that Texas has plenty of. Well, I'll get the wagon off in the trees so's we won't start any stampede."

To Vinnie, the dull thunder was like troops marching, only louder, like the Yankees who had burned their home and fields and Papa's oil. She shivered and made to put her arm around Thos but he shrugged away, eagerly intent on the sea of horns and long-legged, limber-tailed cattle ambling into view, roan and dun, black, white, mouse-colored, some wildly splotched, a bovine rainbow. And those horns! Some grew upward, some had double curves, and most were as wide from tip to tip as a tall man, some even longer.

One of the riders saw Amos's wagon and rode over to thank him for pulling aside. His pants were ragged but he wore hand-made boots, and with his red scarf and wide-brimmed hat, he was the most dashing young man Vinnie had ever seen. As she blushed delightedly, he swept off his hat to her.

"Looks like a lot of cows to take for a stroll to the Kansas border," Amos remarked.

The rider laughed. "Haven't you heard? Joe McCoy's just got the railroads to agree to build a siding at Abilene, Kansas, and ship our cattle to Chicago. Twenty dollars a head for these old mossyhorns we just choused out of the brush south of San Antonio. Here, if you sold one at all, you'd get maybe five dollars."

Amos remained skeptical. "How're you going to get them to Abilene?"

"McCoy fixed that, too. Long as the herd's shipped out of the state, we can trail through if'n we don't come within five miles of anyone's land without his say-so in writing." He grinned at the farmer. "I tell you, man, we're goin' to get rich sellin' those damn Yankees all the beef they can chew! Better trade that wagon for a running iron and go get you some cows."

With an airy wave and another dip of his hat to Vinnie, the rider fell in beside the herd. "By grannies, I may just do that!" Amos called to him. The cattle took a long time to pass, but Vinnie didn't mind the fine particles of dust and manure that tickled her nostrils. Here was hope. Here was something happening.

Thos's eyes shone. When they started on their way again, he said, so only Vinnie could hear him, *"Now* we're in Texas." Vinnie smiled but in her heart she knew she'd never feel at home till they got to Uncle Kirby's.

Amos let them out upon the rutted wagon road that led west to Kane's Fort, near which Kirby McCready had taken up land back before the war.

At Kane's Fort, really just a double log cabin with a log palisade, the storekeeper told them what they could scarcely believe.

Vinnie gazed at the big white stone on the bank above the river, at the names crudely scratched with a knife, three names and one date.

Lorena and Kirby McCready
Their little girl baby
Killed by Comanches
April 3, 1867

Aunt Lorena and Uncle Kirby had been killed just a few days before Vinnie and Thos had left West Virginia with the Prichards, a month after their mother died of pneumonia. Vinnie shivered. That poor little baby! Not even Yankees had killed babies, though they'd stolen all the food and burned fields and houses.

The Comanches had burned, too. Only a few charred logs were left of the cabin on the knoll above the graves. The outbuildings had been fired and a wagon lay splintered and overturned. The Kane's Fort folk who buried the bodies must have taken off anything the Indians might have left. There was a rosebush near the house, and though one side was withered from heat, the other part of the thick green mass was brilliant with yellow roses. The great live oak shading the yard had some withered limbs where the flames had reached but these were almost hidden by deep green leaves.

Every step hurt Vinnie's cracked feet, but she ascended the gentle slope and picked all the roses, every velvet-petaled sweet-smelling bloom, except the buds. She scattered these over the mounds and pulled Thos down beside her as she knelt. She tried to remember the words the preacher had used at Mother's funeral but grief overwhelmed her. How she'd hoped Aunt Lorena would be like their mother, that she and Thos could belong to a family again! And now there was no one left of their kin. Papa had died three years ago in a Yankee prison.

"'In my Father's house are many mansions—'" Vinnie's voice broke, and she added the only other words she could remember. "'The Lord be with you and with your spirit.'"

Thos snuffled. His face was puffed with mosquito bites and he was scrawny from short rations and ague, smaller than a nine-year-old ought to be. What he needed was some good broth. And a long rest.

"Vinnie," he whimpered, "what are we going to do?"

She caught in her breath, dizzy-sick with fear. Mr. Kane back at Kane's Fort had offered to take them in. For a few minutes, she was mightily tempted. She was tired, so tired, and now all their journey had brought them to was a gravestone. Her gaze wandered to the burned house. For the first time she noticed the apple orchard beyond it. There must have been several dozen trees and most were heavy with fruit. The raiders had raced horses through the corn but some eared stalks were still standing.

Her heart lifted just a little, enough to keep her from crying in front of Thos and scaring him worse. Uncle Kirby *had* left them something after all.

"We're going to stay here."

Thos's eyes widened. "But the cabin's burned! And those Comanches—"

"Mr. Kane said the Yankee soldiers went after them. Not likely they'll be back."

Gulping, Thos ducked his yellow head, whispering as if the dead might hear. "I—I'm scared to be where people got killed."

"Now, you look here, Thomas Benjamin McCready! This is our aunt and uncle and little cousin. If they're still around, they'll watch over us, not bring us any harm."

A tear streaked the scabby, sunburned face. "But we don't have food or beds or— we don't have nothin'!"

"I bet we can swap apples at the store for what we need worst. And we've got our sacks and what's in them."

Mrs. Prichard had sewn both of them sacks of heavy cotton, long enough to sleep on. These held their few extra clothes and, since their parting with the Prichards, their tin cups and spoons, flint and steel and a fry pan. Vinnie wore their father's hunting knife at her waist. It had heartened her considerably. "Come on, Thos. Maybe we can find some other stuff to use."

"Vinnie, I—I feel bad. I'm real thirsty."

Fear gripped her but she kept her tone matter-of-fact. "Well, then, let's fix you a nice bed and I'll bring you a drink."

She spread both sacks on the grass and bunched up her extra dress for a pillow. His poor little face! Mosquitoes had stung every inch of his bare skin; his fever might be coming from that. She wished she had some of the oil that seeped out of the ground on their place in West Virginia. It was good for bites and wounds. Pa had brought up the oil while drilling for salt, and since there was some market for it as medicine and for greasing wheels and machinery, he'd made a good sideline of it. The Yankees had set fire to the holding pond, which ignited other seeps and destroyed all the corn and sorghum.

Vinnie smoothed her brother's hair, once new-chick yellow, now dull and scruffy. "I'll be back right away." She got their cups and glanced down at the river.

They had drunk dirtier water but maybe there was a spring someplace. A path led down the rocks to the river but then veered in among high outcroppings where water splashed down the mossy stones. In high-water times, the river probably rose almost to the fresh water. She drank deep from the murmuring freshet as she filled both cups and noticed that the flow came from a small cavern. If it were big enough, it might be a place where they could shelter till something else could be contrived. She'd come back to see after she'd tended to Thos.

He drank both cups of water. She cut the ripest apple she could find into small chunks and got him to eat them. Then she went on a scavenging expedition.

A lot of melons had been split by hoofs and had long since rotted and dried to rinds, but there were a dozen good ones. She gleaned roasting ears for supper, rejoicing that there were some ears that neither raccoons, birds, nor Indians had ruined. The garden had been totally disdained by the raiders. It was full of beans, leathery but edible, onions, collards, and squash. There was even a rank, tangy stand of dill and what Vinnie thought were basil and rosemary plants.

Besides the blessed surprise of the garden, she found a dented bucket, a broken hoe, and an axe buried in the skull of a cow who had run out into the orchard to die. Vinnie felt they were gifts from her aunt and uncle and firmly decided to go on feeling that way; otherwise, she and Thos couldn't live here.

It lacked about an hour till sunset. She took the bucket and started toward the spring, circling the top of the small cliffs this time instead of going by the river. On the other side, she saw a scum-topped little pond. The water was thick and foul, yet oddly familiar. Going closer, she wrinkled her nose at the smell, then dropped to one knee, poking a finger into the blackish ooze.

Oil! Just like on the West Virginia farm. Leaving the bucket, she took as much as she could in her hands and ran back to Thos, smearing his face, throat, hands, and ankles. As she hurried to the spring, she rubbed the last of the oil on her own bites. It was like a sign, finding the familiar healing liquid. Besides, it was another thing she could sell if she could get some bottles. She'd call it Seneca Oil, like that sold for medicine from seeps the Senecas had used back in the East.

Vinnie set the bucket on the rocks beside the spring and entered the cavern. Inside the cool darkness, she waited till her eyes could make out a low chamber about ten feet wide through which the spring had cut a channel. The room narrowed to another passage, but she didn't want to venture farther without a light. The chamber was dry except for the stream. There didn't seem to be any bats or rival inhabitants. It was also a good hiding place. If Uncle Kirby's family had been here instead of at the cabin . . .

Vinnie swallowed the lump that rose, hot and choking. As long as she and Thos were alive there was at least something left of the family, what they had been, what they had hoped. If she ever had a little girl, she'd name her Katharine Lorena after her mother and aunt. And the first boy would be John Kirby for Father and his brother. But that was a long way in the future.

Leaving the bucket, Vinnie crept back through the opening and sped up the path to her brother, glad she'd found shelter, for the sun was almost down by then.

When she made a fire by the entrance, she saw that many others had done the same thing. The sides and roof of the cavern were smoked and pictures had been scratched here and there as if to while away time. Perhaps there had been storytellers too and children playing.

"It's scary!" Thos complained. "And you look like a witch or devil, daubed with that smelly old oil."

"So do you," she returned cheerily, setting roasting ears to cook in the bucket while simmering collards with onions and dill.

"We won't get wet if it rains, or hot when the sun's out or very cold at night. You don't have to carry water. I call it pretty snug."

"What if there's a bear or catamount in that next hole?" Thos fretted.

"If there was, we'd have met him by now." But to reassure Thos and satisfy her own curiosity, she took a flaming branch from the fire and, thrusting it ahead of her, crawled through a narrow corridor. The chamber she found herself in was no wider than the corridor but considerably higher, allowing her to stand. Water rushed from rock here, the source of the spring flowing out to the river.

Another hiding place.

On the third day of their stay in the cavern, Vinnie loaded a sack full of apples and walked the long five miles to Kane's Fort, following the overgrown wheel ruts.

"So here you be!" Mr. Kane was plump and rosy-cheeked with a little brush moustache and bald head. His small store and post office occupied one side of the double log cabin. "When you young'uns didn't come back the other day, some of us rode over to your uncle's place but we couldn't find hide nor hair of you." He lifted the sack up to the counter. "What's this you got? Apples!"

Vinnie explained their needs.

"I'm sorry, little lady," Kane said, rubbing his round chin. "Except for squirrels and such the boys bring in, no one's got real meat around here—won't till slaughtering time in a couple of months. I can let you have sowbelly and salt, a little sorghum and some cornmeal. Could be the missus'll spare a couple of eggs seein' as your brother's sick."

Eggs? Vinnie screwed up her courage. "Maybe there's a hen—a real old tough one?"

He gaped at her, scandalized. "The fight we have to keep varmints out of the henhouse, there's no way my woman'd part with one." He chuckled suddenly. "If you want a chicken, you'd ought to go over to Judge Bluebelly Sevier's. *He's* got chickens and pigs and cows and horses—everything the rest of us don't."

"He's a Yankee?"

"Hope to tell you he is." Kane spat on the warped puncheon floor. "Colonel in the war, he was, and lost an arm. Damn shame the minié ball didn't take the other arm and his legs, like it did our boy's. Anyhow, Colonel Judge Sevier inherited the best farm around from a cousin—who got killed fighting on the *right* side."

"Where does he live?" Vinnie asked.

It was wrong to steal—even from Yankees—but the starched-aproned black girl who came to the judge's back door wouldn't even talk about trading. Vinnie had sorghum and salt, cornmeal and two carefully wrapped eggs in her sack. She meant to add a chicken, even if she had to wait till it was dark. Mother used to make chicken soup when they were sick. Good hot bowls of it would surely put Thos on the mend.

If only one of those clucking creatures would jump over the sides of the pen! But no, the stupid things just ambled up and down, pecking here and there, often squabbling over the same tidbit.

Vinnie sighed and shifted on her haunches. Might as well admit it, she hungered for some chicken, too. But, she added piously, in case her folks somehow knew what she was doing, she wouldn't st—take a chicken if Thos didn't need it so bad.

The boards of the fence were too close together to reach through and the pen opened in view of the big white-painted house. Any prosperous-looking place that was painted and kept up these days you could be pretty sure was a Yankee house. Vinnie sighed again and slapped at a buzzing horsefly. It wasn't even noon yet! She couldn't squat here till night.

How could she make one of the hens flap over the pen? Nobody was visible in the yard, so maybe she could get away with causing a little commotion.

She tossed a small rock into the pen. Only the nearest hens squawked and hopped away from it. A thump on the fence didn't do much, either. Vinnie said cuss words under her breath and stealthily hunted for something to drop. A dead branch with numerous smaller limbs seemed just the thing. That bluebelly colonel judge would probably reckon it dropped of its own accord and harrowed up his chickens.

Making sure again that no one was around, Vinnie dropped the branch into the pen. Immediate din, shrieks, flying dust, and feathers. Not one but several plump red hens escaped their prison. Vinnie didn't overdo it, though. She grabbed the closest one, shut her eyes and twisted the neck.

It was awful! The thing flailed and jerked and struggled,

scratching Vinnie's arms and face. If she could have put it down and given back its life, she would have, but it was hurt too bad now. She had to grit her teeth and keep on twisting.

By the time the bird was limp, so was Vinnie. Never again would she kill another chicken, not unless somebody was starving. She shuddered at the way the lids had closed over its eyes, like transparent skin. Stuffing her victim in the sack, she swallowed the rise of bile in her throat and made off through the trees as fast as she could go.

While water heated to scald the chicken, Vinnie scrambled one egg for Thos and got him to eat it along with a little cornbread. Then, grimly, she took the bucket of boiling water outside and plunged the hen into it as she'd seen Mrs. Prichard do. The rank stench of soaked feathers turned her stomach but she carried the chicken some distance from the cave and plucked it, saving the feathers for a start on a pillow. The naked white skin looked so human that she knew she wasn't going to eat any of this bird. Thos could have it all. She cleaned it, clenching her teeth as she cut off the stiff yellow legs, and put it on to stew with herbs and salt and onions.

Suddenly the entrance darkened. She ducked back, snatching up the knife as a man entered. Even hunched over, he looked big, a monster. And he—he had only one arm!

The bluebelly colonel judge! Would he hang her? Put her in jail?

Gripping the knife, she crouched in front of Thos. "Get out of here!" she hissed. "You—you're trespassing!"

The man laughed, dropping to one knee but not crowding them. His eyes were so brown they could have been black except for their warmth. His hair was brown too, thick and curly with a glint of red, and so was his neat beard. His nose was large and hooked like an eagle's. He had a smile and a way of dancing his eyes that made you want to trust him even if you had just stolen his hen.

"Well, young woman, you could bring charges, but since I'm the judge, I doubt I'd give myself a long sentence. Suppose we say we're even—my trespassing and your, um, appropriating one of my fowls."

Vinnie thought of how ashamed her folks would be—a

McCready a common thief—and wished she could sink through the bottom of the cave. "I shouldn't have stolen it," she admitted, head drooping. "I'll work for you long enough to pay it off or—or I'll bring you a lot of apples."

He looked grave, even sorry. Was he going to say he was the law and couldn't let her off? "If you were hungry, child, why didn't you just come to the door and say so?"

She flushed even deeper. "I'm not a beggar!" Realizing that it was scarcely better to be a thief, she attacked from the depths of her humiliation. "You Yankees stole everything we had! You can't blame us for trying to get something back!"

"Indeed?" he asked coolly. "If you'll tell me what I stole from you, I'll make haste to replace it."

"Maybe you your ownself didn't, but Yankees burned up my pa's oil and our house and fields and woods."

He sighed. "I'm sorry for that. But you know it wasn't all on one side, little girl. I came home from the war to find out our neighbors had hanged my father, and forty other men, over at Gainesville because they were for the Union. And my mother died of sorrowing."

Vinnie didn't know what to say. He hadn't mentioned his missing arm but that must have hurt something awful. She'd never thought about bad things happening to the other side. "But you won!" she cried, exasperated.

"Someone had to." Neither of them had anything to say for a moment. Then the judge scooted forward a bit to peer at Thos. "Is the boy sick?"

Vinnie nodded. "He's had the ague and mosquito bites and when we got here and Aunt Lorena and Uncle Kirby were dead—" Tears overwhelmed her and she bit her lip to keep from sobbing. She wouldn't beg from a Yankee. If this man put her in jail, she'd have to see Thos was taken care of. "Why'd you sneak up on me?" she demanded. "Why didn't you just grab me at your place? You must've seen me take the chicken."

He grinned. "You're not the first to pillage my henhouse. I meant to follow you home and take it up with your parents. But when I saw you coming here, I decided to wait a little and find out what you were doing holed up in a cave."

"It's on our uncle's place! We have a right to—"

"Live like coyotes?" His gaze inventoried their few items

placed neatly against the wall. "This won't do, child. Your brother needs attention. You both should have proper food and clothing. I'm going to take you home with me for a while."

"This is our place! There's apples and collards and—"

"Don't be ridiculous," he said flatly. "As judge, I'm placing you both in my custody till something can be worked out."

Vinnie gripped the knife tighter.

The colonel judge shook his head. "Listen, if the apples mean that much to you, we'll drive the wagon over and pick them. You can save the money for when you're ready to leave my place."

She hesitated. Thos did need better care than she could give him. She was scared to trust a Yankee but she didn't have much choice. He certainly seemed lots nicer than Mr. Kane. "Can I work for our board? We won't take charity."

"If you're set on it, Hester'll keep you busy—after she feeds you up."

Hester must be his wife. How was she going to feel about two strange children, rebels, she'd probably call them? Vinnie pushed that worry away.

"When we come for the apples I'd like to bring some bottles and collect oil to sell. That'll help pay for any clothes we need."

The judge started to say something, but then his long mouth quirked and he only said, "Can you help me get your brother outside? Then I can carry him."

Vinnie turned to the steaming bucket. "But the soup! We can't just waste it! Not after—after—"

He laughed. "If I dine from my own hen, then it's no longer contraband, is it? All right. It smells good and we'll eat before we go." Vinnie sheathed the knife and reluctantly began to put their things into her sack.

An hour later, Mark Sevier lifted Vinnie with his one strong arm into the saddle of his handsome blood bay gelding. He set Thos in front of her before he led the horse up the slope past the burned shell of the cabin.

II ————————————————————————————

Tremendous oaks shaded the grounds of Belleforest. Tall white pillars reared from the ground to support the veranda roof, and there was a brick basement showing four feet or so above ground level. Broad stairs led to the veranda and into the hall with hand-carved columns on either side. There were five rooms on either side of the hall on the ground floor and the one above it, too. The hall was an open breezeway. Each room had a big fireplace that made Vinnie wince to think how much wood had to be cut, chopped, and carried in.

Of course, most of the upstairs rooms weren't used, the music room with its rosewood piano and satin-covered chairs, the drawing room with its somber paintings, sofas, and serving tables, or the formal dining room with a huge bevel-edged mirror that reflected the massive polished mahogany table and tapestry-upholstered chairs. The master bedroom was upstairs too, but the judge didn't use it, preferring the one downstairs next to his study. The adjoining family dining room had a comfortable-sized cherrywood table. The kitchen was behind that smaller dining room.

Across the breezeway were the library, two bedrooms into which Vinnie and Thos were moved, and Hester's room at the end. Out back was a brick bathhouse with a fireplace and big copper tub, a clapboard privy painted dazzling white with curtains

15

at the high windows, a smokehouse, wellhouse, stable, pigsty, and the fateful chicken pen.

The people who worked at Belleforest, or at the sawmill, which was owned jointly by them and the judge, had cabins scattered among the trees, most with garden plots and chicken pens. They had nearly all been slaves at Belleforest under its former owner. Some had drifted for a while after being freed but the government hadn't done much to help them get started, and when word passed that the new owner was hiring, many had been glad to go back to the familiar place. They had a clapboard church that served as a school during the week, and the community looked a good deal more prosperous than the scatter of farms around Kane's Meadow.

Hester, it turned out, wasn't the judge's wife but his housekeeper, once his childhood nurse, sold out of Indian Territory as a child by the Cherokee planter who was probably her father, for her skin wasn't much darker than Vinnie's sun-browned face. Hester was tall and straight and wore her thick black hair coiled at the back of her head. It was impossible to guess her age but she must have been nearly fifty because Mark was thirty-five. Her dark eyes slanted a bit above high cheekbones and her nose was straight and a bit snubbed, so that her profile put Vinnie in mind of a beautiful cat's. She wore her starched white apron only when supervising the cooking and her dresses were deeply flounced, maroon or blue or green. Always she wore gold chains and earrings.

She didn't make over Vinnie and Thos when the judge brought them home, but she knew what to do for the sick boy right enough. "No child that filthy goin' into my clean sheets," she said with her first glance.

"He's got ague," protested the judge.

"And lice too, I'll be bound."

"He doesn't!" Vinnie cried. "Most of that's oil on him!"

Hester scanned her. The straight mouth might have curved slightly at the ends. "You could do with a bath too, child. But your brother's first. He'll feel better clean."

He looked better anyway, smelling sweet of soap made with rose leaves, his yellow hair curling fluffily. Hester tucked him into the big bed herself and instructed him in a no-nonsense voice to drink the brew she'd made for him from a bitter pungent bark.

Grubby as it had been, the oil had taken away the mosquito swellings. Propped against plump pillows in a white shirt of the judge's, he looked so angelic that Vinnie whispered fearfully, "He—he's going to be all right, isn't he?"

"Why," said Hester, smiling for the first time, "give him a couple of days, he'll be frisky as a young tomcat. And now, missy, it's time for your bath!"

A tub of just-right warm water was placed on the stone hearth of the fireplace in the room that would be Vinnie's. As she scrubbed with scented soap, feeling as if all the bruises and weariness of the long ordeal were being washed away, she looked with disbelieving wonder at the carved poster bed with its blue canopy and flounced coverlet, the big polished dresser with a huge oval mirror, the pretty little "primping" sofa, the handsome wardrobe.

Could such elegant comfort be for her? As soon as she had dried herself on the soft towels, she put on the too-large dress Hester had found for her and slowly moved around the room, admiring the furniture, smelling the roses on the bedside table, stroking the satin coverlet. It was like a dream, she thought, blinking back thankful tears. But the colonel judge wasn't a dream. Oh, no! He was the most real person she had ever known. She felt that if she had to go away from him, then it was she who wouldn't be real anymore.

"There must be something you could call me besides 'Judge,'" Mark Sevier said plaintively that night at supper.

"I don't want to call you 'Colonel,'" said Vinnie, "because that—that's—"

"A Yankee rank?"

She dropped her eyes and nodded, squirming as Hester snorted. He had been mighty good to them even if he was a—

"'Bluebelly' won't do," he said, as if reading her mind, and laughed as she went crimson. "How about 'Uncle Mark'?"

"You're not our uncle." But that wasn't the whole reason. Nor was it his siding with the Union that made her unwilling to name him so. There was something deeper, something disturbing, strongly felt, though she couldn't identify it.

"Well, then, how about just 'Mark'?"

"Oh, no, sir! That wouldn't be respectful." She thought a minute. "Would 'Mr. Mark' be all right?"

He grimaced. "It beats 'Judge,' I reckon."

When they had finished big hunks of sherry cake with chocolate frosting, he took out a cigar. "With your permission, Vinnie?"

There was a twinkle in his eye but he wasn't being condescending. "Please do, Mr. Mark. I have to go see how Thos is."

Returning the cigar to an inlaid box, he rose and pulled back her chair. "I'll go with you."

Hester was just rising from the bedside, picking up a tray with an empty soup bowl and obviously diminished fruit plate. "He's drifted off to sleep," she murmured. "Ate good, though, and he's not fevered."

Vinnie thanked her. Thos did look almost himself again, though he was still peaked. She touched his hair, softly so as not to rouse him. When she glanced up, Mark was watching them with pain in his eyes, but he quickly smiled and bowed as he stepped out of the door to let her go first.

A few days later Thos was able to come to the table for meals, and by the end of the week, he was fishing with the other boys, running in the woods with them, and helping with chores. The laundry was done by the women who helped in the Big House, out under the shady tree where the white things could be boiled in a huge iron kettle and where there was plenty of room for tubs for washing and rinsing.

Determined to earn their keep, Vinnie tried to help in the kitchen but the cook, plum-skinned, billowy Cressida, would give her cake bowls to lick or offer tastes of whatever was cooking. It was Cressida's daughter, Fanny, who had turned Vinnie away the day she'd come asking to trade a chicken. At first she darted suspicious glances at Vinnie, but when she saw Vinnie wasn't going to betray her, she relaxed and was friendly.

Hester, seeing that Vinnie was in earnest about helping, suggested that she take care of her room and Thos's. When that didn't salve Vinnie's conscience, the housekeeper let her polish furniture and keep flowers in the vases that graced each room.

Vinnie was rubbing beeswax on the mahogany desk in Mark's study when he paused in the door, quizzically lifting one dark eyebrow. "What's this, child? I didn't bring you here to work."

She raised her chin. "McCreadys don't take charity, sir."

Startled laughter showed in his eyes and he coughed. After a moment's pondering, he asked, "Vinnie, can you read?"

"Yes, Mr. Mark. Mother taught us."

"You can write?"

She nodded. "I can cipher too, but I'm not good at fractions or square roots."

He nodded. "I think we can get along nicely without that." He crossed to the desk and sat in the straight-backed chair. For once he didn't turn his body to hide the pinned right sleeve. "What I really need, Vinnie, is an amanuensis."

"Sir?"

"A scribe." He grinned. "One who writes from dictation or copies manuscripts. I've tried to write with my left hand but it's well nigh impossible even for me to decode my hieroglyphs once they're cold. My records are in deplorable condition. Letters I should write are neglected, the journal I kept during the war lies untranscribed. I don't need another house servant, my dear, but I am in dire need of the aid you might be able to provide."

"But, sir! I just know a little, not the big words you'd use. And my penmanship's not very good. We didn't have any paper, just a slate."

"You can learn if you want to." His mouth twitched. "Of that I'm convinced." His eyes caught hers and wouldn't let them go. For the first time, she saw him as a human, not the powerful colonel judge of Belleforest but a mortal—godlike though he had become to her. "Vinnie. Be my right hand."

Tears blurred the face before her. She suffered physically for what had been his pain, for his irrevocable loss. She wanted to drop to her knees and press that other hand to her face.

Instead she said, "Teach me."

On days when he wasn't holding court at Pleasanton, the county seat, ten miles away, Mark sat in a big chair facing the desk and Vinnie took down his letters, decisions, charges to the jury, and, if there was time, wrote out his war journal as he read it, with the additions and changes he wanted to make.

He halted when he came to the first battle. "Maybe this isn't a good idea, Vinnie. What follows is ugly." He closed the journal. "I'd better employ a male secretary to do it."

"No!" she cried jealously, and gave a bitter laugh. "After all, we were right in the Yankees' path. They burned everything we had. I know what ugly things look like."

"I was on their side," he reminded. "That's bound to make it worse for you."

"I want to write it."

So he continued, but she was sure he was changing words, maybe leaving some out, for her sake. She put down the pen. "Make it true."

"You're so young."

"Forget about me." He looked dubious.

"You asked me to be your hand. I can't if you don't trust me."

After that, he softened nothing. Vinnie couldn't be just a hand, of course. Perched on the edge of the chair, she sometimes fought back tears or had to swallow bile that rose in her throat. She was seeing a man's soul, watching that man forged from a young man who fainted at the sight of blood to an officer who had to lead farm boys to slaughter and care about each one, yet go on—and lead others—when one was wounded or killed. *"I feel like a murderer, less of the Confederates than of these boys I have to urge onward, youngsters who've barely sipped of life. I doubt if most of them have ever had a woman. Certainly most have never sired a child."*

Mark closed the journal. "Enough for today, Vinnie."

Rising, he turned his back. She closed the ledger and dared to touch his arm. "Mr. Mark, those young ones, I bet they were proud to be your men. I bet they were mighty glad to follow you."

"That makes it worse. They're dead. I feel that I betrayed them because I'm alive." He shrugged and touched her hair. "Yet I'm glad to be alive. Especially since you came."

That light caress lit a glow of happiness within her though she was fearful of such bliss. It might be taken away.

"Maybe you have to live for those who died. Maybe you have to make up for what they didn't get to do." That was the only comfort she'd found for her mother's death; to remember her and try to raise Thos as Katharine would have done. "Anyway, you're writing about them. Their names, and what they were like, will be there, a hundred years from now."

"When you talk about a hundred years, young lady, none of us will have anything left except our reputations."

"There'll be our children's children."

His mouth twisted. "Twelve years old and talking like a matri-arch! You're an odd child, Vinnie."

"I don't know what that is," she said, hurt, "but twelve isn't —well, it's not a *young* child!" Besides, she'd turn thirteen in December.

His derisive look vanished. "I suppose not," he reflected. "In four or five years I expect we'll have young rascals tethering their horses three deep at the hitching post."

"I don't want any beaux."

"You'd better not, at your tender age!" He chuckled and caught her hand. "Come along, Vinnie. I'm starved and it smells like we're having biscuits for lunch."

She longed to understand Mark, so when, in writing or speak-ing, he used a strange word, she looked it up in the fat dictionary on its pedestal stand. A matriarch was a woman who was head of her family and rules them and her descendants. Vinnie couldn't do that. She wanted her husband to take care of any ruling that needed to be done and let her love the babies and tell them stories, take care of anyone who was sick, and have big family dinners with all kinds of good things and everyone happy. But she would never marry as long as Mark needed her.

School started. Hester taught reading, writing, and spelling to over twenty children from five to fifteen, including Thos, and on afternoons when he wasn't in court, Mark taught geography, his-tory, science, and civics. One of the freedmen who could read and write held classes at night for the grown-ups, and Mark spent an evening a week at the school, mixing history with how the gov-ernment worked and the rights and responsibilities of citizens.

To her delight, Mark asked if she would like to attend his classes. He opened a whole wonderful world with his globe and books. When Vinnie timidly asked if she might borrow Herod-otus, he took her to the library and showed her his favorites, especially recommending some that he placed on a table.

"Tell me what you think of these when you've read them. Don't struggle through something that doesn't make sense to you, but go on to another volume. And feel free to read anything here. After what you're writing down for me, nothing should shock you."

One afternoon as they left the schoolhouse, he frowned at her dress. "Can you ride a horse in that rig, Vinnie?"

She had been on horses a few times and just hiked up her skirts but now she realized that might not be ladylike. "I don't know." She held out the full skirts of sprigged muslin and regarded them critically. "Hester made this dress extra full and long since I'm growing so fast. I *think* I could ride."

Her heart leaped. There were some beautiful horses at Belleforest, and she loved to watch them, especially colts, gleaming chestnut, sorrel, black, and buckskin in the green pastures, cantering in play or resting heads across another's back. Horses were surely the prettiest things God ever made. She often took a carrot or apple to feed Mark's bay gelding, Selim, but she never dreamed she might be allowed to mount one of the splendid creatures.

"Let's give it a try," Mark said. "If you can't get aboard, we'll get Hester to fix you a riding habit, though they're a damn nuisance with all those yards and yards of skirt." He dropped his hand on Thos's shoulder. "You come too, son. I think we've got a pony just about your size."

They had a glorious ride. Vinnie was reluctant to go back to her own feet after the freeing excitement of skimming along beside Selim on a golden-cream mare with a silvery mane who was called Glory. Thos's eyes shone as he stroked a small, sturdy horse with dark brown spots on white.

"Do you like him?" Mark asked, giving Selim a pat on the muzzle as Lonnie, one of the stable men, came to lead the gelding away.

"Oh, he's—" Thos choked. "He's the best horse in the whole world, I bet!"

"Don't let the other horses hear that," said Mark, laughing. "Patches is yours, then. Go with Lonnie and learn how to rub him down and take care of his feet."

Thos stared, then let out a wild whoop and threw his arms as far as he could around Mark. "Oh, I—dang it, Judge, I—I'll work for you all my life and never ask for wages! I—I won't even go off and be a cowboy!"

Mark tousled the yellow hair and gave the boy a little shove toward the stable. "Oh, I think I can get Patches's price out of you by the time you're old enough to want to wander. Just remember

that you tend your horse before you worry about yourself. And
have a care for him; you're the one with the bit and the bridle. Be
sure he can trust you."

"Yes, sir, Judge!"

Smiling, Mark turned to Vinnie who had managed to slide
from the sidesaddle unassisted. "Does Glory suit you?"

"Oh—" Overwhelmed, it took her a minute to catch her
breath. "She's too wonderful, Mr. Mark! You can't give her to
me."

"Mmm." He rubbed his beard. "Well, maybe I could give you
custody of her, then, just as I'm in charge of you and Thos.
Would you take that responsibility? See that she has a nice trot
around when the weather's good?"

She looked at him suspiciously but he was grave. "I want to
groom her, too."

"Lonnie can do it."

"No, please! If I'm going to ride her, I want to look after her."

"All right. Take her to the stable."

She did, caressing Glory and whispering to her. Tears stung
her eyes. Mark was so good to them. How could she ever, ever
pay him back, even a little?

He hadn't forgotten his promise about the apples and oil, either. Caleb, the graying servant who had been with him through
the war, collected several of Thos's friends and took them, Thos,
and Vinnie over one Saturday in the wagon with a lot of empty
boxes which they filled with apples.

Proudly delivering most of the crop to Kane's store, Vinnie
took some of the value out by letting the pickers select fifty cents'
worth each from Kane's shelves. She tried to pay Caleb but he
shook his head; he was a deep brown man who didn't have a
wrinkle but whose dark eyes seemed to know all the grief in the
world and some of the joy as well.

"The colonel's done taken care of that, Miss Vinnie."

"Well, at least I want you to carry a box of apples to your
wife," Vinnie insisted. "Two boxes are for the Big House, but the
rest are for everybody."

"That's nice of you, Miss Vinnie."

"Not as nice as you all are to me," she said and smiled, enjoying the heady pleasure of having something to give.

It was pleasure of another sort to put almost eight dollars in a marmalade jar Hester gave her. It was kept on the marble-topped mantel of the fireplace in Vinnie's room along with her other treasures; the family Bible she'd carried all the way from West Virginia, and a rose, dried now but still fragrant, that Mark had given her one morning. It was past the time for roses. She'd found a few on the bush by the ruined cabin and taken them to her aunt's and uncle's grave. She'd never asked but she hoped they were buried together, with their baby in their arms, not shut off in separate places.

The memory brought a sharp stab of longing for her mother and father. It was hard to believe she'd never see them again, never in this world. Something that hurt her so much she could scarcely bear to think about it was that her mother had never had a lovely room like this.

Desolation washed over Vinnie, grief for what could not be remedied. She got the Bible down and pressed it to her cheek, thinking of the many hands that had held it since the first entry made a hundred and fifty years ago in an English village. Maybe, in trying to console Mark about his dead comrades, she had been right. She couldn't do anything for her mother but she could do things Katharine would have liked to do. She would try.

Besides that inner promise, this was a day she wouldn't forget because she had tasted the delight of giving, and of possessing money of her own. It was impossible to say which felt better but each made Vinnie feel powerful.

At the store she had bought bottles and some candy for Hester. The first time Mark had to attend court, she asked if she could ride over to what they had started calling the Orchard Place. Yes, said Mark, if she took Caleb.

On that morning she filled the bottles at the oil seep above the cliffs. Mr. Kane paid ten cents a bottle. He said he could use about ten bottles a month. More money for the jar. For, happy though they were, she and Thos couldn't stay at Belleforest always. When they went to live at the Orchard Place, she didn't want Mark to think he had to get them started. She meant to have a start.

The sidesaddle Vinnie used was beautifully made with silver mountings. One afternoon she asked if it had been Mark's mother's.

His shoulders tensed. "It was my wife's."

"Your wife's?"

"Yes."

"But—is she dead?"

"I don't think so." At Vinnie's amazement, he sighed. "Regina's family favored the Confederacy. After my father was hanged, she went back to live with her parents. I'll credit them with giving me shelter when I came home to convalesce after losing my arm. It was hard enough on Regina to have a husband with the Union; she couldn't stand my not having the arm— shuddered when I held her. I went back to the front. She went off to Louisiana with a second cousin who'd gotten a genteel wound in the leg, just enough for a heroic limp."

"You don't know where she is?"

"No. And I damn well wouldn't care, except she has our son."

Again, Vinnie echoed, "A son?"

Mark nodded. "He must be your age by now. Maybe they told him I was dead. Maybe they made him ashamed of me."

Ashamed? Vinnie ached. For the first time in her life she knew hatred for a person, not the fear-hate she'd felt for the Yankees when they burned everything, but loathing for the woman who could desert Mark. Now Vinnie understood the hurt in his eyes when he was watching Thos.

She tried to learn a little more from Hester but the tall woman's face only looked more carved. "He's well shut of Miss Regina and Mr. Fayte too, I reckon. Always liked to hurt animals, that boy did. Good thing he won't never have slaves."

"Was—was Miss Regina pretty?"

"No. Beautiful. Creamy skin and hair between gold and fire that shone brighter than either one. Eyes like wood violets the sun never touched. Moved like a queen. Mr. Fayte took after her, more's the pity for the women he'll ruin."

"Fayte? That's a peculiar name."

"Short for LaFayette. Always been a LaFayette in Miss Regina's family back to the war with the Britishers."

"I wonder if—if they'll ever come back?"

"I pray not," Hester said. "Every night when I ask the Lord to bless Mr. Mark, I ask for that."

Maybe she was right. It might be better not to have your son with you than to have him break your heart. All the same, Vinnie suffered for Mark.

III _____

The marmalade jar filled several times in the next two years.
Vinnie traded coins for bills and small bills for larger ones. There
was over a hundred dollars. She was selling more oil through Mr.
Kane because people were using it as a lubricant. Now that fields
were producing again, wagons rolled north to market in Waco or
Dallas, and of course, since the war, there had been a venture-
some stream of dispossessed Southerners heading west to settle in
lands still roved by the Comanches who took their tribute of yellow hair and captives.

The cattle drives multiplied, bringing new prosperity and
creating great ranches, but except for their chuck wagons, the trail
drivers didn't need Vinnie's oil.

On her trips with Caleb to collect oil, Vinnie always left
flowers or a bouquet of winter pods and grasses on her kinfolks'
grave and cleared rubble away from the cabin. It would be a
lovely place to live, above the wooded river, gazing across gently
rolling slopes, gold or green, according to the season, that met the
serene blue of the sky. In spite of the awful thing that had happened there, Vinnie had a sense of great peace, as if Aunt Lorena
and Uncle Kirby were glad she was at their earthly home.

It was a tranquil life at Belleforest. They didn't attend church.
The war, with both sides claiming God's support, had made Mark

scornful of organized religion. Every six months or so, he took
Hester, Vinnie, and Thos to Waco thirty miles away. While Mark
tended to business, the others shopped and wandered around the
live oak-shaded town. Theirs was one of the first carriages to use
the suspension bridge that replaced the old ferry in early January
of 1870.

That bridge, the judge complained, was the ruination of Waco.
Almost overnight, its sleepy old-South dignity was lost in the roar
of trail herds and freighting wagons. Cowboys and buffalo
hunters let off steam in false-fronted hotels and gambling dens.
Mark declared the city unsafe for women, and after that, Hester
and Vinnie gave Mark lists for Waco. Not that they needed much
that wasn't made at Belleforest or available at Kane's.

One crisp autumn day when sumac was flaming and oaks
turning yellow, Vinnie and Caleb left their saddlebags of bottled
oil at Kane's and rode silently, enjoying the fine day with its trace
of summer, heat mellowed to a caress. They were in sight of
Belleforest's outbuildings when she saw a bright-haired man sitting on a stump, engrossed in something that fluttered in his
hands. Even at this distance she could hear a faint, desperate
cheeping.

Maybe he had found an injured bird. But . . . what was he
doing? Tossing feathers away? At a touch of Vinnie's heels, Glory
stretched into a gallop. The man—no, he looked close to Vinnie's age though he was tall—glanced up as she halted.

Shock took her breath away. The eyes that looked her over
were Mark's, warm brown with thick dark lashes and strongly
arched brows. But one of the hands that held a convulsing bluebird was poised to pluck out more feathers from an almost naked
wing.

"Stop that!" she cried, scrambling down from Glory, tripping
on her skirts in her haste. "Why are you doing that?"

"I wondered if it could fly without feathers."

"You—you—" She found no words for her horror. "Give it to
me!"

He turned lazily to Caleb, who had pulled up to gaze at him in
undisguised consternation. "Tell her who I am, Caleb."

"What are you doin' here, Mr. Fayte?"

The thin-faced, handsome lad hunched a shoulder. "Not a fit-ing way to welcome the young master home, old man. This must be the orphan the judge took in."

"I don't care who you are," Vinnie cried, advancing. "Give me that bird."

His eyes narrowed as he studied her, then glinted with amusement. "All right."

He put it in her hands. The other wing was already stripped. The bird had stopped struggling and its eyes were dulling. Vinnie cuddled it to her breast but the heart ceased thudding beneath her fingers. It wouldn't start again.

When she was sure it was dead, scarcely able to see through tears as furious as they were pitying, Vinnie took it over to a hollow in an oak trunk, made it a nest of leaves and covered it with more.

Fayte was still there when she finished. He seemed less cocksure now. "I suppose you'll tattle to the judge."

"No. I don't want him to know his son would do such a thing." She hated to meet those eyes so like the ones she loved. "I hope you go to hell."

Caleb helped her mount and they rode for Belleforest, with dread, this time. Was Regina there? Even if only Fayte had come, Belleforest no longer seemed like home.

Vinnie was glad she could slip into her room without passing Mark's study, from which came voices, one of them a crystal slash across Mark's deep, muted tones. Vinnie went cold with apprehension though she tried to tell herself that if Mark still loved his wife, it was good she had returned. That didn't quench the elemental serpent-writhing of jealousy. As Vinnie put the oil money in the jar, she told herself she might need it sooner than she'd thought.

It later seemed to Vinnie that Regina grasped the strands that made up the contented peaceful fabric of their lives and snarled them into a tangled mess. The only comfort was that she spent much of her time upstairs in the elegant rooms that were opened up for her and Fayte. She refused to take meals in the homey little dining room by the kitchen. Vinnie, writing letters for Mark, was an unwilling listener to arguments that changed their relaxed, pleasant suppers into stately meals in the formal room above where, in shimmering mockery, great French mirrors reflected the constrained household.

"Really, Mark," began Regina, sweeping into the study without apology or a glance at Vinnie and breaking into Mark's dictation. "The least you can do is acknowledge your wife and son by dining with us."

Mark gave her a blank stare. It was impossible to guess what he felt for the woman whose violet eyes fixed on him in accusing appeal. Regina's golden-red hair was piled in a knot at the top of her shapely head from which waving locks strayed over creamy smooth shoulders. A widow's peak softened her rather long face to a piquant heart shape. Her small teeth were perfect, her lips a trifle thin. She had a high, virginal bosom that made Vinnie feel that her ripening breasts were gross.

This sense of awkwardness was compounded when they stood near each other, for though Regina carried herself imperiously erect, Vinnie was several inches taller and felt all bony legs and arms and hands; Vinnie's cuticles and nails were always ragged, and she chewed and tore at them the more because Regina's were so exquisitely kept.

As Regina advanced on Mark, Vinnie tucked her fingers out of sight. She needn't have bothered. Regina ignored her as Mark passed a weary hand across his eyes. "It was your choice to dine upstairs," he reminded his wife.

"It's the correct place for the *family.*"

He got up and strode to the window, turned his pinned sleeve aggressively toward her. "Regina, I have eaten downstairs with more content and pleasure than ever I did in that damn room of mirrors."

"I brought our son back so you'd teach him how to take his place in society. You owe it to him to behave like a gentleman."

Mark gave a strangled laugh. "I've behaved like a gentleman —or a damn fool—in not throwing you out." He saw Vinnie and clamped his jaws shut. His eyes warred with Regina's. "If we're to occupy the same house, there must be compromises. We'll dine upstairs though I shall have my other meals below. And you, madam, will undertake to teach our son, by word and example, that the recent war settled at least one thing in this country. There are no slaves."

Regina colored. "Nor decent servants, either, Mark! I vow

I've never seen such a parcel of insolent lazy darkies! Hester's the worst. Just because she stuffed your mouth with sugar tits when you were an infant, she acts as if she were mistress here, not I!"

His eyebrows drew together. "I thought I'd made it clear, Regina. You are not mistress here, in truth, as you are no longer, in truth, my wife. For Fayte's sake and to discourage scandal, you may keep the semblance of both so long as you behave with some discretion."

The regal head bowed. Tears sparkled beneath dark lashes. Regina took a step forward, putting out a graceful hand. "Must you be so bitter? Mark, I—"

He swung around so abruptly that she almost touched his empty sleeve. She recoiled. "Damn you!" Her skirts swirled as she turned and stalked from the room.

"I'm sorry you had to hear that, Vinnie." Mark came to stand by her, gave her a crooked grin. "Not very seemly, was it? But note that she got her way. We'll all sit around that mammoth table at night, mum as boiled oysters."

Vinnie's stomach shriveled. "Not Thos and me, Mr. Mark! Mrs. Sevier said family."

He scowled. "You are my family. Anyway," he added in that tender, teasing tone that made her heart swell, "you'd never condemn me to be up there without a friend?"

What else could Vinnie do but brave Regina's frozen gaze and take her place that evening at the huge table? At least she and Thos faced each other across the broad expanse of damask, china, and silver, and if they stretched, they could pat each other's toes.

Regina could not believe that Vinnie was capable of serving as Mark's secretary. When his war memoirs were accepted for publication by a prestigious New York publisher, his wife could not contain her spite.

"It's bad enough that you fought against your homeland, Mark. Now, when people are just starting to forget that, why do you have to rake it up again? And no doubt you crowed about winning?"

"Nary a crow," he said with the calm good nature he ordinarily used with her. "If you'd read the manuscript, you'd know it's about the tragedy of young men dying because old men on both sides couldn't settle their differences."

"You can't blame me for not wanting to wade through a manuscript that was bound to be full of misspellings and errors."

"Doctrinal errors as you see them, perhaps." Mark's smile had an edge. Vinnie knew he had been hurt when Regina scornfully refused to even glance at his book, and she suspected, from the way she sometimes saw him watching his wife, that he still loved her though he continued to sleep downstairs. "However, Vinnie spells much better than you, my dear, and immeasurably better than Fayte. His education must have been sadly neglected in Louisiana."

"What would you expect with a war on?" Regina jabbed. "He can ride and shoot, you must admit. A gentleman doesn't need to burrow around in books and ledgers."

"He'd better be able to keep accounts or examine the ones prepared for him," Mark returned. "And unless Fayte intends to be a doctor or lawyer, he'd better improve his penmanship. He hasn't the faintest idea of geography and his history consists of parroting your Louisiana kinsmen's opinions on why the Confederacy lost the war. He has, in short, all the prejudiced ignorance of Southerners from a generation ago."

"How dare *you* complain of *him?* He thrashed a bigger, older boy almost to death because the boy taunted Fayte with your being a bluebelly!"

Mark sighed. "That's what I mean. He has to learn violence won't wipe out facts. A small academy is opening in Pleasanton. I've enrolled Fayte."

"He's not riding that far in bad weather to suit a whim of yours!"

"No. He'll stay at the school through the week and come home weekends."

"He—he's too young to be away from home."

"He's nearing fifteen. Boys that age fought in the war. He needs instruction, discipline, and most of all, he needs to get away from constant spoiling."

"You're jealous!"

"I confess that I'm sorry we aren't better friends. But you brought him home because you decided rather tardily that he needed a father. I'm going to do my best to see that he grows into a decent, capable man even if neither he nor you thanks me for it."

Regina's teeth showed between her thinned lips. "I came home because my cousin died gallantly for the South and his family was left too destitute for me to burden."

"And you preferred appealing to your bluebelly husband to going to work," Mark said unemotionally.

"I came to give our son his rightful place."

"Most devoted of you. And I intend to see he's fitted for it." Mark rose and escorted Regina to the door. "Kindly see that he has whatever clothes he needs packed by Sunday. We'll take him in the carriage so that you may scrutinize the place and satisfy yourself that it's not the Black Hole of Calcutta."

When Regina was gone, Mark turned to Vinnie who, face averted, was diligently making a copy of the draft of a letter Mark had read over and verbally corrected. Except for a half-embarrassed smile, he had long since stopped apologizing when Vinnie was forced to witness Regina's tempers.

"It seems set up as a good school, Vinnie. Would you see if Thos wants to attend?"

She thought of the carefully hoarded money in the jars. She hadn't thought about school for Thos beyond what he got at Belleforest. But how pleased their parents would have been for one of their children to attend a real academy! Why, with that sort of start, Thos might become a doctor or lawyer or—or anything! If he were willing, he should go, and if it took more money than they had, she was sure Mark would lend it.

Thos demurred with genuine horror. "I'm learning all I can use right here," he said. "I'm not like you, Vin. I don't like to read as long as I can be outside doing something. Anyway, I reckon it'd cost like hallelujah."

"We've got over a hundred dollars, Thos."

"That's to start our farm. Of course, I'll earn a bunch more when I'm a cowboy."

"A cowboy! They spend all their wages drinking and carousing!"

He grinned, brown from the sun, hair bleached almost white. Nearly twelve, he had started shooting up so fast that he could look directly into Vinnie's eyes, and she was five foot six. "Sounds like fun to me. You're the one ought to go to school, Vin."

"Now, that's a good idea, Thos, even if I don't want to lose my right hand." Mark stepped into the downstairs dining room where Vinnie was setting the breakfast table. "Waco University admits females to be educated along with men and there are several other estimable female institutes in Texas."

Vinnie had never dreamed of further schooling. Now she had a rapt moment of imagining teachers who could explain all the things she didn't understand. But Mark did that already. His library had hundreds of books she hadn't read, with more continually coming in. She loved helping Mark but someday she wanted to make a home at the Orchard Place, farm, and have a family.

"I don't need to go to school, Mr. Mark. You can tell me everything I want to know."

"That's flattering, but it won't be true much longer." He shrugged at her determined look. "Don't be too proud to tell me if you change your mind."

Except at formal evening meals, Vinnie had seen little of Fayte, and she was relieved to know he'd soon be gone most of the time. Regina moped and was more brittle-tempered than usual. Fayte came home the first weekend with a black eye, but when his mother wailed and fussed over him, he evaded her.

"It's all right, Mama. I gave the one who did this two black eyes and a split lip. He bossed the class. Now I do."

"But darling—"

"The masters are bores but some of the fellows are fun. Clay Mannering's asked me to his place next week. He's got some fine hounds and we'll go hunting."

"You'd rather racket around with some coarse backwoodsman than visit your mother?" she asked in wounded tones.

"For Pete's sake, Mama! It's deadly dull here!" He caught her hand and wheedled. "Let me go with Clay this time, Mama, and I'll come to Belleforest the next weekend."

"It'll be good for Fayte to make friends and be out on his own," Mark said.

After that, Fayte spent more weekends with other boys than he did at the place he never called home. Regina brooded but then began to entertain, though, as she told Mark crossly, the best old families had either been ruined by the war or would have nothing to do with the family of a judge who had fought for the Union, even if he hadn't compounded his odiousness by being appointed by the hated Reconstruction government.

But since there were plans for a railroad to pass through, a few acceptable professional people had moved to Pleasanton. So a doctor, an attorney, some railroad executives, a few large property owners, and their wives were invited to elaborate dinners or musical evenings when Regina, glorious hair flaming in the light of the crystal chandeliers, sat at the rosewood piano and played so skillfully that the other ladies' performances were pathetic.

Such beautiful music! Vinnie and Thos didn't join the company dinners, but Mark urged them to be in the drawing room for at least the early part of the musicales. One night as Vinnie longingly watched the deft grace of Regina's long fingers on the keyboard, Mark gave her a searching gaze. At the first pause in the program, he said, "Vinnie, would you like to take piano lessons?"

"Oh, I— The piano's too grand for me to touch."

"That's what it's for."

The day after Mark's next court day, Herman Gottfried appeared. He was short, ruddy-faced, and his waistcoat bulged, but his hazel eyes were shrewdly kind. When Vinnie protested that she could never learn, he said briskly, "Do you think me so poor a teacher, Miss Vinnie? Slow it may be for I am thorough, but if you will practice an hour a day, in a month you will be playing tunes. In six months you will be a pleasure to hear."

"So go along with you," Mark commanded. "I have some cases to study and the letter we were doing can wait till morning."

Herman was the son of immigrants. Like most Texas Germans, they had been loyal to the Union, and Herman had fought for it. The stout little man with frizzy hair that formed two horn-like protuberances above his wide forehead certainly lacked a military bearing, but Mark told Vinnie that Herman had dared withering fire to rescue a wounded comrade and drag him to safety beneath the shield of his body. Herman never mentioned the war. He devised finger exercises that sounded like music and was so encouraging that Vinnie, in her free time, read less and practiced more. She tried to do this when Regina was paying calls or riding, but one day her absorption was pierced by an uneasiness that grew till she glanced toward the door.

Regina was watching with a faint smile. Crossing to the piano, she examined Vinnie's hands, which turned lifeless. "Such stubby short little fingers," Regina murmured, curving her own tapering ones with their perfectly shaped, rosily buffed nails, around Vinnie's. "A pity, when you practice so strenuously, that you'll never have the reach for really good playing—like this."

Sliding Vinnie almost off the bench, Regina effortlessly played what Vinnie now knew enough to recognize as a technically demanding piece, smiled brilliantly, and rose. "Never mind, dear." She gave Vinnie's scratched, rough hand a pat. "You won't have any occasion for performing, will you, once Mark feels he's fulfilled his duty to you and your brother?"

"Duty?"

"Of course. You can't really think Mark wouldn't be better served by a real secretary?" Regina's laugh was like tinkling crystal. "It must be that, through you two, he's trying to make up for the orphans of Confederate soldiers he killed."

Having taken down Mark's journals, Vinnie knew better than anyone that such guilts did afflict him, but she didn't completely believe Regina. She doubted if Mark could have bared his feelings to another man, perhaps not even to another adult, but the memoirs were done. The thought that Mark kept her on out of duty was intolerable.

As soon as Regina's steps stopped sounding on the polished oak floor, Vinnie carefully put down the top of the piano and went to Mark's study.

"No, I don't want a male secretary," he told her with asperity. "I don't even have to dictate most of my letters anymore, just give you the gist and you deck it out with all the polite verbiage." His furrowed brow smoothed suddenly. "Have you decided to go to school, Vinnie?"

"No, I—I just thought maybe you needed someone experienced."

He snorted. "Devil take it, you are experienced. You've had two and a half years with me. It's been a blessing not to have to train you away from habits learned elsewhere. You fit me like a glove fits a hand."

At the last word, they both glanced involuntarily at his empty sleeve. He sighed and touched her cheek. "Vinnie, I won't be selfish. Someday you'll marry and I'll be happy for you. But till then, unless you want to go to school, can't we take it for granted that we're both content unless one says otherwise?"

Marry? She couldn't imagine there'd be a man for whom she'd

want to leave Mark. The only dream she had that was separate from him was the dream of living at the Orchard Place.

Her throat was tight. She nodded, and after a moment was able to ask in a normal tone if there was anything he wanted her to do.

She had no heart to practice, though. When she started to raise the piano cover, she saw how Regina's slim hand would do it, how smoothly those white fingers would range over the keyboard.

"You have not been practicing," Herman accused at their next lesson. His eyes dwelled on her with reproachful surprise. "I had not expected, Miss Vinnie, that you would prove lazy."

Her cheeks burned. She spread out her hands. "Look, Mr. Gottfried! My fingers don't reach far enough! I'll never be able to play very well. There's no use in your wasting time on me."

His eyes widened, then grew thoughtful as he tried to smooth down one of his frizzy horns. "Child," he said, "how well do you want to play?"

Vinnie frowned and considered. "I love making music," she said at last. "I guess that's mostly it. But I'd like to be able to play for—for people I care about. When there are things words can't say, I'd like to play them."

"You do not, then, crave to be a concert pianist? Or play for a large church?"

Even had she possessed the talent, nothing could have induced her to do either one. Her laughter echoed through the drawing room. "Gracious, no, Mr. Gottfried."

"Then why deprive yourself of the joy?"

"I won't have a piano after I leave Belleforest." At his puzzled look, she explained. "I won't have enough money to buy one."

He chuckled. "Oh, if that is all! You may be able to buy a dozen pianos before you're my age. You might even marry a man who'd give you one." She looked doubtful. He smiled in the way that made a person forget he was short and fat and funny-looking. "If you learn while you're young, it will come back to you when you're ready. And meanwhile you can have the pleasure for as long as you're here. Now then, try those scales again. Not timidly! Make the notes sing!"

IV _____

No one except Regina was glad when the school year ended and Fayte was home again. He had cronies now, though, and spent much of his time with them. The drawback to that was times when the rowdy crew swooped down on Belleforest like plunderers. Raiding Hester's fresh baking and deriding the lemonade she and Vinnie served, they drank it thirstily enough while Clay Mannering, a hulking sandy-haired lout, and some of the others bragged that *their* fathers let them drink whiskey.

This may have been true. More than once Vinnie smelled alcohol on them. Fayte had turned fifteen in March. Tall as his father but willowy in build, his hands and feet and head looked too big for the connecting parts. He would be a handsome man but Vinnie didn't like to look at him. She always remembered the way they'd met.

On June 19, the Belleforest people celebrated "Juneteenth," the anniversary of the emancipation of Texas slaves. Mark provided a beef to barbecue and the feasting and dancing went on until morning. At dinner, Regina looked icily at Mark.

"You have no respect at all for the brave men who died for their country, do you? Encouraging those darkies to prance and shout about their freedom while your homeland is a conquered province with Yankee heels still on our necks!"

"As soon as Texas ratifies the Thirteenth, Fourteenth, and Fifteenth Amendments, it'll be readmitted to the Union."

Fayte sneered. "If niggers get the vote by law, I bet they can still be discouraged plenty. Once those bluebelly troops leave the state—"

Mark's voice cut into Fayte's. "Son, I'll remind you that I wore that uniform."

Fayte turned dull crimson. "You don't have to remind me, Judge. Do you think I'm ever allowed to forget it? It's lucky my friends don't hold what you did against me."

Mark looked at his son till Fayte dropped his eyes, so like Mark's yet so unlike. "No doubt you shout the Rebel yell louder than anyone," Mark said. "Do you ever give a thought to the grandfather who put you up on your first pony and was so proud of you? Do you ever think how it was for him—and thirty-nine other men—to die at the hands of their neighbors?"

"The fellows at school say they were Jayhawkers," Fayte muttered.

"Do you believe that about your grandfather?"

Mark's white-hot anger quelled Fayte. "No. I mean, I didn't know what to think."

"I can tell you that your grandfather never did a dishonest thing in his life. I know the people who hanged him and the others gave out that they'd been to blame for Indian depredations and other thievery, but most of them died pure and simple because they were Union men." At Fayte's sullen look, which said plainer than words that he considered that reason enough, Mark took a deep breath. "You were too young to remember, son, but a good third of Texans didn't want to secede, Sam Houston among them. He was governor at the time and when he wouldn't take an oath of allegiance to the Confederacy, he was put out of office and died two years later, an impoverished old man. That was his reward for winning Texas's independence from Mexico. Once the state seceded, most citizens went along, but at least two thousand men fought for the Union. It's your right to think we were mistaken, but there was nothing treacherous about it. *We* thought the treachery lay with those who voted to secede."

Fayte's eyes blazed. He trembled as if swayed in a high wind. "Sir! If you weren't my father, I'd call you out for that!"

"Well, then, isn't it lucky for both of us that I am?" Mark

inquired equably. He had control of himself now and his smile must have infuriated Fayte even more. "Dueling's been against the law for years, my boy. You need to realize that the life your Louisiana cousins led is gone forever."

"There still is honor!"

"Yes. Several definitions of it, I'm afraid."

A few days later, Vinnie and Thos rode over to the Orchard Place to bottle oil. As had become their custom in hot weather, once their filled bottles were packed in the saddlebags they swam in separate holes in the river and ate their lunch in the coolness of the cave, drinking from the cold rock-born spring. They had started up the cliff when they heard distant cries and baying hounds.

"Whatever they're after, I hope they don't catch it," Vinnie said. "Sounds like they're headed this way."

Glory and Thos's sturdy pinto were hobbled near the cabin ruins. Anxious as she was to avoid a group of hunters, Vinnie snatched time to take roses down to the family grave. In her mind, though she knew differently, the great white stone had come to mark her parents' grave as well as her kinfolks', and she sometimes talked to them when no one was in earshot. As she hurried back to Thos, a bent-over figure veered past the orchard, stumbled, dragged himself up again. The hounds clamored, and Vinnie expected them to burst into view at any minute.

The man fell again and Vinnie saw that he was dark. He might be a killer, maybe a thief, but Vinnie felt for anything hunted like that. Thos was already in his saddle and she tossed him Glory's reins. "I'm going to hide the man in the cave," she cried. "Ride over our tracks, Thos! Try to keep that pack away from the river!"

The fugitive was struggling to get up. His skin was the color of strong coffee with a dash of rich cream and his thick black hair was clotted with blood. His mouth was bleeding, his face swollen. He had taken a bad beating. Vinnie had never seen him before, she was sure of that, but he looked hauntingly familiar somehow.

"Put your arm around me." Vinnie bent and slipped her right arm around him. The man tried to push her away.

"No use you getting in trouble, miss." His voice was familiar too, though his words were muffled by his puffed lips. "I got a knife off one of them when I got away—I'll give a few of them something to remember me by." To her amazement, he chuckled.

"There's a cave," she said, trying to drag him forward. "Hurry up!"

"River cuts down there?"

"Yes. Come on!"

"All right, pretty lady. If you're bound and determined, we sure can try." Thos had ridden in between them and the pursuit, leading Glory behind his horse. He milled the horses, starting slowly over the way the man had come, which would at least make the scent harder to follow.

As Vinnie helped the stranger past the oil seeps, taking the easiest way down the cliff, he glanced at her. The brown of his eyes was mixed with green so that they changed color with the light. He must be at least part black, she knew, but his nose was long and straight and his mouth, before the beating, must have been handsomely shaped.

"Don't you want to know why they're chasing me?"

"You can tell me later." Just in case he was some kind of scoundrel, she added, "My guardian's a judge. If you ought to be in jail, he'll put you there, but I don't think the gang that's chasing you would take you to court."

"Judge Rope was what I was about to get. They didn't like it because I was riding a good horse, and most of all because I didn't get out of the road for them. They caught me last night, and I guess if they hadn't wanted to stretch their fun before they stretched my neck, I'd be dead. They got drunk, including the one who was supposed to be watching me. The hounds roused them, though."

His accent was different from any she'd heard. "You're not from around here?"

"The Indian Nation." He laughed. "Up there I never got out of the road for any man." She had heard Mark speak of the lawlessness in the territory just north of Texas; he had also said the federal government was much at fault for not letting Indian lawmen and their duly constituted courts deal with white criminals. This man might be part white and he might be part black. She was sure he was part Indian. Cherokee, maybe. He had a look of Hester about him, but that wasn't all.

"Let's go to the river," he said. "I'll wade, try to lose the dogs. Where's that cave?"

She showed him where tall grass and bushes hid the mouth. "There's another chamber back of the first one. Maybe you ought to hide there if you can squeeze through. In case that bunch does follow, you could bash in their heads with a rock."

He laughed at that, then sobered.

"You go along back, miss. If they pick up my trail, don't try to stop them. You've done plenty and I sure do thank you."

He grinned through those battered lips, leaned on a tree to work off his boots, and splashed out into the water. Vinnie rushed up the cliff. A knot of horsemen had gathered around Thos up beyond the orchard. Dogs circled, sniffing, whining, but they hadn't separated their quarry's scent from that of the horses.

Would they smell the hunted man on her? Vinnie stopped where the oil oozed brackishly, smeared her hands and arms with it. That ought to disguise any other smell. She always wore her oldest clothes when she came for oil so at least she hadn't ruined a nice dress. As she started toward the riders, Clay Mannering reached out and grabbed Thos's arm.

"What are you doing?" Vinnie caught up her skirts and ran. "Let go of my brother!"

"Well, here's Miss Tar Baby herself!" Fayte grinned, whirling. He let go of Thos but the boy was penned in by the manhunters. "You see a redbone come through here?" Redbone meant a mix of black and Indian.

Vinnie wasn't a liar and she blessed the way he'd put his question. "I didn't see any red bone," she said. "But you're on my property. I'll thank you to take these hounds and horses out of here."

"Your property!" Fayte gibed. "You talk grand for a pair of beggars!"

"This is our land and if you don't get off it I'll tell your father!"

"Oh, you would!" Fayte danced his big sorrel toward her, but though she was terrified, she wouldn't move and the horse stepped around her in spite of Fayte's spurs. "You need a lesson and someday I'm going to give it to you!"

"You may learn a few things yourself," she retorted. "Real soon, if you don't—"

One of the dogs gave voice, down near the cliffs. In a flash, the rest of the pack was after him. "So you didn't see him?" Fayte derided. "Get on your mare and come along! Do you good to see what happens to people who don't know their place!"

He caught Glory's reins from Thos but Vinnie picked up a rock and smashed it down hard on his wrist, seizing the leathers as he howled and let go. Mounting, she cried, "Ride, Thos!"

If Fayte came after them, that would be one less after the stranger. By now, he must be in the inner cave. She prayed anyway that the dogs would lose him at the river.

Fayte spurred after the other five young men, leaving Vinnie and Thos.

"I'm going to tell the judge!" she screamed.

He turned and laughed wildly. "He can't do much after we've hanged that bastard!"

Either Fayte didn't think Mark would punish the lynching or he was too worked up to care. There was no way Vinnie could stop the gang. But if the man from Indian Territory had reached the mother cave, he might be able to hold his enemies off long enough for help to reach him from Belleforest.

"Thos! Let's take off the saddlebags and cut across country!"

They did, and then they flew.

"Stay here," Mark ordered as Caleb saddled for him and then turned to ready his own horse. Both had Sharps rifles thrust into saddle scabbards; both carried a pair of Colts.

"I have to know!" Vinnie pleaded.

Mark gave her a hard stare. "All right. But keep out of the way if there's shooting. Thos, you wait here." At the boy's disappointed groan, he said sharply, "This isn't a Sunday outing."

As it chanced and to Vinnie's unspeakable gratitude, there was no need for firearms. They met the chagrined cavalcade a little way from Kane's store. Mark reined up and surveyed the party, all of whom looked everywhere else except for Fayte who glared at his father defiantly.

"You don't have to ride any farther, Judge. We couldn't catch the damn redbone. Lost his tracks at the river."

Relief melted Vinnie's bones. Mark looked at each youth in turn. "You're almost as lucky as the man you hunted," he said.

"Had you killed him, I'd have had you in court. Why were you after him?"

The boys exchanged glances. "He wouldn't get out of the way," one mumbled. Fayte cut in. "He was riding a horse that he'd surely stolen!"

Mark's single hand tightened on the reins till his knuckles showed white. "You'd hang a man for keeping to the road on a horse you thought too good for him?"

None of the young men met his eyes. After a long moment, he said, as if reading an indictment, "Charles, Clay, James, Nigel, Harry: none of you are welcome at Belleforest. I intend to speak to your fathers. Fayte, get yourself home and wait for me in my study."

"Why aren't you coming now?" Fayte cried. "Has *she* got him hid?"

"You've got questions to answer, not to ask," Mark said.

All the boys were armed and if they shot as well as Fayte they'd be a dangerous force. Mark made no move for either revolver or rifle but after tense seconds Fayte started off toward Belleforest. His companions rode away in other directions.

The man was in the cave. They got him into Caleb's saddle. Both eyes were swollen nearly shut but he managed to grin. "I sure do thank you folks. And I most specially and eternally thank this young lady. Weren't for her I'd be dangling on one of these trees."

"I owe her almost as much thanks as you do," said Mark. "My son was in that group. For that I ask your forgiveness. If we can't recover your mount, you can have your pick from my stable and I'll make any other restitution I can." He put out his hand. "I'm Mark Sevier."

The battered man peered through his slitted eyes. "Of Belleforest?"

Mark nodded. The stranger took his hand and pressed it. "I was coming to you, sir. My mother, I believe, is your housekeeper."

"Hester?" Mark looked dumbfounded. "I didn't know Hester had a child."

The stranger made a soft sound. "I don't remember her. For some reason or other I was brought up by an aunt and used her name—I'm Talt Ransom—but Mother always sent money and wrote once I learned how to write back. I reckoned I'd just come down and meet her. Didn't tell her." He added slowly, "Maybe I should have. Don't want to cause her any trouble."

"No reason why you should," Mark said heartily. "My mother was strict and pious; that must be why Hester couldn't keep you. But you're welcome to stay at Belleforest as long as you like."

No one said that might be uncomfortable with Fayte seething about the good fortune of his intended victim. When they reached the saddlebags, Caleb helped Vinnie fasten them on Glory, and when they got to Kane's, carried them into the store. She answered the storekeeper's curious questions as briefly as possible, collected her oil money, and soon caught up with Mark and Talt Ransom.

Hester had a son! But never had she mentioned him. There was something peculiar about it. Vinnie hoped with her whole heart that Hester would be pleased—though she wouldn't be at the state he was in. Vinnie wondered what Mark would do to Fayte, and with a shiver tried not to imagine what Fayte would do to the next black man he had a chance to mistreat. Now that the fight was over, she felt sick and went to bed that night without anything but the soup Hester made her sip.

That very week, over his mother's tears and raging, Fayte was sent to a military academy in Massachusetts. "Up among all those Yankees!" Regina sobbed. "How his own father can do such a thing! I'd never have brought him to you, Mark, if I'd dreamed—"

"You and your cousins filled his head with pernicious nonsense that almost led to a man's death. Doesn't that concern you at all, woman?"

She shifted her smooth shoulders. "That redbone tried to run the boys into a ditch."

"Is that what you want to believe?" Mark's jaw set rigidly. "Let me warn you that you're fortunate the boy's going to the academy. Had he and the others succeeded in hanging young Ransom, I do assure you they'd all be bound for prison."

Regina's eyes widened. "You wouldn't!"

"I would."

"You've lost your mind as well as your arm! Coddling that

riffraff, letting him strut around Belleforest while you exile your own son!"

Mark said wearily, "Hester deserves some time with the son my mother was too prim to allow her to raise. Even if that weren't so, I'd be glad to have Talt. He takes over a lot of the things I don't have time for."

Regina twitted, "You mean you need an overseer!"

"I need a manager. Fayte took absolutely no interest in the place though he's old enough to see to a lot of things instead of helling around the countryside."

Regina changed her tactics. Tears sparkled in her beautiful lavender eyes. "If you'd give him another chance, Mark!"

"I have. He's going to an academy instead of to prison for assault and battery."

"It's not fair! Clay and the others—"

"Are also bound for schools out of the state. I've talked with their parents."

"Oh!" wailed Regina. "People will really shun us now! I was just beginning to develop a few connections and you've ruined everything!" She fled the study. Again, as she had so often, Vinnie continued to copy a letter, pretending she'd heard nothing.

There could be no doubt of Hester's almost fearful joy at being reunited with her son, or of her pride in him. At first she was timid with him as if expecting rebuff, but he went to some pains to make it clear that his childhood with his aunt had been happy.

She'd been the freedwoman of a Cherokee master who had given her a good farm and used his influence to see that Talt was allowed to attend one of the excellent schools maintained by the Cherokee Nation. He'd been in his second year at a seminary near Tahlequah when the smoldering feud that had divided the Cherokees since 1835 erupted bloodily as the Civil War tore open old wounds that had never healed.

The bitterness went back to when most of the Cherokees still lived in the eastern states. Many, especially those long intermarried with whites, had fine plantations and were well educated. However, their fertile lands were coveted by whites. When it was clear that in spite of solemn treaties, the tribe was going to be forced to move west, some leaders tried to make the best terms possible by signing an agreement. This treaty was repudiated by the tribal council and most of the Cherokee Nation but the Indians were driven from their homes. A quarter of the Cherokee Nation perished of disease, cold, and starvation on that "Trail of Tears." Once settled in their new territory, the signers of the "false treaty" were killed in what one side called executions decreed by tribal law and what the other faction considered brutal assassinations. The Civil War fanned these hatreds to a blaze and left a devastated region of burned homes, fields, and schools.

After seeing his aunt to Kansas, where many Indians fled to escape ravaging by both Confederate and federal troops, Talt served with an Indian regiment in the Sixth Kansas Cavalry. Like countless refugees, his aunt and her former master died in Kansas from hunger and cold. There was not an animal, fence, or building left on the farm Talt returned to after the war. He joined the Cherokee Light Horse, the tribal policemen, for a while, but his old world was gone, and he decided to find his mother. He knew her whereabouts for through the years she'd written often and sent money for his keep and education.

He soon became invaluable at Belleforest. A good blacksmith, especially deft at shoeing horses and mules, he could repair wagons and tools and carve beautiful rifle stocks. He had learned about crops on his aunt's farm, and since he worked right along with the Belleforest hands, they didn't resent his suggestions. Talt was unobtrusive about what he did but it was plainly evidenced by the neatness and good repair of everything from ploughs to carriage. He lived in one of the cabins but at Mark's insistence took breakfast and the noon meal in the small dining room. These meals, in their easiness and good-natured banter, contrasted sharply with the cold formality of dinners upstairs.

Strangely enough, after Fayte's departure, Regina smiled and chatted with Mark, gazed at him fondly, sought his opinion on clothing and hairstyles. "After all, dear, pleasing you is more important than what other women say."

He raised an eyebrow at this but after a time of being wary of her efforts to charm, he began to soften. He gave her a pearl necklace for her birthday in late August, and when Vinnie and Thos excused themselves from the table that evening, Regina was holding out her goblet for more wine.

They made a handsome couple. Vinnie tried to crush the jealousy that barbed through her. When she and Thos were out of earshot, Thos wrinkled his freckled nose. "What's got into old Regina? She trying to soft-soap Mr. Mark into letting Fayte come back?"

Vinnie herself had wondered if Regina was trying to protect her residence at Belleforest, so she turned savagely on her brother. "Why shouldn't she be nice to him? He's everything a man ought to be. Maybe she's woken up to the fact that she's lucky to have him."

"You don't need to bite my head off," Thos grumbled, casting his sister an amazed blue stare. "All I said was—"

"Don't say it!" And then, to her brother's horror, Vinnie burst into tears.

Next morning as Vinnie passed Mark's room on her way to breakfast, she saw the bed hadn't been slept in. Transfixed by the realization of what that meant, she stood rooted. Her heart stopped. Then it began pounding hard, as if she were running from some terrible threat.

Mark didn't take breakfast downstairs that morning. It was a court day so he was in a hurry as he came into the study with a sheaf of notes. "I'd appreciate it if you could have these copied and arranged by subject tonight," he said. He had a high color and his eyes glowed in a way that made Vinnie painfully aware of his splendid masculinity, and of how it had been stifled. "Don't toil all the day, though, Vinnie. Get out for a ride this afternoon." He touched her hair—as, she thought, he might have patted a dog—and strode down the hall, a high-spirited lift to his step.

Vinnie set to work, but a suffocating tightness compressed her lungs. Her eyes kept blurring. After tears had botched several pages, she gave up and fled to her room. She found some relief in weeping though she scolded herself ferociously.

It was wrong to feel this way; spoiled, ungrateful! Unreasonable too, for hadn't she often winced at Regina's subtle cruelties to Mark, wondered how anyone could behave like that to him? Ashamed that she wasn't glad for him, Vinnie sobbed harder. At last, though her head throbbed, she returned to the notes and kept at them doggedly till Talt looked in. "Mother's got hush puppies and fried catfish," he said. His face had almost healed and his eyes, in the shadow, looked more brown than green as they gazed warmly at her. "Come on, Missie Vin." His teasing name for her.

"The judge won't want you working yourself to a nub. Why don't we go riding this afternoon?"

She liked Talt though she thought he might have shown a bit more respect for her nearly sixteen years. "I have to finish these notes," she said.

Talt crossed his long arms. At twenty-two, he had his full height but was still filling out. "I'm standing right here till you come eat." She scowled but blotted the last line with care and rose to go with him.

She was back at the notes when Regina looked in. "Poor child, slaving away for your hero!" She strolled over and examined Vinnie's work. "You put your funny little heart in it, don't you, dear? A pity your competence doesn't equal your devotion."

There was a sheen on her, a sated complacency that made Vinnie's nape prickle. Regina sat down with a rustle of skirts and held Vinnie's eyes. "Tell me, Vinnie, how long do you intend to take advantage of Mark's generosity?"

Meeting the mocking eyes, Vinnie felt as if a flash of lightning had suddenly, irrevocably, illuminated the depths of her being. She loved Mark as a woman, no longer as a girl child adores a father who seems all-powerful, all kind.

Belleforest—and Mark—had a mistress now. It was impossible for Vinnie to stay on.

She didn't speak till she believed her voice would hold steady. "Whatever you say, Mrs. Sevier, I've been useful to your husband. You're quite right, though. It's time I got started over at the Orchard Place. As soon as Judge Sevier finds a secretary, I'll leave."

Regina's jaw dropped. "I didn't mean . . . If you're going to tittle-tattle—"

"I know what you meant. Don't worry, I won't upset him." Vinnie sat down and picked up the pen. "And now I really must finish these notes."

She had dismissed Regina, but the flicker of triumph died in a wave of desolation that left her feeling more lost and helpless than she had since the day she'd found a tombstone instead of her aunt and uncle. Her lungs were so constricted she could scarcely breathe. She told herself grimly that Mark needed a wife much more than he needed a secretary.

V

Vinnie was chagrined that her replacement proved very close at hand. Talt's spelling wasn't as good as hers but his penmanship was boldly legible and he could cipher complex problems in his head. He could do everything Vinnie could and some things she couldn't. Regina must have hated to see the man she considered responsible for Fayte's exile becoming indispensable to Mark, but she was clever enough not to make an issue of it.

When Vinnie told Mark her decision, he stared at her with such baffled hurt that it was all she could do not to yield to his persuasions. "You and Thos can't go live by yourselves, Vinnie. You're still children!"

"I'm not a child! I'll soon turn sixteen!"

He caught both her hands in his single one. The rise and fall of her breast was as swift as if she'd been running. His touch made her blood run heavy and warm as if mixed with honey and sun. Unable to meet those beloved eyes, she gazed at the streaks of gray just beginning at his temples, longed to smooth them, longed to embrace him.

"No," he said, "you're not a child."

Abruptly, he let her go, turned to look out the study window at the gold and scarlet leaves. "I'll send some men over to build your house, dig a well, and get things in order." When she started to protest, he swung around. "I owe you a lot more than that."

"No you don't. Thos and I were to work for our board and room—and—and—" She fought a rush of tears. "You've given us so much more!"

"You've worked a lot harder than I expected." He leaned over, awkwardly did quick sums with his left hand, and thrust the result under her nose. "Besides room and board, I'd have had to pay a secretary at least twenty dollars a month. If we reckon Thos's earnings covered your clothes and sundries, I still owe you six hundred and eighty dollars." He shook his head and again his smile was the one that made her heart glow. "After you have your house, well, outbuildings, and implements, I imagine I'll still have to throw in a few cows to even things up." He chuckled. "You'd better take some chickens, too."

Vinnie blushed at the reminder of how they'd met, then laughed along with him.

Because of the sawmill, all kinds of cured lumber was stored at Belleforest; hewn logs and kiln-dried maple, cherry, walnut, oak, and hickory. Mark told Vinnie she could have a frame house but she preferred a cabin of pine logs felled on the property. These could be used green so the building was soon under way. Thos, who grumbled considerably at leaving Belleforest and his friends but sulkily rejected Vinnie's suggestion that he stay on at Belleforest without her, didn't care what the place looked like. But Talt made excellent suggestions. It was his idea that the roof of the dogtrot or breezeway that connected the two big rooms, actually separate cabins, be extended to cover an area big enough to hold a year's supply of wood. This aroused Thos's first enthusiasm.

"Hey, I can just step out the door and fill the woodbox!" he gloated.

Talt dropped a hand on his shoulder. "That's right, but first you've got to fill the space up." When Thos's face fell, Talt grinned. "Don't fret. I'll help you get the wood chopped."

He helped with a great deal else. Talt had the difficult knack of precisely shaping dovetail notches at the corners that locked wall logs in place so securely that they would stay without any other fastening or support as long as the logs themselves endured.

The rock foundation was laid on the site of the first cabin, which had only a packed earth floor. Vinnie paid no attention to some of the workers' mutterings about ghosts; she thought Aunt Lorena and Uncle Kirby would like to have family living in their place. There was still an occasional Comanche or Kiowa raid much farther north or west, but the return of federal garrisons protected the principal settled parts of the state. Talt said it could only be a few more years before even the wide-ranging Quahada Comanches of the vast Staked Plains were forced to a reservation inside Indian Territory.

"Along with the rest of us." He grinned wryly. "Anyone who thinks Indians are all alike should take a jaunt around the Territory. The Five Civilized Tribes were farmers and stock raisers long before they were hustled west, but Kiowas and Arapahoes are rovers and would a sight rather have buffalo than beef. Then there's what's left of other tribes who had the bad luck of living where whites came—Shawnee, Sauk and Fox, Osage, Delaware, Potawatomi, Kickapoo. It's like scrambling up what might be left of all the European countries after a big war."

Talt could speak as correctly as Mark, or near it, but he usually didn't. He probably knew it made most whites uneasy to hear English superior to theirs coming from a man who was obviously part Indian and perhaps part black. Such people doubtless resented Talt's striking good looks, but nothing could conceal them. In spite of his advancement at Belleforest, he was well liked because of his good nature and willingness to put his hand to any kind of work.

After the first well caved in, he managed to direct, without seeming to, the making of the next one, using methods acquired while drilling for salt water in the Territory. Much of his aunt's old master's wealth had come from salt evaporated from such brine and sent by wagon to Arkansas and Missouri.

Selecting logs about twelve inches across, Talt drilled with an auger through sections eight to twelve feet long, tapering one end to a point so it fit the funnel shape of the next section's end. When this casing was in place, water bubbled up through the center. Talt reamed out a hole in the top section and fitted it with a smaller drilled log that connected to others, unbelievably bringing water right to the cabin door, to be turned on or held back by a handled bar. "Leaks a little," Talt admitted, "but that'll just water your posies." For the yellow rosebush Lorena McCready had planted was still flourishing.

Caleb was a master at splitting shingles and floor boards with a froe and mallet. Belleforest's best mason made the rock fireplaces and chimneys and constructed an outdoor fireplace to hold the big iron wash kettle. He also made a watering tank by the snug barn that was already completed because it didn't require all the finishing that the cabin did, though it was well chinked with clay.

In less than a month, the cabin was finished: oak floor boards smoothed by a two-handled drawing knife; windowpanes set in frames that could open and close; doors hung on heavy iron hinges; smoke drifting from the chimneys to prove they drew properly. Next to the barn was a chicken coop and within the fenced pen strutted a proud rooster who unchivalrously snatched morsels from under the diligent beaks of his dozen snowy white hens. The two fawn-colored Jersey cows were fresh, each with heifer calf close to weaning age. There were stalls in the barn for horses, but Vinnie had absolutely refused to accept Glory as either gift or further "payment" and Mark just as adamantly refused to sell Glory for the hoarded apple-and-oil money Vinnie offered him.

"Glory's yours," he insisted. "She won't be ridden here and she'll miss you. If you care about her, you ought to take her with you."

Vinnie loved the mare but she was horrified at the labor and expense she had cost Mark. His best carpenters had put in shelves and made sturdily handsome furniture from well-cured cherry and walnut. She stared dolefully at her rejected money. "If you won't sell Glory, I guess I'll buy another horse later on."

"How'd you get so stubborn, Vinnie?" His tone was as plaintive as it was indignant.

"Well," she countered, trying to make him laugh, "I'll steal another chicken if that'll make you feel better."

"I feel better because Thos is keeping Patches," he retorted. "And that's between us, young lady, so keep out of it."

"Yes, sir, Colonel Judge." She cast him a demure glance and they both burst into laughter.

When the dwelling was ready, Mark on Selim, and Thos on Patches, rode ahead of the wagon Talt drove, Vinnie and Hester on the seat beside him. Mark had charged Hester to assemble everything needed for housekeeping. A big cedar chest was filled with embroidered sheets, pillowcases, quilts, and towels. Blue delftware was tucked among them and in the pillows and feather ticks spread over boxes and crocks of staples and cooking gear. Talt had already delivered the iron wash kettle, tubs, a wheelbarrow, and tools. Vinnie's sadness at leaving Belleforest was momentarily alleviated by the excitement of having her own home—and such a beautiful one!

The orchard was still a blaze of gold and copper behind the long house, and there were still a few roses, seeming like a welcome from Aunt Lorena. The cows and fawn-eared calves grazed on the slope and the rooster proclaimed his dominion from the chicken pen. The roofed shelter adjoining the dogtrot was piled with wood divided by size from kindling to logs big enough to hold a fire overnight.

Mark helped Hester and Vinnie down from the wagon. Vinnie turned to gaze across the trees and small cliffs along the river to the rolling plains beyond, out to the meeting of earth and sky, dun-yellow and sparkling blue.

Her face showed her feelings and Mark said softly, "It's your place, Vinnie. You were right to come here."

Talt built fires in each room while Thos unhitched the team, rubbed them down, and grained them. With everyone helping, it didn't take long to have the place ready for living. The east room was partitioned with shelves that left room for the fireplace heat to cross over. Thos's bed was covered with a Mexican serape in brown, black, cream, and gray. There were pegs for his clothes, an oak dresser, and a bench. He had already stowed some of his treasures on the shelves that were made with a single back to face both directions.

The shelves on Vinnie's side held books Mark had given her, sewing things, and oddments. Her quilt was of blue flowers—

bluebonnets, bluebells, flax, and asters, with a light blue background and a graceful border of green vines, Hester's work and gift. The wide dresser had a big mirror framed by carved birds and flowers. There was a bearskin by Thos's bed but a braided rag rug by Vinnie's, in many shades of blue. There was a blue patchwork cushion in the rocker by the fireplace, and on the small table beside it stood a lamp of the kind that had once burned sperm whale oil. Now that the great whales were diminishing, rock oil or kerosene was used instead, refined from crude oil like the oil in the seep near the cliff. If there had been a refinery anywhere close, they could have sold the ooze quite profitably instead of supplying only Kane's store.

There was another lamp on the hand-rubbed cherrywood table in the other room. Besides three chairs that matched the table, there were two comfortable large cane-bottomed chairs near the fireplace. The big old family Bible lay on the mantel and Father's hunting knife hung from a peg near Thos's shotgun. A long table for preparing food ran beneath shelves of dishes and pegs that held pans, skillets, and utensils. The cabinet beneath the table was for dishpan, kettles, and Dutch oven. Cabinets set against the other wall held food and supplies, and the rock-lined root cellar Uncle Kirby had dug in the slope behind the former cabin had been cleaned out and filled with bins of potatoes, onions, and apples that exuded a pungent fragrance.

When everything was in order, Hester rang the cow bell Talt had fastened on the branch of a great live oak that sheltered the house. She and Vinnie covered the table with good things from the wicker basket they'd prepared that morning: ham, deviled eggs, crispy fried chicken, corn pudding, relishes, cornmeal muffins, baked potatoes reheated in the fireplace, peach cobbler, apple cobbler, pumpkin pie, spice cake with a caramely burned-sugar frosting, steaming coffee, apple cider and buttermilk.

The sun was kind that day. After they'd filled their plates, everyone went to sit on the benches in the dogtrot.

It was a feast and a dream come true. Looking around at her friends and brother, Vinnie was joyously content as she realized that people she loved best in the world were gathered at *her* house. Regina and Belleforest seemed worlds away. If only they could be all together always. Just like this.

* * *

It had been the happiest hour of Vinnie's life but after Talt and Hester waved a last time from the wagon, after Mark turned in the saddle and flourished his hat, after they dipped out of sight behind a slope, there was a cold glitter to the sun and the summerlike balminess of the November day vanished in a sharp, sudden wind.

It was over, more than three years of having a home. She had insisted on leaving it, and if she wanted another home, she would have to make it: That took a lot more than a comfortable house. After a surge of panic which made her want to run after Mark, she straightened her shoulders and turned to Thos. Her brother was running his arm across his eyes. Her heart smote her. "Thos, you can go back—you don't have to stay here because I am."

He shook his head, darkened now from its childhood yellow to tawny brown. "No, Vin. There's just us left. We have to stay together. Besides, you need me for the ploughing and heavy work. But you'll have to find a man of your own when I go off to be a cowboy." He grinned at her. "Hey, I'd better milk before that old sun goes down."

"I'll help," Vinnie said. "I don't have to cook supper, we've got enough leftovers for a week."

"Think you remember how?"

Vinnie had helped with the milking in West Virginia till the Yanks drove off all the cows, but she hadn't done it since. Thos liked being around animals so that had been one of his Belleforest chores.

"If I don't remember, I'd better learn," she retorted. Her first few squeezes were awkward, but then it was as if she had only the evening before coaxed streams of warm creamy milk into a pail. Thos turned the cows into the corral with their calves and strained the milk, pouring it into pans where the cream would rise. Vinnie collected the eggs and fed the chickens before shutting them in the coop, safe from marauding skunks and coyotes.

Now that humans were gone, the animals took on new importance as companions. Vinnie stopped to caress Patches and gave him some apple peels she had saved from the chicken scraps. As his velvet lip rubbed her hand, she thought with a pang of Glory. Maybe, in time, Mark would change his mind and sell her to Vinnie.

Thos built up the kitchen fire. The heart of the fiery chunks glowed and sparkled, curling flame around the logs, sending out warmth. Vinnie lit the lamp, brooding a little over having to buy rock oil when there was plenty of it a hundred yards away if there was only a way of getting it refined. It would burn as it was, of course, but with such an odor and blackness that no one could use it indoors.

Replete from the big dinner, they had bread and milk, sitting by the fire. Thos glanced at Vinnie and grinned. "Know what, sis? This sure beats eating upstairs with old Regina watching us like a chicken hawk to see if we break any of her dumb rules!"

Vinnie laughed, glad to be jarred out of her longing for Mark. Three hours since she had seen him and it seemed as many years! She was going to have to take herself firmly in hand. Rising, she said, "Why don't we read out loud each night before we go to bed? We could take turns."

"Aw, Vin, that's like school!"

"No it's not. You can read anything you want to." At the mischievous light in his blue eyes, she added hastily, "You choose the first book, I'll pick the second, and so on."

"All right. Mark gave me some books, too." Thos returned in a few minutes and brother and sister, while wind whined through the boughs of the big oak outside, sat snug by the fire with the lamp between them, and were soon shipwrecked with Robinson Crusoe, exploring his island.

Thos continued school at Belleforest, taking the five-mile shortcut after chores and breakfast. He was home in time to do the milking but those first days were heavily lonesome for Vinnie. Till spring, there'd be little outside work and the house was so well supplied that for the time being she had only to see to regular tasks, churning butter, baking, cooking, and cleaning. She washed on Saturday when Thos could carry water from the wooden pipe to fill the huge kettle and rinse tubs. Vinnie started a crazy quilt but there was no urgency since it wasn't needed. She gathered acorns to roast and feed the chickens and roamed the woods for hickory nuts and black walnuts. The walnut husks had to be broken off before they could be cracked and shelled, labor which occupied several rainy days. Vinnie put the biggest meats in a jar to take to Hester, who vowed there was nothing like black walnut to flavor an applesauce cake.

Many times those first few weeks, Vinnie almost started to Belleforest but stopped before she was out of sight of her house. She was welcome and intended to visit now and then whether Regina liked it or not, but she didn't trust herself there till the Orchard Place was more securely her home.

Thos said that Mark often came by the school and asked how they were getting along. Vinnie was a little hurt that he hadn't been over, but it might be that he too needed time to grow accustomed to the change. Talt had come several days after the move, when Vinnie was at her lowest.

As they walked by the gravestone, Talt pulled out his beaded leather tobacco pouch and sprinkled some of the fragrant leaves on the mound. "In case your uncle might enjoy a smoke," he said.

Touched, she glanced up into those light brown eyes with their depths of green. "Thank you, Talt."

"My pleasure, Missie Vin."

"Do you have to call me that?" She frowned. "It sounds like I'm a baby or you're—" She broke off, flushing.

"A slave? I reckon, Vinnie, I'm close to being yours." He took her hand, placed it against his heart so that her palm felt its strong, steady beat. "I expect my meat would've rotted off my bones by now if you hadn't hid me. I just hope someday I can pay you back."

"You have," she said, confused. "Notching the cabin logs, running water to the house . . ."

He held her hand between his hands, which were strong-muscled and work-hardened, but the fingers shapely and long as Mark's. Those Mark had left. Her heart constricted with yearning.

As if he guessed her thoughts had left him, Talt released her. "I owe you a life, Vinnie."

He turned abruptly and walked to the seeps. Kneeling, he skimmed a finger through the ooze. "Lots of this up in Indian Territory. A few places have been fixed so people can take baths in it—drink it if they can get up enough nerve. Lewis Ross, the Cherokee chief's brother, was deepening one of his salt wells back in 1859 when oil came spewing up all over the place. That was a few months before Edwin Drake hit oil at Titusville, Pennsylvania. The difference was that Drake was close to markets and transport."

Vinnie sighed. "Yes, that's the problem here, too. So I'll just have to buy kerosene and sell what I can of this for greasing wheels."

"That'll change." He tasted the oil, made a face and wiped his hand. "You know what, Vinnie? I've always been sorry I missed the Gold Rush. Even if I never struck gold, it sure would have been fun to try—see if you could find it. It may just be that this stuff will turn out to be a new kind of gold."

"I don't see how." Vinnie sniffed. "All the lamps in the world won't use that much, or so many machines need oiling."

"You never can tell. Supposing boats and trains that run on steam could be powered by oil instead? And if it can be used for lighting, someone'll figure a way to use it for heat, too. Shucks, we used to stick a pipe in an ooze, light it, and keep warm."

"Oh, I know it'll burn." Vinnie remembered all too well the blaze of her father's oil spreading across the fields, taking everything. Shivering, she pushed away the memory. "If you're so interested in oil, Talt, why don't you go work where it's being produced?"

"That's what I'd reckoned on doing after I visited a spell with my mother. Work on the wells till I saved enough to do my own drilling." His eyes sparkled. "That's where the kick is, Vinnie, hunting for a place you think has oil and getting down to it, bringing up what's been hidden in the ground forever."

"Why don't you do it, then?"

He gave her a weighing look. "If I did, would you come back to Belleforest? Help the judge?"

"I can't!" Taking his gaze for reproach, she caught her shawl tighter about her and quickened her pace.

"So it *is* like that."

"Like what?"

"The way you care about the judge."

Vinnie started to deny it but the expression in Talt's eyes withered the lie. He looked sad, regretful, yet accepting. She had never talked about her feeling for Mark though she suspected Hester had known it before she did. It was a relief now to tell someone how wonderful Mark was, how he had been a wise, kind father and friend to her, taking the place of all she'd lost.

"Why did the way I love him have to change?" she grieved, as she finished.

Talt brushed her hair. "Because you're growing up, honey." His smile seemed forced, and he gripped his hands behind him.

"I wish things could have stayed the way they were."

"Stay thirteen for always?" He shook his head and laughed. "No, you don't, Vinnie. You're alive. Live people grow and live and take chances and lose and win and learn. Live people change all the time."

A comforting doctrine but upsetting to Vinnie's vague notion that when you grow up, you just *were* and had no more struggles with your own nature. "You must think I'm a coward."

He stopped, put a hand on either side of her face and looked down into her startled eyes. Something between them was changing, too. He was a man, not only a friend. But how could she be aware of him when it was Mark she loved? Unable to bear his gaze, turned gold by the nooning light, she closed her eyes.

"You're afraid sometimes, Vinnie. Only a fool isn't. But you're brave. I'm betting that's one thing you'll always be." Abruptly, he let her go.

VI ────────────────────

Vinnie didn't think much of Thanksgiving because Abe Lincoln had proclaimed it a holiday, but it was kept well at Belleforest. Talt rode over in the morning, leading Glory, who whickered joyfully at Vinnie and accepted dried apples from her hand before they left for the sumptuous dinner.

Strange, thought Vinnie, how the place that had been her home for three years no longer seemed so, even though, when she left her cloak in her old room, she saw that nothing had been changed.

Regina was cordial though her eyes darkened when they rested on Talt, seated across from Vinnie and Thos, where Fayte should have been. The drawn, tight look was gone from her face; she was in the full bloom of her beauty, so lovely that Vinnie, with a dull ache, had to admit that it was no wonder Mark watched her fatuously. Regina coquetted with him as if they were new lovers. Perhaps his sending Fayte away, angry as it had made her at the time, had restored the way they'd felt about each other before the war, before so many things.

Tormented, feeling like an intruder, Vinnie was grateful when it was time to leave. Downcast and silent as they rode along, she responded briefly to Talt's remarks and Thos's elation over the whole pecan pie Hester had tucked in with a bundle of elegant leftovers. But as they came over the rise that gave them the first glimpse of the cabin and orchard, she reined in and turned to Talt.

"It's home. It's really home!"

His mouth quirked. "Why then, it's been a good Thanksgiving, hasn't it?"

Her heart was too sore to go that far but she gave Talt a reluctant smile. "At least I've learned something."

His smile was a caress. "Sometimes that does more for you than being happy."

The red-streaked western sky cast a soft glow on the house and outbuildings, mellowing the new logs. It had a welcoming look that Belleforest, with its stateliness, never could. Mark wasn't there, but he had built it for her. It was a sign of his love, and if that love wasn't the kind she wanted, it was still her greatest treasure.

Vinnie's birthday was the twelfth of December. Hester had always baked a scrumptious cake and fixed Vinnie's favorite dishes. It was no fun to bake your own cake and Vinnie felt thoroughly dampened when Thos went off to school without remembering her birthday and wishing her a happy one.

It was chilly but bright. There had been rain the Saturday before so laundry was piling up. Vinnie decided to drown her mopes in soapsuds. The white things were flapping in the breeze by early afternoon and she was wringing out the coloreds when she heard distant creaking.

Who could it be? Talt was the only one who ever visited and this sounded like a wagon. Hurriedly wringing out the last of Thos's pants, she pegged them up, pulled down her sleeves, and ran into the cabin to brush her hair. The rumbling came nearer with each moment.

Glad that her private celebration of the day had included wearing her nicest everyday dress, gray-blue the color of her eyes with dark blue trim at the flounces and collar, Vinnie regretted the lack of time to do her hair up but tied it back with a blue velvet ribbon. The mirror gave back a face broad at the forehead, narrowing to a firm, clefted chin, the mouth full, eyebrows winging up to give a perpetually questioning look.

Sixteen and—yes, pretty! Not beautiful like Regina, but perfectly satisfactory. Nodding at reflected eyes that sparkled with anticipation, she fastened the last buttons at her throat and hurried to greet the vehicle that was rolling to the cabin door.

The sandy-whiskered driver climbed out of the wagon, while a slighter black-haired man jumped down from the other side and hitched the mules. "You'd be Miss Vinnie McCready?" asked the flat-nosed bushy-browed driver.

"Yes." She stared at the large hulk in the wagon, its shape lost in a swaddling of rugs and canvas. "But that can't be mine."

"Reckon it can't be nobody else's," said the driver with a grin. He reached in his coat and brought out an envelope. "This'll tell you all about it, ma'am, but for now could you just show us where to put your pianny?"

Piano? She thought instantly of Mark. "I can't take it."

The man scratched his reddish hair. "It's paid for, ma'am. We sure ain't cartin' it back to town. Tell us where it goes or we'll just have to chuck it out in the road."

She'd fight it out with Mark later. The men were already stripping off the coverings. Vinnie went inside and surveyed the main room. If the dining table were shifted nearer the fireplace, the piano should fit against the wall where there'd be good light from the window.

It wasn't till the lovely little spinet, walnut buffed to a satiny sheen, was in place and the wagon was rattling off that Vinnie opened the letter. Talt's confident writing didn't surprise her; he would be doing Mark's correspondence. But the words amazed her so that she had to read them twice before she grasped their meaning. *"I owe you a life. This is interest on the debt. Practice up so you can play for me next time I'm over."*

Talt! He could afford the rich gift less than Mark but there'd be no arguing with Talt. Slowly, delight overcame misgivings. The top opened to reveal a scrolled brass music holder supplied with several books. She stroked the keys, enraptured at their response, and sat down on the needlepoint stool that had come with the piano.

Mr. Gottfried would have cringed at her first efforts but her fingers began to remember their training. Leafing through the music, she found an easy tune she knew, and played through it till she thought her teacher would have applauded.

What a marvelous present! She didn't think she'd ever be

lonesome again, not with music waiting for her to play it. Why hadn't Talt come so she could thank him?

When she heard hoofbeats, she thought he had. Running to the door, his name glad on her lips, she caught it back. "Mr. Mark!"

He smiled before he swung down from his bay. "Happy birthday, Vinnie." He had been leading Glory, and now he put the golden mare's reins in Vinnie's hand.

Caressing the slim muzzle, Vinnie said, "Oh, Mr. Mark, I can't! She's too valuable."

"She's lonely," he said. Something in his dark eyes made Vinnie wonder if he was, too, though of course that was impossible now that he and Regina were lovers again. "However, if it'll ease your conscience, my stubborn little one-time chicken thief, you can earn her. I've got a serious business proposition."

She eyed him dubiously. "What?"

"My publisher wants another book."

"Oh, Mr. Mark! That's wonderful!"

"What is this 'Mr. Mark'? Now that you're sixteen, I demand you stop it or I'll start calling you 'Miss McCready'! Anyway, this book will be about the effects of Reconstruction."

"You can certainly do that—Mark." How deliciously intimate that was.

"Not without you."

She gaped. "Why, you have Talt."

"I do, and he's excellent. But he handles a lot of Belleforest's management as well as my personal business. Besides, it's not his fault and it doesn't make sense and you can call me cantankerous —but I can't think aloud with Talt the way I could with you. Letters, legal things, that's different. But a book—I can't."

"Have you tried?"

"Of course I have." He looked at her reproachfully and her heart began to race. "Aren't you going to ask me in? I could do with coffee if you have some."

She helped loosen Selim's cinch but hesitated over turning Glory into the corral. "Go ahead." Mark grinned. "Whether you'll help me or not, I won't take that poor lonesome mare back to Belleforest."

Vinnie led the horse into the enclosure, took off the sidesaddle Mark had bought for Vinnie after Regina reclaimed hers, slipped off the bridle, and couldn't keep from throwing her arms around Glory's neck.

"I hope I can keep you, beauty," she whispered. "I've really missed you." She gave the mare some fragrant meadow hay and joined Mark, who was surveying the piano with considerable astonishment.

"So that's why Talt wanted some wages in advance." He touched the open songbook. "I see you didn't throw *his* present back in his face."

"I couldn't. He sent some men along with it."

"Wise fellow." Mark's tone was dry.

Vinnie made coffee. It was the first time he had come to her house alone. She felt as if she must be giving off a visible glow at the happiness of sitting across from Mark by the fire as if they were . . . her thoughts stuck at the word, then defiantly added . . . as if they were married. She had taken herself away from his beloved daily presence though it was like denying sunlight; she had done her best to be glad Regina was truly his wife. But she couldn't help the way she felt.

"Your publisher must really like your journal, Mark." She had long called him that in her mind but it was strange to say it. "When will it be published?"

"Next summer. And they'd like to have the next one done by fall so that it could be brought out the next spring. Please?" He held out his cup. She filled it and added cream, the way he liked it. "So, Vinnie, would you scribe for me when I'm able to work on the book? I'd like to put in two good days a week when court permits. I'd come here after breakfast and carry through till midafternoon if you'll feed me."

If? Taking care of him, doing things for him, was the greatest joy she'd ever known. She missed it terribly. Probably the reason he could allow her to be the hand writing down his thoughts was that he'd formed the habit while she was a child, not an adult to whom he'd have had to justify his opinions. That didn't bother her. But something else did.

"We can have soup or something that'll cook while we're busy," she said. "But Mark, will—won't Regina . . ."

He chuckled proudly. "You wouldn't believe how pleased she's becoming about her husband being an author. Since most of her friends don't read, she can neglect to tell them my story's written from the 'wrong' side of the war. She even suggested that I ask you to come work at Belleforest, but I didn't think you'd like that, your having become such an independent young lady."

Had it been necessary for his book, she'd have gone to Belleforest, but this would be sheer bliss! Two days a week with him, making good things for him to eat, resting sometimes like this in the companionship that she'd rather have with him than all the vaguely imagined raptures of making love with anybody else. If God let her have that much, she'd promise to be grateful, never ask for more.

Afraid that he could read her feelings in her eyes, she poured more coffee. "I'm glad you can come here." She glanced around the cozy, tidy room, grateful that her lack of a pressing occupation had driven her to clean house even when it didn't need it. "I love this place, Mark."

"I see you do." He sighed. "That's good, though I miss you. I still can't believe you've settled into your lifelong nest at this early age."

She looked at him. "I'll be perfectly happy to live here all my days." *In the place you made for me, though you cannot share it, at least not through the nights when I turn against the pillow, dreaming you are there, where you can never be. But I would rather have the dream of you than real arms and mouth and flesh of any other man.*

"Thos, though, I suppose he'll go away some day."

"So will you."

Not while you're alive. Not while I can see you. She shrugged to cover the moment, suddenly grown tense. "I won't go if you need me. When will you be ready to start on your book?"

After weeks of hunting tasks, her life now overflowed. When the weather permitted, she rode Glory on days Mark didn't come. She practiced the piano every day, listening for errors as if part of her were Mr. Gottfried. And above all, there were the days when Mark came shortly after Thos left and they had hours together, in her own place.

He made her stop if he thought her fingers were cramping and they would have coffee or walk through the orchard or down to the river. On fine days, they ate outside, and sometimes, when the thoughts wouldn't come clearly, Mark asked her to play for him.

"But Regina plays so much better," she objected at his first request.

"Yes," Mark agreed. "But she is she and you are you and I like to hear you both."

Talt came almost every week. He always asked her to play for him. Then, depending on the weather, they talked by the fire or walked. As spring came on, he helped her and Thos fence the garden with posts interwoven with pliable willow branches.

During the winter, Thos and Vinnie had tossed over the intended fields and garden with manure and trampled hay scooped out of the barn. This was now worked into the earth as Thos hitched Patches to the plough and filled the air with the smell of fresh-turned sod. Vinnie dibbled corn, pressing soil over it with her foot, and planted potatoes, carefully cut so that there was an eye in each section.

She planted according to Caleb's directions about phases of the moon, and looked forward to a bountiful array of onions, carrots, cabbage, peas, green beans, squash, and yams. Caleb had brought her some strawberry plants. In a few years, there should be a thick patch of them.

Caleb had also brought sturdy saplings, plum, peach, and cherry, that would bear in three or four years. The redbud trees Vinnie had planted last fall at the front of the cabin were now in full blossom, rich pink shading to red at the stems. Birds courted and chose nesting sites. Tender green leaves hid the river that had shone naked through the winter trees. Everywhere life quivered and budded. The very air was tremulous.

Vinnie felt the stirring. In spite of her resolve to be thankful for what she had of Mark, she began to long for more. If only he would kiss her, hold her against him—a wicked thought! He was married. She forced the image away, but in her dreams, that happened; that and more. The dreams weren't happy ones. They ended with Mark watching her in horror and disgust.

She would rather have died than have him look at her like that. It would be unbearable if he guessed her feelings. At the same time, she was resentfully humiliated in some female depth of her that he seemed so steady while her hands trembled, that he smiled benignly while she wanted to cry out her frustration. To him she seemed a useful hand, not a woman with a body that ached for him.

Despite her inner storm, the pile of manuscript grew steadily. "It'll be done ahead of time," Mark said, pleased. "My editor's already hinting that he'd like a third book, one about Union sympathizers in the South during the war."

For a moment, Vinnie almost hated him. This was fine for him—Regina to love, and Vinnie to do his manuscripts until she was a dried-up old maid. Well, she wouldn't! She couldn't!

"If you're going to keep writing and writing, Mark, you'd really better get used to dictating to Talt," she said, putting down her pen. "Or," she added with what she meant as humor but came out brittle, "you might start looking for another child."

He looked shocked. As soon as she had spoken, she wished she hadn't. But it was too late. His dark eyes searched hers, baffled, hurt. "Has the work gotten boring?"

"No!" Hating herself, she got up and walked to the window. Even if she hadn't loved him, she would have found his ideas intriguing. "It's just that . . . this can't go on."

"I hadn't understood that you found it so disagreeable," he said gruffly. "That you do certainly destroys the special way I could talk to you." He picked up his notes, fumbling a bit with his single hand. "I'm sorry to have imposed."

Aghast, she blocked his way to the door. "Mark, I didn't mean— Please! Let me take down this book!"

"I've no wish for you to suffer out of gratitude."

"But—"

He shook his head. "It would be intolerable, Vinnie. The flow we had, from my mind and words through your hand—it really was as if you were a part of me. That's gone." His smile was forced. "Don't look distraught, my dear. You've been patient and kind, but how could you go on with my maunderings feeling the way you do?"

She couldn't bear for him to think that. Though it was the hardest thing she'd ever done, she looked straight into his eyes and said, "The way I feel is that I love you."

"Well, of course."

She shriveled inside, blushed with shame as comprehension dawned in him. He stepped back, shaking his head, taking her hands in his. "Vinnie, dear, you love me as you would a father."

"Don't say that!"

He tried again. "I haven't wanted to face that you're old enough to be courted, that you should be meeting young men."

"It wouldn't make any difference." She held herself rigid, drawing away from him.

"My poor little girl, what have I let happen? I hoped perhaps you and Fayte—"

She gave a harsh laugh. "If Fayte and his friends are examples of young men, I'd rather not know any. And I'm not your poor little girl! I'm a grown-up. Don't you dare feel sorry for me or—or think I don't know what I mean!"

As if she'd slapped him, he went to stand in the door. "That's why you left Belleforest."

"Yes." Why had she ruined everything? She *had* behaved like a child. No wonder he watched her in that amazed, almost horrified fashion. "When you wanted to work here, I was so glad," she said despairingly. "I thought it would be enough."

He gave himself a bemused shake. "I don't know what to say. You are so dear to me, Vinnie. But in a year or two the right man will come along." He glanced at his sleeve. "A whole man, young enough to make a whole life with you. I hope then we can—can be the way we were."

She didn't argue. But they could never be that way again any more than she could go back to being twelve. In the long silence, he put his notes with the pages she had done into his satchel. She felt as if he were taking away some private precious part of her. He was. He was taking the work that had been their special bond.

If only she'd said nothing! Yet even in the pain of seeing him go, of losing the joy of serving him, she knew she could no longer be his hand. She wanted to be his woman, even if she was so foolish and so young.

Vinnie helped saddle the bay, held open the corral gate. As he rode through, Mark touched her hair. "Vinnie, if there's anything you need, ever any way I can help, you'll let me know? Please, let's not stop being friends."

She would love him till the day she died. She pressed his hand to her lips, allowed herself that. Managing a smile, she said, "Yes, we'll always be friends."

She watched him out of sight. Then she spread out her arms on the ground and lay on her face and wept.

VII _____

The fruit trees passed from masses of white and pink bloom to tiny nubs. Delicate sprouts in the garden grew into plants and beans, and pea pods swelled daily. Fluffy yellow chicks followed after their mothers. Talt came by the evening Vinnie was cooking the first marble-sized new potatoes with tender peas, said there was nothing he liked better, and accepted the invitation to supper.

He must have wondered why Mark didn't work with her any longer, but he never hinted for a reason. Vinnie was grateful that he always gave news of Mark without waiting till she asked.

Many times she went back and forth over that last encounter, upbraiding herself for lacking the strength to do the one thing she could do for Mark, but the end of these fits of remorse and longing was the same; she couldn't have gone on. She didn't know if she could go on this way, either, so close to him, yet distanced.

Much as she loved the Orchard Place, she began to think of leaving when Thos finished school. She could never bring herself to sell the farm, though, so when she thought of going away, it was as if she were tugging at roots already locked deep in the earth.

She felt in between: one life had ended and a new one hadn't begun. That nature, all around her, followed its cycle without hesitation or apparent misgiving made her feel all the more estranged from everything. Talt seemed restless, too. He prowled the room as she set the table, sliced bread, and put out a crock of fresh-churned butter.

"The judge sure is having a time with this book. We cross out three lines for every one we keep. I think he'd forget the whole thing if he didn't believe it was something that needs doing."

Bracing against a wave of guilt, Vinnie poured the creamed potatoes and peas into a blue bowl. "Maybe when his journal comes out, it'll encourage him."

"I hope so. But Fayte and the book ought to get here about the same time."

She dropped a spoon. "He's coming back?" She didn't like to think about Fayte, and as he was far away, she seldom did.

Talt nodded. "Mrs. Sevier begged, I guess. Seems he's kept his nose clean. So he'll have the summer at Belleforest and go back to the academy in the fall."

Vinnie sighed, picked up the spoon and washed it. "I hope he's learned his lesson. Anyway, I don't suppose he can cause much trouble in so short a time."

Talt said nothing. She called Thos and put on a bowl of wild greens flavored with rosemary and poured glasses of buttermilk. Talt praised the food but she could tell that he was distracted. After, at his insistence, he and Thos did the dishes, and then he suggested a walk.

The early summer twilight was reluctant to give way to night and the air was heavily sweet with blooming as they took the familiar path along the river. "I don't see how Fayte and I can last all summer under the same roof," he said at last. "It'd sure be better if I went off and worked somewhere else till fall. You reckon, Vinnie, you could help the judge till then?"

Put like that, it seemed unreasonable and ungrateful to deny the request. And to see Mark again! Just for the summer... Vinnie battled the longing. "I'm sorry, Talt. I just can't."

For a long time he said nothing. When he stopped and turned to her, it was dark enough that she couldn't see his expression. He was just a tall dark looming man. "Vinnie, will you forgive me for speaking plain?"

"Talt—"

"No, listen. I'm not the one to say this but there's no one else to do it. The judge is the best man in the world, honey, but he's got a wife. You got to quit thinking on him."

His putting it into words left her feeling as if he'd stripped off her clothes. Shamed, burning, she smudged away hot tears. "You know so damn much! Tell me how I'm supposed to do that!"

He brought her against him, holding her arms between their bodies. She was too startled to avoid his mouth as it found hers, warm, seeking, so desirous that the trembling wracking him shook her also. She had no will or strength to resist.

It was Talt who finally drew away. "Vinnie," he whispered. "Vinnie!"

Raising her hand to her lips, she was filled with horror, sickening revulsion. How could she feel like that with someone besides Mark? And Mark—oh Mark, if anyone!—should have given her that first kiss from a man. She struck out blindly, at herself more than Talt. He didn't flinch but, as her hand stung across his face, she did.

"Talt," she cried, half sobbing. "Why'd you have to go and do that? Why—oh, why does everyone have to *change?*"

He made a muffled sound as he whirled, moved up the trail ahead of her. She followed, dazed, knowing that just as her confession had irrevocably altered things between her and Mark, so Talt's action had changed their brother-sister closeness. If this was growing up, she didn't like it. Most wretched of all was the thought that perhaps Talt cared for her as she did for Mark.

She was amazed when, in sight of the house where Thos had lit the lamps, Talt swung about and laughed. "I'll beg your pardon if you want, but I was just trying to jar you into realizing that some things can be mighty nice even if you aren't in love to start with. How do you know there's not another man for you, Vinnie, if you won't give one a chance?"

Anger that he'd taken such a way to teach her a lesson was smothered by relief. He didn't love her! She hadn't lost him, then. Not that he wouldn't get a piece of her mind!

"Men haven't exactly been knocking down my door," she said acidly. "Even if they were, it wouldn't be honest to—" She broke off, blushing to remember the quicksilver his kiss had sent through her.

"Folks have to live the best they can. It's sure not always

honest." The savagery in his tone squelched her intention to give him a lecture. "You'll have to find your own way, I reckon."

He didn't say good night.

Talt didn't come again till early June after Thos was out of school, and then he acted as if nothing had happened that night by the river. "The judge sent this," he said, taking a parcel from his saddlebag.

Carefully opening the package, Vinnie stared at the thick book with what she thought of as a Yankee-blue binding. Stamped in gold were the words: THE WAR JOURNAL OF COLONEL MARK SEVIER, U.S. ARMY OF THE REPUBLIC. She wiped her hands on her apron before she ventured to open the pages. Across from the frontispiece was a picture of Mark in uniform; a picture from when he'd still had both arms. Her fingers trembled as she turned the page. She read a few words before her eyes filmed and she couldn't see.

Thos, peering over her shoulder, read aloud. "This book is dedicated to the young people who must heal our nation, and most especially to Lavinia McCready, without whom it could never have been." Thos gave a piercing Rebel yell.

"Sis, you're famous!"

How would he dedicate his second book, which, if he finished it, would be no thanks to her? Vinnie hugged the volume to her breast, so proud she thought she must burst. This came from his mind and her hand—something they had made. Not a child, but something wonderful, something to last.

Talt's voice roused her.

"The book was on sale in Massachusetts before Fayte left there. He came home having conniption fits, carrying on about how his friends around here are going to feel about what he calls Yankee propaganda. He won't even read it and he's gotten Mrs. Sevier crying and upset after she was so proud and excited. It's too damn bad they let him come home."

"How awful for Mark!" Vinnie gasped.

"Pretty rough."

"Can you get along with Fayte?"

Talt gave a wry chuckle. "I'm sure trying. So far, he's mostly pretending I'm not there. He spends most of his time racketing around with Clay Mannering, who must have talked his folks into letting him come home for the summer, too." Talt shrugged. "I sleep better knowing that the rest of that bunch that tried to hang me won't be back this year."

"Now that you work for the judge, they wouldn't dare try anything."

"Nothing they'd be caught at, no. But I come from where there was a lot of bushwhacking, Vinnie. There's many a man shot from his saddle and the killer never known."

A chill crept down Vinnie's spine. That could happen to Mark. With hatred over the war and Reconstruction still high, it was a wonder it hadn't. Caleb stuck close to him, of course, but two or three men undercover with rifles could easily blast them both.

That would bring in federal troops, though ironically Mark detested Reconstruction, military government, and the law barring Confederate soldiers from the vote if they wouldn't take the "ironclad oath" of allegiance to the U.S. government. The previous November, in 1869, after Texas ratified the Fourteenth and Fifteenth Amendments, giving black men citizenship and the vote, Texas held its first elections since the war.

With military authorities supervising, it was no wonder Republican E.J. Davis had taken office in January. But at least Texas was recognized as a state again, not conquered territory. Mark predicted that the next election would return the Texan government to more acceptable people.

"I'm a Texan, Vinnie," he had said last November. "I don't like the way the radical Congress has humiliated the South after its defeat and terrible losses. But there's one thing to remember. Part of what the Confederacy defended was the right to go on owning human beings, treating them like livestock, selling away their children. There were good masters and bad masters, but there shouldn't have been *any* masters."

Vinnie eyed the young man who would have been born a slave had Mark's father not freed Hester, despite the fact that he was less than a quarter black since his Cherokee grandfather had also had Scottish blood.

If white blood was so superior, why didn't a preponderance of it make the possessor white? Mark had told her that the Spanish in Mexico had worked out an elaborate system whereby mixed-bloods, by marrying white, could eventually reduce their Indian or Negro strain till they were legally white.

Here, one drop of black blood made you black. "Talt, you'll be careful?" She laid a hand on his arm.

"You bet I will. I didn't ride over here till Fayte took himself off to Clay Mannering's. I don't want to have to kill the judge's son but I sure don't want him to kill me." He paused, then reluctantly voiced what was on his mind. "If Fayte rides over here, Vinnie, starts pestering you, let me or the judge know. Please."

She remembered Fayte as she'd first seen him, pulling feathers from a bluebird's wing. Fear coursed through her but she fought it down. "Why should Fayte bother about me?"

"He knows you took down the judge's book. And he won't ever forget that you kept him from getting me and how that sent him up north. On top of all that, Vinnie, you've become a mighty pretty girl. So whether he comes at you with fair words or foul, don't you trust him."

"I couldn't if I tried."

"Good," said Talt.

Whenever they were caught up on field and garden work, Thos rode to Belleforest to fish or ramble the woods with his friends. "Hester's worried," he told Vinnie one night. "She's heard that Fayte and Clay Mannering are running with some Ku Klux Klan."

Vinnie stared. "Their Grand Wizard disbanded them last year."

Thos shrugged. "Must be some diehards."

"Has Hester told Mark?"

"She doesn't want to. Hester did tell ole Regina, hoping she'd take Fayte to task, but Regina just went into a tantrum and accused Hester of having it in for her precious darling."

"Talt knows?"

"Well, sure he does, but he doesn't want to tell the judge, either."

"I wish it were fall and Fayte were back at the academy."

"I expect the judge does, too. Fayte's tried to get him not to let the hands celebrate Juneteenth. Hester says he's in a powerful sulk because the judge told him he wasn't running the place yet."

Vinnie hurt for Mark. It would have been better if Regina, having saturated her son with poison, had never brought him back to the father he was bound to clash with. Mark would have gone on mourning his lost son, but that would have been better than grieving for one who was a constant source of disappointment.

Several days later, Thos had gone to Belleforest and Vinnie had just punched down bread from its first rising and set it to double in the sun, covered with a clean towel, when she saw a horseman coming from the direction of Kane's Meadow. He was too far away to recognize and there were many dun horses in the region. Vinnie washed her hands, smoothed her hair, and just for safety's sake set a chunk of wood by the door.

The only weapon they had, apart from their father's old hunting knife, was the shotgun Thos always carried with him in case he had a chance at a squirrel. Vinnie wished he wouldn't kill them and refused to cook them so he took them to Hester.

Deciding she might as well have the knife handy too, Vinnie stuck it inside the door frame. She was probably being silly. Chances were the rider just wanted more oil than Kane had at the store; every now and then someone came with a bucket or jar they wanted filled. Vinnie was glad to oblige them and not split the money with Kane.

Something made her wait just outside the doorway, though, rather than going to meet the visitor. As the smart clop of hoofs softened in the grass out front, she was glad she stood close to the knife, for it was Fayte.

Why did his eyes have to be so like his father's? It was close to a year since she'd seen Fayte. His lanky frame was filling out, and he was going to be bigger than Mark, though with Regina's slenderness. His hair still blazed red-golden as he swept off his planter's hat with a mocking bow.

"How are you, Miss Lavinia?"

"Thank you, I'm well."

He smiled lazily. "But not pleased to see me. Too bad. I thought it only neighborly to pay you a call."

"That's kind of you, but I'm busy."

"You won't ask me in?"

"I'll bring you coffee or buttermilk, and something to eat if you're hungry." Her heart was thudding so hard that she feared he would hear it, and her mouth was dry.

"But you won't let me cross your threshold?" The smile became a show of small white teeth. "That's not very hospitable."

"Do you want a drink?"

He came out of the saddle in one swift motion, tossing the horse's reins in front of him so the mount would stand. "I want you to ask me in, Vinnie, the way you do Father and that damn redbone. I'll wager you don't keep them standing outside."

"And I wouldn't you, if you were like them."

"You like traitors and red niggers?"

She yanked the knife out of the frame and stepped toward him. "You sorry varmint, don't you call your father a traitor!" She choked with fury. "And Talt—he's ten times the man you'll ever be!"

Fayte went crimson but he laughed, narrowing his eyes. "How do you know, you white-trash slut? Have you tried him in bed? He been playing with your titties? That why they've gotten so big in a year?"

"You get out of here!" Vinnie raised the knife as she advanced on him. "Git, and don't you ever come back!"

"I can give you harder and bigger than that nig can."

Only the thought of Mark kept her from attacking that taunting handsome face. Their eyes dueled. Then he dived, catching her wrist, tumbling her to the ground. He wrung the knife from her hand. They rolled over and over, wrestling, he trying to tear her clothes and straddle her, she throwing him off, going for his eyes.

He was stronger and heavier but she was well grown, resilient, and wiry. Also she didn't mind getting hurt so long as she hurt him, too. She yanked his hair and bit his wrists and when, finally, gasping for breath, he managed to get on top of her, she brought her knee up to his crotch.

He howled, doubling up as she wrenched out from under him. She was barefoot, but she turned and drove her heel into his belly, then into his face, before she snatched up the knife. Soothing the dun who had skittered away, she hauled Fayte's expensive rifle out of its scabbard, ran down to the oil seep, and tossed it in.

When she got back, Fayte was crawling to his knees, face blanched and sweating.

"I saw my daddy cut a boar once," she said through her teeth. "I'd fix you right now if it weren't for the judge."

"God damn you, you going to tell him?"

"Think I want him to know what you're like? Stay away and I won't tell. But come on my place again and I sure will do my best to kill you."

With a glance of sheer hatred, he limped to the horse, groaning as he dragged himself up. His face was contorted when he looked at her. "I won't ride back here, you slut, but you'll come begging to me someday. Maybe after you crawl on your belly, I'll let you in my bed if you—"

She took a long stride forward, brandishing the knife. He spat at her and wheeled the horse away.

Next morning a grim Talt knocked on the door. Thos was hoeing corn and Vinnie was churning butter. She had a bruised jaw and cut lip. Fortunately, most of her scratches and marks were hidden by her clothes and Thos had accepted her story of bumping into a tree branch while she was out riding.

Talt took one look at her, clenched his hands, and said some words she'd never heard before.

"I'd mighty well love to wring his neck!"

"Whose?"

"You know whose, Vinnie McCready!"

"He told you?"

Talt gave a hard laugh. "He came home looking like he'd tangled with a wildcat. Told his folks he'd tried to jump a fence and fell off in some briars. But I had a kind of notion. Fayte and me, we had a talk after his parents went to bed. He lied some, of course. Said you jumped him with a knife like you'd run crazy and he got all those scratches trying to calm you down without hurting you."

It was Vinnie's turn to laugh. "I hurt him a lot more than he hurt me," she admitted cheerfully. "But the first part's true. I did go after him with Daddy's old knife."

"Why?"

"He called Mark a traitor." No use repeating his words about Talt.

Muscles ridged in Talt's jaw. "The filthy— How he can be the judge's son!"

"But he is."

Talt's eyes blazed tawny green. "And you weren't going to tell me!"

"I didn't see any use dragging you into it. I think he's learned not to come around here."

"You don't understand much about people like him if you

think that. He'll have to get even to prove he's what he sets up to be. He may have just wanted to fool around with you, but now it's turned into more than that. I hate it like hell but I better talk to the judge."

"Oh, Talt, no! I couldn't bear for Mark to know. He'd be so ashamed!"

"He'd be more than ashamed if that young devil really hurt you. Fayte's not going to grow out of his meanness, Vinnie. He'll get worse."

"Please, Talt!"

She implored with her eyes. At last Talt growled. "I'm bringing you a good watch dog. And you need more than that old shotgun."

"Fayte's rifle's down in the oil seep."

Talt whooped. "Let's have a look at it."

He fished it out of the black ooze. After a careful cleaning, he loaded it, fired, and declared it good as new. Talt's rifle used the same cartridges and he put all he had with him in a bowl on a shelf.

"All right, Vinnie," he said grudgingly. "Keep this rifle loaded and close to the door. Carry it when you go riding. And when you're working outside, at least carry your daddy's knife. I don't reckon Fayte'll shoot you. Getting his paws on you will be what he wants."

"I'll be almighty glad when he goes back to the academy."

"Sure. And if the judge can get him into a university, that may keep him out of the way for several more years. But then what? It's like letting a rattler go till it's got more poison."

"He's still the judge's son."

"More's the pity." Talt moved his broad shoulders. "Guess we can always hope he'll get taken care of up in Massachusetts." Holding her gaze, Talt said in a tone that brooked no argument, "I'll bring that dog today. And you've got to promise me, Vinnie, that you'll tell me if Fayte comes around, even if he doesn't do anything."

She gave a reluctant nod. She was going to have to warn Thos, just enough to make him cautious without exciting him into thinking he had to fight the older boy to avenge his sister. Vinnie heartily wished the summer over and Fayte gone north.

VIII _____

Rufus was a young but huge reddish part-mastiff with droopy ears and a wise, sad expression usually belied by his wagging tail. He was immediately protective of Vinnie but Thos was his god. Vinnie pretended not to know that Thos smuggled him into bed at night, though the sheets got twice as dirty in half the time. Loving was good and Thos, so young, had lost many of those who loved him best.

When Thos went to Belleforest, he ordered Rufus to stay home and the dog obeyed with an audible sigh. He made Vinnie feel safe as she went about her tasks. More important, he was company.

She'd told Thos that she and Fayte had quarreled and she'd thrown his rifle in the seep, that she doubted he'd be more trouble, but it wouldn't hurt to be careful. Thos had fired up and wanted to tell Fayte to keep away from his sister, but she persuaded him not to. Less said the better. They'd just be watchful.

It turned out they were watching the wrong place. Juneteenth came and Thos went off early for the celebration. Since it would go on most of the night, Vinnie didn't expect him home till next day. It seemed strange without him. She barred the doors though they were usually left open for cooling these sweltering summer nights. She sat up reading till her eyes began to close and she

79

thought she could sleep in spite of her nervousness. Rufus curled up on the rug beside her bed and thumped his tail when she told him she was glad he was there.

She rubbed the sensitive spot behind his ears, blew out the lamp, and lay down, pulling up the sheet for a sense of protectedness, though her thin cotton gown was already moist with sweat. She was tired, first from chopping weeds out of the corn, and then from sitting up so late. She heard coyotes on the river, the calling of owls, and then she was asleep.

Fire roared black-edged from the oil pond, licked across the fields, devoured the heavy-eared corn. From the woods, crouching by her mother and Thos, Vinnie moaned in terror as flames swept to the cabin. The blue-clad soldiers who had torched the oil rode off like a pack of demons. Katharine McCready hugged her children to her. "We're alive," she said through her tears. "That's what matters, kiddies, we're alive."

But she wasn't. Not anymore.

Vinnie roused at Rufus's whining. He was licking her hand. Had she been making sounds in her sleep? "Sorry, boy." She stroked him. "It was just a bad dream."

But the hoofbeats she heard were real. Galloping in the dark was a good way to get a broken neck, but a drunken man might not care. Vinnie sprang out of bed, fumbling for her clothes in the blackness. Rufus ran growling to the door. Vinnie didn't light a lamp. By the time the horse stopped in front, she was dressed and holding the rifle.

"Vinnie!" Thos's voice. He pounded on the door. "Vinnie!"

She leaned the rifle on the wall and drew back the bar. Thos fell inside, panting, sobbing. She dragged him up, shaking him. "What is it, Thos?"

He clung to her as he hadn't since he was small. "Fire! The Big House—"

She felt as if she herself had caught aflame. "Mark?"

Gulping, Thos said, "Talt got him out. They're both burned bad. Fayte—he was with the gang of Ku Klux—he went in after his mother but the wall fell in—"

Mark was hurt. Questions could wait.

* * *

As they rode for Belleforest, Vinnie finally sorted out what had happened, as much as Thos could tell her. The barbecue and dancing had been in full swing when a dozen or so white-robed, hooded riders swept through the clearing, scattering fires, food, and people, striking out with bull whips. Caleb's wife was trampled and a lot of people were burned or lashed, but no one seemed seriously hurt.

After charging back and forth, yelling that if the blacks wanted to celebrate Juneteenth, the Klan would help them, the raiders were starting to go when the kitchen of the Big House blazed up with explosive force. The horses must have carried a brand that set fire to the back of the place and ignited tubs of fat Hester had been collecting for soap.

Terrorizing blacks was one thing. Burning out a powerful judge was something else. The Klansmen left faster than they'd come except for one who shucked off his robe and ran around to the front of the house, shouting for his mother, the fire rolling through the dry old wood.

Hester, knocked down by a horse, was crawling for the house, calling Mark's name. Talt soaked his shirt at a water trough and, yelling at his mother to keep back, ran crouched through the breezeway. Mark must have been coming to see what the commotion was, for Talt found him under a collapsed beam. Somehow, burning his hands terribly, he pried it up enough to pull Mark free. Dropping to the stone floor, he managed to drag Mark to safety before passing out.

Caleb and several others tried to go around the front way to save Regina and her son but the porch and stairs fell. "Fayte burned up his own mother," Thos wept. "And hurt the judge and Talt."

"Did someone go for the doctor?"

"Caleb did." The late-rising moon cast eerie light. Vinnie asked no more questions but leaned forward, urging Glory on.

In spite of injuries that made her limp, Hester directed that the burned men be fully immersed in water troughs with heads supported so they could breathe. By the time Vinnie and Thos galloped up, the other victims had been cared for and several smaller fires put out. The house still blazed, lighting the whole yard. A bucket brigade tried to quench it, but soon abandoned the effort when it was clear the mansion was gutted.

Giving Glory's reins to Thos, Vinnie slid from the saddle and ran to kneel by Hester between Talt and Mark. Talt was wanting to get up but his mother commanded him to stay under the water.

"You're burned bad, son. But I've seen some awful burns heal pretty as a baby's bottom if they were put under cool water right away and kept there a spell. Nothing else you need to do—you got Mr. Mark out."

"Mrs. Sevier—"

"Nobody help her now but God."

Talt's eyes closed. Vinnie whispered, "Talt, thank you."

His hair was scorched but the damp shirt must have protected his face and also shielded Mark's, for Mark's features too were unmarred.

"So you got here, Vinnie." Talt's eyes opened slowly.

She leaned over. Tears mingled with the kiss she gave him. He grinned faintly, said so softly that Hester couldn't hear, "I won't be as mean to you as you were to me for doing that. Don't cry, honey. Neither of us fixin' to die." He tried to turn his head, grimaced and fell back. "Judge come to yet?"

"He's got a bad bump on the back of his head." Hester was applying wet towels to it, propping the towels in place. She looked around at the people who weren't much hurt and were taking care of those who were. "Find out who needs to see the doctor while he's here, and make sure everybody's got a roof."

"None of the cabins burned," Lonny, the stableman told her. "The barn caught but we put it out."

Everyone looked at the Big House. They may have been thinking, like Vinnie, how ironic it was that Fayte hadn't harmed the blacks seriously while destroying his own home—and killing his mother.

Hester limped off to Caleb's house to see his wife and brew some comfrey tea, which she considered good for healing. Vinnie stayed with the burned men.

Mark breathed stertorously, his mouth slack. While Vinnie prayed for him to rouse, she also dreaded it. What would he do when he learned his wife and son were dead—worse, when he knew why? The only terrible comfort he would have was that Fayte had tried to save his mother.

Aside from shock at anyone dying that way, Vinnie couldn't mourn Fayte. But her horror over Regina was full of guilt. Vinnie had never wished Regina death or misery but she had sometimes remembered wistfully how it had been before Regina came, and she'd imagined how it might be if Regina took herself back to Louisiana.

Without opening his eyes, Talt muttered, "The judge?"

"The same."

Talt stirred and winced. "Wish that doctor'd get here. But the judge is a strong man, Vinnie. He'll pull through."

What if he didn't want to, once he learned about his family? Vinnie found herself hoping that he wouldn't regain consciousness until his body had healed too much for the shock to cause harm. She kept one hand lightly on the back of his neck and prayed for him.

Dr. Spellman was aghast at Hester's water treatment, but after he examined the men, he admitted that the burns looked better than they would have if treated with salves or fresh butter.

"Judge Sevier's burns are concentrated on his legs and arm." The doctor rubbed his gray moustache. "I'll salve and bandage them, but since the water seems efficacious, the affected limbs might be soaked from time to time. If this causes infection, send for me at once. Judge Sevier has a concussion, I believe, but the only cure for that is rest and nature."

"Would it be dangerous to move him in a wagon?" Vinnie asked.

Dr. Spellman glanced from the smoldering Big House to the scatter of cabins. "After he regains consciousness, it might be better for him to recuperate somewhere else." He coughed but didn't mention Regina or Fayte. "I would say the risk would be minimal, provided several mattresses are placed on the wagon and someone holds his head to keep it from being jarred. It would be simpler for me to attend him, of course, if he were moved to town."

"You've said there's not much you can do," Vinnie pointed out. "Hester, you'll come, won't you? We can move Talt and look after them both."

"Master can have our bed," protested Caleb, tears leaking from his old eyes.

"Your Tillie's hurt," Hester said. "You need to take care of her, Caleb. But you can come over and see the judge anytime you want."

"I'll go help Lonny get a wagon ready," the old man said. "Everyone'll want to loan their mattresses. We'll pick the best. Dr. Spellman, sir, you goin' to have a look at my woman?"

"I'll see anyone who needs it," the doctor said firmly, and turned next to Talt.

Mark had Vinnie's bed. With difficulty, they kept Talt in Thos's bed for two days but then he insisted on getting up and taking his turn watching by Mark, though he submitted to immersing his burned arms, hands, and shoulders in a tub several times a day. Mark groaned and muttered incoherently but hadn't regained his senses. At least the burns hadn't formed cracking, painful scabs or become inflamed.

"Could he just—stay this way?" Vinnie forced herself to ask the doctor when he came out three days after the fire.

"I've never seen such a case." Before Vinnie could take comfort in that, the kind-faced gray-haired man added reluctantly, "What can happen, sadly, is that a blow may have a permanent effect."

"Effect?"

"He might regain consciousness and be physically well, but his mind could be impaired."

Mark's brilliant incisive brain ruined? Why, that was what made him who he was! Vinnie shuddered to remember an imbecile back in West Virginia, a grown man with vacant eyes from whom people ran when he shambled in their direction.

Not Mark! Better he had died.

"We know so little about these injuries," Dr. Spellman went on. "Occasionally a person functions normally most of the time but now and then has seizures—what's called the 'falling sickness.'"

That didn't frighten Vinnie so much. Mr. Prichard's aunt used to have fits during bad storms and about all the attention anyone paid was to put a stick in her mouth so she wouldn't bite her tongue. *Oh God, if Mark has to have anything, let it be only that!*

When the doctor left, Vinnie went where she could vent her feelings, hurrying to the creek and into the cave. She sank down in the inner chamber where she could hear the play of water rushing out of the crevice.

In the ancient dark, she tried to bargain with God to take her life, maim her, anything, if Mark could get well. She crouched there a long time. Soothing cool darkness, the music of water, the sense of timeless grace gradually calmed her.

She, Mark, everyone, was mortal. All fated in the end to die. But in between there was joy and work and beauty and what people were to one another. If Mark's mind could not return, she'd still take care of him and love him. As long as they lived.

She bathed her face and went back to the man who lay in a blackness deeper than that of any cave.

Ten days. Two weeks. Caleb reported that grass had already spread over the grave in the Belleforest cemetery marked by a stone with Regina's and Fayte's names. Caleb had hunted through the ashes for hours but the charred bones he found were so few and unidentifiable that they were placed in a single coffin. A warrant was out for Clay Mannering and others suspected of taking part in the raid, but none of them could be found. It didn't seem to matter. All the rest of their years they'd have to live with the flames of Belleforest.

Dr. Spellman was amazed by how cleanly the burns had healed. Wearing thick gloves, Talt was beginning to use his hands. Mark's legs were pink but only the deepest burns had a slight crust at the edges. The doctor could give them no hope about the head injury, though. "If someone's going to recover, they usually show signs of it before this."

"He has opened his eyes a few times," Vinnie said. "Once I thought he knew me."

"Well," said the doctor, patting her hand, "who knows?" It was clear he had given up.

Watching beside Mark that night, Vinnie took his hand, kissed the dulling scars. Slow tears ran down her face to the warm but lifeless-seeming fingers. When he had done everything for her, why couldn't she help him? "Mark," she whispered. "Come back. Please, please, come back."

After a time, she drowsed, her face on the bed beside his hand. It was a movement of his fingers that brought her awake— *live* movement, with purposeful intelligence directing the movement. Scarcely daring to look, she straightened. His fingers touched her hair and her cheek.

"You look like you've been crying, Vinnie." His voice was husky. His gaze wandered to the lamp, strayed about the room. "I'm at your house. What's happened?"

She didn't want, God above, she didn't want to have to tell him. "You were hurt." She got to her feet, light-headed with relief yet dreading this. "Would you like a drink? Something to eat?"

He caught her wrist, amazing strength in his hand. "My damned head! It's splitting! But—I heard a commotion and started outside. There was smoke and fire. I started back for Regina . . ." His eyes widened. His fingers bit deep into Vinnie's flesh but she welcomed the pain. "Where is she? Where's my wife?"

When Talt got better, he'd given up his bed to the women and moved into the kitchen with Thos and Rufus. Hester now rushed out of Thos's room and threw herself on her knees by Mark, taking his face between her hands, laughing, crying—Hester, who had been stoical every moment up to now.

"Lord love you, Mr. Mark, you can talk! Bless God, bless Jesus, you're in your right mind!"

He dropped Vinnie's wrist and seized the hand of the woman who had taken care of him since he was a baby and she a young girl. "Hester, where's Regina?"

Hester got control of herself. She stroked Mark's hair, weeping quietly. "She couldn't anyways be got out of that fire. Mr. Fayte ran around to try—"

"She can't be dead!"

The wounded cry brought Talt, scrubbing sleep from his eyes. His glad shout faded as Mark buried his face in Hester's breast, shoulders heaving, body writhing.

"There, boy," Hester murmured, rocking him. "There, there, my honey boy. Can't give up."

At last, he drew away. Perhaps he had known all the time in those layers beneath consciousness. Maybe that was why, for so long, his mind had refused to join his body. He shivered in spite of the hot July night. Hester started to pull up the coverlet but he fended it off, hitching himself to a sitting position.

"Fayte?" he asked, the name tearing its way from his throat. "You say Fayte was there?"

He'd find out, but it was crueler than even Regina's death. Hester was silent. Vinnie tried desperately to think of a way to evade the question till he was stronger, but Talt dropped to one knee so that he was on a level with Mark's gaze.

"Fayte went in after his mother. Never came out."

Mark flinched as if flames seared him afresh. "But he went to Pleasanton that day. He was on a tear because of Juneteenth."

"Reckon he was." Talt took a long breath. "He and some friends came back. Rode through the celebration, scattered fires." At Mark's stricken look, Talt said quickly, "It was just meant for a kind of mean little lark, Judge. They didn't much hurt anyone at the barbecue. They sure never dreamed the Big House would catch fire."

Mark stared off into some place that must have been more terrible than the war. "The Klan?"

Talt shrugged. "They wore white robes and hoods."

"Have they been arrested?"

"Sheriff tried. Can't find hide nor hair of any of them."

"Who got me out?"

Talt didn't answer but Vinnie said, "Talt did."

Mark fell back wearily. "I've got to thank you, though right now I'd just as soon have gone with my family." Then he took the small comfort there was. "At least the boy tried to save his mother. He never meant—what happened."

IX _____

Vinnie had thought if Mark's mind came back, she'd have nothing left to ask of heaven. Now she found herself despairingly thinking that if he went on as he was, he'd sorrow himself into a grave beside the one that held the blackened bones of his wife and son.

He scarcely ate or drank. He had moved into Thos's bed and Vinnie, now sharing her bed with Hester, heard him toss restlessly. When he slept, he groaned, calling Regina's name.

It was seldom he slept, however. Most nights he rose after a while and went outside. Days, Selim was saddled for him and he started riding to Belleforest. Caleb said he spent hours searching the ruins of his home or sitting by the grave.

"He's so thin," Vinnie worried to Hester. "I don't think he's had an hour's solid sleep since he came out of that stupor."

"Takes time. Even when someone's sick or old and you expect them to die, it takes a long time to grieve through a death. Mr. Mark, he's got two to mourn. Besides that, he hates the Klan. Fayte died to him twice."

As soon as he was strong enough, Mark resumed his court duties, and with prompting from Talt, slowly began to catch up on his business and correspondence. "I've imposed enough on you," he told Vinnie one night as he picked at the fresh corn soufflé Hester had made especially to tempt him. "Talt, would you go over tomorrow and help Caleb pick a house site? I don't need anything fancy, two or three rooms, maybe situated on the knoll on the far side of the sawmill."

"Judge, that's a long way from the Belleforest people."

"Maybe Caleb and his wife will move over there, and if you and Hester are with me, I won't need any other help. I don't want to be in sight of the old house."

"You could stay here, then," Vinnie offered. "There's plenty of room to build another house or we could add on to this one."

How often she had wished that Mark lived at the Orchard Place—but not like this, broken inside, brooding. He was her love, though. She would do for him whatever he'd allow.

A faint smile softened the tight line of his lips. "Bless you, Vinnie, I'm bad company. I shouldn't go on inflicting myself on you."

"You took us in, Thos and me, and gave us everything."

He sighed. "I'll admit I'd rather be here, at least for a time. Later, perhaps, I may take a house in Pleasanton. Is it all right for the men to build on a room? And run up a cabin for Hester and Talt?"

"Of course." Vinnie nodded. Relief warmed her. If he was starting to plan his life, that must mean he intended to live it. She was startled as Talt's chair grated back.

"No need to make room for me. I'll see to the building, Judge, but then I'm leaving."

Hester said nothing but she drew in as if compressing her flesh into a shield.

Talt gone? Vinnie felt a rush of desolation. He had become such a steadfast presence, watching their needs without seeming to, always there. Mark must have felt the same.

"Leave? I'll be glad to raise your wages."

Talt shook his dark head. "You already pay double what I'm worth. But I never meant to stay here so long—just wanted to see my mother before I settled in to making a living. Got a notion to buy a drilling outfit and dig wells for folks in between poking around for oil."

"There's oil right here," Vinnie said. Every moment, she less and less wanted him to go. "You can have all you want."

"I bet you won't always say that." He grinned. "Drilling's a mess. You wouldn't want this pretty place all mucked up, Anyhow, like you said, this is too far from transport and markets. But somewhere pretty near a railroad, well, it'll be fun to see what I find." His eyes glowed.

Mark said slowly, "You really do want to go."

"I've done about all I can around here. Debts all paid." He looked at Vinnie; he was telling her that he had given her the life he'd owed. "I'm not leaving you in trouble, Judge. Vinnie can take over—and I bet your book moves faster with her than it ever did with me. It's due this fall, remember."

Mark frowned. "It was lost in the fire. I've been intending to tell my publishers that I can't deliver it."

Talt chuckled. "You'll have to give them another excuse. The first draft did burn, Judge, but I'd been making a fair copy every day or two all along and putting it in a box I kept at my cabin." As everybody stared, Talt went over to the chest where Vinnie'd let him store his things. He took out a ledger and set it in front of Mark. "My aunt lost some valuable papers once and she sure impressed on me that it was smart to keep separate a second copy of important things."

Could he also have worried about what Fayte might do to the manuscript? However that was, Talt had used canny judgment in waiting to produce it till Mark was beginning to think about work. A few weeks ago Mark might have thrown it away.

Opening the book, he read swiftly before he gave his head a bewildered shake and laughed for the first time since that frightful night. "It seems I'm trapped. I'd better start work on it tomorrow if I'm to meet the delivery date." He turned to Vinnie. She could see in his eyes that he remembered not only the day and the reason she had ceased to be his helper but also all the kindness and laughter and comfort that had ever been between them.

She remembered all of it, too. He was alive and he had laughed, and if all she could be was his hand, she was joyful to be that. The time she had scorned life's simple gifts because he couldn't be her lover seemed long ago, in an incredibly selfish childhood before a fire swept away two lives and the great old house, before she had prayed through despairing nights that Mark would come to himself again.

Before he could ask, she leaned forward. "Talt says this book is even better than the first. I don't see how that can be, but I'm ready when you are."

That night, instead of going outside alone, Mark read his manuscript and asked Vinnie if she would play the piano. It was Talt who watched her for a while and then went out.

It was decided by general consultation that the best arrangement for the new quarters would be to build another set of cabins about ten feet behind the existing ones and join them by walkways covered with small branches to make an inner court that would be cool in summer and protected from harsh weather in winter. Grapevines would be planted along the walkways and trellised across the top.

A cabin was going up for Caleb and Tillie, too. Tillie had recovered from the trampling but she cried every time she looked at the ruined Big House, and Caleb had been with Mark too long to give it up. Tillie was used to lots of trees so she had asked that her house be raised by a stand of live oak on the other side of the cornfield. The Belleforest lumber barns hadn't burned, so there was plenty of cured wood for where green wouldn't serve. Mark's cabin was done and furnished in a week, a spacious study with a small bedroom partitioned off with bookshelves. These weren't completely bare. Mark had many books at his town office and started bringing home a full saddlebag each court day. Also, upon learning of the disaster, Mark's publishers shipped a copy of every book they had in stock that might suit his tastes. By the middle of August, all the building was done.

"I guess," said Talt at supper, "I'll move along tomorrow."

Hester's hand went to her throat. She didn't say anything but she looked at her son in a way that made Vinnie's eyes sting. Thos hero-worshiped Talt, more than ever since the fire. He put down his bite of cake, his appetite gone.

"Aw, Talt! Don't go! You can hunt oil around here."

Tousling the boy's hair, Talt grinned. "My feet are getting itchy, pardner. Got to see some new territory. Who knows, when your sis thinks you're old enough, you may want to hunt me up and help me make our fortunes."

Blue eyes lighted. Vinnie saw the old dream of being a cowboy fade in a twinkling. "Oh, Talt, could I?"

"Why not? Even if I make my first million before you turn up, I won't have it long, so we'll make another."

Thos whirled to Vinnie. "Hear that, sis? Hey! Could I go right now? I'm almost fourteen!"

"Certainly not!" She glared at him and Talt, her stomach twisting. Was this how it would be one day, the brother she'd cared for since their mother died eager to go, breaking loose, tearing her heartstrings as he went? "I need you right here, Thomas Benjamin McCready. Don't you even think about leaving home till you're at least sixteen!"

He yelped in protest but Talt laid a hand on his arm. "That's right, young'un. You want me to take you on as partner, you either be sixteen or have a note from your sis. And don't you act up and cause her grief, hear?"

Thos's round face lengthened but Talt's eyes bored into him, demanding the promise. "All right," he said, "but let us know where you are once in a while, because the minute I turn sixteen I'm on my way."

It was rare for a boy of spirit to stay home that long. Better for him to be with Talt who'd watch out for him than roving alone in rough company. Still, it hurt that he was so ready to go. And because it was moonlight, the minute dishes were done, Thos called Rufus and went hunting.

Talt asked Vinnie if she'd walk with him. She was tempted to refuse till she remembered this would be the last time. The moon shone in serene fullness behind scudding clouds, some thick enough to obscure it, others forming blue or silver traceries around it. Vinnie thought of the times and seasons they had walked the river. "I wish you weren't going," she said. "We'll miss you something fierce."

"You'll get along without me just fine." His voice turned wry. "Have you stopped to think on it, Vinnie? You've got what you wanted, the judge over here with you, needing you more than he ever has."

"I didn't want it this way."

"That's the trouble with wanting something real bad, honey. The *way* it comes . . ." He shrugged. "You're the most important person in his life now. Take care of him."

"You've got nerve to say that when you're leaving!"

He grimaced. "Vinnie, I can't stay here any more than you

could live at Belleforest. The day I kissed you— God, Vinnie, don't you know I love you?"

Her flesh shrank. "Oh, Talt, please don't—"

"Not much I can do about it. Except go where I won't have to pine after you while you pine after the judge." She hung her head. After a moment, Talt gave a small bitter laugh. "Just as well you only love me like a brother. That's all the law allows us. Even if I didn't have black blood, whites can't marry Indians. Bed with them, sure—I'm proof of that."

"It's a wrong law. If—if I loved you that way, Talt, we'd go someplace where we could marry. Or I'd claim to be part Indian."

He chuckled at her indignation. "I bet you would. But that's all *if*s, and on my part it's dreamin'. Anyhow, Vinnie, I had a couple of reasons for asking you to walk with me. One was to tell you, send for me if you ever need me. The other. . ."

Without waiting for him to ask, she moved into his arms, lifted her face, let her hands caress the back of his neck. She would give him whatever he wanted. She held him almost as dear as Thos. He had rescued Mark.

His kiss seared away thought, questing from mouth to throat, the curve of jaw beneath her ear, back to her startled lips. It wasn't charity that melted her against the taut, warm length of him, made her blood flow heavy as molten gold. She clung to him with roused woman-need. He was going away. Mark would never take her. What would it matter?

Long hands trembled for a heartbeat on her breasts, then fixed hard on her shoulders, holding her away. "No, Vinnie." He was gasping, shaking his head. "Not that way!"

Faces pale in the light that strayed through the trees, they stared at each other. Talt whirled around as they heard a twig crack. A clublike something smashed against Talt's head. He reached for the shadowy form that had risen from behind the rocks, but his knees buckled and he sprawled on his face. A hand choked off the scream rising from Vinnie's throat.

"Thought I was going to get to watch that redbone lay you," Fayte rasped. Her first thought, that he was a ghost, vanished at the cruel grip of his hands, the weight of his body forcing her to the ground. "Guess I'll have to do it myself. Then I'll slit your throats, nice and quiet, and go set fire to your shacks."

A blade pressed the side of her neck. A cry would be sliced off before it left her mouth. "Your father's there."

"I know. Goddamn bluebelly sellout's alive while Mother's dead! He won't be for long!"

"You didn't go in after her," Vinnie said, knowing it was true. "The fire was too much. You ran away. Could you hear her screaming?"

He struck her so hard that moon and clouds crashed down. She fought her reeling senses, knew she had to divert him till she had a chance to battle him or till Talt roused. But what if Talt's skull was crushed? What if she was the only barrier between death for her and Talt and the people in the cabins?

She pretended unconsciousness. Fayte wouldn't enjoy his vengeance so much if she didn't feel it.

"Bitch!" He slapped her again, but lightly. "I've waited every night for you to come down here. Found that cave where you must of hid that red nigger the day we almost got him. If you hadn't stopped us—" He shook her by both shoulders. The blade no longer pricked her throat. "Come out of it, damn you! I want you to know what I'm doing."

Trying to keep her body limp, she mentally tensed, readied herself. *Talt, Talt! Wake up! Help me!* Fayte's hands snarled in her hair, yanking it brutally.

She screamed as loud as she could, praying it would travel to the cabins, and heaved upward in the same instant, clawing for his eyes, screaming again. They grappled for the knife. He got it.

Hot red pain seared through her shoulder. She sank her teeth in his arm, bit till her teeth grated together. He hissed. Spitting out his blood, she saw the blade glint, flung herself away from him, rolling down the bank, too breathless to scream anymore. As he lunged after her, she got behind a tree, heaved up a rock she had stumbled on and dashed it in his face. He shrieked. His nose poured blood. He sprang around the tree, bearing her down, his hands digging into her throat.

From far beyond the blackness sucking her down, she heard Mark calling her. Then there was impact, a tearing at her throat as fingers drove in desperately and then were gone. A rush of air burned her throat. She gulped it in, leaned against the tree.

Black against the moon, two men contended on the rocks

above the river. Back and forth they swayed, one slighter than the other but taller.

"Vinnie!" Mark's cry echoed through the cliffs. She opened her mouth but an answer stuck jaggedly in her crushed throat. The man who had to be Talt slipped, dodged aside as the knife flashed down.

An explosion shattered the night, sending birds crying from their trees. Fayte was spun around. The knife clattered as he threw up his arms, facing toward the river.

He fell or dived. Hester leaned Fayte's rifle against a tree, hurried over the rocks to Talt. "You all right, son?"

"Sure, Mama. Vinnie?" he cried out hoarsely.

Stumbling, Vinnie moved out into the light. She still couldn't speak but as Mark reached her, she took him in her arms.

They hunted that night with torches but couldn't find the body. A search in daylight was also futile. The river was running high. Fayte might be carried for miles before he washed ashore or caught in debris. Talt had seen the wound. Entering the chest, the cartridge tore badly as it came out the other side. Fayte's shirt had been soaked with blood when he went off the ledge.

Good trackers explored the banks a long way in both directions and found no sign. Mark helped search, but when there was no use in looking further, he shut himself in his cabin. Vinnie called him for supper, but he said he didn't want any. His words were slurred. But Mark never drank more than a glass or two of wine! When Vinnie told Hester, the older woman scowled, then sighed.

"Lord help him, whiskey could be the best thing for a little while. But his pa was a notable drinker. I don't aim to see him go that way."

On the third day, Mark was still locked in. Caleb admitted fearfully that he'd been sent to the store for more whiskey—anything that'd keep a man drunk. Hester glanced at Talt. Suddenly her eyes flashed. She snatched off her apron and caught up a butcher knife.

"Mama!" Talt called, following her, "what you fixin' to do?"

"Get his nose out of the jug!"

She pounded on the door. "Mr. Mark, you open this here door!"

"Go 'way, Hester."

"I'll not. I'm staying right here till you come talk like a human 'stead of denning up like some snake-bit pup!" Vinnie hurried after Hester and listened with a thudding heart as shuffling came from inside. Finally, there was the scraping of the bar across the door. Mark was unshaven and red-eyed. His hands twitched.

"All right, woman. What do you want?"

"I want you to throw out that whiskey."

He started to shut the door and she seized his hand. "Mr. Mark, if you blame me for shooting that boy, you take this knife and cut my throat. I can't stand your carrying on this way!"

"Hester!" He seemed shocked into sobriety. "What else could you do? I'd have done it myself. But to lose my only son . . ."

She gave him a long look between pride and sorrow. "Fayte's not your only son."

"Mama!" Talt cried. "Don't say—"

Mark turned to him, staring at the younger man. Vinnie scrutinized their faces, the same strong jaw and high forehead, the same eagle nose. As she studied them, Hester nodded.

"Talt's your son too, Mr. Mark. Your mama knew. You were so young—not sixteen. I wanted the baby—how I did! But she made me see going up to have him at my sister's and leaving him there was the best way. I'm not telling this to make you feel bad. Just look at him, though! Isn't he a boy you can be proud of?"

Then Vinnie understood. Why Talt had stayed with Mark instead of rambling off after oil and adventure. The why of many things. Her eyes stung as Mark reached out his arms, blindly, and Talt went into them.

Talt left a week later. He was glad to be acknowledged as Mark's son but ferociously set against benefiting from it. As he told Vinnie good-bye, he kissed her cheek and murmured in her ear, "Remember, send if you need me."

Embracing his mother and father, he turned last to Thos. "I'll get us that drilling outfit and find us some good sites. But till you're sixteen, you be a good help to your sis." He mounted.

At the last rise, he turned to wave. They all waved back. When he was out of sight, they started to the cabin and Mark's hand closed on Vinnie's. "We'd better get to work. Book's due soon."

"Yes." Her eyes met Hester's and Vinnie recalled what she'd said to Hester when they were alone after the revelation. "You really loved him!"

"I loved him always," Hester said calmly.

You still do, Vinnie thought, ashamed at her own demanding, vowing to be lessoned in what love could be.

"Yes," she said again, pressing Mark's hand. "It's time to work. And live!"

Book Two ─────────────────

KATIE

I

Katharine Lorena Sevier O'Malley looked to see if the corn bread was almost done and glanced at the thick dark bear steaks Esau had broiling on the outdoor grill by the cookshack. Bear meat was so rich and sweet that some didn't like it, but Katie served it about once a week as a change from venison, pork, and beef. Unlike most staples, meat was cheap in Baygall, eight or ten cents a pound. Katie had moved to the new boom town eight months ago after her husband, Dan, died from lungs seared as he helped battle a horrible blaze at Spindletop that had threatened to engulf the whole field.

Katie could have gone home to the Orchard Place but she was a woman now, twenty-five years old, three years married. Besides, at home she would have been constantly reminded of Darcy, Talt's son, who had grown up with her after his mother died of tuberculosis up in Oklahoma, which had been the Indian Territory till lands were opened to whites. Uncle Thos and Talt were still working there, and Darcy had joined them when he was old enough. Darcy's mother had been the daughter of a wealthy part-Scots, part-Cherokee rancher and his mostly French wife, who'd have been glad to raise their grandson, but Talt had brought the black-haired, gray-eyed eight-year-old boy to Vinnie and Mark and his own mother, Hester.

Katie couldn't remember a time when she hadn't worshiped Darcy. He had mended her toys, made her new ones, taught her how to swim and ride. The Orchard Place was full of memories of their happy times together, and that heartbreaking time when their feelings changed from those of brother and sister to a tremulous desire. Their blood relationship might have been ignored—Talt was not officially Mark's son—but they couldn't marry because of Darcy's black and Indian blood. She begged to go with him anyway, but he rode off without telling her good-bye.

For over a year she grieved, refusing to accept calls from eligible young men. Then Dan O'Malley came to try to lease the place for drilling. Son of Irish immigrants, lilting-voiced, laughing-eyed, he'd teased and courted and blandished her into marrying him. A fiery but tender lover, he came as near to making her forget Darcy as any man could. From their honeymoon, they went to the fields near Beaumont, accompanied by Esau, Caleb's son.

Dan lost his savings drilling one dry hole, then hired out to build another stake. That was when he was killed. Since the Lucas Gusher blew in wild at Spindletop ten years ago, January of 1901, spewing oil 225 feet in the air, drilling in coastal salt domes had brought booms at Saratoga, Batson's Prairie, Sour Lake—and here, Baygall, a wide boggy street lined with rickety buildings and tents with the shacks and palmetto-thatched huts of families on one side and brothels at the far end. The cattle drives that had helped bring Texas prosperity after the Civil War were long over, though Texas beef still fed Northerners. The new bonanza was oil, oil that was changing the world. People from all the states flocked to its promise, and Baygall was one of many oil towns that sprang up overnight.

There was a community-built church that used Methodist hymnals but was attended by everyone of a religious bent. It also served as a school. A livery stable that doubled as a mortuary was at one end of the street. Next to it was one of two dry-goods stores, a drugstore, and a grocery. There were two frame boardinghouses, two tent ones, and an elegant, dilapidated hotel, frequented by lease dealers, investors, and promoters, that went back before the War Between the States when Baygall had been famed for its mineral baths. Locals liked to say that if Sam Houston had soaked himself here instead of at Sour Lake, he'd have been cured of his arthritis.

The remaining forty establishments were gambling dens, saloons, dance halls, brothels, or mixtures of any or all of these.

The graveyard shift that worked from midnight to noon was heading for the restaurant, and Katie hurried to finish setting the three long plank tables with blue enamelware and tin forks, spoons, and knives.

When the men got off their twelve-hour tours, which they pronounced "towers," they scrubbed off as much dirty oil as they could with tow sacks or rags before bathing in the hottest water they could stand. Lots of them wore their work clothes till they rotted from the crude oil, but Negro women carried big kettles and tubs around, asking for laundry, and more fastidious workers let the women do their best with the stiff black garments.

Once changed into comparatively clean clothes, the men consumed vast quantities of food and coffee. Some then fell into bed, often a cot they were allowed to use for only eight hours before the next man took his turn. Others got drunk, gambled, whored, and fought, sometimes managing all these pastimes before catching a little sleep, then going to another grinding twelve-hour stint.

As the men dragged up chairs and benches, Esau brought pungent steaks and Vinnie passed big pans of corn bread. Each table was supplied with washbasins of fluffy mashed potatoes, big bowls of gravy, and bowls of okra stewed with tomatoes, onions, and peppers.

Katie prided herself on good, plentiful cooking and fresh butter on each table. Her food was so renowned that lots of men who paid full board at boardinghouses in order to have a bed came to her place to eat, paying the extra money.

Rance Gorman, a driller, grinned at Katie as she filled his cup. His lean, sunburned face was attractive in spite of pits left by acne or disease, and his hazel eyes appreciated her warmly. Dan had known him at Spindletop and said no one was Rance's peer with a rotary rig.

"What's for dessert, Mrs. O'Malley? I need to find out before I plumb stuff myself on your good corn bread."

"Fresh blackberry cobbler with cream," she said with a smile.

"My favorite," sighed Bailey Scott, his snub-nosed freckled face assuming a beatific look. Man-grown though barely eighteen, Bailey was a roughneck. When his hair was clean, it was light blond and his eyes were sky-blue. Katie sometimes slipped him an extra helping of dessert.

"More coffee, please, ma'am?" drawled Joe Young.

His short-clipped sandy hair couldn't hide the dozens of ridges and scars all over his head. His nose was squashed flat, and he was missing several teeth. Only a few years older than Bailey, he looked middle-aged. His arms and shoulders pitched forward as if he were carrying something heavy, his face was traced with broken veins, as were his arms. Straining as he helped build the big wooden tanks that stored the oil had caused those broken veins, and the scars were from fights.

Tankies were toughest of the tough; Joe had to be the toughest of the tankies since he was the tank-setter who bossed a crew, but he'd never picked a fight at Katie's, except when a newcomer once made a suggestive remark to her. Joe's fist lifted the stranger off the floor and into the street and the man would have gotten stomped if Katie hadn't stopped her avenger.

She liked these men. Those who had been Dan's friends at Spindletop seemed almost like family. She wrote letters for the ones who couldn't, listened to their troubles, and kept their money safe in her strongbox. This was an exhausting life, one she wouldn't want to follow for many years, but it paid better than anything else she could do and left no time to grieve for Dan or yearn for Darcy.

The last of the blackberry cobbler vanished. The last coffee was drained. When all the customers were gone, Katie and Esau cleared the tables, dumped the dishes into a washtub of soapy hot water, and filled their own plates, sitting on stumps beneath the shade of a big gum tree. They would have to serve another big meal around eleven for these same men before they went to work, and another right after midnight for the men coming off the day tour.

"I think I'll make buttermilk biscuits tonight," Katie said, sopping corn bread in okra stew. "Grits, redeye gravy, green beans. You fix the meat and I'll make apple upside-down cake."

A tall, thin man in a cream-colored suit and planter's hat was picking his way along the edges of the miry street. Katie groaned. "Lord help us, it's that Fayette man!"

"Whyn't you just duck inside your room?" Esau suggested. "I'll fix him a meal if he's bound to have one." Esau slept in the cookshack and Katie lived in a small room connected to it by a dogtrot.

"He sees me," Katie said, shrugging. "I don't want him to think I'm afraid of him."

But she was. Not that the wealthy promoter had said or done anything offensive in the several weeks since he'd begun to stop by after the men were gone. It was just the way he looked at her and the fleshiness of his lower lip in contrast with his narrow, hard-angled face. It was hard to guess his age, but she put him in his late fifties because of the silver that gleamed in thick, waving red hair.

Striding to the edge of the restaurant floor, he took off his hat. "If your darky can hustle me up a plate, Mrs. O'Malley, perhaps you'd keep me company."

"Esau isn't 'my darky', Mr. Fayette. The war settled that. And I'm afraid the food's cold. You'll dine better at the hotel."

"Oh, I doubt that." Not in the least discomfited on her rebuke, he sat down. Deciding to have it out with him, Katie got to her feet.

"I serve meals at eleven and twelve, night and noon. You're welcome then if you can find a seat but I simply can't bother with people who stray in at odd hours."

He kept smiling. "Boy," he said to Esau, "bring me some dinner."

"Don't," she told Esau before advancing on her unwanted customer. "This is my property, Mr. Fayette. Kindly take yourself off it."

He showed small, even white teeth. "Are you going to throw me out yourself, ma'am? If that nigger touches me, I'll shoot him dead."

Katie had never needed the loaded shotgun she kept by her bed, though Dan had taught her to shoot. She went inside and got it. "I won't kill you, Mr. Fayette, but if you don't get out of my restaurant right now you'll get you a load of shot in your legs."

His dark eyes flared like flame edging a blowout. After a moment he laughed and rose, gave her a mocking bow. "We'll meet another time, my dear. When you don't have a shotgun or your nigger."

Lighting a cigar, he lounged away. Esau shook his head. "Wish you hadn't done that, Miss Katie. Porter at the hotel says

Morgan Fayette killed two men over at Sour Lake just because they wouldn't get out of his way."

"I'm not a man," Katie said, trying to laugh.

Esau hesitated, then burst out, "Miss Katie, why don't we go home? The judge and Miss Vinnie would sure be glad to have you. With your Uncle Thos and Talt and Darcy wildcatting up in Indian Territory, it must get lonesome for them, and they're sure not gettin' any younger."

Katie felt such a longing for the Orchard Place, for Vinnie, still trim and sweet-moving, and the judge, who still seemed taller and wiser and handsomer than any other man. They'd had their sorrows even after they'd married, two children lost in infancy, but the judge, in addition to his court duties and writing his records of the Civil War and Reconstruction, had served four terms in the state legislature before returning for good to country life.

It would be so good to go home—to rest in the peace and love that were almost tangible in that house. But that would be retreating from life, warming herself in the glow of her parents' dearly won content. Katie straightened and spoke bracingly to Esau. "If Fayette makes me trouble, he'll have all our friends after him. I'll bet we don't see him again."

All the same, her appetite was gone. She put up the shotgun and began doing the dishes.

Katie was at the grocery store when a commotion broke out in the street. Another fight. Fights were so common that she scarcely glanced at the crowd gathering around the contenders till someone yelled, "Rip her clothes off, Annie! Get ahold of that yaller hair! Let's see if it's real!"

Halting, Katie stared. Why, there were Sheriff Calhoun and Justice of the Peace Morris Sopworth. The men had a disgusting weekly practice of lining up arrested prostitutes on the balcony of one of the boardinghouses, calling out each one's fine to the men below, and awarding the woman's company for a day to the first man to reach the JP with the money.

Katie had futilely protested to both sheriff and JP. "Why, Miz O'Malley," Sopworth said unctuously, "that's where we get our salaries. Them women, they don't care. Kind of good advertising." He chided, "You oughtn't to even notice their sort, ma'am."

"We're all women. This is like putting slaves on the block.

You don't arrest the men who visit the brothels, do you? In fact, didn't I see you coming out of The Bird Cage a few nights ago?"

The JP had an immense dough-armed wife. Imagining the scrawny little cadaver atop her was like picturing a praying mantis astride a tub of lard. "You—you see too much a lady shouldn't!" he whinnied. "You run your restaurant, Miz O'Malley, and me'n the sheriff'll run the town."

Now he and the sheriff were standing in front of the dry-goods store, collecting money that was being shoved into their hands. "Five on Annie," Katie heard a man bellow, and the next one shouted, "Ten on Hook-nose Nell!"

Calhoun and Sopworth had found another way to make money off the women men used and then despised. Some boom-town followers were prostitutes as hard as nails, robbing their customers, depraved by drink and dope. But they'd all been young girls once. Plenty still were—young in years.

Katie recognized a number of her customers. So respectful to her only a few hours ago, Rance Gorman now whooped encouragement to Nell while Joe Young cheered on the black-haired Annie. Bailey Scott called out delighted, obscene comments.

Katie put down her groceries and pushed through the throng. She caught Bailey's arm. "You think gawking at these women'll make you a man?"

He gaped. She whirled on Rance and Joe. "You ought to be ashamed!" Furious tears filled her eyes. "If Bailey was your son, would you want him here? If Nell or Annie were your sister, would you think this was entertaining?"

"Now, Miz O'Malley, ma'am," began Joe, scratching his scarred head, face scarlet. But she didn't stay to listen. She advanced on the JP and sheriff.

"Isn't it your duty to keep order? *Stop* fights?"

Tubby, freckled Sheriff Brick Calhoun didn't take off his grimy hat.

"This ain't no place for *ladies*. Push in where you got no business, Miz O'Malley, and you'll see a lot you don't like."

"If you're taking bets on this, gambling's against the law."

"Bless your heart, ma'am, we got nuthin' to do with bets the boys're makin' on the side." Calhoun chortled. "Me'n Morris, we're just collectin' a dollar a head from them as wants to see the show."

"And you're going to give the money to Hud Walters's widow and kids," said Rance, who had come up behind Katie. Bailey and Joe flanked him. The driller's hazel eyes flicked from Calhoun to Sopworth. "Right?"

More of Katie's regulars closed in. "Yeah," said a brawny driller, "and let's just take what we all bet and add it to the kitty. Miz O'Malley, you want to take the collection to Hud's missus?"

Katie's wrath was stemmed by a need to laugh. "Oh, I think the sheriff and the justice ought to do that, boys, but Amalia would certainly appreciate it if you all went along with them."

Rance took charge of the wagered funds, and as the men marched the officials toward the widow's shanty, Katie turned to the panting women who were trying to drag their ripped garments around their scratched, exposed flesh. Nell was pretty despite her crooked nose. Annie was older, a plump matronly woman. Both watched Katie warily.

"Why were you fighting? You weren't mad at each other, were you?"

"No'm. But the sheriff said we wouldn't have to pay our fines if we put on a good show." At Katie's shocked look, Nell shrugged. "What's the difference? We're a show for 'em one way or the other."

"If you'd like to work for me, I'll hire you," Katie said. "But it's hard work and I don't allow drinking or—or—"

Nell grinned at her floundering. "Throwin' our fannies? Honey, I make five bucks a whack. And I gotta have a bottle."

"Me, too," said Annie. "Thanks all the same." She spat in the dust, rubbing blood from a split lip. "We'd do fine if that slimy JP and sheriff let us alone."

They moved off, arm in arm, apparently the best of friends. Katie looked after them with regret before she shrugged and picked up her groceries. Hud's widow would have a bundle of money to help her get on her feet; and she didn't think Calhoun and Sopworth would organize any more such battles.

Several days passed without a glimpse of Morgan Fayette and Katie began to hope he'd left town. Trouble was brewing, though. One oil company was hiring Negroes to drive teams and make earthen reservoirs. Most of the men Katie knew were in favor of leaving them alone so long as they didn't try to "take a white man's job," but there were many who feared that if the blacks got a toehold, they'd take over the fields since they would work for less. A delegation of independent drillers and workers had told the company's superintendent that he'd better fire his Negroes. He hadn't, but he also didn't seem like a man who would protect his men.

The men working graveyard and those coming off the day tour had all been fed. It was almost two in the morning. Smudge pots smoking around them to keep off the mosquitoes, Katie and Esau were doing dishes when they heard shouting and jeers from nearby where a sludge pond was burning off.

Dark figures were silhouetted against the blaze. It looked like an ungraceful dance, men weaving and flailing their arms. The howls were chilling, like hounds baying. Figures were running and stumbling, falling, lying prone and then dragging themselves up, trying to dodge the blows of their tormentors.

"Lordy God!" breathed Esau. "They've got them poor niggers!"

Katie's blood froze. No use going to the sheriff. He didn't like blacks any more than he liked women. Esau ducked inside for the shotgun. She yanked it out of his hands. "Don't go over there! You could get killed."

"You 'spect you to watch while they toss my folks in that fire?"

"Get to the boardinghouse! See if you can find Rance or Joe or some of our friends."

"What you fixin' to do with that shotgun? Them men's all worked up, Miss Katie."

"I don't think they'll hurt a woman. Hurry! Send someone to help!"

She was terrified, though, as she cut through town to the glow of the burning waste that made the men, victims and persecutors both, look like creatures in hell. She had seen plenty of fights but never a mob. It was as if the workers forming the gauntlet weren't men at all but mere bodies, possessed by blind lust; it reached her hotter, more searingly, than the fire.

If Esau could find help soon!

"You shouldn't be here, Mrs. O'Malley." Morgan Fayette stepped out of the shadows. The blaze reflected in his dark eyes.

"Neither should you! Did you start this?"

"I can't claim credit, my dear. I only stood a few rounds of drinks and let the men decide they'd better get rid of the niggers or see their jobs taken over at nigger wages." A steellike hand closed on her elbow. "Come, I'll take you home. You're insane to be out at this hour on any night, let alone this one."

She thrust the shotgun into his side. "Let go of me!"

"You won't shoot."

Laughing, he reached for the weapon. He was right; she couldn't shoot. But she wrenched free of him and swung the double barrel as hard as she could against his head. He pitched forward. She hoped she hadn't cracked his skull but wasted no time thinking about him.

Running into the smoky, eerie space near the pond, she discharged the shotgun into the air, then shielded with her body a black man who'd been beaten to the ground and was covering his head with his arms.

"Stop this!" she shouted in a voice that pierced through the howling. She recognized some of the men, though none of her favorites was there as far as she could tell.

They all stared. Then someone yelled, "Get on back to your crib, sweetie!"

"She's no whore," growled a robust tankie. "That's Miz O'Malley as runs the restaurant. Now, ma'am, you sure hadn't ought to be here."

"No one should."

A tall driller said, "This is men's business, lady. Don't be mixing in what you don't understand." He dropped his club and started toward her. "Come on, I'll see you safe to your place."

The shotgun was empty. She gripped the barrel and raised the stock over her shoulder. The injured Negro had crawled against her skirts and his blood soaked her feet. The driller stopped.

"Please, ma'am," he coaxed.

"You're the ones who ought to go home!" she choked. "My God—I've seen some of you in *church!*"

There was an uneasy shifting. The dozens of blacks, herded into a mass, who hadn't yet run the gauntlet, watched hopefully. Then the shotgun was wrested from her with such force it numbed her fingers.

Fayette tossed the gun aside. His head was bleeding but he was steady on his feet. He gripped both her wrists. "I'll get the lady out of here, boys. You go ahead and take care of what has to be done."

"I reckon nothing here's worth doing," drawled a lazy voice. A man eased out of the darkness. Light glinted off the barrel of his big Colt revolver. His hand-stitched boots had never slogged through oil muck and he wore a new-looking silver-gray hat. "I'm a Texas Ranger, boys. My commission's good all over the state. If you don't make tracks, I'll start making arrests."

"He's bluffing!" Fayette shrilled. He reached inside his vest and brought out a derringer.

"Inciting to riot," murmured the stranger, bringing the barrel of his gun crashing down on Fayette's head.

Men were running toward them from town—Rance, Bailey, Joe, others. Some had guns; all had at least a piece of pipe or a club.

The Ranger stepped toward the biggest man on the gauntlet, but before he could touch him, the roughneck backed away. "I'm goin', Captain, I'm goin'."

The mob melted into the blackness. The massed blacks came forward to pick up their battered comrades. "You don't have to leave," the Ranger told them. "I'll be around town to keep the lid on." He stirred Fayette with his elegant booted toe and turned to Rance and the other would-be rescuers. "Let's tote this bird down to the sheriff. And by the way, where *is* the sheriff?"

"Gettin' his take off the gamblers and madams, most likely," Rance said. "Good thing you was in town or there'd likely been some killin'." He spat. "Not that some couldn't use it."

"Sounds like you're from Virginia," said the Ranger. "Funny, you taking up for Negroes."

Rance gave him a direct stare. "Wasn't takin' up for 'em. Takin' up just for Miz O'Malley." The injured black had been carried away but his blood stained her skirts. "God Almighty, ma'am! You hurt?"

"No." She suddenly felt like her knees were dissolving. "No, Rance. Thanks for coming."

"Esau had to root us out of a saloon or we'd have got here quicker. C'mon, Joe, give me a hand."

They hoisted Fayette and moved off, careless of his dragging hands. Esau came forward. "Miss Katie, don't ever let your folks know I let you get in such a fix! If this gen'man hadn't come . . ."

The stranger laughed and holstered the revolver. "Got me off to a flying start here. The captain heard there was maybe going to be trouble and sent me to take care of it." He took off his hat. His hair was taffy brown and curly and his eyes were the gray of a blue norther. "Hardy Alastair, ma'am." He grinned and she realized how young he was, probably only a few years older than she. "Seemed a lot of guys wanted to take you home tonight but it looks like I'm the winner."

He slipped his hand firmly beneath her arm and something sweet and wild coursed between them. He laughed, "I sure do like to win."

II _____

Hardy was like no man Katie had ever known. He might surprise her with an armful of hothouse roses shipped expensively from Dallas, or, with as much flourish, present a few sunflowers from the roadside. He might dry dishes for her, or, with Esau's support, untie her apron and sweep her up to the hotel for dinner with champagne. He didn't try to kiss her but seized every chance to help her up and down stairs or across miry spots in the road. Each time he touched her, wild sweet flame swept through her.

She loved Darcy. In another way, she had loved Dan. But this intoxication was different; she distrusted it because it had flashed between them from the start and because, in spite of working till she usually fell into immediate sleep, she still had times of hunger for love, for a man's strong arms and caresses that would lead to the flowering of the private female self she had stifled since Dan's death.

His laughing banter would have kept anybody from guessing that Hardy had faced down one mob and continued keeping order without drawing his gun. Word sped through saloons and dancehalls that he was a deadly shot with either hand; the most drunken tankie hadn't cared to make him prove it.

Hardy's mother had died when he was twelve and after that he'd trailed with his Ranger father, growing up among men whose mere presence often was enough to quell a riot or, as it had in this case, to send tinhorns and crooks out of town as fast as they could go. To Katie's relief, Morgan Fayette was gone, too. He hadn't been chained to the big oak like other malefactors. Sheriff Calhoun had gotten him packed and on the train. Hardy had let him go, but he'd called on the blacks' employer and chastised him for not protecting his men, strongly suggesting that those beaten too badly to work should be paid while they recovered.

That same day, Katie invited the solid element of Baygall to meet at the restaurant. They formed a justice committee, following the example of citizens over at Sour Lake where decent folk had organized to put an end to lynchings of black and Mexican workers.

Baygall needed to be prepared. Hardy couldn't stay there long and the sheriff and JP were pretty much useless.

Ten days after his arrival, Hardy told Katie that he'd been ordered to Batson's Prairie to clean up the town that had boomed at the same time as Baygall.

Esau was in bed, for Hardy had dried the dishes after the graveyard shift breakfasted and the day tour had supper. The town was as quiet as it ever was, music and rowdy laughter coming from the red-light district.

At the news that Hardy was leaving, Katie's smile faded and her heart went bleak as if parched by a searing wind. "Oh. We'll miss you," she said woodenly.

"Will you?"

He didn't touch her but the lantern darkened his gray eyes while radiating light from their centers. A rush of fear mingled with urgency, an inner trembling, made her shrink back. He touched her hair, then her cheek, laughed softly. "You can't be scared of me, Katie, not after the way you stood off that whole damn boiling of rowdies. I hope God strikes me dead before he lets me bring you a second's grief."

The elemental depths of her vibrated with the resonance of his deep voice; it was as if it had entered her body, stirred warmly through her veins. She couldn't move. She couldn't speak. She only looked at him.

"I love you, honey." Warm, strong fingers dropped to her throat, paused at the pulse leaping beneath them. It was as if he had his hand on her very heart. "You must know that." The temptation was strong to close her eyes and lift her mouth for his kiss. Her body smoldered with hunger long-denied. Yet she had felt guilty about loving Darcy throughout her marriage to Dan. She couldn't let that falseness taint whatever this was she felt for Hardy, even if it sent him away from her.

He held her by the soft caress on her throat, only that. She stepped back and was amazed that her voice could be so steady when she was a chaos of swirling desires and warnings. "Hardy, I care a lot for you. But I love someone else."

"Your husband? He's dead, sweetheart. But I can wait till you're ready."

She shook her head. "Someone else."

Hardy's eyes narrowed. "Then why hasn't the fool married you?"

"He can't. Not ever."

Hardy thought a moment, turning a little, and she saw his high forehead and strong chin in dark profile against the light. "Is it someone in camp? Someone you've met since Dan?"

"No. He was before Dan. He was . . . almost all my life."

"But you married Dan." His words were cool.

"Yes. Dan was so—alive. He made me laugh and I could feel the way he loved me. I thought I could love him back. And I did, in a way."

"In a way! Your husband? The man who held you every night, slept with you in his arms?"

She couldn't answer. Silence thickened between them. She wanted to fill it with defenses but pride forbade that. After a space of heartbeats, he turned away.

"I've got to think about this, Kate. I'm leaving tomorrow but I'll be back."

Suddenly, he spun around, brought her close against him. That first kiss was not gentle, not kind. It compelled, demanded. Crushed against his heart, her breasts ached. Her starved, dry tissues seemed to soften and swell like drought-withered plants opening gratefully to rain. She moaned and went soft against him, her arms clasping around his neck. She thought of her narrow bed. Would he take her there?

Abruptly, he let her go and she caught the edge of the shack to keep from reeling. "Maybe I can't marry you," he said roughly.

"But I could have had you tonight. You need a man, Katie. Think about that."

He strode away.

Katie couldn't sleep that night. How could he make her feel like this when she loved Darcy? And why had she believed she had to tell him the truth when her love for Darcy could never be fulfilled? Why hadn't she kept it to herself?

Hardy didn't stop by on his way out of Baygall. She wondered as she went mechanically about her tasks if he would come back at all or if he would forget her.

After Hardy left, Katie drove herself. She worked all the time except when she went to bed after everything was ready for the next day. Then thoughts she could no longer keep at bay came crowding in, memories of Hardy, the comfort of his strength, the way he could make her laugh like a child. But it was Darcy she loved, she had always loved.

What was this feeling then that she had for Hardy? It was more, much more than bodily need, wilder than friendship. But he was no man to take second place. Was she never to have a lover again? Darcy had urged her to marry, told her bluntly that he'd have women where he found them, the same as he intended to eat and drink. That didn't, he had said, have anything to do with how he felt about her.

Katie grimaced. Perhaps men had no problem in separating love from lust, but she needed to care about a man before it was possible to lie beside him. She thought of her mother, who had for so long, and with apparent hopelessness, loved the judge. After her cruel childhood, Vinnie deserved happiness and Katie was glad for her, but she saw no chance of her own love ever being fulfilled.

The repelling power of the kerosene-soaked rags she'd hung beneath the cheesecloth netting must have worn off, for she heard insects whining. One had slipped through her defenses and hummed maddeningly around her ear. She slapped at it. The sibilance continued. Tossing off the thin sheet, she dipped the rags in the odorous fluid, wrung them out, rubbed her oily hands along her temples and ears, and went back to bed, but not to sleep.

* * *

Ten days after Hardy left, Katie was coming out of the grocery when she glimpsed a rider on a big steel-gray horse like his gelding, Smoke, at the far end of the straggling main street. She couldn't see the rider's face, but as he dismounted she recognized his easy grace and the light gray hat. Her heart began to pound. She started forward, then checked.

It wouldn't do to rush after him when she wasn't sure how she'd answer if he spoke of love to her again. Better to wait for him to come by the restaurant. She hurried back, put on her prettiest apron, and smoothed her hair before starting the hominy grits. Esau glanced up from the kettle of beans he was seasoning. "What happened to you, Miss Katie? You got a shine like dew on a rose!"

"I've just been walking fast."

Esau eyed her keenly. "Frilly new apron when the other was fresh this morning? Could be Cap'n Hardy's back."

Katie turned to hide her blush. "I think I saw his horse."

"His horse!" Esau snorted. "Lot the horse cares if your hair curls or your apron's pretty." He added dourly, "You best not let the cap'n get away again, missy. You need a good man, 'specially if you're studyin' to live in boom towns 'stead of going home to your folks."

She pretended not to hear. Any minute now Hardy should be along. She'd be cordial and welcoming but she mustn't let him see how delighted she was or he'd jump to conclusions. She'd missed him terribly. But loving, she still didn't know about that.

He didn't come at noon or between meals, and he didn't come at midnight. Puzzlement changed to disappointment, then to hurt and anger. If he'd changed his mind, if he'd fallen out of love or decided that he should, he might at least have told her so.

She was scrubbing viciously at a kettle when a shadow loomed and a long arm reached for the dish towel. "I'll finish up, Esau." Hardy's tone was as airy as if he'd never been away. "And don't worry if you hear Miss Katie hollering at me. We've got some real serious talking to do."

"Long as you're with her, I sure won't worry, Cap'n. Glad to see you back." With a chuckle, Esau deserted.

Katie concentrated on the kettle. "Aren't you going to say 'Hello,' 'Good night,' or 'Go to the devil'?" Hardy's tone was amused but there was an undercurrent of iron that made Katie go defensively rigid.

"You left without saying good-bye."

"That was because I was coming back." Luminous shock pulsed between them. Katie's strength drained away. She summoned up grievance to keep her voice cool.

"How long have you been in town?"

"Rode in this morning."

"You didn't exactly break your neck getting here."

"Had things to attend to, Katie. I'm leaving the Rangers."

"You're *what?*"

"I'm kind of tired of cleaning up boom towns. Same kind of cheap riffraff over and over. I might as well be a policeman!"

"What will you do?"

He shrugged. "Country's going to hell up here, autos and roads and swarms of people. I'm heading for Mexico."

Desolation washed through her. "You are?"

"Had an offer of a good job while I was in Sour Lake. Delivering payrolls for a British company that's drilling out in the forests beyond Tampico. Between Indians and bandits, it gets to be pretty interesting. That's why companies are hiring all the Rangers they can get."

"It sounds just wonderful—if you like to shoot and get shot at!"

"It's top money. I want to get into oil, Katie, but not just as a roughneck. If I earn enough for a stake, I'll get some partners and start drilling."

Going to Mexico! So far away, and no telling when he'd come back, if he ever did. Katie set the last utensils to drain. "I hope it goes well for you, Hardy. That you get your stake and bring in a gusher."

He draped the dish towel over a branch and brought her around to face him, heedless of the soapy water that dripped from her hands. "Do you, Katie? Enough to come with me?"

She didn't know if it was joy or terror that stopped her breath, made her feel that she was falling. It was exhilarating, headily seductive. "You—you've thought about what I told you?"

"Haven't thought about much else. But it comes back to this."

With deliberation, he gathered her to him, cupped her chin in his hand, fingers molding her jaw. He held her, not with strength, but with an intensity of longing which shook her to the depths and made her tremble.

He may have lowered his lips; she may have lifted hers. However it was, the kiss melded them. She willed the crushing sweetness of his embrace until her body flowed against his, shaped to its strength. He was the one, at last, to draw back, voice deep with triumph and possessive tenderness. "Whoever it is you think you love—did you kiss him like that?"

"I never kissed him at all."

He frowned. "That's worse, I reckon. Dreams can be what a real man's not. But you're a real woman in my arms, Katie. It's up to you. Marry me, have all the caring there is in me, or go on wanting what you can't have."

He didn't touch her. She knew it was on purpose, that he wouldn't try to persuade her with lovemaking. A proud man, Hardy Alastair. So much more the wonder, then, that he'd come back. Had he tried to take her by storm, she'd have resisted. As it was, he forced her to meet squarely the question of what she intended to do with her life; blight it by yearning after Darcy or join it to this man who watched her gravely, with a sort of compassion. She'd told him the truth. If he wanted her anyway, could she be fainthearted? She took a deep breath.

"I'll marry you."

She moved into his arms. Before his mouth claimed hers, he said, vowing, "Someday you'll love me."

They were married at Old Orchard, as the Orchard Place was now called. Vinnie, slim as a girl, played the piano. Katie didn't didn't think her mother would ever look old. Silver-blond hair wouldn't show white, and though her early years had been hard, Mark had cherished her so lovingly that there was a glow of serene happiness about her. If only Father weren't so much older! Katie couldn't imagine Vinnie without the judge. Still, at almost eighty, he was more vigorous than men half his age. He still presided at court and was working on his fifth book, an account of the Gainesville lynchings that had taken his father. Katie had grown up used to his empty right sleeve, but as he smiled and offered his left one, escorting her to the minister, she thought how cruel it must have been for a young man to lose an arm. Of course, as he was fond of saying, Vinnie had been his right hand since he brought her home with him rather than put her in jail for stealing his chicken. That had been at Belleforest, never rebuilt, though a small community flourished around the sawmill.

Hester's dark face was still handsome though she was over ninety. Time was the master carver that had refined the flesh to a thin cover for strong bones, the bones Darcy had inherited, though he had his father's gold-green eyes. Hester, too, looked peaceful. She had loved Mark all his life, through his marriages to two other women, had been dear as a grandmother to Katie. She exemplified a definition of love that awed Katie, who didn't think she could ever achieve Vinnie's sweet dignity or Hester's wisdom. Their examples adjured her to put all her might and will into this marriage. As her father gave her into Hardy's keeping, she made an inner vow more fervent than the one spoken.

After a gala dinner, Katie opened gifts, all manner of crystal, china, linen, and other house gear from neighbors and friends. Most of it would have to be stored, joining gifts of the same kind brought to her wedding to Dan. Still, she reveled in the sheen of mellow silver, embroidery on snowy sheets and pillowcases. She wouldn't always live in oil camps, have to travel often and light. From her parents came a toy piano with the promise of a real one when she could use it, but the most unusual gift was the one Esau presented on behalf of all the men who'd come to her restaurant in Baygall.

It was a gold derrick four inches high, executed in exact detail. On the derrick floor was engraved, "May all your wells be gushers!" But the gift that made Katie's eyes mist was a forked hazel branch of the kind dowsers used when witching for water or oil. Around it was fastened a legal-looking document that declared: *"When as and where ever Katharine Sevier O'Malley Alastair and Captain Hardy Alastair drill for their bonanza, we, the undersigned, solemnly swear to aid and assist in said drilling in return for beans and beds. Good luck in Mexico, folks, and let us know when you're ready to dig a well."* It was signed by Rance Gorman, the driller; Joe Young, the grizzled tankie; and young Bailey Scott.

Hardy chuckled. "Well, we've got a crew. Now all we need's a stake." He had resolutely refused to use any of her Baygall savings, insisting that she ask her father to invest it safely. Nor would he accept the judge's offer to sponsor a well. "I don't want to start out borrowing from your family," he said. His eyes danced. "Besides, I'm itching to see some new country, have a little excitement."

"I'd just as soon it didn't get too exciting," Katie said. "Father's worried about a revolution. Díaz kept things quiet but now he's exiled and Madero's having trouble with the other leaders like Zapata and Villa and Carranza."

"Honey, you won't be guarding payrolls." He took her in his arms, murmured in her ear, "I'll always take care of you, sweetheart. I may act crazy but I'm not stupid."

It was good to be married at home; to have her name and Hardy's written in the family Bible by the judge; good to sense her parents' liking for Hardy and their relief that she wouldn't be living away from them and unprotected. But Old Orchard brought back legions of memories, mostly of Darcy. Though Hardy was eager to know about her growing up, she couldn't bring herself to show him the cave, that special place for Darcy and her.

The night of the wedding, after Vinnie and the judge had gone to their sleeping quarters behind the main cabin, Katie finished her wine. Before she had a chance to grow nervous, she went to her husband and kissed him. He trembled but didn't draw her down on his lap. His eyes asked, hoped, desired. He was allowing her to make a gift.

That grace enabled her to take his hand, blow out the lamp. The bed she slept in as a girl was made with new linen sheets but the quilt was the one of blue flowers that Hester had made for Vinnie long ago when Vinnie first moved to the cabin. Katie's wedding night with Dan had been spent at the best hotel in Pleasanton. To be in her own room with Hardy gave her a feeling that she was still herself, though the reflected light in Hardy's eyes sent a strange languor through her. A girl had married Dan. She was a woman now. She thrilled rather than tensed at Hardy's hands as they smoothed her throat, moved like a moth's brush to her breasts, shook as they undid the buttons of her pale green-silver satin.

A candle glowing on the dresser, reflected also in the mirror behind it. Hardy bent to kiss the hollow between her breasts, let his lips graze toward her nipples, delicately, shyly, as a deer might feed. *With my body I thee worship* ... He filled her with wonder, a feeling of richness in what she could give. She stood proudly as he slowly slipped down her dress and lacy underskirt, took off her chemise, and stepped back to look. No one had seen her naked since she could remember. Blushing, she started to cover herself.

"Don't. Please." Hardy's voice was husky. "You're so beautiful I can't believe it. Let us have the light."

She moved into his arms. Lambent flame passed between them. Suddenly, she was not the gracious giver but a seeker, needing him, whispering endearments, stroking him, undoing his shirt. The male body had always abashed her but she wanted to see his, wanted to fondle and admire and make friends with that part of him that would yield them both so much joy in that miracle before it subsided like a spent flower. He didn't take her quickly, only after she moaned and arched against him, offering, pleading. His hard mouth, the rhythm of his body, the clasp of his hands lifting her to meet him, hurtled her into a sweet fury she had never known. She surged ahead of him, exploded into rosy fire. He throbbed with silent force, showering her soft darkness with pulsing that dissolved into bliss.

They rested in each other's arms. It was only after Hardy slept, the smile on his mouth making him seem a boy, that she allowed herself to think of Darcy, beg him to forgive her, will him to be happy.

III _____

Katie was used to the damp heat of the Texas Gulf but Tampico was worse. The Indian village ravaged by Cortez had been reestablished by a priest, sacked by pirates, and resettled just in time to be a battleground during the war for independence from Spain. Built on a bluff above the Río Panuco, the wharves and waterways had schooners, brigs, steamers, tugs, and lighters anchored along the noisy waterfront reached by stone steps descending from the town.

Long the country's busiest port and now headquarters for British and American oil companies, it woefully lacked the charm Katie had expected though she made what she could of the cobbled streets, the Plaza de Armas with its gardens and bandstand surrounded by the municipal palace, cathedral, and best hotels, the rowdy Plaza de la Liberación a block away, the ruffling palms, brilliant flowers, and pink, yellow, and blue wood or stucco houses with overhanging balconies and grilles made of wood because iron would have rusted.

The hotel was rather grand, but she longed for a place of their own. She panicked when Hardy announced, pleased, that he'd been hired by the Eagle Oil Company, a big British concern, to deliver payrolls to outlying camps.

"Some are quite a way back in the jungle." He laughed, hugging her. "But the money's good, and when I'm not traveling, the company will train me as a driller at Jarocho."

Katie had a drowning feeling of being abandoned. He had told her his plans before she'd agreed to marry him, but it had all sounded so dashing and colorful then, so different from the reality of being alone in a foreign town without even a house to keep.

"Where's Jarocho? And what is it?"

"It's about fifty miles inland, the company's training camp for drillers and a depot where supplies and equipment shipped up the river are sent on by narrow-gauge railroad to outlying fields."

"I'll go with you."

He stared. "But, honey! It's in the middle of the jungle. A bunch of rough men, bandits on the prowl, and there's only a barrack for living quarters."

"We'll find something—or build it. I'm not going to stay here while you're off all the time."

He frowned. "Jarocho's no place for a woman."

She laughed. "Some might say that Baygall wasn't."

"At least it was in the United States. Besides, I'll be gone half the time delivering payrolls."

"And how often would I see you if I stayed in Tampico?"

"When I came for payrolls," he admitted ruefully. "But Katie, there are other oil company wives here. We'll find you a nice house and maid—"

"I'll go back to Texas or go with you." Angry tears made a blur of his startled face. "It may suit you to see me a few days each month and then get back to your adventures, but I didn't come down here to play cards and gossip with other bored women."

"Katie! I'm just trying to take care of you."

"I don't want to be taken care of if it means being useless and twiddling my thumbs."

He considered her grimly for a moment. Then he laughed and swept her up in his arms. "All right, woman! I'll even promise not to say 'I told you so!' when you take one look at Jarocho and want to leave."

He carried her to the bed and put her down on the coverlet patterned by shafts of light slanting through the grilles. They had learned each other's bodies well in the month since their marriage, knew how to excite, tantalize, prolong, or urge to cresting release. Cooled by the breeze from the sea, they rested and loved each other again before bathing and going down to a meal of *huachinango,* fresh red snapper, huge avocados, black beans, rice with shrimp, French wine, and Mexican coffee so strong that the flavor dominated the added half cup of hot milk.

"When are we leaving?" Katie asked.

He cocked an eyebrow at her and said with smiling challenge, "How about tomorrow?"

Long pale masses of mangrove roots looked like tangles of drowsing snakes along the riverbanks. Bamboo grew forty feet high and Katie had never seen so many shades of green, so many shapes of leaves, as on the vines and trees towering above the mangroves. Orchids and air plants that grew from the branches were so thickly interwoven with moss, lichens, and vines that they often formed gardens in the air where hummingbirds glinted as they fed. Egrets, herons, and roseate spoonbills waded in shallows as they searched for dinner. An anhinga spread his plumage to dry and Katie cried out with pleasure. "Why, I've seen him in East Texas!"

The chug of their launch motor sent parrots in scolding flight and provoked the curiosity of monkeys who clamored as they followed along in the trees. Sometimes children stared from thatched cane huts along the bank, each with its beached dugout, for the river was the only road. Occasionally, they passed barges loaded with pipe and other equipment for the company's outlying fields.

In spite of Hardy's argument that it would be better to wait till they knew what they'd need, Katie had collected all the portable housekeeping things she could locate, and as they traveled farther and farther into the wilds, she only wished she'd had time to gather at least all the essentials. Hardy said there was an Indian village at Jarocho but she doubted if she could buy anything there besides fruit, though she hoped for eggs. There were no other passengers on the launch, which was steered by an expert young Mexican who chatted with Hardy, and tried out his few words of English on Katie. She responded with the smattering of Spanish she had learned from Hardy, who spoke the colloquial language well because of serving along the border.

It was evening when they drew up at one of several docks.

Barges were being unloaded despite the late hour, railroad cars being packed with supplies for the other fields. Though this was a small patch with only about ten derricks thrusting out of oily black muck, the clamor was deafening after the calm of the river. Walking beams moved to the throbbing growl of the engines, and the workers were black with greasy mud.

Katie hung back a moment, then lifted her chin and laughed, "Just like home!"

"You won't say that after a day or two, my dear lady."

They whirled to face an immense young man with sun-bleached yellow hair, eyelashes, and moustache. His nose was raw from sunburn, and the few places where he wasn't peeling, he was newly roasted. He had a baby's chubbiness on a frame that loomed a head above Hardy's six feet. Delphinium eyes searched Katie's before resting on Hardy. Then, with exquisite formality, the giant extended a hand.

"I fancy you're Alastair. Hope you last longer than the payroll men we've had lately. I'm Tom Hanford, the general superintendent."

They shook hands. Hardy introduced Katie. She received a very English bow. "Welcome to Jarocho, madam. I applaud your pluck, if not your wisdom, in following your husband. Fortunately, you can get a ride back to Tampico almost any day you decide this won't do." He coughed delicately. "It won't, you know. Isn't done, a lady in an oil camp."

Katie made herself as tall as she could. "I don't know about English women, sir, but a good many American women live with their husbands near oil fields. I was at Spindletop and Baygall." *And now I'm mightily glad I was.*

"Ah, Texas!"

"Yes, Texas."

He grinned, and in spite of her ruffled feelings, she suddenly liked him. "Right!" he said expansively. "Let's get you settled. Would you prefer a warehouse or part of the barrack?"

The buildings in the Indian village across the railroad tracks were of cane thatched with palm fronds. She resolved to ask Hardy to pay some Indians to make them one. But for the night . . . She glanced at the long frame barrack with its thatched veranda. Men lounged there, smoking, drinking, playing cards. Hardy suppressed a grin before he said, "We'll try a warehouse."

The warehouse was thirty feet wide and a hundred long with thick mud walls and great double doors of solid mahogany. Two of the three sections were stored high with boxed supplies, but Tom Hanford had one of the camp *mozos* clean out debris from the empty part and set up cots rigged with mosquito netting. Boxes to hold their suitcases and another with an enamel washbasin, pitcher, and lantern completed the arrangements. The leather payroll bags, containing heavy silver coin and American dollars because workers had grown suspicious of Mexican paper, were locked up in the superintendent's safe.

Katie put clean sheets over thin, lumpy cotton mattresses, and was glad she'd bought feather pillows in Tampico. She wanted a bath but Hanford had invited them to dine with him, so she washed in the basin, tucked a clean shirtwaist into her cadet-blue duckcloth skirt, and did her hair while Hardy freshened up, trying vainly, as usual, to flatten the wave of his thick light brown hair.

The dining hall was simply a thatched roof over long plank tables surrounded by benches. The superintendent's table had deerskin-covered chairs and seated four, but there was no difference between the food served to the men and that served the superintendent, black beans, rice, fish, fried bananas, and *cocada* for dessert, grated fresh coconut boiled with milk and sugar to a creamy pudding.

The fourth person at the table was Hal Martin, a rangy young American geologist starting on his first survey for the company. Wistfully, he told Katie that his bride had planned to come to Tampico but the guerrilla risings in the north and fears of a general revolution had led her parents to insist she stay in New Orleans.

"Madero's doing his best to keep the machinery running and placate the hotter heads," Hanford told Hal. "Without British and U.S. investors, Mexico wouldn't have railroads or much industrial development at all. All we have to do is stay out of the country's politics, except for judicious 'presents' when necessary. Send for your wife, old chap." Hanford smiled paternally at Katie though he couldn't have been over thirty. "By the time she gets to Tampico, I daresay Mrs. Alastair will be there to keep her company."

Katie smiled, too. "Don't bet on that, Mr. Hanford."

His blue eyes weighed her before he turned to Hardy. "We've

found the best way to handle payrolls is to deliver them a different way each time and on different days. We've packed them in pipe and stoves and cylinder heads of pumps, in bales of cotton, tool boxes, gasoline drums, and just about every other container you can imagine. How do you want to do it?"

"I think I'll just put the bags on a pack mule and follow the tracks."

Hanford stared. "My dear fellow, that'd be a dead giveaway."

"I hope so," Hardy returned sunnily. "Because the bags will be full of dirt. But I reckon whoever stops me will be dead by the time he finds that out."

"You could be the dead one."

Hardy shrugged. "If it's my time."

Their eyes locked. After a moment, Hanford gave a brief nod. "It's your job. I'll send a couple of our best Indians with you."

"No, thanks. If there's shooting, I don't want people in the way."

"Bandits have shot other Texas Rangers, Alastair."

"It happens," Hardy acknowledged.

Hanford gave up and began to advise Hal Martin on what he'd need for his journey. Katie and Hardy said good night and rose to leave. Getting to his feet for Katie, Hanford bowed, again displaying surprising grace for such a large man. "Be sure to shake your clothes and shoes out before putting them on," he warned. "Besides scorpions, centipedes here can be a foot long. I had a whole tribe of them take up residence in a jacket pocket."

"Sleep well yourself," Katie retorted, laughing, but before they got into their cots that night, she held the lantern while Hardy shook out the sheets, looked under the cots, and examined her nightgown.

The cots were drawn together so they could rest in each other's arms. They were too tired for anything more. "Hardy?"

"Mmm?"

"Why don't you take a few men tomorrow? Or hide the payrolls on the train?"

He kissed her thoroughly but his tone was final. "This is my job, honey. Let me do it."

And if you're killed? She clamped her lips shut. He had let her accompany him. She couldn't carp and wheedle. "If you faced

down that Baygall mob, I guess you can take care of a few bandits," she said to cheer herself.

She kissed him again. His arms tightened, one hand straying
to her breast, along her loins, resting warmly there before, so
slowly that she gasped, his fingers spread glowing eagerness
through her thighs and secret parts. Weariness vanished as they
loved each other, and then, deliciously exhausted, she went to
sleep with her head on his shoulder.

Night didn't pass blissfully, however. It was still pitch-black
when Katie woke to scurryings and squeakings on the crossbeams
above. Rats, she decided after a terrified moment. They were bad
enough, but that swishing meant bats after insects. She refrained
from rousing Hardy. He needed his sleep and there wasn't much
he could do anyway, but she resolved not to spend another night
in the warehouse.

Her nerves were further unsettled by Hardy's shaking a huge
black, red, and yellow centipede out of his boot as they were
dressing. He was off at dawn, his shotgun in his saddle scabbard,
and a short, sheathed machete slung from the other side. His twin
Colts were out of sight beneath a loose cotton jacket.

"I expect I'll be back tonight," he said as he kissed her good-
bye. "But don't worry if I'm not, because I mean to keep going
till something happens." He chuckled. "Won't it be a joke on me
if I make it all the way to the Tupan camp without getting robbed?
The men would be kind of sore that I had rocks instead of
money."

"Be careful," she said, and forced a smile as she waved him
on his mission.

She would be anxious till he returned so the best way to com-
bat fear, grief, or loneliness was to get busy. She found Hanford
talking to Hal Martin. As soon as that young man was on his way,
she asked the superintendent if she could hire a few of his Indians
to build her a house.

"I didn't think you'd stay in the warehouse." He smiled. "But
dear Mrs. Alastair, the barrack at least has a floor. Those thatched
huts look romantic but I doubt you'll find one satisfactory."

"I'd like to try it."

"Very well," he said with a shrug, and called over three men.

* * *

The house went up like magic. Clad in loose white shirts and
trousers tied in at the ankle to keep out pests, the three Indians cut
corner posts while Katie selected a site as far as possible from the
derricks without moving into the jungle. The river curved just
below and she planned on finding a secluded bathing spot. When
posts for two rooms were firmly planted, the men fastened bamboo uprights and braces together with vines and bound them in
place before fastening palm leaves over the sides and the roof
poles. They even made a standing shelf, table, and beds of split
bamboo and bamboo chair frames.

One Indian went to the village and returned with several deerhides. He was followed by a pretty young woman dressed in a
white blouse and hand-woven black skirt patterned in black, red,
and blue. She had a big-eyed golden-skinned baby in the shawl
draped around her back and she carried a sweet-smelling grass
mat.

With a shy smile at Katie, she spread it on the earthen floor
while the men strung the deerhides to shape sling chairs. Katie
touched the mat and held up three fingers. *"Tres más?"*

The woman shook her head and Katie realized the people
probably spoke their own language, not Spanish. In pantomime,
she showed that she would like to spread other mats on the floor.
With a giggle of comprehension, the young mother hurried off. In
a few minutes she returned leading five women, all of whom were
carrying mats.

Katie decided it wouldn't hurt to cover the entire floor. She
spread Mexican coins on the table and indicated that the women
should take what was right. Their smiles vanished. One of the
men said, "Present. Give."

Katie blushed. She signaled the women to wait, went to the
warehouse and selected jars of jam, marmalade, and syrup. Her
visitors were delighted and withdrew with laughing murmurs.

While the men moved the Alastairs' belongings, Katie sought
out Hanford, who assured her the workers would be pleased with
an American dollar apiece. Katie let each choose a tin of fruit or
meat in addition, and they went off as happy as she was.

It was late afternoon. She made the bed, sighing at the lumpy
mattresses, but disguising them as best she could with a bright
coverlet. A woven tablecloth and vase of crimson flowers made

the other room more like home. The only books they'd brought were her father's essays, a Spanish dictionary, Prescott's *History of the Conquest of Mexico*, and A.E. Housman's *A Shropshire Lad*. She arranged them on the top shelf and beside them placed the small gold derrick, a tangible remembrance of their friends, which she had brought for luck.

When this was done, she rested for a bit, admiring the house. But worry over Hardy permeated her content and she attacked the problem of what to do with their clothes. Underwear could be left in suitcases but, left packed that way, their outer garments would be masses of wrinkles. There were a few leftover bamboo poles, and she fastened one of these across a corner for a hanging rod and a longer one in front of it, blessing her purchase of wooden hangers and heavy homespun meant for curtains.

Each room had two small windows. Hemming the closet curtain had used up her never-extensive patience with the needle for that day; she decided to leave the window and door curtains for tomorrow, though she could cut them to size and hang them makeshift for the night.

As she was finishing this task, Hanford called from the door. "Time for supper, Mrs. Alastair. I say, won't your husband be astonished at coming home to a new house?" She asked him in and he looked around approvingly. "You ladies have a gift. Jolly comfortable it looks. Tomorrow I'll have the men stretch a canvas above the roof. That'll make it cooler." He smiled coaxingly. "Please, you will join me for supper?"

She knew he wanted to alleviate her increasing concern for Hardy and flashed him a grateful smile. "I want to cook as soon as I set up a kitchen, Mr. Hanford, but I'd be delighted to dine with you. Just let me tidy up."

They sat talking over coffee long after the men had retired to the barrack for cards and probably some serious drinking before they went to bed. "We don't run at night," Hanford explained. "These wells produce more salt water than oil, and this field isn't intended for production, only as training for crews who haven't worked with cable tools."

"How long have you been here?"

"A year this November. I began as a rig helper and learned every job up through drilling. Didn't seem quite the thing to take charge till I knew the work." Katie was more impressed with that than with what Hardy had told her—that the sunburned Britisher's father was Lord Hanford and a key investor in the company.

"Wouldn't you like to oversee some drilling for actual production?"

"Of course. But the manager's watching. He'll move me when I'm ready." Her surprise at this easygoing attitude was so obvious that he chuckled. "Not your American 'get up and git,' is it? Your husband, for instance. I'd wager that within the year, he'll be drilling on his own."

If he doesn't get killed. My God, while we sit here chatting he could already be dead. Or wounded or beaten.

Again Hanford read her thoughts. "Your husband was following the tracks, Mrs. Alastair. If he's not back before morning, I'll send a supply train to the camps and have the men watch out for him. But it's not likely, don't you know, that he'll travel after dark. I daresay at this very moment he's in the Tupan barrack playing a few hands of poker before tucking in."

"I hope so. And you must be tired, too." Appreciating his kindness, she managed a smile and got to her feet. "Good night, Mr. Hanford."

"I'll see you home." He picked up a lantern and escorted her to the new house. In the darkness, both camp and village seemed far away. "If you'd like to spend the night in the barrack . . ." he began.

No one would be surprised, but they'd think Hardy's wife didn't have a fraction of his courage. And she had insisted on coming here. "Thank you," she told the superintendent. "I'll be fine."

"I'll just wait till you light a lantern and have a look around."

No scorpions in the bed. No snakes nestled under the table or chairs. No centipedes, plain or fancy, in her nightgown. Hanford nodded in satisfaction and told her good night.

The only worse nights she had spent were those after learning that she and Darcy couldn't marry and those following Dan's death. There were no rats overhead but the silence of the jungle seemed to be waiting. Every now and then the hush was broken by a strangled cry or a sudden thrashing in the brush as some predator found its meal. Jaguars or *tigres* were no threat to humans, but she shivered at a vivid picture of one tearing at the soft throat of one of the pretty little deer. Away from the sea breeze, it was much hotter here than in Tampico, but she felt too exposed, in spite of mosquito netting, to sleep without a sheet over her. She turned from side to side, flipping her pillow from sweaty side to cooler one, and behind her skittering surface thoughts loomed clutching fear for Hardy.

She finally got out of bed, shook out her slippers, groped her way to the table, located the tiny derrick, and got back in bed, placing it on her pillow; a talisman from dear friends, a goal for the future. She prayed for the safety of Rance and Joe and Bailey, prayed for Hardy, and at last slept fitfully.

IV ─────────────────────────────

Hardy rode in at noon next day. He didn't have the pack mule and empty leather payroll bags were tied behind his saddle. Katie sprang up from Hanford's table and ran to her husband. He was stiff getting out of the saddle, but it wasn't till after he kissed her and stepped back to greet Hanford that she saw the dried patch of brownish-red that stained his right trouser from his thigh to the top of his boot. A hole had been blasted through the cloth.

She cried out but Hardy squeezed her hand. "I'm all right, honey. You ought to see the other guys." He nodded as he met Hanford's questioning gaze. "We can load the real payroll now."

"It can wait till tomorrow," the superintendent said. "Do you have a bullet in your leg?"

"Carved it out with my jackknife. It didn't hit the bone. I'm sorry about the mule. You can take him out of my wages."

Hanford made an impatient sound. "Hang the mule! Come sit down and eat and tell us what happened."

Hardy gave a brief account between bites of grilled fish. It took questions to get details. Five bandits had blocked the way when he was nearing Tupan. Armed with machetes and rifles, they ordered him to unload the mule and not to reach for his shotgun. He did their bidding. One of them sighted with his rifle as the others swarmed toward the bags.

134

Before the robber could pull the trigger, Hardy jerked up his revolvers. The bottoms of the holsters were cut away so that he could shoot through them. He killed the man who was trying to murder him and fatally wounded another, dodging behind the mule. A bullet bored right through the animal and buried itself in his thigh. When the shooting was over, the bandits were dead, all five.

While Hardy was digging the bullet from his wound, a mule-drawn supply train stopped. The drivers helped load the bodies on top of some pipe and said they'd deposit them in the plaza of the village of Tupan, near the camp. These bandits had been the scourge of the region, abducting women, torturing peons, killing anyone who objected.

"So things ought to be pretty quiet for a while," Hardy said, patting back a yawn. "I spread my blanket beside the tracks but I didn't sleep much last night. Too many mosquitoes. If you're sure the payrolls can wait till tomorrow, Mr. Hanford, I could do with some rest."

"You've earned it, old fellow. But I'd better have a look at that wound. I'm not a doctor but I have a big medicine chest."

"I can take care of it," Katie said. "I brought a good supply of medicines, too."

"Call me if you need anything," said the big man. "I suppose they warned you in Tampico to have some quinine every day, did they? Malaria's no joke."

Hardy made a face and grinned at Katie. "Don't worry about us, sir. My wife came prepared. At least she lets me wash down the quinine with a slug of bourbon." Hanford laughed and went his way.

Hardy was amazed at the house and its improvised comforts. "You're a marvel, Katie." He winced and grunted as she cleaned his wound with alcohol, swabbing as deeply as she could. "Owww! That's enough, sweetheart! How about pouring me a drink and letting me snooze?"

"After I finish." She tweezed out some bits of cloth, poured on more alcohol, and applied a good dollop of arnicated carbolic salve before fixing a clean gauze pad in place with court plaster.

She brought his drink. When he had sipped it, tension visibly draining from him, she checked the bed for pests and helped him undress. His body was spare but perfectly proportioned, beautifully muscled.

That bullet could so easily have found his heart or brain. She shuddered. "Stay with me for a while?" he asked drowsily. "For once, ma'am, all I can do is hold you. But I'd love to do that."

She lay down with him. For the first time, she pillowed his head on her shoulder, stroking the damp curls. His breath warmed her flesh beneath the thin gown. She couldn't love any man as she loved Darcy, those roots were too deep, meshed in her blood; but this one, so strong yet so boyish, had grown dear to her heart and body. Giving thanks that he'd come back to her, she drifted into sleep.

Hardy insisted on riding off next morning with the payrolls. He was back late the third day. "No trouble," he said to Katie's anxious look, coming out of the saddle a bit gingerly but hugging her with abandon in spite of onlookers in the dining hall. "I guess a story's gotten around that I've got horns and a forky tail. Things ought to be smooth till a new bunch ease into the territory, figuring they're tougher than the last gang was."

Katie had utilized his absence and her nervousness over it to establish an outdoor kitchen a safe distance from the house. The Indians who had built her house quickly constructed a thatched open-sided structure, and then made a fireplace from mortared stones and mud. A grill for fish could be placed over the fireplace, as could an old gas tank top that served as a griddle or a support for kettles. Her oven was a tank bottom, cut off about eighteen inches high, that fitted tightly on the tank top.

Placed on uprights, an old mahogany door made a splendid table large enough to be worked on while also holding utensils and containers of beans and flour—anything heavy enough not to be knocked over by curious monkeys or other creatures. More vulnerable supplies were kept in stretchy woven slings hung from the rafters of the dining room.

The boy fishermen of the village took turns bringing their catch, so varied that even Hardy, a confirmed beef eater, didn't complain. Mangoes, avocados, bananas, coconuts, and other tropical bounty were offered by the women who supplied the camp cooks, two Chinese who probably created the best food ever served in an oil field. Most of the villagers had chickens, so there were plenty of eggs. In all, Katie found it easier to devise good meals here than she had in Baygall, with its abundance of meat but little else.

The Alastairs had a permanent invitation to Hanford's table, but when Hardy was home they usually preferred privacy. Katie sometimes asked Hanford to join them, however, if she had concocted some special treat.

Her worst problem now was keeping occupied when Hardy was gone. Each week he went by barge or boat to Tampico, collected the payrolls, and returned. Sometimes he could do this in a day, other times he couldn't reach Jarocho till the second day. Delivery to Tupan and to Xo and Zapote, the other two camps, and the return from them, took close to three days. Which meant that Hardy was at Jarocho three days a week at most, and then he was busy learning the oil business, working different jobs.

Katie watched his initiation. As Hardy reported for work one morning, Mike O'Brien, a stocky, bull-chested redhead from Oklahoma who was in charge of novice drillers, called out to Hardy from the lazy bench of a rig where he was handling the temper screw attached to the drilling cable and tools. "Come over here, lad," he cried jovially. "You need to learn the feel of when the tools reach bottom."

After that, Katie couldn't hear what was said because of the commotion—wells spewing as tools or bailers were pulled out, men shouting, boilers blowing off steam, the chug of engines— but it was easy to tell what was happening. Hardy held the big screw, which was almost as long as he was tall, and stood there intently for several minutes. But at last he shook his head. Mike took over, gave the screw a twist to lower the tools a bit more, and again relinquished it to Hardy. Again, after a longer spell of concentration, Hardy ruefully made a negative gesture.

Mike shrugged and gestured at the walking beam. The engine was stopped while Hardy got up on the walking beam. He straddled the end, holding the cable that was fastened to it. Starting the engine, Mike let the beam move slowly up and down. Every now and then he called a question to Hardy, who occasionally nodded, though more often he shook his head.

Hardy was already bouncing. Suddenly, Mike gunned the engine. The beam lunged and pitched. Hardy held on to the cable with all his might, trying not to get pitched to the derrick floor. Even above the racket, Katie heard Hardy yelling, "It's on bottom! It sure'n hell's on bottom!"

Mike eased the tempo. He lowered the tools. Hardy still gripped the cable. After he'd relaxed a little, he grinned with satisfaction, raised his free hand. Mike cut the engine and Hardy jumped down. He was bruised and that noon Katie picked several big splinters out of his seat, but he laughed as heartily as Mike, who slapped him on the back and let him have a chance at the screw.

Katie knew the rough jokes of the oil fields, and though she'd been frightened as the beam plunged like a mustang, she was proud that Hardy'd kept his good humor, shown that though deadly with guns he could take a joke. Katie was glad to see him being accepted, but she felt more isolated than ever.

Hardy had too much to do and she had too little. María, the pretty young mother who had brought the first mat to the house, communicated that she wanted to do their washing in return for canned foods and other small luxuries. Housekeeping was a matter of frequently changing sheets and daily shaking out the grass mats. Katie enjoyed cooking but that absorbed only a few hours a day.

During the hottest part of the afternoon, she swam in a bend of the river not far from where the village women bathed, and then she studied Spanish for a while, practicing phrases Hardy taught her and writing a journal in Spanish, using her dictionary. She was also picking up all the Indian dialect she could by chatting with María, the fish boys, and the fruit bringers. Her salvation, though, was in writing letters. Each day, she added to a letter to her parents, mailed on Hardy's weekly trip to the city. She tried to keep these interesting, dramatizing camp incidents and what she could learn about the village.

"Shoot fire, honey!" Hardy said when he hefted an envelope containing thirty pages. "Why don't you just write a book?"

She stared at him. "Maybe I will. *Letters from Jarocho*—how does that sound?"

He grinned indulgently but she expanded her journal from a few short Spanish sentences to an account of camp life even more detailed than the one she sent her parents. Probably nothing would come of it but at least it might entertain their grandchildren one day.

After the day she gave María some paregoric to soothe the baby's fretfulness and diarrhea caused by teething, Katie unwillingly acquired the reputation of a doctor. Fortunately, most of her patients were children with minor cuts or burns who used the excuse to visit Misalasta, as the villagers called her, because of the cookie or piece of Adams' Pepsin Tutti Frutti Gum she might give them.

When they learned that Hardy wasn't unreasonably jealous, some of the oil workers stopped by to be treated, and unless their complaints were serious enough to require a visit to a doctor in Tampico, Katie dispensed headache powders, paregoric, slippery elm lozenges for sore throat, soda mint tablets for sour stomach, and arnica for sprains.

But there was still not enough to do, and one day when she was waving Hardy off to Tupan, she felt an overwelming surge of envy. *She* would like to be delivering payrolls. Or work on a derrick. Or even be camp cook. What frayed her nerves wasn't being marooned out in the jungle but the lack of something important to do, work that would make her feel like a person, not just Hardy's wife. She could scarcely run off the Chinese cooks, however, and she had to laugh aloud at the consternation it would cause in company offices if a woman applied for a paymaster's job.

All the same, she thought rebelliously. *All the same* . . .

Joining Hanford for the noon meal, she noticed that several buttons were missing from his shirt. "You need a wife," she teased him.

"You're the only woman I know who'd come here," he teased back. "When all the buttons go, I'll get another shirt."

Appalled at such waste, she said, "I'll sew on your buttons, Mr. Hanford. Just bring your pile over this afternoon." And then, without thinking, almost as if it were another woman speaking, she added, "I will, that is, if you'll teach me to drill."

Almost as amazed as he was, she started to smile and make it a joke, but as his blue eyes widened and he choked on his coffee, a reckless impulse swept her along. Why shouldn't women do whatever they were strong and smart enough to handle? Why should a healthy woman feel herself rusting? If she'd had a baby —but there was no hint of that yet. She thought of her own mother with a wave of longing.

Had Vinnie ever been this confused and frustrated? Probably not. Vinnie had married her childhood idol while little more than a girl, had written down his books for him, had created the gracious, loving home in which Katie grew up. But you couldn't do that in an oil camp with a husband who was gone most of the time.

Well, if you were settled, if Hardy came home every night, would you be satisfied then? No. With Darcy, it would have been enough to be his wife, to make his home. At least, she'd thought so.

She needed to *do* something. She watched Hanford as he gasped, "Dear Mrs. Alastair, dear, dear Mrs. Kate!"

She said inexorably, "I can't move heavy things and I don't ask for a twelve-hour shift. But drilling's more skill than muscle. Someday Hardy and I want to make wells. It could come in handy if both of us knew how to drill."

Her cool tone brought a heavier dew to his peeling forehead. "Have you discussed this with your husband?"

"I want it to be a surprise." She beamed.

Hanford groaned. "Your husband, dear lady, is not a man I'm keen to have angry at me."

She chuckled. "Tell him I held you to ransom for your buttons. Don't worry. If he's mad at anyone, it'll be me."

"Your shirts'll get caught in the wheels and cable," he said hopefully.

She had inherited her parents' heights, and though her waist was much smaller than Hardy's, her hips, as they had laughingly discovered, were nearly as wide as his slim, tough-muscled ones. "I'll cut off a pair of Hardy's pants. And I brought riding boots."

He eyed her with dread, then admiration, and his smile gradually widened. "Have a go, then. But it's purely unofficial, mind! And if your husband says you can't, that's it!"

"That *will* be it," she agreed, though they were talking about different things. "Let me have your shirts. I'll be at the field as soon as I change."

* * *

She felt she truly had changed when she emerged from the house twenty minutes later. Hardy's tightest, oldest pants were snugged to her waist with a piece of rope. She wore her own plain duck shirtwaist and boots. Her hair was completely covered by a bandanna, tied back.

It was more than the strange ease of movement, the freedom from skirts and underskirt that gave her an exposed feeling that was uncomfortable at first but then became exhilarating. By the time she reached Hanford, who was standing by the derrick where Mike O'Brien was drilling, she was walking in longer, easier strides as if invisible hobbles had dropped away. Well, weren't high heels, pointy-toed shoes, and long skirts hobbles?

As the men stole glances and tried not to stare, her face heated. What would they think? That she was a loose woman? Unsexed? Would they feel sorry for Hardy?

She simply refused to try to predict Hardy's reaction. Surely he would understand that she couldn't just sit around when he was away. Neither could she shame him before others, however. Dressed as a man, working like one, she must be more than ever a lady.

By the time she reached the derrick, her polished boots were gaumed with oily mud. Mike O'Brien's blue eyes slitted. He cut the engine and rocked back, hands on hips. Like any true driller, he wore expensive laced boots that cost ten times what work shoes did and a slush-spattered Stetson. "So, missus, you're after wanting to learn to drill? You ken it's a daft notion!"

She smiled. "Mr. O'Brien, I'm hoping you won't try to buck me off the walking beam. I already know how the bit feels on bottom. My first husband was a driller and he showed me enough to let me understand his work."

O'Brien's frown deepened. "Driller, was he?"

She answered the unspoken question. "Yes. His name was Dan O'Malley. He was killed fighting a tank fire at Spindletop."

"Dan O'Malley. Hell!—beg your pardon—I was his tool dresser over at Corsicana! Sure was sorry to hear about him. He knew well diggin'. A mighty good man."

"Yes." Hearing Dan spoken of so warmly brought back the flash of his smile, the jaunty tilt of his head. All that strength and hope and energy, did it still exist somewhere? Tears filled her eyes.

"Well then, missus," said O'Brien. "Come along on up here." His toolie, a swarthy, hatchet-faced Cajun named Tony St. Cyr, watched them, bemused. O'Brien's grin widened. "But you've got to promise not to let that Ranger of yours take his pistols to me if you make a boss rope choker before he does."

"Don't worry about Hardy," she said, gaining the derrick floor. She pushed her own doubts away.

There was a lot more to drilling, of course, than sitting on the lazy bench and adjusting the temper screw to lower the bit as it pounded away a thousand feet below. Nor did Katie find it difficult to tell from the vibration of the cable when the tools were on the bottom, though O'Brien kept a close check on the cable and tried to educate her on when the bit was hitting full force and just right.

"Too much slack, missus!" he yelled above the engine chug and creak of the walking beam. "You'll drill crooked!" She tightened the screw and he howled again. "You're not hitting bottom. Can't dig well that way!"

He fixed the screw and had her keep her hand lightly on the cable till the screw ran out. Unhitching the cable from the screw to hang loose from the crown block directly above the hole, O'Brien reeled the tools out.

"A string weighs five or six thousand pounds, missus. Bit, a set of jars, stem and socket. After we bail, on goes that new bit Tony's been pounding at and we do another screw."

Under his direction, Katie lowered the bailer with the sand line and reeled it up. When the bottom was opened, mucky cuttings and mud sloshed into the slush pit and Katie got her baptism. O'Brien watched quizzically as she rubbed the black mess off her face. At his nod, she sent the bailer down again.

When she quit that evening, she was filthy, exhausted, and happy. She couldn't swing Tony's sixteen-pound sledge to dress the bits and she couldn't break and make up the tool joints without help, and she'd never be the carpenter, steamfitter, plumber, blacksmith, and mechanic that a driller had to be; but she hadn't done anything crazy. If she and Hardy got their own drilling outfit someday, she could be a real help.

That morning she'd set a tin tub of water behind the house to heat in the sun. It was as hot as she could tolerate. She soaked and scrubbed off the mire, put her clothes to soak in a bucket, and fell into bed after a quick supper of scrambled eggs. That night, she had no trouble sleeping.

It was considerably harder to get up the next morning. She stirred and yelped at the pain in her neck and shoulders. Moving would help—if she didn't die first. Pushing herself up, she forced herself to stretch. By the time she'd had breakfast and two cups of coffee, she could move without wincing. In Hardy's second old-est pants and a gingham shirtwaist, she pulled on her mud-caked boots and started for the rig.

On the third day of her apprenticeship, she intended to quit early, bake Hardy's favorite pie, and be sweet, clean, and pretty when he came home. There was nothing she could do about the black grime staining her nails and cuticles, or the calluses she was swiftly acquiring, but maybe he wouldn't notice till she'd time to—well, find the right time to tell him.

Tony and Mike were by now reveling in having her with them. Teaching her added novelty to the grind, and the other men's chortles had changed to envy. Mike and Tony couldn't stop swearing but would hastily apologize till she grinned at them and said, "Look, boys, I was married to a driller and I ran a restaurant in Baygall. I don't even hear what you're saying."

That removed the final constraint. And she wasn't so stiff anymore, either. Giving the screw a twist, Katie smiled in satisfaction at the feel of the cable. As soon as it was time to bail, she would leave for home.

She jumped as a shout cut through the racket. "Katie! What the holy *hell* are you doing?"

Lord help us, this wasn't what she'd planned at all. His yelling at her in front of everyone brought blood to her face and she cast him a fiery look over her shoulder.

"What does it look like?"

He bounded to the derrick floor. "By God! You've got on my pants!" Clenching his hands behind him, he took a few deep breaths. "Come on. Let's go home."

Hollering at her like she was a mule or dog, and now giving orders! Furious tears smarted. "I'll come when this screw runs out."

"Miss Kate—" Mike began.

"I'll see you later," Hardy said grimly to Mike.

Without another glance at Katie, Hardy stepped down from the floor and strode away. "You better go, Miss Kate," Mike said unhappily. "Don't get your back up at him, huh? Seeing you here was a mighty big shock."

He's got more shocks coming, she thought but managed a smile for Mike and Tony. "I'll go. Soon as the screw's done."

V _____

Hardy wasn't in the house when Katie got home, or anywhere in sight. Her heart plummeted. All the while she'd been concentrating on keeping the bit hitting properly, another part of her mind had grappled with how to make up with Hardy while maintaining her right to learn the business.

Damn the luck, that he'd come on the scene cold, without any preparation, when he was tired from days in the jungle. He needed time to cool off, and she resolved to keep her temper.

When there was no sign of him, her stomach twisted into a tight knot. Good heavens, had he gone to pick a fight with Hanford for letting her on the derrick? He didn't seem even to have changed clothes, and fastidious as Hardy was, that was a bad sign.

With growing unease, she bathed and started to put on the lace-trimmed pale green lawn dress that was Hardy's favorite, then dropped her hand from its hanger and instead selected the blue-gray tailored piqué. She had planned to blandish Hardy with every possible means but, after the way he'd yelled at her, there'd be none of that. No tears, and no sweet persuasions.

She fixed supper, hesitated over the coconut she had shelled for the cream pie, and decided it would be no sign of weakness if she made it. She began to prepare the crust.

* * *

It wasn't easy to get baked goods from the oil-barrel oven that were neither half-raw nor burned, and Katie was proud of the pie with its light golden peaks of swirled meringue. There were crisp corn pones to go with black bean soup flavored with fresh orange juice, grilled fish with a subtle herb sauce, and a fruit plate arranged in a medley of colors—pineapple, papaya, mangoes, bananas, and melon.

Everything was ready. Hardy didn't come.

At last, Katie left the house and walked to where she could see the open dining hall. Hardy was not at Hanford's table or anywhere in sight. Blindly, Katie returned.

Her appetite was gone but she knew she could handle whatever was going to happen better if she was physically fortified. She compelled herself to chew but she couldn't eat much. The thought of the rich pie was revolting.

Unless he had left camp, which seemed unlikely, the only place Hardy could be was at the barrack. He loved cards and there were games every night, but he hadn't played because he was with Katie so seldom that he hadn't wanted to intrude on their time together. She had known before she married him that he'd never saved money because when he wasn't on duty he enjoyed gambling and an occasional all-out drinking spree. Beyond a few beers or a dinner glass of the French wines amply supplied by the company, he hadn't drunk since the wedding. There'd been no discussion. He just hadn't.

Katie had congratulated herself on satisfying him so completely that he'd lost the inclination to binge. Now she realized that he had probably denied himself those diversions because of her. And now she had violated his idea of what a wife should be, so he was retaliating. Katie put away the food that would keep and took the rest over to María. In the twilight, she saw lamps shining from the barrack. Could she ask Hanford or Mike, who were still in the dining hall, to tell Hardy she wanted to talk to him?

Angrily, she smothered the impulse. Trying to fill the time by learning something that would benefit both of them was not at all the same as his gambling and getting drunk. She wouldn't beg for reconciliation.

She knew with a sick, sinking heart that this might be the end of their marriage. She didn't want that, but she wouldn't surrender, either, and play at being his ideal little woman.

She cried herself to sleep.

Hardy hadn't come in by dawn. Katie, rousing with a dull weight on her heart, didn't at once remember why. Then she saw his unrumpled pillow and her body contracted, doubling as if to protect her woman parts. She straightened and stood up.

The gray piqué lay over a chair. Clean work clothes were folded on her suitcase. For a moment, Katie could scarcely breathe. Her lungs felt squeezed too thin to draw in air. Then she put the piqué back in the closet and dressed in her derrick clothes.

Mike O'Brien frowned as she approached the derrick. "Miss Katie, you better not."

"Do you mean I can't?"

"No," he said unhappily. "Far as I'm concerned you're doing fine. Just sure do hate to see you spattin' with Hardy." His blue eyes met hers levelly. "Most men would feel the same. I would."

"I suppose I *could* drink, to while the time away. Or go to Tampico and play bridge and gossip. Or take a lover."

The big driller's jaw dropped. "Crazy talk, Miss Katie. Listen, Hardy slept in the barrack last night. No one's there now but him. Why don't you take him coffee and—and talk things over?"

"I wouldn't want to disturb him before he's slept off the booze." A maddening thought struck her. "Mike! Did he—did he ask you not to let me work?"

Mike sighed. "No, ma'am. Fact is, he told me strong to let you if you'd a mind to." He gulped. "But, Katie girl, wheesht! Don't be cuttin' off your nose to spite your pretty face."

She looked at him. He got up, shrugging, and let her have the lazy bench.

Hardy didn't come home that night. Katie, between sobs, downed three glasses of wine, navigated to the bed, and woke next morning with a dismal headache that exploded into blinding rockets as she sat up.

She went to work. This time, Mike didn't argue. Both he and Tony watched her so commiseratingly that she trembled. Did they know something awful, something they didn't want to tell her? She was afraid to ask. But, my God, this couldn't go on much longer! Day after tomorrow, Hardy would leave for Tampico. They had to talk before he left.

Did they? He didn't seem to think so. Or, more likely, he intended to drink and gamble till she left the derrick and came crawling. However much she'd offended him, what he was doing to her was much worse—sulking in the barrack, making them the talk of the camp!

She was dumping the bailer when Hanford approached. He called over the engine, "Mrs. Alastair, I need a word with you."

Had Hardy sent him? Katie brought an arm across her face to clean it, only smearing it more. Mike whispered, "Good luck, Miss Katie."

Hanford looked so grave that a fleeting hope that Hardy had asked him to mediate died before Hanford cleared his throat. They reached the edge of the field and comparative quiet, and he said, "Mrs. Alastair, I'm frightfully sorry, but I must ask you not to work."

She flushed. "Hardy got you to say this?"

"Not at all."

"Then—"

"My dear lady!" The incongruity of his polished speech and her scroungy appearance would have been funny if she hadn't been both angry and afraid. His gaze, usually indulgent, was hard. "I am responsible for this field. I regret that I erred in consenting to what I supposed would be a quickly abandoned whim. Certainly I did you no favor."

"Hardy's behaving like a child! Why should I—"

"Children, even in Texas, don't drink themselves sodden every night and gamble with IOU's it'll take a month's wages to settle."

Staggered, Katie stared at the Englishman. His eyes were kinder now but his voice was firm. "Since neither of you seems prepared to stop this—this duel, I must."

She couldn't blame him. Hardy, not she, was important to the company. But she couldn't keep from saying, "So you tell me to get off the rig, but you won't tell Hardy to quit carousing?"

"He's not doing anything most of the men don't do."

She gave him a bitter smile. "That's what it comes down to, isn't it, Mr. Hanford? Men can do just as they please but women have to please them."

"I didn't make the rules," he said wearily, though she thought he turned redder beneath his perpetual sunburn. Then he burst out in exasperation, "For heaven's sake, old girl, all you have to do is clean yourself up and go over to see him."

"And fall on my face like Vashti before the King of Persia, hoping he'll pardon my insolence in coming without being sent for? Well, I guess women have advanced a little in three thousand years. Our husbands can't legally kill us if we don't keep our place."

Not fair, not bloody sporting English cricket, but she was too humiliated and angry to care. She whirled and walked fast to her house.

Damn them, damn them all! So smug and patronizing and in control! *Their* work was important; even in this place. *They* had diversions. But *she* couldn't enter their lair and play a hand of poker though she'd bet she could skin most of them!

Her steps slowed. Wait a minute! True, the men drank and gambled for entertainment, but what else was there for them to do?

She thought back to Baygall and Spindletop, at how the men had flocked to her restaurant, not just for food but for a chance to be around a woman who reminded them of mothers or sisters or wives, a chance to be for a little while in a place like home where they didn't need to bristle and fight and prove they were tough.

She couldn't run a restaurant here, but what about an alternative to the barrack? A place that served fresh fruit juice and coffee and different kinds of pie? With tables for games or just talking? Her mind raced.

Some of the men had harmonicas. There was at least one accordion. Mike O'Brien had a pennywhistle his father had brought over from Ireland. She had heard Tony singing snatches of Cajun songs. There could be music, then, maybe a barbershop quartet. And when she could pay for it, she could import a stereopticon or even a moving picture machine, a Graphophone—why, there was no end to what could happen if she could make the place attractive to enough men.

As abruptly as she'd left him, she turned and hurried to where Hanford was sifting bailings through his fingers to see what they contained.

"Mr. Hanford, if it's not breaking company rules, I've got a proposition."

* * *

Half a dozen Indians worked swiftly that afternoon alongside Katie. By the time the workers were sitting down to supper, a large thatched open-sided shelter was ready, furnished with tables, benches, and chairs. Another warehouse door set on uprights made a sturdy serving table that displayed golden-brown latticed dried apple pie and canned peach pie, three coconut cream pies and three banana cream, covered with a clean cloth to keep away insects.

Company cooks had lent pie pans, coffeepots, cutlery, and cups and allowed her to bake in their ovens so long as she finished before they had to start the evening meal. Pressing María and her widowed mother, Sara, into grating coconut, slicing bananas, whipping eggs, and other such chores, Katie rolled out crusts till her shoulders pained, but she was too full of hopeful excitement to care.

Hanford thought it a wonderful idea. He was in favor of anything that might cut down drinking and the resulting fights. Injuries from these sometimes kept men off work for several days or even permanently disabled them. He said he'd feel justified in asking the company to provide a moving picture machine and Graphophone.

Her hands shook nervously as she changed into the pale green dress and tied on a fresh ruffled apron, added securing pins to her hair, which was threatening to escape in a mass of waves.

If the men would only come! And surely curiosity would bring Hardy to investigate. He couldn't quarrel with what she was doing; it was close enough to the way she'd earned a living when they met. Still, as she approached the dining hall and didn't see him, much of her excitement dulled.

Was he drunk? Sleeping it off? Would he persist in his mulishness now that she'd hit on a way for them to make up without either one abjectly submitting to the other?

She forced her worries to the back of her mind and paused, smiling, beside Mike and Tony, who were sitting by the entrance to the dining hall. They hastily got up, dumbstruck by how different she looked from the last time they'd seen her.

"Boys, I'm opening a sort of club. No alcohol, though you can bring your own beer if you prefer it to juice or coffee. You can play cards, though I'm hoping we can get some singing and music going. There'll be moving pictures as soon as we can get a machine. And there's four kinds of pie."

"Pie? Tonight?"

Katie nodded, and Mike promised, "We'll be there with a full head of steam!" He beamed. "Miss Katie, ma'am, I'm sure glad you—well, that things are going to be all right."

He thought she'd straightened things out with Hardy. A pang stabbed her, but she thanked him and moved on to Hanford. A cook rang the gong and as talk and laughter subsided, Hanford stood beside Katie and made the announcement.

As fifty men streamed into the club, some eager, some looking hard to convince, Katie panicked. But she remembered that she'd served two sittings of eighty men, twice a day, with only Esau's help. She wished Esau were there now. María's husband didn't want María around so many strange men, but old Sara had on her best skirt and smiled toothlessly from behind the coffeepots.

"Please come choose your pie and what you'd like to drink," Katie called. "Once you're settled, we'll keep your cups and glasses filled."

"I'd like a cut of each kind of them pies," Tony said. "But not to make a plumb hog of myself, how about a hunk of peach?"

"You can have two if you'll sing in a little while," Katie begged.

"Sure," said dark, narrow-faced Tony, "if you'll keep the boys from throwing their boots at me."

"I'll squeeze out the tune on me accordion," said Chunk, a broken-nosed, scar-headed tankie. "That'll cover you, Tony."

By the time all the men were seated, all the pies had vanished except for one piece of coconut cream that Katie had tucked away hopefully, for Hardy. Now if they wouldn't just devour and run! And why didn't Hardy come? She and Sara circulated, collecting plates and pouring coffee.

"Nifty idea, Mrs. Alastair," said a balding driller she remembered from Spindletop. "Your pie's as good as ever."

"Thanks, Jerry. How're you liking Jarocho?"

"Lots better now that you've started this. Okay if we play some monte?"

"Go ahead. This is your club. Just no hard liquor and no fighting." The men at his table watched her approvingly and she guessed that Jerry had told them about what had happened to Dan. Oil workers always passed the hat for a widow and did what they could to help.

She relaxed as she saw that cards were coming out at many tables. Chunk had his accordion ready, and a strapping tow-headed Texas boy had his harmonica. After a conference among the three, Tony launched into "Dixie."

That brought all the Texans and Southerners to their feet, singing lustily. Illinois scissorbills and Pennsylvania starving owls, called that by the West Virginians who mocked them for not being able to make a living in their own state, retaliated with so many verses of "John Brown's Body" that Mike broke in with a shrill blast of his pennywhistle.

"Who's for a jig?"

The tune he played was so lively that even some engrossed in card games quit to do fancy footwork in the center of the room. Chunk soon recruited three other accordion players, and after pre-liminary harmonizing, they soared resonantly into "The Girl I Left Behind." Soon they responded to shouts for "My Old Kentucky Home" and "Sweet Rosie O'Grady," then rested while Mike played "The Wearing of the Green."

Katie would have been ecstatic if not for the spreading cold feeling in the pit of her stomach. Was Hardy dead drunk? Or vengefully unforgiving? Her smile stiffened as the night wore on.

She was getting a fresh pot of coffee when someone at her elbow said, "Please, ma'am, can I have a cup?"

She spun around, almost dropping the pot. He was so close their bodies brushed. Awareness flooded her along with relief that swept the heaviness from her heart.

"Oh, yes, sir! There might even be some pie."

He was shaved and clean though his eyes were bloodshot and he looked thinner. As she hurried to serve him, he said softly, "Well, Katie, here you are feeding folks again. Just like Baygall."

"Yes." She gave him a straight look, not wanting to anger him but needing to have it said. "And now I can help you drill if we're shorthanded after we get our own outfit."

His mouth tightened. She met his stare with a look that meant business. After a moment, he laughed and shook his head. "We'll see, Katie. That might be all right if we're off to ourselves—but no wife of mine's going to wear my pants and work with men."

"And no husband of mine's going to gamble and drink for three days straight!"

His eyes flashed like sheet lightning behind a storm cloud. "You started it, sweetheart."

She started to thrust back at him, but she had to chuckle at the sudden realization. "We sound all of five years old."

"Maybe six?" He grinned. "Call it a draw. I know you're different. Hell, it's part of why I love you. But honey, you're smart enough to think of all kinds of ways to stay busy without making me look like a damn fool."

"And how do you think you made me look—hanging out in the barrack?"

Hanford, watching them, got to his feet. "Eleven o'clock, chaps. Time we turned in. But let's give Mrs. Alastair a cheer for giving us a club and the best evening we've had at Jarocho."

They gave her three. Then, with hearty good-nights, compliments, and envious glances at Hardy, the men moved off to the barrack.

Hardy finished his coffee. Katie couldn't tell whether he was angry at her last retort or not. After a few words with Sara who cackled her delight, Hardy gave her two American dollars and slipped an arm around Katie.

It felt so good, so strong! "Sara'll clean up," he murmured, warm breath in her ear sending tremors through her. "Hell, sweetheart, let's quit fighting. We've got a lot of loving to catch up on before morning."

"Yes." She melted against him, her need warmly, ardently aroused in spite of her weariness. "Yes, my darling, we do."

He carried her to their house, to their bed that had been so lonely without him. They loved each other, teasing, pleasing, more abandoned and urgent than they had been on their wedding night. In the soft shadows before dawn, she woke to his stroking, his kisses roaming from eyes to feet. She touched him, exulting at his gasp. When they lay tenderly sated in each other's arms, she thought contentedly that this was almost enough for being completely happy.

Almost. Darcy, Darcy, will I ever stop needing you?

VI ────────────────────────────

Katie's problem now was finding time for all she had to do. But she enjoyed running the club. Not all the men came every night. There were usually high-stakes, whisky-powered games going in the barrack. Most came for pie, though Hardy insisted it was to see Katie, and a surprising number stayed on for cards and coffee or to hear whoever was performing that night.

The company, at Hanford's request, had ordered a moving picture machine, a pool table, and a stereopticon lecture series in color. Officials had scoured Tampico and within a week of the club's opening had sent several guitars; a banjo; an astounding assortment of books that ranged from Horatio Alger to Marcus Aurelius; a Graphophone with a carton of records; and a roller organ equipped with over a hundred rollers that played polkas, waltzes, quadrilles, and songs that ranged from "Rock of Ages" to "A Hot Time in the Old Town Tonight."

Backgammon, dominoes, and a Ouija board also came from Tampico, and Hanford produced a small chess set with exquisitely carved ivory and ebony figures, a gift from his sister who knew how much he loved the game. He offered to teach anyone who wanted to try. To his surprise, several of the men knew the game well enough to give him a real contest.

The club benefitted the village, too. María and three other

154

women helped with the pies. Sara and another widow served pie and refilled cups. Gathering and squeezing fruit for pitchers of juice occupied four families, and men who were too old to work for the company did the cleaning up and made sturdier chairs.

"It's transformed the camp," Hanford said one night as Katie cut him a second wedge of his favorite lime pie. "Fights have dropped to a couple a week instead of that many every night. Fewer accidents, less swearing." He grinned at her, the corners of his eyes crinkling with shrewd good humor. "It was a good thing for Jarocho that you got bored, Mrs. Alastair."

"I enjoy it. When Hardy and I leave, the club can keep going. By then, María and Sara should be able to run it."

"Splendid idea! I think the company would even hire a manager if need be. They're so impressed with results here that they're trying to set up similar clubs in other camps. But no one can make lime pie like you do."

Katie laughed at him. "María made this."

"Did she, by Jove?" Hanford took a bite. His skeptical look turned beatific. "Mmm." He sighed. "Do you suppose she'd make me one of these—a personal one, mind you, every day?"

María was pleased to oblige. After a month of private pies and wages, she showed Katie how much she had saved and hopefully asked if it was enough to buy a sewing machine. When the women washed sheets and clothes for the workers, there were often tears and holes. Wouldn't the men pay to have everything neatly mended?

Contacting an oil official, Hardy bought a handsome used Sears and Roebuck cabinet sewing machine that became the pride of the village and something approaching an industry. Katie quit worrying that, when she was no longer at Jarocho, María would cease to prosper. Though only eighteen and properly respectful of her husband and elders, she had in her the stuff of a matriarch who could choose what was good from the foreigners and use her influence against what was bad.

Each week, Hardy banked the club's profits. At the end of the month, when he deposited his wages—$400 because of the hazards of his job—he returned with the deposit slips, handing them to Katie with a half-rueful, half-proud smile.

"Look at that, honey! You earned more than I did, even after getting the club set up and paying wages to half the village!"

"You're complaining, Mr. Alastair?" She made a teasing face and kissed him hard. "All the sooner we can start drilling on our own!"

"Sure. But damn it all, Katie, I want to take care of you—hit a gusher and buy you a mansion and Rolls-Royce and anything else you can think of."

She looked at him and suddenly it was as if he were a child, eager, striving, *her* child. A flash of foreknowledge chilled her. "Hardy. We'll have all that someday. But I doubt we'll ever be happier than we are right now while we're working and saving and hoping, with all our life ahead."

He laughed, and cradled her against him. "For us, things'll just get better all the time. Like the way I'm taking you to bed right now even if it is the middle of the day!"

She gave touch for touch, kiss for kiss, meeting his ardor with fiery abandon. But even as they moved into that radiant ocean of desire, floating like spirits freed from time and place, she felt that edge of warning. She had been close to this happy with Dan, as fulfilled as she could be without Darcy. And then they had brought him home, so charred there was little to show he had been a man.

Shivering, she turned to Hardy again. He smiled lazily, smoothing her hair, but as he sensed her urgency, he raised on one elbow and gazed down at her, gray eyes piercing her secret darkness with their light. Calling her name, he began to trace her body with breath and lips and hands.

It was two months since they'd come to Jarocho; late autumn and the rains had abated. It was warm except when a norther, having chilled Texas first, howled in with fog and rain and sent temperatures down as much as forty degrees in an hour. After these *nortes* the weather would be fresh and pleasant, bringing a tang of home. Katie longed to see her parents, but she kept her letters cheerful and combatted her yearning by helping the cooks plan a Thanksgiving dinner and making "pumpkin" pies out of squash.

Hardy returned from Tampico in time for the gala dinner. He had a letter for Hanford and brought startling news. Eagle Oil was being bought by an American company with holdings down near Vera Cruz. Since he'd quelled bandit attacks on the paymaster in this region, Hardy was being sent to deliver payrolls to jungle camps farther south that had been losing payrolls to an especially formidable gang headed by an American known as El Tigre who seemed to have a special grudge against that company.

"I'll be on the road all the time, honey. Just in Vera Cruz overnight to pick up the payrolls. You could stay there, but I think you'd be happier here."

"Can't you say you'd rather stay on this route?"

"I did. But they're doubling the pay."

"That means they've been losing a lot of payrolls—and paymasters."

He shrugged and grinned. "That's why the salary's eight hundred dollars a month. Of course, when things quiet down . . ."

"You mean when you kill all the bandits or they kill you."

"That was my job as a Ranger, remember. What's the difference? Besides, we'll make our stake a lot faster."

"If you don't get ambushed!"

He drew her down on his lap. "Katie, I won't go if you're set against it, but it was made pretty clear to me that if I don't I'll have to find another job. I can do that, sure. We can even go back to the States."

"But you'd rather carry the payrolls? Don't you see what's happening, Hardy? Anytime there's trouble somewhere, the company's going to send you to stop it. If you go often enough, *you'll* get stopped one day."

He held her close and murmured against her throat, "Not as long as I've got you to come back to. This won't be forever, sweetheart. I figure I can get the message across to this El Tigre in a month or two."

"Then what?"

"The company says I can have this route back—at the same eight-hundred-dollar salary—provided I agree to take over payrolls at any of their operations when the regulars have trouble."

"You might as well be back in the Rangers."

"I'd never save up a stake in the Rangers."

Both fell silent. Katie wished they could go home. But they'd come down here to get enough money to drill.

"All right. If you think it's the best thing to do. I'll stay here and run the club," she told him.

The relieved heartiness of his kiss told her that he was actually glad to be going where there'd be danger. He was getting bored with his uneventful trips to Tupan and the other camps. That frightened her. Then she grimly reflected that he'd never be bored on an oil rig; there were a hundred ways of getting killed or maimed. Some ways were beyond anyone's control, while others were the forfeit paid for a second's inattention.

"The sooner we get you digging wells, the better," she said. "When are you leaving?"

"They'll send a man tomorrow to deliver these payrolls. I'm to be in Vera Cruz next week. I'll go by steamer. When the branch director found out I was married, he suggested I bring you to Tampico and have a few days' vacation before heading south. Nice of him, wasn't it?"

Surprising, too. Oil companies paid so much better than other employers that they considered salary alone ample compensation for primitive living conditions and family separations. Eagle Oil was the first outfit she'd known that tried to make life better for its men.

Oh, well, maybe the new owners were similarly embued with the wish to keep employees satisfied. It would be lovely to have a few days with Hardy, and she could shop for some things she needed before returning to Jarocho. María and Sara were perfectly competent to run the club.

Casting off her reservations and doubts, she placed her hands at the back of Hardy's strong neck and kissed him long and deliberately, enjoying the power she had to make him tremble, thrilling to his eagerness.

"Little witch!" He rose, carrying her to the bed, kissing her as he slowly bared her flesh, arousing her till she burned to be naked and open to him. "How will I last a month without you?"

She laughed shakily. "We'll get a room with a balcony so the sea wind will keep us nice and cool. And we won't sleep much."

"Just enough to get strength for more of this," he whispered.

She arched against him, demanding, wanting, needing. He came into her with one long, throbbingly sweet plunge and rested within her, charged bodies communing, till she cried out, moved, and he answered, carrying them both through the tempest.

Katie expected to be back at Jarocho in four days, five at most, so she packed lightly. If Hardy hadn't been going so far away and on such dangerous duty, she'd have been delighted at the prospect of this excursion. But forebodings plagued her.

She felt as if this were the end of their marriage, in some way, or at least that things would never be the same. Instead of growing closer, each of them would have to manage alone. She knew Hardy wasn't abandoning her, but at some deep, mindless level, no matter how she chided herself, she felt as desolate and frightened as if he were. She couldn't let him guess that; he would need his full concentration on the new job, need to be alert to the slightest signal. The last thing he should have on his mind was a panicky wife.

She took her prettiest gowns and the Italian leghorn straw hat trimmed with pale green velvet ribbon, dainty white kid sandals with a bow on the strap, knitted lace hose, and Hardy's favorite intimate garment, a transparent black chiffon sacque that ended just below her hips. She wouldn't need a nightgown.

American Eagle Oil, as the company was now called, had reserved the Alastairs a suite in the hotel with an immense bed, marble bath, and balcony facing the Gulf. Flowers were on the dresser, on the bed table, on the grilled window of the bath, on the mantel, and on the veneered French tables in the gold satin-draped sitting room.

"They really want to keep you happy, darling!" Katie laughed after the first astonishment. "Now if we only had champagne . . ."

"Here it is."

Assuming he was joking, she followed him out onto the balcony. In a silver ice bucket nested two bottles. Crystal glasses were beside it on the low marble table. There were more flowers, and a silver platter of fruit with knives and porcelain plates.

"I don't know what this is all about," Hardy said. "The new owner's coming down soon. Maybe the hotel gave us his rooms by mistake." He grinned and swung her in a circle. "What the hell, let's enjoy it till they throw us out."

"There's a card with the fruit."

He picked it up and read the fine copperplate writing: *"With the compliments of American Eagle Oil to Mr. and Mrs. Hardy Alastair. Mrs. Alastair is welcome to occupy the suite as long as she wishes. Mr. Alastair should be at the dock Friday morning. A messenger will inform you of the time early enough for you to report to the office before you sail. Enjoy your holiday."*

Hardy reached for the champagne. "I've never been treated like this, honey, but I could sure get used to it fast."

She smiled, but as they sat in the wicker chairs, sipping champagne, savoring the sweet chilled pineapple and melon, Katie felt as if she'd walked into a dream beginning like a fairy tale and ending horribly. This, she thought, was all too much like giving a condemned man his favorite last meal.

They bathed and made love in the huge bed, drowsed luxuriously, and playfully fondled and admired each other for a while before bathing again. They went down then to the chandeliered restaurant with its marble floors and splashing fountain surrounded by palms, scarlet hibiscus, and bougainvillea in every rosy shade from salmon to fuschia. White-jacketed dark waiters were deft and smiling, the man at the grand piano concert-quality, the food superb.

Watching candlelight play over Hardy's lean brown face, Katie was overcome by tenderness. He was her man, handsome and strong and daring, but often like her child. She loved him. Not as she did Darcy. But he was her husband and their lives were meshed together.

She would make these two days something they would both remember. And yes, she was ready now; she hoped to conceive his child.

After jungle camp, it was exhilarating to stroll the flower-bordered walks on the Plaza de Armas and roam the Pánuco riverfront from railroad station to docks, stopping at the market to buy hammocks and straw hats to send to Vinnie, Mark, Hester, and the other Old Orchard folk. A company touring car and driver were placed at their disposal and they drove to a clean white beach where they swam naked in a concealed lagoon, dried in the hot sun, and feasted on a picnic lunch. That was their last day, and it was perfect.

The driver took them to the docks next morning and waited for Katie until she'd waved Hardy out of sight. The desolation she had kept at bay shrouded her like a fog as she walked slowly toward the gleaming Pierce-Arrow. She didn't want to stay in the suite with its memories, so like an unexpected honeymoon. The sooner she got back to Jarocho, and work, the sooner she could shake this irrational feeling that Hardy had left her for good.

"Please wait at the hotel," she told the driver in her recently learned Spanish. "As soon as I can pack, I want to catch the next boat or raft to Jarocho."

"Muy bien, señora."

She was hurrying through the grand foyer when the manager intercepted her. "Madam, the new president of your husband's company hopes you will do him the honor of joining him on the terrace and having breakfast with him."

She was in no mood for conversation, especially with a stranger. "Do me the favor, sir, of conveying my regrets. I have already breakfasted and I'm in a rush to get home."

The manager's smooth olive face looked pained. "Forgive me, madam, but surely it would be wise to accept the courtesy? The gentleman said expressly that he looked forward to making your acquaintance." He spread his hands. "You will at least join him for coffee?"

The man was obviously distressed at having to carry a refusal to the company president. And she reminded herself that the new management had gone beyond all bounds to give Hardy and her an opulent holiday. She nodded, resigned, and the manager led her up the grand staircase to a second-floor terrace facing the sea.

There was only one person on the colonnaded porch. He was almost entirely hidden by a bank of flowering vines. As he rose and moved toward her, there was something about the arrogant head, its ruddy hair traced with silver . . .

Warning shot through her. She halted. Before she could speak, the manager left her.

Her feet seemed mired in quicksand. She couldn't move as Morgan Fayette strode gracefully toward her. His white linen suit was impeccable. He wore a black string tie. Diamond rings shot dazzling fire. He was no taller, really, than Hardy, but his thinness made him seem taller. His narrow face was like a mask. She had never seen anyone so handsome yet so chilling.

"Mrs. Alastair." He bowed. "My dear, most dear lady! What happy chance to find you here."

It was a moment before she could trust her voice. "If you're Eagle Oil's new owner, then I doubt there was much chance about it."

He chuckled, revealing small white teeth, even except for the incisors, which were long and curved. "Mexican oil's too tempting to ignore. I didn't know I was acquiring your husband till the deal was negotiated. But when I learned, the possibilities enchanted me."

"You haven't—*acquired*—my husband, Mr. Fayette. I can't imagine that he'll want to work for you."

"He's ambitious, I hear. Eager to start wildcatting. I'm prepared to make him such a profitable offer, Katie, that I doubt you'd want him to refuse." He put a hand beneath her arm. "Come, sit down, and let's talk about it."

His touch was dry, almost raspy, though his fingernails were buffed and the cuticles pushed back, showing pale crescents. Katie stepped back with deliberate slowness, forcing herself not to jerk away. She must not let him know how much he frightened her.

"I shall certainly advise Hardy to have nothing to do with you, Mr. Fayette."

"I think he will like my proposition. Business is business, my dear."

"You'll have to take it up with him. There's no point in discussing it with me. Good morning, Mr. Fayette."

Turning abruptly, she told herself, *Don't worry. Don't let him see he has you scared.*

The back of her neck prickled as she heard the light pad of his footsteps. It was like being stalked by a great cat, and nearly impossible to keep from either running away or whirling to face him. Then suddenly he was in front of her, blocking her way.

"You're wrong, Katharine Sevier O'Malley Alastair. I know firsthand that Captain Alastair is a formidable fighter, and Hanford's report is that he'll make a competent driller. But I can hire hundreds of men equally good in either capacity. My benevolent interest is inspired exactly and precisely because he is your husband." He smiled charmingly. "So you see, it's with you that I must strike my bargain."

"How did you know my names?"

"Bless you, I know a lot more than that. Once, Katie, I was closely associated with your parents. But that's ancient history. You and I are here and now."

He stood a man's length away, but she felt as if those cold

hands manacled her. "All right. Tell me what you want. I'll tell you no, and then we can both go about our affairs."

"I never do business standing up."

He wouldn't let her go till she'd listened to him. She let him escort her to the opulent dining room. Once they were seated, the manager and a waiter were beside them. "A roll?" Fayette suggested. "Perhaps some melon?"

"I'm not hungry."

"Pity." He ordered coffee for two, pastry, and a bowl of fruit. He sat back and studied her with an intensity that made her flesh feel as if it were shrinking against her bones. "I hate to admit it, but marriage has brought a bloom to you. At Baygall, you were almost scrawny. You're a magnificent woman, or will be when you hit your prime."

"I'm not a racehorse, sir. Surely my looks don't enter into your business matter."

"They do." The lines at the edge of his eyes were one of the few signs that betrayed his age, and they crinkled now as he laughed. "Very much."

"I want to get back to Jarocho, Mr. Fayette. Please say whatever's on your mind and let me catch my boat."

"American Eagle's boat, surely?"

She shrugged and didn't answer, envying his power, or rather, the freedom it gave. If she and Hardy had his wealth, he wouldn't be maneuvering them like Hanford moved pawns on a chessboard. The best thing about having lots of money would be that you wouldn't need it. The absurdity made her smile.

Fayette leaned forward. "Something pleases you?"

"I was thinking about when Hardy and I have our own company."

"Ah, yes." He paused. His eyes were the crystalline green of frosted glass. She clamped her hands tight beneath the table to keep from shifting uneasily under his gaze. "That company is yours, Katharine. For just a word."

She considered him warily. "I don't understand."

"Don't you, my sweet?"

There could be no pretending. "You say you can buy men like Hardy. Wouldn't it be easier to buy whores?"

There was satisfaction in seeing his eyes dilate. Then his arm moved across the table and hard fingers bruised her arm. "Listen, you priggish little fool! I want you for my mistress. Not to while away a night or a week, but for the rest of my life. I'd marry you, but I have a wife whose fortune has been exceedingly helpful."

Though she knew he desired her, Katie was astounded. She started to rise but his hand held her fast. "Wait. Hear the rest. I'll make your husband a partner—or if you prefer, set him up as an independent and let him drill some proven fields of mine in Louisiana. You'll stay married. That would give a name to any child we have, but of course I'll have exclusive access to you. You may choose and have title to your own house."

She shook her head. "I can't believe this. You sound like the Sun King with Madame de Montespan. This isn't the seventeenth century. Nothing in heaven or hell could make me agree. And even if I would . . ." She choked with anger at his estimation of Hardy. "My husband's not a pimp."

"He could have a regrettable accident."

She froze. "Are you threatening him?"

"My dear, I never threaten. I point out probabilities." She tried to wrest free. Without apparent effort, he held her arm and smiled, tightening his grip till she nearly cried out. Abruptly, he let go of her. "No, Katharine, I don't want to lose Hardy. Also, I believe his business sense is superior to yours, that he'll convince you to strike the bargain."

Rising, he escorted her to the door. "A launch is waiting for you. Godspeed to Jarocho." He raised her hand, pressed his lips to the palm. The kiss was cold; cold, yet it burned.

"Think about it, Katharine." He placed his hand on the pulse of her throat for the briefest instant before he smiled and left her.

VII _____

Tremors of physical fear went through Katie as she hurriedly packed. Was there any way of letting Hardy know that the man he'd struck down the night of the mob fury at Baygall was now his employer and not to be trusted?

It wouldn't do any good to follow Hardy to Vera Cruz. He was being met by company officials who would send him as far as possible by boat and narrow-gauge rail. After that, he'd go horseback. He hadn't known the jungle camps' locations, so it would be impossible to find him without going to the company, and she was sure Fayette had told them not to let her reach Hardy or send a letter.

She sat down on the bed and hugged her husband's pillow, drew in the faint scent of him. It calmed her a little. Hardy had risked his life countless times in the Rangers. It wouldn't be easy to kill him, except by treachery. Fayette seemed to believe that Hardy could be bought; it would suit his devious methods best if his mistress had a complacent husband.

Hardy should be safe at least till Fayette talked with him. That could scarcely be till after Hardy had made his new route safe for paymasters. Hardy would quit, of course, hire on with another company, or they might even go back to Texas. A wave of homesickness swept over Katie. If Fayette planned to stay in Mexico, then she wanted to leave. It would take longer to save for their rig, but she would breathe easier far away from Fayette. Meanwhile, all she could do now was go back to Jarocho.

It would have been a relief to tell Hanford about Fayette but it wouldn't be fair to embroil him. She did ask him if she could send letters to Hardy.

"Of course, but he may get back before they find him. They'd have to go with other company dispatches and correspondence sent out of Tampico."

She looked so disappointed that he added in a kind voice, "If someone from here finishes training and is assigned near Vera Cruz, he could try to deliver a letter for you."

Katie brightened. Crews were always coming and going, and surely a number would be needed at the expanded company's southern holdings. "You'll let me know?"

"The minute any such orders come in." Hanford smiled at her. "Sorry Hardy's away but we're glad to have you back. Not only for your pretty face, Mrs. Kate, but because, though their efforts are commendable, none of the women can match your lime pie!"

"I'll make you one right away," Katie said with a laugh.

As she unpacked, she wondered how she could manage a month or more of mounting dread, of never knowing if Hardy was safe.

She stayed too busy to be lonesome. But the nights were terrible. Though she was bone-weary, she tried to imagine what Hardy was doing, to assure herself that he could handle payroll raids down south just as thoroughly as he had on the way to Tupan. But Morgan Fayette's green eyes seared her.

Why was Fayette so determined to have her? He was past the age of headlong passion, surely. He desired her, she could feel that, but there had to be another reason. When had he known her parents? She intuitively knew that his obsession was rooted far back, and since he was about her mother's age . . .

Katie thought of pouring out her anxieties to her parents, asking if they remembered Fayette, but that would trouble them without helping her. There was nothing they could do to help her beyond sending, as they already did, frequent loving letters with news of Old Orchard and people she knew.

A week after her return from Tampico, Hal Martin, the rangy

young geologist who'd been surveying leases, stopped through on his way to headquarters. He was delighted with the club. He talked late one night to Katie about his hope that the new management would send him back to Louisiana so he could be near his wife.

"I miss Amalia something awful," he confided, his face like a boy's. He rubbed a festering mosquito bite on his ear. "Even if I didn't, I've had a crawful of snakes, tarantulas, and bugs. Worst things are these doggoned ticks. *Garrapatas* and *conchugas* are bad enough but you can at least smother them with tobacco leaves soaked in *aguardiente*. The pinhead ones, though, they like to settle in your eyelids or behind your ears, and I've had nasty sores from the little devils. Not to mention that fly that lays eggs under your skin to hatch out as grubs. I hate to sleep around pigs because they like to come up and rub their backs on a guy's bare feet. That's how I got an egg sac under a toenail, and if you think *that* wasn't a mess!"

"I know," said Katie. "I've had to slit Hardy's skin with a razor blade to get the sac out without breaking it and scattering the nasty things."

"Amalia could never do that. She faints if she sees a spider."

"Then it's lucky she stayed in New Orleans."

"Sure, but what's the use of being married if you don't see your wife for months on end? The money's good here—it sure should be—but I'd take a fifty-percent cut to go home."

"It won't hurt to ask." Most of the others had left the club by then and Katie was exhausted. "Would you like more pie? Coffee?"

"Thanks, I've already put away a whole coconut cream." He grinned and got to his feet. "Good night, Mrs. Alastair. You're a brick, setting up this club and staying as close as you can to your husband. Hope he'll be back with you real soon."

She smiled and offered her hand. "So do I. And I'll hope you're immediately assigned to Louisiana and Amalia." As he turned to go, she stopped him. "Mr. Martin, while you're in Tampico, if you meet someone who's going to the company's camps beyond Vera Cruz, would you ask them to carry a letter to my husband?"

"Be glad to, ma'am. Or I can send it by company courier."

"Please, I'd rather this passed directly to him."

He chuckled knowingly. "I understand, Mrs. Alastair. I sure wouldn't want people to peek at some of the letters I've sent Amalia. Write your letter and I'll do my level best to send it by someone trustworthy."

She sat up late, tearing up several letters that would have been either too alarming or not emphatic enough. At last she composed one that simply stated that Fayette was the new president, that she believed him dangerous, that Hardy should be on guard, and if at all possible should come to her before reporting to Tampico. *I think you'll have to resign,* she wrote. *If you'll tell me where to meet you, I'll come to Vera Cruz. Otherwise, I'll wait. Please come, darling, as fast as ever you can, or let me know how to find you.*

She handed the letter to Martin at the dock next morning and waved him on his journey, feeling more hopeful than she had since the confrontation with Fayette.

Three weeks crept by. By now, with any luck, Hardy should have received her letter. To come overland would be a long, dangerous jungle ordeal, but she began to meet every craft that approached the dock.

One afternoon Hal Martin jumped to the planks from a boat. She gave a glad cry that died the moment he looked at her because of the pity in his eyes. She couldn't move. It seemed to take him forever to reach her, and when he did, he took her hands and gulped.

"Mrs. Alastair—Mrs. Alastair, I . . ."

She gripped his fingers. "What? What is it?"

He shuffled miserably. "Ma'am, I'd give anything if I didn't have to tell you."

"Hardy?"

Martin nodded very slowly. "El Tigre's men seem to have left the country. But rebels raided the camp, *federalistas* jumped the rebels, and Hardy was hit in the crossfire."

"He—he's dead?"

A brief nod, then he dropped his gaze, unable to meet her anguished eyes. "How do you know?" she whispered. "Maybe— there could be a mistake."

"No. I'm sorry. I was there when it happened.

"You?"

"Yes. See, when I talked to the manager about going back to Louisiana, he said I could if I'd first go check out some land adjoining the Vera Cruz leases. So I carried your letter myself." He hesitated. "Whatever was in it sure upset Hardy, ma'am. He said he was getting back to Jarocho as quick as he could. But that was the night it—it happened."

Blackness closed in on Katie, thick and suffocating. She fought it with all her strength, Martin's hands steadying her.

"Where is he? Is he buried there?" At least he had no close family to mourn him, no aged parents who'd have to be told. But she hated to leave him in the jungle, so far from home.

"I hope I did what you wanted, ma'am. I brought him back to Tampico. He's being embalmed. If you want to see him before he's buried, I'll take you as soon as you can get ready. This boat'll wait for us."

Katie packed hastily, too numb to cry. She couldn't believe it. When she saw his body, she would have to. She picked up the little gold derrick. That would rest with him. That, and all their dreams.

Hal Martin was so ill at ease and fidgety that she finally said, "I'm not going to jump overboard, Mr. Martin. You don't have to stay with me. Please don't misunderstand, you're very kind, but I need to be alone and—and think."

He got up, plainly relieved. "I'll be with the captain if you need me."

She nodded assent and gazed blindly at the tangled growth along the bank. Hardy, Hardy! Strong, so much a man, yet so tender. She took comfort from believing he'd been happy with her except for those few days of conflict. Yet she was bitterly ashamed that Hardy had given her his whole heart when there were parts of hers he could never fill.

But he had filled her life. Held her in his arms at night, eaten her food, shared common things that wove him into the fabric of her days. She would miss him as one misses daily water compared to the longing for Darcy's presence, a heady wine.

If only they'd had a child, a boy to carry Hardy's eyes and smile and name! Someone to save this from being such a terrible waste.

The thought brought her up short. Her flow was a few days

late, not an unusual thing for her when she was upset or overtired. But there'd been those last days in Tampico, the idyllic nights . . .

Oh, she prayed it was so! If she could love and nurture a child of Hardy's, keep something of him alive in the world, she'd feel less guilty.

Sustained by that hope, she faced the problem of where to bury Hardy. She wanted to take him to Old Orchard, have him rest beside Great-aunt Lorena and her family, but the body would start decomposing before she could get home. If she had him cremated, she'd carry his ashes home. Or she could bring him to Jarocho; he had friends there. After the camp was gone, perhaps María would see to his grave.

Fervently she hoped she wouldn't see Fayette again. She'd rather forfeit Hardy's wages. If Hardy had died any other way, she'd have suspected Fayette, but even he could scarcely have arranged the deadly chase between rebels and *federales*.

The journey to Tampico seemed eternal, but as the boat steered through the other craft to the wharf, she wished she'd never have to arrive, would not have to look on Hardy dead. For a moment, she cravenly wished that Martin had buried him at the fatal camp, but her husband deserved better than that. He would have all the honor she could show him.

Martin helped her ashore and a deckhand carried her valise.

"Would you like to go to the hotel first?" Martin asked uncertainly.

"Where's Hardy?"

"At the embalmer's. Look, there's a company touring car. I'll ask the driver to take you there." A sleek Pierce-Arrow pulled up, perhaps the very one she and Hardy had used. Martin opened the door and almost thrust her in.

"But—" she protested.

The door shut hard and the powerful engine roared. Only as the auto sped across the railroad tracks, jarring her sideways, did she realize a man was on the other side of the wide seat. "My dear."

She reached for the door handle. Iron fingers closed on her wrist, hauled her into a crushing embrace. A cruel mouth closed on her scream. When horror had robbed her of the strength to resist, Morgan Fayette moved back and smiled. "So here you are, my lovely."

Hope warred with paralyzing dread. "Hardy? Was—was all this a lie?"

He held her hands tightly between his. "It's a prophecy."

"Then Hardy's alive?"

"Yes, Katharine. Whether he remains alive is entirely up to you."

"But Hal Martin said—"

"What he was told to, in order to be assigned to Louisiana. Don't blame him too much. I swore you'd be treated like a queen, and that this deception was necessary only because you clung to your marriage vows in spite of having fallen in love with me."

"He couldn't believe that!"

"He wanted to, so he did." Again that taunting, watchful smile. "You could believe it yourself, sweet, if you tried. It would make things happier for everyone."

Her heart felt as if ice water were being pumped through it. "How do I know you haven't had Hardy killed?"

"You'll have to take my word for it. If you're sensible, I'll arrange for you to meet . . . eventually. He's more likely to believe you've chosen me if he hears it from you."

"He never will!"

"In that case," Fayette said, shrugging, "he'll be told that Hal Martin and you were lovers, that Hal brought that wild tale to Jarocho as a cover for eloping with you without causing protests from Hanford and the other men who think you're so pure."

"If Hardy believed that, he'd hunt down Hal Martin and get the truth."

"Which is why he won't find Hal."

"You—you'll kill Martin?"

"He's traveling by company ship. He's going to get a little drunk one night and fall overboard. His widow will receive American Eagle's condolences and a generous check."

Though Martin had betrayed her, Katie shuddered. Now he would never see his Amalia. "Don't do that, Mr. Fayette. Let him go."

"Can't risk his blabbing, my dear. He's too weak for this business, too tied to his wife."

Useless to plead, but she cried, "Why are you doing this? I don't believe you're going to all this trouble for someone you barely know." She took a deep breath. "When did you know my parents? Do you want to hurt me to get back at them for something?"

He was genuinely surprised. "I don't wish to hurt you at all, Katharine. But yes, it will be the high point of my life when the judge and Vinnie learn you're my mistress. I'd marry you if I could, but I have a wife who's given me a fortune and a son."

"I'm surprised that bothers you. What's bigamy compared to abduction, rape, and murder?"

He showed his teeth. "Among other things, it'll warm me for the judge to know that his grandchildren are bastards."

The viciousness of it stopped her cold. "Why do you hate him so?" she finally asked.

Fury tightened the narrow, handsome face before the mask slipped back in place. "That's a story well nigh as long as my life. You'll hear it all in good time." He probably guessed, rightly, that not understanding why this was happening deepened her fear, her sense of being helpless against powerful unseen forces set in motion before she was born.

"I'm not a person to you," she said raggedly. "I'm a weapon to use against my parents."

"You wrong yourself, my lovely. I would want you even if you weren't who you are. Do you know the Rule of Capture?"

She blinked, bewildered by the sudden switch. "Of course."

Oil pools usually extended beyond the property of one owner and weren't fixed in place like coal or gold or iron. A well drilled into a formation created low pressure at the bottom into which oil from surrounding areas would be forced by gas. The Supreme Court of Pennsylvania finally solved the ticklish problem in 1889 by declaring oil and gas to be of a feral nature and governed by the Rule of Capture applied to wild game—that they belonged to whoever captured them on his own land regardless of where they originated. This led to the wasteful, heavy drilling of wells, each operator trying to pump all he could from the same formation, with the result of lowering gas pressure so that much of the oil couldn't be recovered.

Katie frowned. "What does that have to do with me?"

His tone caressed her as disturbingly as if his slender pale hands were stroking her. "A lot. There's wildness in you, Katie, a need for freedom. I don't doubt that you've been faithful to your husbands and tried to act the dutiful wife, but it's clear that you have to act on your own, earn your own money. I never heard of another woman trying to learn to drill. I admire your spirit. It's the wildness of you I want as much as your body."

"I won't be wild or free as your whore."

"You could be. Listen, Katharine, I'm giving you the chance to be true to your nature. Throw in your lot with me and I'll make you an executive of the company with a hefty share of stock. You'll have money and power—freedom to do anything you choose, unfettered by a husband or conventions." His eyes challenged her. "Can you honestly say that doesn't appeal to you?"

It did, of course. Not that she cared about controlling others; she just wanted not to be controlled herself. She was beginning to believe that the only way to avoid that was to have power or money, unless one took the path of ascetic denial of things she still very much desired. But the price Fayette asked would destroy her.

Though she shrank inwardly from the cold fire in his eyes, she looked straight at him. "I'd rather be a hooker in the cheapest crib in the worst boom town than have you in my bed."

As deliberately as she had spoken, he drew back his hand. She managed not to flinch from the stinging slap, gauged to be more humiliating than painful.

"So much for freedom, then. Get this through your head, Katharine. I'm going to have you. Unless you kill yourself or me, I'll keep you as long as I like. Your only choice is whether to cooperate and save your husband's life, or to stay locked up while he has an accident."

Humid air clogged her lungs. She couldn't breathe. The world narrowed to hypnotic eyes, glinting out of whirling darkness. As if he saw her slipping beyond him, taking refuge in shock, he said quietly, "I'm going to show you, Katharine, what will happen to Hardy if you sacrifice him. But first I'm going to have you. If you'd rather be raped than adored, that's up to you."

It was rape. He laughed at her struggles, increasingly enflamed, till she bit deep into his wrist. He stunned her. When she revived, he was lunging to his climax. Desperately, she hurled herself sideways. His semen spilled against her thighs, a thin scalding.

His fingers bit into her throat. "Do that again, and I'll have my men spreadeagle you!" She thrashed beneath him, clawing at strangling hands that tightened till she spun into flame-shot blackness.

As consciousness returned, each breath tortured her bruised windpipe. She lay on the huge satin-covered bed feeling that if she moved she would crumble into pieces like fractured clay. She looked slowly, fearfully around.

He was gone. But his semen was drying, corroding her flesh. It had an acrid scent like decaying fungus, not at all like the clean-salt odor of Hardy.

Oh, Hardy! What can I do? I can't let you die. But this—how can I let him—

She sat up, her head throbbing. Her throat hurt. Fayette could have snapped her neck. In revulsion at what he had done to her, she almost wished he had.

Not quite, though. As long as she lived there was a chance to get away, a chance to protect Hardy. A terrible thought edged into her mind. At first she recoiled from it. Her parents had taught her the value and sweetness of life, especially the judge, who had seen so much slaughter of young men. She'd never dreamed of killing anyone, even the night of the Baygall riot. But now hard cold clarity possessed her.

She would kill Fayette if she could. And a chance would come, if he didn't do her to death first. The resolution sent strength through her bruised, violated body.

Rising, she winced at the pain in her ravaged parts but made her way to the marble washstand bolted to the deck of the spacious cabin. They were on Fayette's yacht, bound up the coast to whatever it was he hoped would cow her to his will.

As she washed his smell from her, put on the clothes he had roughly torn away, a part of her mind stayed remote, functioning like a machine. Fayette, now, couldn't do worse than he had. The intelligent thing would be to pretend capitulation, promise whatever he demanded to buy Hardy's life. She should simulate first reluctant, then increasing passion, playing on Fayette's vanity till he was lulled into relaxing his guard. It wouldn't be enough to escape. If he lived, she and Hardy would always be under threat.

She would have to kill him. And God help and forgive her, she would.

VIII _____

The dying sun reddened the waves where the yacht was anchored in a crescent bay. A uniformed steward invited Katie on deck, where Fayette rose to seat her at a table set with linen, porcelain, and silver. The steward brought a crystal tray with fresh fruit, clear soup, crusty rolls, and cheese. Katie compelled herself to eat. She would need her strength. But she refused chilled Sauterne and sipped instead at a mixture of fresh fruit juices that at first stung, then soothed her aching throat.

Avoiding Fayette's appraising eyes, she gazed at the white shore, the palms and low scrub out of reach of the tide. "When will we dock?"

"In the morning." He smiled lazily. "We'll enjoy our comfortable bed but leave early enough to be back on the yacht before the worst heat."

His glance struck something beyond her that made him reach for his field glasses and sweep the coastline. "Splendid." He gave a nod of satisfaction. "The drilling crew I sent here three weeks ago already has the derrick up. I'll stop by tomorrow and see how they're doing. I had to pay premium wages to get anyone to drill this near Dos Bocas but it just may pay off handsomely."

"Dos Bocas?" She searched her memory. "That was the first

175

big gusher drilled in Mexico, wasn't it? Blew in wild while the crew was eating lunch, caught fire, and cratered."

"My dear, one could boil the Book of Revelations down to those last two phrases and miss all the magnificent terror. Rock and fluid erupted, opening cracks around the well and boilers. Gas and oil flamed up till no one could come close enough to control the blaze. The cracks widened and then the whole surface collapsed—derrick, drilling rig, boilers, pumps, the whole she-bang sank into the crater. It could have been another Spindletop. Instead, it's a growing lake of boiling salt water spewing up sulphurous gases and masses of thick black oil, the closest thing to hell you'll ever see on earth."

He was telling her this for a purpose. Dread weakened her but she gave a deliberate yawn and smothered it. "I can't understand your interest in the field if it's that hopelessly lost."

Those white incisors touched his lower lips as his grin widened. "I have a legitimate interest, Katharine, as well as a personal one. In all these coastal fields called the Golden Lane, many wells have been ruined by drilling into salt water that contaminates the oil. Drillers have noticed a critical temperature change from oil to water, the water generally being about five degrees hotter. This can be measured by lowering self-registering thermometers in a heavy tube fastened to the bailer. By reading temps after the drill hits the Tamasopa limestone, a driller can stop when the bottom temperature suddenly shoots up. That way, he can produce whatever oil's above the brine."

"I still don't see what that has to do with a well that cratered in 1904."

"Everything. It's sound theory to correlate temperature data from other wells with the current reading of Dos Bocas. The more accurately we can peg the critical temperature, the more oil we can recover without making just one fatal screw too many."

"So?"

"Recording Dos Bocas temps at various levels will be a fascinating job. It should appeal to your Ranger's thirst for adventure."

"Hardy's no geologist!"

"He doesn't have to be. All he has to do is lower the thermometers, leave them in place five minutes, and read them. He'll do it if the bonus is attractive enough. After all, aren't you saving for your own outfit?"

"But you'll make sure he slips!"

"The footing's treacherous."

"It seems an elaborate form of murder when you could simply have him shot."

"I devised it for your edification, my dear. When you've seen that forty-acre crater pumping its daily hundreds of thousands of barrels of scalding salt water into the lagoon, I think it'll make an impression that will keep you from doing anything foolish. I think you'll gladly promise to tell your husband anything I require." He rose and stretched.

"Come, love. There's nothing more delightful than amorous play when there's a full moon and cool sea breeze."

Silver light cast Fayette's shadow eerily across the glimmering white satin bed. His face above her was half darkened, half ghostly pallid, so that he looked like a corpse.

Katie felt like one as he sheathed himself within her.

Morning came at last. Drawing her close a final time, Fayette gauged each stroking, each caress and exploring kiss, trying to draw response from her, but she could no longer connect what he was doing with the part of her that lived and cared. She knew what was happening but it was as if she had nothing to do with the body he cursed viciously because its inertness didn't give him the stimulus he needed to reach climax after night-long excesses that would have drained a young man.

"You'll do better after you've seen Dos Bocas," he panted, sliding off her. "It'll take some enthusiasm on your part to keep Hardy in good health."

"Why are you so set on me?" she whispered. "Why?"

He pondered, then laughed. "I had intended to tell you when you bore my first child but you might as well know now. You do attract me, Katharine, more than anyone has in years, but I'd hardly take this trouble over that." He polished her thigh with his hand. "I wanted your mother when I was young. I wouldn't have her now, of course. She's old. And I want revenge on your father, the judge."

"*Why?*"

His laugh was soft and terrible. "The judge is my father, too."

She couldn't take it in. Paralyzed beneath his stroking hand, she choked, "You—you're lying! The judge's only legitimate son drowned!"

"After he tried to rape your mother?" The man beside her chuckled. "It was best everybody think so. I went to Pennsylvania and became a lease man, then a producer. I really struck it rich in Oklahoma, though. Give those damn Indians a red Cadillac or a purple hearse and they'll sign away rights that would make them millionaires. I came back to Texas figuring to break the judge and Vinnie but stopped to look over the field at Baygall. When I found out who you were—well, what could be more perfect? Possessing you is much more pleasurable than burning out Old Orchard or turning Belleforest into an oil field—though I may do that someday. I've always intended to turn up at the judge's funeral and press my claim to his estate."

"You're the bastard, not Talt."

He laughed again. "I've already fixed him and your Uncle Thomas. Drilled wells along their leases in Oklahoma and sucked them dry, broke their little two-bit company. They're drifting around doing contract drilling, and they're awfully old for oil work. Jobs getting harder and harder to come by."

"They can come back to Old Orchard."

"Sure. Worn-out old wrecks with their tails between their legs. Nothing to do but drink themselves to death. Talt's already made a good start on that. Been hitting the bottle hard ever since his squaw died."

"She wasn't a squaw! She was half French and Scots."

"Indian enough to be on the tribal roll and own some prime oil locations." Again that awful laugh. "So there you have it, little sister. All the reasons. And the only thing that'll make me happier than I am now is when I send our parents a photo of us with our child. A bastard born of incest. It might even be an idiot, or misshapen."

"Nothing could be as twisted, as malformed as you."

"We'll wait and see, won't we, my sweet?"

She had to kill him. But no chance came that night. When he drowsed, he kept a leg or arm thrown over her so she couldn't move without waking him at once.

But there'd be a time. Soon or late, there'd be a time.

This grim resolve nerved her to dress and get down a roll and coffee. One of the crew had been dispatched to the new rig to borrow a truck that could negotiate the wasteland to Dos Bocas. When the truck appeared, stopping high enough up the beach to keep from getting stuck, Fayette wondered impatiently why the crewman didn't bring back the small boat.

"He's not there!" Fayette lowered his field glasses in disgust. "Must be some whores hanging around the camp, or someone offered him a bottle. Well, no matter. We'll use another boat."

They were soon aground on the fine bleached sand. Fayette kept his hand controllingly beneath Katie's elbow as they walked toward the truck. The driver, hunched over the wheel, had a greasy Stetson pulled low over his eyes. Mortified at anyone, even a stranger, knowing that she'd spent the night with Fayette, she didn't look at the driver but averted her face as Fayette got in and drew her up on the high seat alongside him.

"Drive toward that bare stretch," Fayette directed. "Get us as close to Dos Bocas as you can without danger."

"Yessir, Mr. Fayette." The driver slurred the words but there was something about his voice . . . Katie couldn't glance at him without peering around Fayette but she searched her memory.

She'd met thousands of men in the oil fields, and lots of them were now working in Mexico. It was possible the driver had been one of her customers. If so, she hoped he didn't recognize her.

The truck topped a rise and the crater came in view; vast, a forest of dead trees thrusting up remnants of trunks and limbs like black skeletons on the higher rim, while a steaming black spill churned over the lower side.

Far around the seething caldron, the earth was dead. Nothing grew, not a weed, not the toughest cactus. No flash of wings, no hum of insects. The stifling dense sulphur stench of rotten eggs poisoned the air, stinging Katie's eyes, making her choke. The surface of the black lake was a dizzying, ever-changing hell-broth of whirlpools, eddies, and sudden belches of oily brine.

As Katie stared in appalled awe, the center spewed a geyser fifteen feet high of gobbets of tar, yellowish steam, and oily brine. Katie thought of Hardy standing on those undercut banks that could give way at any time.

"You can't ask anyone to measure temperatures in that nightmare," she cried. "It's impossible!"

"Oh, I wouldn't say that, ma'am." The driver's voice, pitched so low it was almost inaudible, plucked at her memory again. "A real long bamboo rod—metal-cased thermometers on the end of a tough cord you'd cast out like a fishing line." She tried to peer around Fayette to see his face but he was looking at the crater, hunched over the wheel so far she thought he must have a deformity. "I could do it if the pay was right."

"You could?" Fayette sounded skeptical but intrigued. "I'd pay handsomely for readings taken from all around the crater and as far toward the center as possible."

The driver braked. "Well, Mr. Fayette, whyn't we just go up and have a look-see?"

Fayette hesitated, turning to watch Katie. He frowned, then smiled. "Somehow, sweetheart, I can't imagine you'll try to run away. Will you wait here, or do you need a closer view to convince you that you don't want your husband to take this assignment?"

The taste of salt blood was in her mouth. "You know I haven't got a choice." The words were bitter in her mouth. Not so bitter as the brush of his lips across hers.

He got out on the driver's side and smiled at her.

"That's good, my lovely. We'll celebrate your decision when we get back to the yacht."

His kiss, the sickening odor, the wasteland as blasted as her spirit, deepened the horror caused by the night's ordeal. She leaned against the cracked leather seat, watching as the two men made their careful way to the crater's rim.

They were of a height. The stranger had suddenly lost his hunch and walked with lithe grace, evoking another troubling memory. He turned, throwing back his head to laugh at something, and everything clicked together.

Darcy! What in the name of God was he doing there?

Hope flooded through her. He'd know something of her situation from what Fayette had said during the drive. Darcy would get her out of this. Blood pulsed through her quickly, a cleansing and revitalizing that swept away thick sludge. She sat up, turning toward the sea breeze that dissipated some of the worst smell, keeping her eyes on Darcy.

Whyever, however he was there, thank God he was. Lightheaded with joyous relief, she fought back hysterical laughter.

The men stood silhouetted on the rim, shadows against the

dead trees and pale sky. Suddenly, as if inviting each other to dance, they raised their arms.

It was no dance in which they came together. They strained on the crater's edge, swaying back and forth, trying for the advantage. Fayette kicked and Darcy stumbled back. Metal flashed in Fayette's hand.

A shot resounded as Darcy half rolled, half lunged toward Fayette. He gripped Fayette around the legs; they wrestled, and then they vanished. A shrill scream rent the air, ended as if a head had been chopped off. Katie tried to scream but it stuck in her throat. Darcy couldn't go like this, so fearfully, not when they were together for the first time in years!

She wrenched open the door and plunged recklessly up the incline, heedless of the crust breaking beneath her feet. Why care whether she plunged too if Darcy was gone?

Panting, she gained the spot scraped and trampled by their battle. She looked over the rim; only tortured oil brine steamed below. Her knees failed. She started to fall to the blackened crust when she saw a motion on her left.

Darcy held to the root of a dead tree that was lodged precariously where the rim had crumbled beneath the two fighting men. Below Darcy swirled and hissed the deadly turbulence that must have already claimed Fayette—no, Fayte Sevier, only son of Regina and Mark.

Katie moaned. Such a fragile hold! It could break any second. If he put more weight on it, trying to clamber up . . . "Darcy! Let me reach down—"

"No! Don't come closer, Katie! Your weight could break the ledge and kill us both. Is there a rope in the truck?"

"I don't know." She was afraid to leave, afraid the root would give way before she could get back.

Glancing around wildly, she fought down her panic. She could break a limb off one of the dead trees. And there was a sturdy-looking trunk. If she tied her ankles to it with her dress, then stretched out full-length and lowered the limb . . . maybe, maybe, with the help of God and all the angels, Darcy could climb out.

The first rotten limb broke in her hands. The second was sound but too short. Then she saw what had been a young tree but was now a pole. She kicked it over, tested it, and stripped off her dress, blessing the strong cotton, the wide, wide skirt that let her tie each ankle securely before she knotted the arms around the trunk. Scarcely breathing, she crawled forward, edging the pole in front of her.

"Darcy," she called. The ties would let her go no farther, and she was unable to see him. "I'm lashed to a tree—I'll be fine. I'm going to lower a pole. Between it and that root you should be able to climb out."

"Katie, run the hell to the truck! That damn ledge can go any second!"

"I won't move till you're up here so quit wasting time," she cried.

She lowered the pole, gripping it hard. Her lower arms were over the rim though she couldn't see him. Would he refuse to let her help? Would he try to scramble up by the root and perhaps fall into that simmering hideousness?

There was a tug on the pole, tentative, then trusting. He gave it more of a grip. Sweat poured down Katie's face, blinding her. She felt a lurch, held on for dear life, cringed at the sound of crumbling earth. But he was still there, he had hold of the tree.

There was scuffling, a moment when it seemed all his weight was on the pole, that she couldn't hold any longer, couldn't. And then he sprawled over the edge, rolling toward safety. She let go of the pole and he swept her along with him as the rim caved in up to within a few feet of them. She was still tied to the trunk as they held each other, sobbing and laughing. They kissed, and he untied the knots and helped her into her dress.

She gazed at him, stupefied, unable to believe he was here, he was alive—and Fayette was gone. She wouldn't have wished that horror even for him, but she was glad he was dead.

Wonderingly, she raised her hand to Darcy's dark-stubbled face. "You're so much thinner, Darcy. I wouldn't know you if it weren't for your eyes." Those ombré gold eyes, startling with black eyelashes and straight black eyebrows, were the same.

He cocked his head at her, the familiar motion. "You're thinner, too, Katie. But I'd know you anywhere."

They reached the truck and he helped her in. "Now tell me what you're doing here. Where the hell's your husband?"

She explained in a few words, yearning to touch the brown hands that skillfully steered the laboring truck. Darcy gave a low tuneless whistle.

"One thing Fayette wasn't lying about was that his southern paymasters were getting robbed. I was doing it."

"*What?*"

"Robbing robbers, Katie. That bastard Fayette broke your uncle and my dad and cheated my mother's kin—got them drunk and had them sign tricky leases that made him rich and gave them nothing. I tried to settle his hash in Oklahoma but he skipped while I was in jail."

"Jail?"

His face was set in harsh lines. "I killed one of Fayette's drillers who wouldn't move his rig off my mother's land. I broke jail, Katie. I'm wanted in the States. So when I heard Fayette was operating in Mexico, I decided to come down and keep him entertained."

"You—you're El Tigre?"

"Yes."

She couldn't speak but her heart wailed. Then he was outlawed here, too. He'd killed men—men like Hardy who were just doing their jobs. Darcy sighed. "Katie, I've earned the bullet or rope that's going to get me. But I want you to know that I've never robbed anyone but Fayette and I've given most of those payrolls to poor Mexicans. And bought guns for the rebels. The Revolution's just beginning. Madero's weak and when he falls there'll be a dogfight till someone comes out on top. I'd like it to be someone who'll give the people a chance."

He stopped in the shade of a thicket and turned to look at her. "So, Katie, we've got to get you to your husband. When the payrolls weren't intercepted, he may have started back to Tampico."

"Darcy, you can stop what you're doing. The judge might be able to get you a pardon—"

"I don't want a pardon. I'd do it all again." He gave a harsh laugh and passed his hand across his eyes. "You don't want me in the States, Katie. I'd kill those sons of bitches who're stealing Indian oil rights just like they stole their land."

"Uncle Thos said some Indians have gotten rich from leases."

"Some have. I know one who has a Christmas tree every month with presents for all the kids in town. But I know more who've been screwed. Listen, Katie, do you know big oil interests put the squeeze on the government to break up the reservations? The Indians didn't want to own little individual chunks of land in place of the big common territory, reservations given to Indian nations in compensation for lands the whites seized earlier. Theirs as long as waters run and grasses grows! Sure. Theirs till the whites smelled oil or wanted more homesteads."

"But Darcy—"

"So much for the Indian side of me. I'm black too, remember? And the Oklahoma blacks who had head rights, a share in tribal income, because they'd been slaves to Indians, don't have even the form of government-appointed guardianship that's supposed to protect the simple Indian. It's open season on blacks. I know of two little orphans who were murdered for their leases and they weren't the only ones." He shook his head slowly. A streak of white began at each temple, startling in his raven hair. "There's no place for me, Katie. I'm throwing in with the rebels. Now Fayette's paid out, I'd like to do something that may count."

She bowed her head, no longer able to fight back tears. To find him again—then hear he meant to throw his life away. "Your father, Darcy, he wouldn't want this."

"No. Dad'll struggle along with Thos and they'll probably get a poor-boy well dug and someday maybe they'll get a producer and sell to one of the big companies in order to drill some more. I'm not that way. I stay mad. Oh, the hell with it, Katie." He gave a deep sigh, then said, "I guess we can put you on that yacht and tell the crew their boss had an accident, tell them they're to take you to Tampico."

Not a word about them! Not a word of love! Maybe he didn't care anymore. She looked up quickly, caught his unguarded expression, the hunger in his eyes. With a thrill of triumph and despair, she knew he loved her.

"Darcy, let me stay with you. Just a little while . . ."

"I can't take you to camp. My men are still celebrating taking over the rig from Fayte's crew. Besides, Katie, you're married."

"Yes. And I love Hardy. But I loved you *first*. I always have. I always will."

His breath rasped. He reached for her, gripping her hard. "You're upset, honey. You'd be sorry later. I'd rather die than cause you sorrow."

She held his eyes and tried to keep her voice from breaking. "Darcy, Fayette—what he did—I feel all dirty and ruined. If—if you would love me, it would make me clean. It would heal me. Please, my darling. Please give us this."

The pupil spread across the gold in his eyes. She took his face between her hands and kissed his mouth with all the need and passion and yearning of the years they'd been apart. And with all the grief for the time they wouldn't have together.

A moan sounded deep in his chest and his arms closed around her. He carried her to where leaves shaded white sand. Their clothing made a bed; and their loving, in spite of its fatedness, made them a heaven.

IX ———————————————————

The yacht reached Tampico that afternoon. Darcy had come on board with Katie and composed a letter about the accident that he instructed the captain to give to American Eagle's Tampico superintendent. Darcy also impressed upon the frightened captain that El Tigre would have vengeance if Katie was not immediately and safely conveyed to the city and sent on to Jarocho.

"This letter tells all that's necessary," Darcy declared. "The señora must not be harassed or questioned, *comprende?* She will go now to the cabin and you will not disturb her beyond bringing food and drink. *¿Comprende?*"

"It will be as you say," muttered the captain, but he dared one glance toward shore. "It is certain, señor? Señor Fayette has perished?"

"If you want to see where he fell," offered Darcy with a grim smile, "I will be happy to show you."

The captain backed away. "No, *gracias*. Thank you many times, that will not be necessary."

Darcy walked Katie to the cabin. His gaze took in, then retreated from, the satin-covered bed. "You'll be all right here? They can rig an awning for you on deck."

She held out her arms. "I'll be all right. If you'll just hold me for a while."

He did, loving her with voice and hands and mouth till at last he tore himself away. "Good-bye, Katie. Be well. Be happy. Don't grieve for me, but always remember you were my only love."

"Oh, Darcy. . ."

But he was gone.

In Tampico, the captain found a launch to take her to Jarocho, and as he helped her into it, asked timorously, "Señora, if—if there is trouble, you will testify that my men and I treated you well? And that we had nothing to do with Señor Fayette's—accident?"

"Yes. If need be." She climbed under the thatched shelter covering half the small boat and sank into drugged heavy slumber from which she did not rouse till Hanford was bending over her. She told him Martin had been wrong, that Hardy was alive. But she didn't, couldn't, tell him what Fayette had done to her.

Hardy arrived a week later with the news that Fayette's son, Bernard Silks Fayette, known in East Texas and Louisiana as B.S., which could stand for bottom settlings or basic sediment, was coming down to look the operation over. Hanford groaned. "Another Yankee boss."

"You'd better not let a Texan or Louisianan hear you call one of them that," Hardy said with a grin.

"No offense," Hanford said gloomily. "All the same, I've got money saved and a mind to try wildcatting. Care to throw in with me, old chap? Mike O'Brien does, and his toolie, Tony St. Cyr."

"I got a bonus for the Vera Cruz stint even though El Tigre had melted away," Hardy said. "But we still don't have much money, Mr. Hanford."

"That'll be cured if we dig a good well." The corners of Hanford's eyes crinkled. He glanced at Katie. "I refuse to do without your wife's lime pie."

How much had Hanford guessed? She had told him only that the company's owner had turned out to be an old acquaintance who had taken her to see Dos Bocas and slipped to his death. Hardy, just arrived, knew nothing so far except what he'd heard in Tampico—that Fayette had been the mysterious new owner and was dead.

Katie smiled distractedly at Hanford's gentle teasing. She was tied in knots, her mind racing. She hated to tell Hardy what Fayette had done to her but she couldn't hold the terrible secret within herself, could she? And what about Darcy? It would do no good to tell Hardy that the man she'd always loved had cleansed her of Fayette by making love to her. A violent headache sledged at the back of her neck.

There was more. Her period had never come, though it would be a miracle if Fayette's brutality hadn't dislodged an embryo. She had bled slightly. But the baby she might be carrying could be Hardy's, or Darcy's, or even, God forbid, Fayette's, begot of incest and vengeance.

She clenched her hands in her lap, scarcely hearing what Hanford and Hardy were saying. If she knew the child was Fayette's, she'd get rid of it even if it killed her. But if the child was Darcy's—oh, if she could have that much of him, she would gladly pay the cost, whatever it was. But Hardy? As she gazed at him with regret and tenderness, she decided to tell him everything.

When they entered their house, Hardy swept her into his arms. She answered his kiss, but when he laughed and moved her toward the bed, she put her hands against his chest. "Hardy. I have to tell you something . . ."

As she spoke, she felt his heart lunge beneath her palms, stop beating, then lurch into heavy pounding.

She told him about Fayette, and he tried to comfort her, but she held him back, getting to Darcy before she could turn craven and conceal that she had begged Darcy to take her. Hardy stiffened, moving beyond her reach. He heard her out without showing emotion except for the muscle twitching in his jaw.

Silence deepened between them, silence as dreadful as that hellish crater in the dead forest. She felt as blighted, except for that small seed growing within her darkness. She felt terrible fear and equally desperate hope: nothing could be confirmed or dismissed till the child came into the light. What she would do if it resembled Fayette, she couldn't bear to think.

Hardy simply continued to stare at her. It was as if she had told him she had some disgusting, incurable disease. "Let's see if I have this straight," he said at last, turning away from her, his tone so muffled she could barely hear. "You may have been pregnant by me. Then Fayette—raped you. Then you persuaded this Darcy—the one you turned me down for at first—to make love to you. Have we missed anyone?"

She cried out at that and his shoulders sagged. "Sorry. Cheap shot. But my God, Katie!"

She winced, waiting, head hanging. When he said nothing more, she swallowed. "If you want a divorce, Hardy, you can have it. What I did was wrong, but you have to know this: I'm not sorry. If Darcy ever came to me, I'd do it again."

Hardy made a stifled furious groaning sound. He plunged blindly through the door. Katie didn't follow. This was how it felt to kill someone you loved, someone who deserved only kindness at your hands. But she'd had to tell him so that he could choose.

Somehow, Katie went on with the club, which María and Sara had kept going. Hardy was drinking in the barracks again, Hanford told her, and scanned her with shrewd, troubled concern. "Is there anything I can do, Mrs. Alastair?"

"Thank you, no. I—I had to tell him something that— Well, it was a shock."

"I'm sorry." Hanford clumsily patted her hand. "But you can bet he'll be home when his head clears. I've turned in my resignation, and as soon as the company sends down a replacement, our little company can get started."

"That's wonderful." She forced a smile. It would be a good way to take her mind off Darcy and the corroding poison of Fayette, to cook for and look after a drilling crew. She craved hard work and new surroundings. But if Hardy couldn't forgive her, she'd have to go back to the States.

A part of her longed for the refuge of Old Orchard; another part shrank from the job of concealing from her parents what the judge's son had done to her. Much, much better that they go on thinking Fayte Sevier had drowned all those years ago.

On the third night after Hardy's return, she had closed the club and was undressing when Hardy came in. "Do you want something to eat?" she asked faintly as he stood there, very tall in the dim light.

"No." His eyes were hammered steel. "Katie, you love this Darcy but he's off to the Revolution. Is that right?"

"Yes."

"And you're going to have someone's baby. His, mine, maybe Fayette's."

"Yes."

Hardy sighed. "Do you want to stay married to me?"

"If—if you want me."

In one step, he took her by the shoulders. "Hell, I want you! I love you, Katie! I've chewed it all over. I hurt for you and I was mad at you and I ached. Blamed myself too for letting that bastard get his hands on you. The only thing I can't swallow is your saying you'd be Darcy's again if he came and asked."

"It's true."

Hardy released her so roughly that she staggered. Then, as savagely, he caught her hard against him, found her lips. "The hell with it! I've got you and I'm going to keep you! I'll father the baby, whoever begat it. We won't ever talk about it again. It'll just be mine."

Weak with relief, she wept against his shoulder, only then allowing herself to realize how awful it would have been to endure without him the months till the baby came—and the time after that when the child would need a father and she a husband. Hardy held her close, stroking her hair, before he turned up her face and kissed her tears.

"You have to know this, Katie. You're my wife. If Darcy tries to see you, I'll kill him unless he kills me first."

Her heart stopped. "If you did that, you'd do better to kill me, too. But he won't come, Hardy. He doesn't mean for me to see him ever again."

She broke into convulsive sobs, reliving all that had happened since Hardy had last held her. It seemed eternity. She had changed and so had Hardy. But he loved her: he would care for her and the child. That was what nerved her to go on after the horrors of Fayte and the loss of Darcy.

"Oh, Lord!" Hardy breathed, drawing her closer. "I'm sorry for you, Katie. For Darcy, too, I guess. But— Well, hell! I won't think about it. We're together, that's what counts."

They lay down. He was tenderly ardent. But when he tried to enter her, his body failed him for the first time in their marriage.

"God damn it," he muttered and turned on his back.

She dared to touch the crisp hair on his chest. "It—it'll be all right, Hardy."

"Sure."

In a little while, it was. But she knew that what had unmanned him had been a revulsion in his deepest nature, instinct far more deep-rooted and inevitable than rulings of his brain, at reclaiming a woman possessed by other men.

Hanford made a deal with a British company to drill on a lease near Tupan for a percentage of any oil the new company of Texerenla found. The name was made from the allegiances of the partners, Texas, Erin, England, and Louisiana.

American Eagle, under B.S. Fayette, was closing down operations like Tupan that were vulnerable to seesaw battles between revolutionaries and *federalistas*. The partners bought drilling equipment at bargain rates, moved it as far as possible by narrow-gauge rail, and took it the rest of the way by pack mules.

Two weeks after Hardy's return, they had a camp on the edge of the axe- and machete-cleared future field, and in ten days, with the help of workers hired from Tupan, the cellar was dug that would give space beneath the derrick floor for valves, fittings, and jointing and unjointing pipe. Heavy timber foundations were laid, and engine house and belt house sprouted at the end of the walkway. The pipe rack was raised, and legs, girts, and sway-braces of the derrick began to form the open tower that seemed to Katie like a crude wood ziggurat offering their prayers to heaven.

Within the week, the derrick reared one hundred and twenty feet into the sky, twenty-two feet square at the bottom, tapering to six feet at the crown-block, the frame mounted with grooved pulley-wheels over which ran the casing line, the sand line for bailing, and the drilling line.

Then came rigging up, connecting the boiler to the engine, putting the rigging irons in their places, and setting up the forge. It was midmorning when Hanford, a mighty grin on his pink-patched face, stepped back from adjusting the temper screw and glanced around at his partners, one of whom was Katie, for she had invested her profits from the club along with Hardy's stake.

"We're all set, folks! Texerenla Britoil Number One is about to be spudded in."

"Faith!" bellowed Mike O'Brien. "Let's do it right, Lord Tom! Just you wait a wee minute!"

He was back quickly with a jug of *aguardiente* and an assortment of cups. Handing one of these to each partner, he tipped in a spill of the clear spirits, overriding Katie's protest with, "Just a nip for luck, Miss Kate."

When everyone was served, he set down the jug and raised his cup. "To our first—to a gusher!"

Everyone drank though Katie sputtered on the fiery draught.

Some hole would have to be drilled before regular tools and walking beam could be used. This was done by attaching manila cable to the wrist pin of the crank, running this cable over the crown-block, and as it dangled over the opening in the floor, fastening on the heavy spudding bit. When all this was ready, Hanford started the engine. Mike O'Brien stood by the hole, keeping the cable steady, seeing that the bit revolved evenly as it raised and dropped, pounding a hole into the earth.

Katie's heart swelled. She laughed, really laughed, for the first time since that false message had come about Hardy. This might be their fortune. At the least, it was a bold venture they were making together. Hardy was at the forge, helping Tony dress the tools. As if sensing her exhilaration, he looked up at her and grinned.

She was happy as she went back to camp. While the bit probed the earth, another mystery grew inside her. As she hoped for success with the well, she hoped her baby would be beautiful and strong—and yes, she prayed it might be Darcy's even if that was a sin. She could give Hardy other children, but this was the only way she wouldn't lose Darcy entirely.

The house, down to the bamboo furniture, was a copy of the one at Jarocho, with the small gold derrick holding pride of place. Tony and Mike had a hut and Tom Hanford a small one. Most of the Tupan workers who'd helped build the camp and set up the derrick had been paid off, but three stayed to provide wood for the boiler, keep the camp supplied with fish, and help Katie. Ysidro, a young Indian with soft brown eyes and a shy smile, helped her with the cooking and cleaning up, peeling fruits with a murderous-looking knife, roasting and grinding coffee beans, fetching water from the spring a mile away, and scouring pans till they glistened. He was so deft and willing that Katie ceased to mourn María, to whom she'd turned over the club.

It was good to be busy feeding her husband and partners who

were sending the drill deeper with every dip of the walking beam. And she was busy: eggs, bacon, biscuits, gravy, and pots of strong coffee for breakfast; fish, beans, and rice for dinner with *cocada* and fresh fruit for dessert; and for supper whatever meat was delivered by the Tupan butcher, more tasty black beans from the earthen *olla,* slow-cooked over charcoal, and sweet potatoes or fried bananas, perhaps sliced avocados dressed with lime juice and cilantro, often a filling soup, and always several kinds of pie.

Hardy insisted that she rest a few hours in the afternoon and wouldn't let her wash his work clothes, much less those of the other men. Ysidro had big tubs of hot water ready for the men to bathe in every night and another boiling soapy one to receive their mucky clothes. He stirred these well, beat them with the paddle, and rinsed and hung them to dry over strong branches.

Katie was relieved to escape that task. She was feeling queasy in the mornings, not actually sick but unable to eat. It was better since she'd remembered something Vinnie had said and started eating a crust of bread or biscuit before getting up. She was in her third month and the faint rounding of her belly was imperceptible, though her clothes were becoming a little tight.

Time to let them out. Time to write Vinnie the news and tell her not to send baby things. If the well was a decent producer, Katie might be able to go home to have the baby. Hardy had already suggested it, though Katie hadn't told him that she yearned for her mother as never before. But if the child looked like Fayte, or even Darcy, how could she manage not to tell Vinnie everything, burden that loving spirit in relieving her own?

The drill was pounding through limestone now. Traces of oil showed in the cuttings. All the men were tense. If there was oil, they'd strike it soon.

Mike O'Brien's big, tough, sensitive fingers had the best feel for what the drill was doing, so he took over the lazy bench, which up to then had been shared with Hanford and Hardy. They lost the tools and Tony had to fashion several fishing tools with which many frustrating attempts were made before the string was hauled up and reattached.

There were seldom three days in a row when the butcher didn't arrive with frightened tales of skirmishes and raids. While government forces hunted the rebels and the other way around,

both sides pillaged the common people for supplies, often giving
villagers the choice of immediately "enlisting" or being shot.

Oil camps were a favorite target because there were usually
explosives, weapons, horses, and ample food. All the Texerenla
men wore sidearms except for the three Mexicans, whose whetted
machetes were never far from reach. Loaded .30–30 rifles were
kept in each hut and in the open-sided shelter that served as
lounge and dining hall. Hardy insisted that Katie practice till she
was able to hit a tomato can at a hundred paces nine times out of
ten.

One day the butcher rode in without any meat, begging to hide
at their camp so the *federalistas* couldn't force him into their
army. Hotly pursued by rebels, they had taken over Tupan that
morning, confiscated all the food, forcibly recruited every male
above the age of fourteen, and barricaded themselves in the
church. When the rebels followed, the plaza would turn into a
battlefield.

"God curse all *soldados chingados*," lamented the paunchy
middle-aged man. "Saving of course those poor devils compelled
to fight, like my three cousins who are with the rebels! *Chis* and
caca on the Revolution!" He spat savagely. "At least in Díaz's
time we only had to dread the Rurales. They were mean *cabrones*
but they kept the bandits down or made them into more Rurales.
Better to fear one big devil than a dozen small ones! If I could
stay with you señores till one bunch whips the other, I will bring
you a tender kid—if God preserves any from those thieving *pen-
dejos*."

Hardy's Spanish was much better than Hanford's. After a brief
conference with the partners, he invited Paco Sanchez to hide his
mule with their horses, which were, for safety, kept in a corral
back in the trees. Paco could help fuel the boilers; and of course,
if either rebels or *federalistas* came this way, he could hide, or if
there were no alternative, he could fight.

Trembling with relief, he thanked Katie for the coffee she
brought him. She smiled and nodded, deciding not to let him
know she understood the obscenities he had rained impartially on
government and rebel bands.

Drilling continued, but the Mexicans were instructed to hide
explosives, saddlery, storable food, and several of the rifles back
in the brush. Most of the company's money was in a Tampico

bank, but the amount needed for operating was hidden in a steel chest that Hanford kept buried beneath the twisted roots of a big sapote tree at the edge of camp.

Ysidro was posted about two miles up the trail to the village. If he brought an alarm, the rig could be closed down and a defense prepared, or, if the approaching force was drunk and numerous, everyone would hide in the forest. Cheated of their most valued booty, the raiders might wreck or burn the derrick, but that was better than being slaughtered.

It was a nerve-wracking day. Deprived of Ysidro's help, Katie had no chance to rest. She was slicing jicama, a crisp turniplike vegetable, for supper, when she heard Ysidro's frantic shout.

"They're coming! Singing, yelling, *muy borracho!*"

The engine cut off. "Which side?" called Hanford.

"*¿Quién sabe?* They're drunk!"

No time to haul the tools up. Tony doused the forge, Mike opened a valve to let steam escape from the boiler. Hanford and Hardy hurried toward Katie, each saying to the other in the same instant, "Take Katie and hide with the *campesinos*."

It was funny but no one laughed. Paco, Ysidro, and the other two men had already snatched up rifles and were disappearing into the brush. Katie stuffed the talisman derrick down her bodice and seized the rifle by the door. "We'd better all go."

"There's been more oil in the cuttings the last few times we bailed," Hardy said, eyes glinting as hard as the barrel of the Colt jutting out of his cutaway holster. "This gang might torch the derrick just for the hell of it. Maybe I can give them some good Scotch and jolly them into moving on."

"You've got a wife to look after," Hanford growled. "Go along, there's a good chap. I'll see what I can do with the blighters."

"Look, Tom, handling mobs used to be my line of work. Take Katie and get going. Since we don't have an army, one man'll actually be better than a couple."

"Always the Texas Ranger, old fellow?" The two grinned at each other. "Come on then, Mrs. Alastair."

As Hanford took her arm and hurried her into the dense growth, she heard Mike and Tony arguing that they should stay, but Hardy prevailed and the two quickly caught up and helped

make a way for Katie through vines, brush, trees, and a particularly wicked type of giant bamboo with barbed stems.

Ysidro called softly. He and the other three Mexicans were
hiding where a stream, now almost dry, had hollowed the bank
into a shallow cave overgrown with rushes.

"Get down and stay," Hanford told Katie. He turned to Mike
and Tony. "I'm going back and have my rifle trained on those
noisy lads. It's all very well if Hardy can fob them off with
whisky and cigars, but I'm not going to let them kill him without
dealing them a bit of grief."

Mike slapped his shoulder. "I'm with you, Lord Tom. Tony,
you ugly little monkey, can you hit anything with that rifle?"

"Reckon I've shot more deer than you've ever seen, you big
lummox!" Tony's hatchet face softened as he gave Katie an encouraging smile. "Don't fret yourself, ma'am. Those bas—soldiers—try to jump Hardy and we'll blast 'em into next July."

Katie wanted to follow but knew the men would turn her back.
She waited till the sound of their movements faded and then
started to make her way along the stream bank. A little farther
down she'd cut back toward camp and position herself where she
too could use a rifle if Hardy were threatened.

"Señora!" came Ysidro's piercing whisper. "Come down here.
Let us guard you as the señores commanded!"

"I must be near my husband, *chico*." Katie tossed the words
over her shoulder and kept going.

In a few minutes, there was a scrambling. Ysidro was ahead of
her, making a path. "Go back!" she hissed. "If they catch you,
they'll make you join them!"

His smooth young jaw was stubborn. "I stay with you, señora." He slashed a thick growth of *mala mujer* with its viciously
spined leaves out of her way and moved ahead, rifle in one hand,
machete in the other.

Katie could hear distance-muffled shouts and drumming
hoofs. She thought she recognized Hardy's voice. She tripped in
her haste and Ysidro turned to help her.

There was a slow twisting in her entrails. And then, as she
struggled to her feet, an explosion rocked the earth.

X ─────────────────────────────

Through the trees, Katie saw a huge pillar of steamy white vapor rise into the air. Gas! Would oil follow? The hole had attracted gas that poured with such pressure into the weakened formation that—yes, as she pushed nearer, she saw that the tools must have been blown straight upward, knocking off the crown block, destroying the derrick down to the second girt, which she could only dimly discern through the boiling cloud. Mounted men had reined in at the far edge of the clearing. A couple fired shots at the steam. In that moment the purity of the geyser changed. Black grease mixed with vapor, spewing like rain, coating the soldiers with glistening oil. The rumble from the earth was like the stirring of an agonized behemoth humping against the surface, thrashing its mighty limbs, trying to get out.

The commander's mouth opened but all the other noise drowned out his shout. With a sweep of his arm, he led his men back down the trail to Tupan.

Katie went limp with relief. Smearing oil from her eyes, she quickly realized that what they faced now was as dangerous as rampaging looters. Texerenla No. 1 had blown in wild and must be capped. If it could be. Sometimes these blowouts cratered. She thought of Dos Bocas and shuddered.

The black plume sprayed four hundred feet into the sky. The

men plugged their ears with cotton and tied their hats down over them before they ran to the wrecked derrick, tarred figures nearly indistinguishable from one another. They would try to close off the flow, but surely this primeval explosive surging would put too much pressure on the iron master gate intended for the well, though the gate weighed two tons. And with the derrick and lines down, how could they get it in place?

Sheltering beneath the thatched dining hall, Katie found a towel and cleaned herself as best she could while watching the men.

They couldn't hear each other and had to gesture. From her years in the oil fields, Katie could interpret what they were doing, adding clamps and rods to strengthen all the connections, fitting a heavier-test valve over the master gate, checking what was left of the derrick and deciding it was strong enough to rig the block and tackle that would swing the gate over the hole.

The biggest tar-man collapsed and the others dragged him a distance from the derrick so he could recover from the gas. Now they all tied ropes around their waists so that, as each one went down, he could be hauled to safety.

One spark from the metal parts and tools they were using would turn the black spume into a titanic blaze. It might take days to cap the gusher. The men would have to eat and, now and then, move a distance away from the gas long enough to clear their heads. Paco and the two workers had cautiously returned, and Katie sent them to help at the derrick. Then, with Ysidro clearing a spot in the brush out of range of the spattering oil, she set up a temporary kitchen, made coffee, and put a nourishing stew on to simmer. Shielded by a poncho, she got to camp in time to see the huge iron master gate swung above the hole and carefully lowered. In spite of its two-ton weight, it bobbled over the flow like a leaf caught by an eddy.

The exhausted men came and sprawled on mats. They were nauseated by the poisonous gas, but after a few cups of strong coffee, they were able to get down bowls of stew.

"A gusher." Hardy's hoarse voice was barely audible above the roaring of the wild well. "All that oil going to waste! We'll be damn lucky to cap it before it catches fire."

"But if it does," said Hanford, glancing around, his yellow

hair as gummy black as his face, "everybody run. We don't have enough boilers and hoses to douse an inferno."

Mike sighed. "Guess you're right, Lord Tom. We can drill another well, but not if we're all burned to cracklings." His teeth flashed white in the dark mask of his face. "It sure sent those soldiers on their way! They got a dandy oil bath they didn't bargain on."

"We need to go to Tupan and see if we can scrounge up a heavier master gate from an abandoned oil camp," said Hanford. "But we can't haul it through the middle of a battle. We'll need a lot of mules, too. Deuce take it! Drilling in this country's hard enough without a blooming revolution going on!"

Katie poured more coffee. Straightening, she almost dropped the big enamel pot as a man stepped out of the brush. Almost at once, in spite of the oil dripping from his wide-brimmed hat, she saw that it was Darcy. Bandoliers crossed his breast and he was armed with pistols and a rifle.

The partners followed Katie's stare and Hardy's hand went to his revolver. Laughing, Darcy swept off his hat. "Miss Katie, as I live and breathe! I ran into some of your old Spindletop customers and they said your husband had gone partners to drill out here." He cocked his head toward the billowing spume. "Looks like you've got a producer if you can get a lid on it. Maybe I can help."

"Where—where did you come from? The soldiers—"

"The lucky ones are heading for the hills. My men have Tupan."

"That's a stroke of luck!" Rising, Hanford thrust out his hand and introduced himself and the others. Hardy nodded stiffly, for even before Darcy gave his name, Katie knew Hardy had guessed who he was. She was certain that Hardy would rather lose the well than accept Darcy's help, but Hardy had no right to rob his partners of a chance to salvage the oil.

Watching Darcy, aching with the joy of seeing him, longing to tell him about the child, Katie scarcely heard what the men were saying till Darcy grinned and said, "I'll be back as soon as I can with the heaviest gate from the old camp. If I can find some boilers and hoses, I'll bring them too in case we get a fire."

"I say!" Hanford said thankfully. "If you help us tame this one, Ransom, you're in for a share."

"I'll settle for one of Mrs. Alastair's meals and a bottle of Scotch," Darcy said over his shoulder, then quickly was out of sight.

Hardy's eyes met hers. For a moment, she was terrified, hearing the echo of him saying, "*I'll kill him.*" But of course he couldn't, not when Darcy had freely volunteered to help them. Hardy turned his back to Katie. "Come on," he said to the men. "Maybe the pressure's dropped enough to let us clamp on that gate."

The well wasn't tamed, though, till Darcy and his men returned with a pack train that must have used every mule in the countryside. They hauled an even heavier master gate than the one the partners had, as well as three boilers and lots of hoses.

Darcy checked the connections himself while the boilers were rigged and hoses readied in case of the dreaded spark. Perhaps the pressure had subsided a little. In any case, with Darcy supervising the lowering of the iron piece, it settled into place. The wild geyser vanished. Like men hastening to bind a momentarily subdued but treacherous beast, the partners and Darcy secured the giant iron with wrenches.

The black treasure was saved, ready to be sold as soon as pipe could be laid from there to connect with the Tupan pipeline that ran to Tampico. That was Britoil's job. Hanford leaned against the blasted derrick and laughed exultantly. "From now on, all we have to do with this well is spend our checks. Ransom, without you we could have had a disaster. You've got to give us an address so we can at least pay back a little of what we owe you."

Darcy was now as black as any of them, which made the gold of his eyes even more startling. "Thanks, but I don't have an address. If you could feed us and give me that Scotch, we'll move along."

While the men scoured off the worst of the oil, Katie and Ysidro hurriedly opened cans. Tinned meat and soup extended the kettle that had never stopped simmering, and she made a huge batch of biscuits and sweet batter to pour over canned peaches for improvised cake. It wasn't the feast she would have loved to give Darcy, but he and his score of men relished every bite. The Texerenla outfit ate sparingly to make the food stretch.

Katie would have given almost anything for a few private

words with Darcy, but after his third cup of coffee, he got to his feet and shook hands all around, except with Hardy who was pouring himself more coffee.

Last of all, Darcy passed before Katie. "Good-bye," he said softly. "I'm glad I got to help you with your first well. Hope there'll be dozens more."

What would it matter when she couldn't have him? When he was determined to throw himself away? "Darcy, if you'd go back to the States—"

"No."

If she could only tell him that she might have his child. He raised her hand to his lips, gave his men a command and, in a few minutes, led them out of camp, a bottle of Hanford's best Scotch wrapped in his poncho.

Mike O'Brien let out a gusty breath. "There's a lad I'd like to have beside me on a derrick *or* in a fight."

Hanford and Tony nodded. Hardy stared after the riders with a face Katie couldn't read.

The partners voted to dig another well close to No. 1 and the whole process began anew. The baby, having quickened when the well blew in, seemed to have absorbed some of its wildness: it moved more vigorously every day. Her waist was thickening and she tired more easily, though the morning sickness faded. "Don't you want to go home?" Hardy asked one morning when she couldn't get her swollen feet into her loosest slippers. "We can afford it, and you'd better go while it's safe to travel."

Katie knew he was right. She wanted her mother, and the reassuring presence of her father, wanted to have her child in the house where she'd been born. She trusted Dr. Newsom, who had delivered her and tended all her childhood ailments, to bring forth this baby. But she hated to leave Hardy. Even more, she hated to leave Mexico where there was a tiny hope of seeing Darcy. She was afraid that after she left, she'd never hear of him again, never know what was happening to him. "I'll go," she said to Hardy, "but there's no big hurry. It's still five months."

She wondered if he both wanted and feared for the child to be born and show its paternity.

Two weeks later, two Chinese cooks arrived, along with supplies. "You can show them how to feed us," Hardy said. "And then, Mrs. Alastair, I'm taking you to Tampico and putting you on a train to Texas."

She started to protest, looked at him, and knew it was futile. Besides, he was right. The journey would be arduous, particularly now that the Revolution had wrecked a lot of trains and tracks and thrown schedules into chaos. She'd better go before such a trip might endanger the baby or bring on premature labor. She greeted the Chinese and took them to the kitchen.

Both Sung and Wu were experienced camp cooks. They took over so smoothly that Katie quickly saw her cooking wouldn't be missed, except for her pies. The other partners had insisted that Hardy escort her to the border, so at the beginning of her fifth month in that spring of 1912, she packed, leaving the gold derrick for Hardy.

She had become very fond of Ysidro. Her eyes glistened as much as his did when she told him good-bye and gave him a scrolled machete with an inlaid handle that she'd ordered custom-made from Tampico. It was to have been a birthday gift but she gave it to him in parting. "Come back, señora," he murmured. "I will take care of your little one." He was not much older than a little one himself. She kissed his brown cheek and hoped that this Revolution would make his world better.

Tom Hanford, Tony, and Mike had become more than partners; they were as dear as family. She made her farewells with a lump in her throat and kissed each man on his cheek. They were spudding in the new well, and for luck, they asked her to put her hand on the cable for a minute. It was the last thing she did before she waved a final time and, with help from Hardy, mounted her horse.

The military commander of the region was in a private car with his staff, and ten other cars were filled with soldiers. More soldiers, heavily armed, served as guards, filling one freight car behind the engine and two more at the end of the coaches. Hazards of travel being what they were, the civilian car was sparsely occupied, mostly by *norteamericanos* on business. A grassy plain with occasional clumps of trees stretched from the coast to the first hills, where the train snaked through a tunnel in the side of the first mountain, then moved along a canyon walled by sheer rock cliffs, the green river cascading below. They wound along a shelf on the side of the mountains. As they entered another pass, the engine laboring up the steep incline, Hardy, sitting by the window, shouted a warning and pulled Katie to the floor, bracing his body over hers.

"What—" she began.

The brakes of the train screeched. The car lurched. A re-sounding crash, an impact that sent the train twisting, an instant when everything froze, then rending, splintering confusion, screams, rocks jutting through wrecked metal and shattered windows.

When at last debris stopped falling, when Katie realized that Hardy wasn't moving and, still dazed herself, tried to shift around so as to touch his face, a deafening explosion convulsed the overturned cars. Something smashed against Katie's head and everything went dark.

A heart was beating beneath her cheek. Its insistent steady pulse somehow strengthened her before returning consciousness told her why her head throbbed, why she felt like poorly glued fragments. Someone on horseback was holding her tightly against him. She knew, even before she opened her eyes, that it wasn't Hardy, and remembering his frightening limpness, she gasped his name.

"Your husband's all right. He's up ahead." The arm around her tightened and a mouth brushed her forehead. "God, Katie, when I saw you . . ." *Darcy.* She rested for what seemed a long time, lost in the undreamed-of comfort of being in his arms.

But soon an awful knowledge thrust through that peace. There was a wrecked train. "You did it, Darcy. There—there must be a lot of people dead."

"Soldiers. And General Lobos with his whole staff. He's butchered whole villages, Katie."

"There were civilians, too."

"I hate that, Katie, but this is war."

"What happened to those who weren't killed?"

"My men have them. We'll leave them—and you—in the next village. Why were you on the train? Are you going back to Texas to—have a baby?"

How she had longed to tell him the child might be his! Now all she said, woodenly, was, "Yes."

The village nestled in a small basin watered by the river and traversed by the railroad. Corn grew on the rocky slopes, anywhere a plant could find a niche. The plaza, facing a weathered little church, was only hard-packed earth with a few stone benches and tenacious flowers. A long low building was connected to the church by a courtyard. Like most of the other structures, it was of roughly cut stone with a thatched roof.

There were fewer men in Darcy's band than there had been, less than a score now. Katie recognized a leather-faced old man and several boys Ysidro's age. The rebels dismounted in the courtyard. Darcy helped her down, and she stumbled in her haste to get to Hardy, who had been held in the saddle by one of Darcy's men. They carried him into the low building, his head drooping. "One of those racks hit him," Darcy explained. "He may have a concussion. We'd better keep him quiet a few days."

Katie helped spread blankets on the cold stone floor, examining Hardy anxiously as the men lowered him to the pallet. There was a gray cast to his tanned skin and his wavy hair was damp. His eyes were closed and his shallow breathing scarcely moved his chest.

What if it weren't mild concussion, but a permanent injury— even a deadly one? Gripped with icy fear, Katie held his head and shoulders in her lap. She couldn't speak to Darcy who stood above them.

"The priest here is a friend, Katie. He says federal troops have been prowling around so, as soon as my men and horses have eaten and rested, I'm sending them back up into the mountains. But I'll stay with you till Hardy can ride, or till you can both get on a train for Texas."

"The tracks must be blocked from the wreck."

"If the crew of the first train that comes along can't clear the mess, the conductor will send someone by handcar to get help."

"How did you wreck the train?"

"We turned an engine loose on it, headed downhill while the train was coming up." Wild engines or cars were greatly feared in the mountains, though tracks might be dynamited anywhere, or trains ambushed from cover. Trains hauling fuel oil were a special target for rebels. Katie had heard all this but till now it had seemed something that happened a long way off to people she didn't know. Now it had struck Hardy, and the man who had done it was her lover.

Unable to meet those tawny eyes, she wiped Hardy's face with the edge of her skirt. Panic rose. Would he die? Was his brain damaged? Might he never be himself again? "Go with your men," she told Darcy. "I'm sure the priest will help us get on a train when that's possible."

Darcy winced. "I'll stay with you."

"This is war. That's what you told me. Why worry about a few people who were in the wrong place?"

"I'm sorry your husband was hurt. But let me tell you straight, Katie. Even if I'd known you were on that train, I'd have done the same thing in order to get Lobos."

"Then there's nothing to be sorry for, is there?"

He walked away. In a few minutes, the priest came, an old Indian with deep sad eyes and a kind smile. He examined Hardy with deft fingers, and while Katie propped her husband up, Padre Garza got most of a cup of some aromatic brew down his throat.

"Keep him warm," the priest cautioned. "He's young and strong, his own best healer. You sustained no hurt, my daughter?"

Only to my heart. Only to my hope that in spite of everything, Darcy might still leave his revolution and make a life in our own country. "I'm bruised a little. Nothing that matters."

"I will be close enough to hear if you call me," he said, rising. "I'll send some food, and you must eat even if you aren't hungry. Rest if you can. I'll look in every hour or so."

His rough sandals scuffed on the stones as he went out. Katie wiped Hardy's face again, smoothed his hair. If only she could pour her strength into him, restore him by absorbing his hurt into her own body; the only other time she'd felt so helpless was when Dan's burned lifeless body was carried home to her. In a way, this was worse. Hardy was alive but she couldn't help him. Mixed with fear for him was guilt for not having loved him better, and a shocked outrage at Darcy that came close to hatred. She could never forgive him if Hardy died or was impaired, yet Darcy's life and hers had always been interwoven, warp and woof. If she had to tear him out of her, she would become raveled, broken threads. If Fayette hadn't cheated him . . . if black and Indian blood hadn't mixed with her father's in his veins . . . if she had been able to make him believe that didn't matter . . . but all those things had been, and were—and what would happen to them all now?

She held Hardy's head and shoulders in her lap, watching for the slightest sign of consciousness. "Hardy? Hardy, darling, it's Katie. Hardy! Wake up!"

He had always responded quickly to any call of hers, a sigh, a frown, a smile. Panicked that he couldn't hear her, she stifled the wailing that rose to her throat, but she couldn't manage to stop the tears.

Spicy smells wafted from the courtyard. From the talk and laughter, it sounded as if the whole village had come to praise the rebels for getting rid of the detested General Lobos. From what she heard, Katie guessed that the soldiers who hadn't been killed in the wreck had been shot afterward. The civilian survivors had been given food and told to rig shelters for themselves and wait for rescue. Hunched in the corner, Katie sank into exhausted torpor, aware of the clinking of bits and stirrups, the creaking of leather, as horses were saddled. Hoofs clopped briskly away as she fell asleep.

Rousing later from exhausted slumber, Katie sat up, flinching as her numbed legs tingled. Changing positions carefully so as not to jolt Hardy, she peered at him. Was his color a little better? His breathing a trifle deeper? From the angle of the sun slanting through the small high window, she thought it was late afternoon. Had Darcy left with his men, without even telling her good-bye? Father Garza's sandals rasped on the walk. He pushed the heavy door open, nudged a stone against it, and placed a big bowl of soup and a basket of tortillas and white cheese on the floor. A young girl followed with fruit and a mint-scented earthen pot with wooden cups. Her soft dark eyes touched Katie as she murmured a greeting, set down her burden, and slipped away.

"The same?" Father Garza sat on his heels and felt Hardy's pulse. "No, I think he's better. Perhaps this good soup will revive him."

While Katie supported Hardy, the priest got a few horn spoonfuls of soup down him, and half a cup of the tea. "He's swallowing. That's a good sign. Now you must eat, my daughter. Get up and move around. I'll stay with your husband."

"Thank you, father, I'll stay here." However, she allowed the priest to ease Hardy from her arms into his. The soup warmed her, the tortillas were paper-thin and fresh, the cheese mildly tangy, and the mint brew refreshing. Father Garza watched her approvingly.

"It's good," she said. "You're very kind."

"What we have is yours." He hesitated. "Except for Señor Ransom, we would have nothing. When General Lobos burned out crops and slaughtered or stole our animals, Señor Ransom fed us and brought us mules and cattle. When the general tortured our *alcalde* to find out if we had any hidden valuables, Señor Ransom broke into the jail and rescued him. The girl who brought your tea is an orphan. Señor Ransom provides for her and for dozens of others."

Hearing Darcy praised caused painful joy. "I'm glad to know this, Father. But why are you telling me?" she asked cautiously.

Wise, infinitely sad eyes seemed to enter her mind. "You are important to Señor Ransom. He is distraught to have caused this harm to your husband. His men have gone but he would not ride with them although it is dangerous for him to stay here. As soon as the wreck's discovered, there'll be soldiers after him." The priest leaned forward. "Go talk with him, señora. If you forgive him, he can go."

Overwhelmed by bitterness and grief, Katie said brokenly, "Until I know my husband will get well, I can't forgive *el señor*. But I wish him well, and I want him to save himself! Please tell him that."

Father Garza shook his head. "Even if you forgive and plead, he might not leave. Unless you do, he certainly will not."

"I am sorry." Katie looked at this man who had heard so many confessions. "I love *el señor*, father. I would give my life for him. But it is my husband's he has touched. That I cannot forgive till I see my husband well and sound."

Without a word, the priest rose and gathered up the empty dishes. As he closed the door, Katie started to call to him, but checked herself. She had voiced what was true. There was nothing more to say while Hardy remained like this. Yet if Darcy were taken . . .

She fell to her knees and prayed for her husband and her lover.

XI ─────────────────────────

The girl brought a pitcher of water, a basin, towels, and a large gourd that she said was for the señor, a perfectly functional urinal with its crooked neck. There were no outhouses and Katie had gone into the trees to relieve herself. She induced Hardy to use the gourd, but it seemed a purely physical reflex, his stupor remaining unaltered. At dusk, Father Garza brought a pot of chamomile tea and basket of *pan dulce*, sweet bread. He helped Katie get a cup of tea down Hardy and sat to talk with her a while. The priest was from a wealthy ranching family of Sonora but his sympathies were with the *campesinos*. During the Díaz regime, he had been jailed twice for preaching against the extermination of the Yaqui Indians.

"The Revolution spread like wildfire all over Mexico. It will blaze till centuries of hatred and rage burn out, maybe for years. I only pray this suffering will bring to the oppressed freedom and the better life fought for by Hidalgo and Juárez." Father Garza got to his feet. "Would you like Elena to sleep in the room? My house is next door. I can hear you if you call."

"That's enough, father. No need to keep Elena from her bed." She hoped he would tell her where Darcy was, but he went out after a murmured good night.

Katie had already removed Hardy's belt and shoes, made him

as comfortable as possible. Now she covered him snugly, took off her outer garments and shoes, and lay beside him, her arm protectively across him. If he lived on in this condition, it would be more horrible than if he died; but if she could get him home, doctors might be able to do something. As long as he breathed, she wouldn't give up. *Please, please, let him wake up. Let him be well.* She repeated the prayer over and over, blocking out thoughts of Darcy, refusing to soften toward him, until at last she slept.

There was more color in Hardy's face next morning. His eyelids fluttered as she and Father Garza got him to swallow a bowl of rich goat's milk. He groaned when they raised and lowered him, but didn't respond to their voices.

"He is better," the priest said positively.

In his body, he was better. But what of his darkened mind? Reading her thoughts, Father Garza said, "It may be some days, my daughter. And though we have no doctor, I think your husband should not be moved till he is conscious."

Each hour brought nearer the time when federal soldiers would swarm in after the rebels who had killed General Lobos. "Please, father." Katie's words choked off. "Please get Señor Ransom to hide in the mountains. Federal soldiers won't hurt *us*, surely."

"Not deliberately. But we are plagued by bandits who'd like nothing better than holding *norteamericanos* for ransom. Unless you yourself persuade *el señor,* he will not leave till you do."

"Where is he?"

"He slept last night across your door. Now, I think, he is in the church." The priest lay down by Hardy. "If you will speak with him, señora, I will stay here with your husband."

"I can beg him to go. God knows I don't want him killed or hurt. But I cannot forgive him—not till Hardy is all right."

Father Garza watched her sadly. Smothering a sob, she got to her feet and stumbled out into the dazzling sunlight. Her blinded eyes caught the glitter of steel and glass from the train; it looked like a toy flung against the cliff. She shielded her eyes as she caught a motion, froze as she made out a string of horsemen following the tracks. They were veering from the pass, heading for the village. She caught up her skirts and ran.

The church was so shadowed that she had to stand inside a moment before she could see Darcy. He knelt before the dark

Virgin of Guadalupe, the beloved patroness of the Mexicans. The images were all fashioned with more love than skill and the pews were rough-hewn, but the altar cloth was beautifully embroidered and from every niche and altar fresh flowers perfumed the air.

"Darcy!"

He turned and rose in one graceful motion. His eyes glowed like the candles. Searching Katie, the luminance faded as he said, "Your husband—he's no better?"

"Better. Not awake." She ran to him, seizing his hands. "You've got to go! Riders are coming this way, lots of them!"

"Soldiers?"

"I think so. Whatever they are, there're too many for you to stop. Get out of here, Darcy! Hide in the brush if you can't reach your horse!"

His mouth formed a hard line. "You and your man are here because of me. I won't leave you."

As they stared at each other, cries of alarm sounded in the village. The drumming of hoofbeats grew louder, rose to a crescendo that echoed in her brain. She threw herself into his arms. They kissed with a yearning that burned away everything except their love. Then he put her aside and walked to the door.

An hour later, she knelt and wept by his body, which the villagers had carried to the dark madonna's altar. He had stepped out of the church to find soldiers herding the village men and boys into the plaza to be shot unless they told where the rebels were. Darcy bought their lives with his, consenting to stand against the church wall and be shot if the men were freed and the village left unharmed.

Katie and Father Garza pleaded for him, but the colonel said, "My general must be avenged. The rebel will not die with a gun in his hand, but like a felon." As Darcy walked to his place, Katie screamed and ran after him; the priest and villagers pulled her away, dragged her into the church.

A volley sounded. Then there was a single pistol shot. It was from the colonel's Mauser, the bullet that killed. The soldiers had all missed or fired wide.

With Lobos avenged, the detachment went to clear the tracks. The colonel offered, through the priest, to give Katie and Hardy an escort to the nearest station, but she refused.

If she could have died in Darcy's place; if she, not Hardy, were in that dark silence... She despaired of her life but life would not leave her. She stared sightlessly at the small wound above Darcy's right ear. The left side of his head had been blown away, but women had covered it with flowers. Weeping, they had closed his eyes, crossed his hands on a crucifix. On their knees, the whole village mourned, from toddler to ancient.

Vaguely, it seemed important to take his body home, bury him at Old Orchard. But this is where he had sought his destiny. This was where he would be remembered. She turned to the priest, spoke her first words since the execution.

"Can you bury him in holy ground? I don't know his religion."

"I will bury him in the grace of God and where the sun will shine the longest on his grave. Leave him with us, my daughter, and I promise that so long as there is a village, there will be candles and prayers on the day of his death."

There was an assenting murmur. Katie understood now why mourners among some peoples slashed their bodies, cut off fingers, lopped off their hair. Physical pain might have lessened her torment. But she had lost a part of herself as surely as if an arm or leg had been severed. As she got heavily to her feet, the baby moved within, and she knelt again at the Virgin's feet, arms across her lover's body.

Let it be his child, she prayed. *Let him live on that way.*

She scarcely heard the footsteps. Strong arms raised her. She looked into her husband's face, cried out, and slipped into muffled blackness.

The village mason was making a stone for Darcy that would tell why and how he died. At the funeral, the *alcalde* told Katie that the people wished henceforth to call their village San Roque de Ransom, as was done to commemorate heroes. Katie had nothing worthy to bury with him, but she had kissed a red rose and placed it by the crucifix clasped between his hands.

That night a northbound train churned up the cleared track and stopped to take them on. Hardy seemed normal except for a severe headache. Katie wanted him to see a doctor at San Luis, Potosí, where one line ran to Mexico City and another to Laredo and the border. He refused curtly. By the time they reached Texas two days later, he insisted he was fine.

They had not talked about Darcy beyond the stark facts. Now Hardy stared at her and said, "Shall I take you home, Katie? Will you be all right alone?"

The coldness around her heart pierced deeper. In her most secret being, she would now always be alone. No matter how she reasoned against it, she felt that because she had not forgiven Darcy, she had traded his life for Hardy's. And just as Darcy had said he would have wrecked the train even knowing she was on it, so, if she had known Darcy would die, she could not have acted differently.

"I'll be at Old Orchard tonight," she said. "There's nothing to worry about. Just you be careful—and write as often as you can."

They kissed, but it was dry and formal. Darcy was between them as he had not been in life. As Hardy helped Katie board her train, she was desolate, for she had lost him, too.

John Sevier Alastair was born at Old Orchard on Christmas Day, 1912. The moment Dr. Newman placed him in her arms, Katie saw Darcy in the furrowed black eyebrows, cleft chin, and mouth. His eyes were indeterminate, a misty green that sometimes shone gold or went dark. He nuzzled at her breast, a small, blind helpless creature, and his searching need drew out of her some of the frozen rigidity that had sustained her these past few months. The hard shell, while protecting, had kept her from being able to reach out to even her mother and father. For one thing, there was so much she must never tell them—about Fayte, about who the baby's father was. Vinnie and Mark had endured enough. They grieved deeply, as it was, when she told them how Darcy had died. He had been their fosterling and was, after all, Mark's grandson. Mark had written Talt at the last known address, an Oklahoma boom town where he was working with Thos, but there'd been no answer.

The place where Katie went for solace was the cave, where Vinnie and her brother had sheltered so long ago, where, a generation later, Katie and Darcy had played or rested and daydreamed on hot afternoons. A few days after her return, it was there that old Hester had found her.

Hearing shuffling in the antechamber, Katie stiffened. For a moment, she thought crazily of ghosts, maybe Darcy's. But it was the bent ancient woman who entered where the sweet spring gushed from the rocks. Hester was almost sightless. It was a marvel she hadn't fallen coming down the bluff above the river. Now she came to sit by Katie and take her by both hands. Enough light came in from the opening that Katie could see the visage from which time had fleshed away all softness, all sex, leaving a taut sculpture of brown skin over handsome bones. It was the face of a priestess or a seer, but this was Darcy's grandmother, who had shared the raising of him after his mother died.

She said simply, "Tell me, child. Tell Hester all about it."

In Hester's hundred years, she had been a slave and Mark's first mistress, borne his son, managed Belleforest for the benefit of imperious, beautiful Regina, been Vinnie's comforter and support, and Katie's nurse. Except for Talt, she was the only person who could bear the truth and perhaps draw comfort from knowing it might be Darcy's baby, her own great-grandchild, who was stirring ever more urgently in Katie's womb.

Katie told her everything. The thin long hands tightened on hers but Hester didn't speak till Katie finished with the story of the village that would forever carry Darcy's name. Then the priestess-seer dissolved into a bereaved old woman who mourned in silence, tears edging down her cheeks.

"Darcy was the sweetest little boy," she said at last. "I didn't get to keep Talt, you know, mistress sent him away. Darcy was my real baby. Maybe it's a sin to church-folk, honey, but I'm glad you got to love each other even for that one time. Do you want this child?"

"More than anything."

"Won't that make trouble with your man?"

"Hardy's alive. He can have more children. This one, if it's Darcy's, is all of him there'll be left in the world."

Hester sighed. "I'm going to live to hold your baby. That's all I ask the good Lord now. I'll see Darcy in the other place and greet him for you and the child. There's nothing bad left over there, Katie girl. Just love and light. Don't feel too bad for Darcy. Go ahead and live your days the best you can. If you get to be my age, you'll know the dead we loved aren't very far away."

Hester *had* held Johnny, kissed him and crooned, and within a week died peacefully in her sleep, smiling as if she beheld someone to whom she hastened eagerly. She was buried by the white stone that marked the graves of Vinnie's aunt and uncle and little cousin killed less than fifty years ago in a Comanche raid.

How swiftly times had changed! The oil seep that had been medicinal and a lubricant now seemed a prime spot for drilling, though Vinnie and the judge refused to sign leases that might have made them rich. They were comfortably off and would have sold Belleforest before permitting Old Orchard to be fouled and ruined, the cave desecrated—for drilling would inevitably fracture the rocks that fed the spring, and probably flood the refuge with brine and oil.

Katie could not mourn for Hester; she had made a good end, happy to see Darcy in the new life just come into being before she passed on to be with him and suffer no more loss.

Vinnie and Mark adored their grandson and Katie's grief tamed as she joyed in holding him, nourishing him with milk that flowed as rich and warmly as her love. Her labor had been long and difficult, but she had nothing to do but look after the baby while she regained her strength, and in this she was helped by Vinnie and by Esau's recently acquired wife, Thaley, a tall golden-skinned young woman with auburn hair and green eyes. Thaley slept in Katie's room and changed the baby before bringing him to be nursed. Pampered by the whole household, tempted to eat by the delicious meals prepared by Corinth, Caleb's daughter, Katie looked neither ahead nor behind but lived in each day like a soldier recuperating from a wound before going back to battle. The only taxing thing she had to do was write to Hardy.

He had sworn to father the baby, accept him as his son; he had said he wanted no discussion of it. Still, he must wonder. It wouldn't do for him to see Johnny unwarned. The likeness to Darcy grew with each day. Of course Darcy had favored Mark, so Katie's parents assumed Johnny was a throwback to his grandfather.

Katie solved the problem by having a photograph made of the baby with the family, another by himself, and one with Mark. She filled her letters with everyday life at Old Orchard, what Mark thought of Woodrow Wilson who would shortly be inaugurated, the increasing concern over the Mexican Revolution spilling across the border, and queries about Texerenla and the partners. She told Hardy she missed him, which was true. She began her letters with "Dearest Hardy" and signed them "Your devoted wife." She could not write "I love you," though she did. Until he had seen Johnny, until they had seen if it was possible for them to go on, she could not write about her feelings. If Hardy wanted to leave her, he must be able to go without any sense of having wronged her.

Hardy's letters were brief, dated a few days apart, though she would get none for several weeks and then, as her anxiety mounted, a whole bundle would arrive. From certain gaps and leaps, she knew not all of his messages were reaching her, but from the chaos he described, it was a miracle that any did. Early in February of 1913, idealistic but ineffectual President Madero was assassinated in Mexico City along with Vice President Suárez. The United States ambassador, far from trying to save him, had backed a traitor, General Huerta, who was now trying to become a second iron man like Díaz. Under President Wilson, U.S. policy condemned the usurper and kept troops along the border. All Mexico was a battleground between Huerta's government and rebels led by Carranza, Villa, Zapata, and Obregón.

"This area's controlled by rebels one week and federales the next," Hardy wrote. *"We pay whoever's around for protection, and sometimes we have to pay twice. But we can afford it, Katie. We have three producing wells, and if we bring in another good one, I'd like to sell out to our partners and come home. Is that all right with you? We can start our own company, maybe hire some of the Baygall boys. I want to see you, Katie, it's been a long time."*

Not a word about the baby. That hurt, but Katie argued that Hardy must have things he couldn't write about, just as she did, the most important things. She answered that she'd be glad if he sold their interests on the spot; she didn't like for him to be in the middle of all that fighting.

She didn't add that they needed to work out their future. Johnny was four months old now, sleeping through the night, and she was physically and emotionally recovered enough to survive whatever happened. Her son was beautiful and it was impossible to breathe in the odors of spring and see the flowers pushing up from the soil without feeling the wonder of new life, new hope.

The orchard was masses of pinky-white blossoms and she loved to walk there with Johnny. One old tree had a low fork where she could sit with the baby. She was laughing at the way he tried to grasp the flowers when she saw someone coming through the trees in a stride too long and confident to be her father's. She slipped out of the tree, heart stopping, then speeding, as Hardy ducked through the boughs. She had forgotten how tall and strong he was, the vital force that radiated from him. Shocking in his lean brown face, his gray eyes enveloped her. Katie ran to meet him. She had forgotten the baby in her arms till Hardy's opened wide enough to clasp them both.

Hardy loved her tenderly that night, ardent fervor making it like a second honeymoon. "I've dreamed of you," he murmured huskily. "But, oh sweetheart, you're more beautiful than any dream!"

"All those stretch marks! And I can't get into some of my clothes!"

"Get some new ones." He grinned, caressing her blue-veined breasts. "Hell, honey, we're fixing to be independent oil producers. Diamonds, Rolls-Royces—"

"Hold on! What if we get dry holes instead of wells?"

"We can stand a few. But I traveled up with a geologist from Standard Oil who told me about some good prospects. Want to go lease-buying with me?"

"Oh, that'd be exciting!" Then she remembered. "I guess I can't, Hardy. I'm feeding the baby and it wouldn't be good to drag him around the countryside, especially now that the heat's starting."

Hardy's stiffening was so imperceptible that she couldn't see it, but she felt it. "I'd forgotten," he said after a moment. "Stands to reason jouncing over bumps in the dust wouldn't do much for the little guy's digestion. It's lucky that you can stay here while I'm scouting around."

Kissing him gratefully, Katie said, "As soon as you've decided where to drill and have us a tent or shack, I'll come and cook for the crew."

"I can hire a cook." Hardy chuckled. "I've got other plans for you, Mrs. Alastair."

"But I want to help."

"It's different now, honey. We don't have to squeeze every dollar till it hollers. Besides, you've got lots of help with the baby here, but it'll be different in a camp." Framing her face in his hands, Hardy watched her. His tone was playful but it was tinged with exasperation. "Katie, for just a year or two, can't it be enough to be my wife and a mother?"

She felt as if she'd had her breath knocked out by an unexpected blow. "I didn't know I'd been a trial to you. I was running a business when we met."

"Sure, and doing a great job of it. Don't think I haven't appreciated the way you went to Jarocho and Tupan, pitched in and helped instead of whining. But Katie, you don't need to do that now. You can have a maid and nice clothes and—do whatever women do when they're well off."

Katie stifled a scornful retort. He had accepted Johnny, taken with good grace the disappointment of her not being able to help him look over lease properties. Johnny probably would take most of her time and energy for the next few years. But after that, well, unless there was another baby, she'd find something she could do, if not with their company then somewhere else.

She smoothed the lines etched from nose to mouth and at the corners of his eyes. "I'm proud to be your wife, darling. I want to be a good mother. But you'll have to make up your mind that I'm not the kind to be happy unless I'm doing something useful."

He groaned with mock despair. "I think you wouldn't mind if I went broke so you could start another restaurant!"

"I can stand being rich. But not being idle."

He laughed and began to kiss her throat, sending warm shocks through her. "Well, then, get busy and see if you can make a tired man able to love you again."

He already was, but she reveled in caressing and exciting him, building their need to an irresistible pitch before she welcomed him completely. It had been so long . . . so long . . . and now he was home.

XII

Hardy was a bit sheepish when he returned two weeks later with some of the leases Standard's geologist had tipped him to, and one he'd promised to drill first for the widowed wife of an old Ranger comrade who was sure there was oil on her hardscrabble farm north of Forth Worth. "I tried to get out of it by making a lease for enough to take care of her and the kids." Hardy rubbed his ear in that way he did when embarrassed. "She wouldn't hear of it. Doesn't want lease money but someone to drill and give her a bigger percentage if they bring in a well."

"Everybody thinks there's oil on their land, Hardy. You can't drill just because of that."

"It's a possible location. There's an anticline—you know, where rock strata arch away from a ridge like a house roof. Some geologists think a formation like that may serve as a tray for oil. Anyway, Eulalia won't be satisfied till a well's drilled."

Kate shrugged. Because Hardy had agreed to father Johnny, would she always feel bound to support his decisions? "Oil's where you find it. Why don't you drill her place first?"

Hardy looked relieved. "I will. But first I'm going up to Oklahoma and hunt for your uncle and Talt Ransom. How'd it be if they came in as partners?"

"Oh, Hardy!" she cried, and jumped up to kiss him.

* * *

It was almost a family outfit that spudded in the Lone Star Eulalia Warren No. 1 about the end of May. Uncle Thos's blue eyes widened every time he looked at Katie. "Can't believe you're the skinny little gal I saw last time I was home," he said more than once.

"That was a good long while ago, Uncle Thos," she reminded. When he and Talt had brought Darcy for Vinnie and Mark and Hester to raise. Oh, yes. Lifetimes ago.

Like Vinnie's, Thos's blond hair scarcely showed its white. Sun and wind had baked him brown as Talt, whose hazel eyes were heart-stabbingly like Darcy's except for being less golden. Thos was in his late fifties, Talt about ten years older, and oil work was a young man's job, but they'd learned economy and sureness of movement. Their scars from broken cables, exploding boilers, and blowouts, the toll of forty years in the fields, were the proud marks of warriors. Katie suspected that even if Morgan Fayette—no, Fayte Sevier—hadn't cheated them, they would still rather hunt for treasure beneath the ground than spend it in a city.

Both had lost their wives long ago and Thos's daughter, Tamara, raised by her mother's parents in New Orleans, had recently married a young doctor, Jewish like Thos's beloved wife, Judith.

Thos drilled while Talt, with Hardy's help, dressed the tools and kept the boilers fired up. Meanwhile, on another lease, Katie's friends from Baygall were fulfilling their pledge, working for a share of any oil they found. Rance Gorman was drilling, Bailey Scott and Joe Young, the former tankie, helping. Whichever crew hit oil first would be treated to a big party in Fort Worth. If neither did, Rance's outfit would go back to contract drilling and Lone Star would proceed on the other leases, hoping to find oil before the money from Texerenla ran out.

Eulalia Warren had solved the problem of a decent place for Katie and the baby by insisting that the family use her spare room with its separate vine-shaded porch. Thos and Talt slept on the big screened-in back porch, and the smokehouse made a good place for the men to bathe after work and change into clean clothes.

Eulalia's brown eyes sparkled as she plied the men with questions each evening, but her gaze rested most often on Thos, and his wedges of pie were a trifle larger than those served the others. Pleasantly rounded, her skin amazingly fresh and rosy for one who'd spent years on a Texas farm, Eulalia bloomed, loosening her coil of soft brown hair so that tendrils waved around her face, wearing ruffled aprons instead of plain flour-sack ones. She doted on Johnny. So did Talt and Thos, vying to hold him in the evenings while Katie helped Eulalia with the dishes.

Probably no one except Katie noticed that Hardy never picked Johnny up or offered him a finger to grip. Sometimes she wondered if she ought to tell Talt this was his grandchild, but that seemed a betrayal of Hardy. Also, she'd have had to tell the aging man—amazingly, her own half brother though she thought of him as a kind of uncle—that his only son was dead. Apparently, Talt didn't worry about Darcy. "I was never one to write," he said with a grin, "and my boy has sure taken after his dad."

So Katie kept her silence. Was that part of getting older? Having more and more secrets that should be kept from people they would wound uselessly? When she held Johnny, smiled into his dove's eyes, an incredibly soft green-gold like sunlit velvety moss, she melted with love for him and sorrow for his father. Would she ever tell him who his father was?

For sure not, if only Hardy behaved like a father. But she was beginning to fear that all Hardy could give the child was a home and a name—and she couldn't blame him.

Lone Star Eulalia Warren No. 1 came in at two thousand feet for fifty barrels a day. At almost the same depth and time, Lone Star James Hagerty No. 1 overflowed the derrick for three hundred barrels a day. The celebration in Fort Worth lasted four days. By then no one wanted even to smell champagne or bourbon. They got Joe Young out of jail, rescued young Bailey Scott from a hooker old enough to be his mother, and went back to the Warren farm to decide on their next locations.

Hoping the fifty-barrel well could be bettered on Eulalia's land, Thos and Talt were left in charge of operations there; they hired a contract driller to dig test wells on the peripheries while they concentrated on the anticline. This was a sensible arrangement, for Thos and Eulalia were married in the parlor of her house the day before Katie and Hardy left to hire a tool dresser so Hardy could drill on a lease near the Red River—the Oklahoma line—where a rancher was complaining that the wells he dug for the water his cattle desperately needed only seeped oil. Rance's crew was drilling around their first producer.

The town nearest the Red River lease, Fortune, was a scruffy straggle of feed store, grocery, mercantile, filling station, and post office. There was no hotel and no house for rent, but the mercantile owner had two rooms over the store for which, when Hardy admitted he was a driller, the owner charged an exorbitant price and said that if the baby ruined the mattress, the Alastairs would have to buy a new one.

The rooms were hot, walls shedding scabrous orange paint onto a floor so splintery that they bought linoleum—from the mercantile—so Johnny could crawl around without hurting himself. Katie made curtains and put the little gold derrick on the table that served for a dresser. She hated the place, but it was foolish to spend time and money to fix it up because they might move on in a few weeks.

They did, after drilling two dry holes. Johnny broke out with prickly heat. He was teething, she was starting to wean him, and he fretted continually. Two more dry holes. Another wretched set of rooms. "For God's sake!" Hardy exploded one night when nothing Katie did would quiet the baby, "I've got to get my sleep!"

"I'd like to sleep, too," snapped Katie. "You can't expect a baby to be good when he's dragged around like this. If we were home . . ."

Hardy swung his legs over the edge of the lumpy bed. "I guess you mean Old Orchard."

"You certainly can't call these dumps home!"

He laughed harshly. "That wasn't exactly a mansion you had at Baygall."

"No, but I was busy, earning my own money, and I didn't have to worry about a child." She bit her lip at once, but it was said. She had vowed never to complain about how difficult this life made it to take care of Johnny.

Hardy didn't say, *That boy is none of mine—you got him all by yourself.* But he pulled on his trousers and reached for his boots. "I'm going to sleep at the rig."

She didn't see him again till three days later when the well came in with enough flow that he could bring another driller in on shares to exploit the formation.

Katie suspected that he picked the next lease because the elderly couple who owned it had a big farmhouse now emptied of children, and were delighted to have the Alastairs in one wing. Mrs. Sauer volunteered to sit by Johnny with her knitting while he had his afternoon nap and Katie took a walk along the shady creek. The white-haired woman made Johnny's second birthday cake and Mr. Sauer hung a swing for him on the big oak, placing a bar across it so he couldn't fall out. Johnny followed the big shepherd dog around the grassy yard, helped feed the chickens, and drank cups of sweet milk fresh from the Sauers' Jerseys.

Rested and relaxed, Katie was able now to enter gladly into lovemaking instead of being so tired that she only hoped Hardy would finish quickly. She had never denied him; she knew the child who wasn't his was the cause of most of her weariness, but a much less sensitive man than Hardy would have noticed the difference in her response. Now they pleasured again in each other. Lone Star Henry Sauer No. 1 was a producer, and Hardy spent the next five months developing the lease, which he then sold to Standard for enough to recoup losses on the dry holes and finance more exploration.

The Sauers' 12.5 percent royalty was bringing in so much money that they planned, as soon as the war in Europe was over, to collect their children and grandchildren, hire someone to take care of the farm, and charter a round-the-world cruise. "Our farm's free and clear," said ruddy-faced, gray-shocked Ernie Sauer, hoisting Johnny to his knee and giving him a bouncy ride. "There's enough in the bank to take care of us to the end of our days. So Anna and me, we just reckoned to use this money on something we'll remember the rest of our lives. Just hope there's something left of the little villages in Alsace where our grandparents came from."

The United States was supplying most of the oil used by the Allies. Besides this demand, domestic consumption had doubled since 1912. Tractors had come on the market, trains and ships were fueled by oil, the number of trucks and motorboats swelled, and now that a Model T Ford cost only $390 and could be bought on installments, a million cars would be sold in 1915—half of them Fords—while petroleum waste supplied asphalt to pave the roads.

"You can take that cruise, Mr. Sauer, and start planning another!" Hardy said, laughing. He lit one of the cigarettes he'd started smoking constantly when he wasn't at the rig. "We're just beginning to use oil. Factories are switching to it, airplanes fly on it—"

"And submarines will hunt on it, like the one that sank the *Lusitania*," said Katie, shuddering. One hundred and fourteen Americans had drowned in May along with over a thousand other people. Outrage was swinging Americans closer to war. And there was still cause to worry about Mexico. In the spring of 1914, U.S. marines who landed for supplies at Tampico were detained for a while. To force an apology from Huerta's government, the U.S. had occupied the port of Vera Cruz and war might have broken out in earnest had Huerta not been forced to resign. So the Revolution ground on. Just this October of 1915, the U.S. had recognized Carranza's government but Villa, Zapata, and other powerful Mexicans had not. Meanwhile, the people suffered. Katie often thought about María, Sara, Ysidro, Father Garza, and the brave folk of San Roque de Ransom, achingly hoped they would survive to win a better life.

Mrs. Sauer's practical voice called her to the present. "It's nice to have the money, but we'll stay on our farm and drive our team and buggy." She sighed as she turned to Katie. "I wish you weren't leaving, dear. We'll really miss you, especially little Johnny."

"We'll miss you, too," Katie said, smiling; but she was flooded again with resentment, remembering how Hardy had overridden her objections to selling the Sauer leases.

"Sure, we could do just fine here," he'd admitted. "I could drill the whole lease, maybe buy others."

"Then why don't you? You know the oil is here."

He stared at her, then said with a startled, apologetic grin, "Yeah, Katie, we *know*. That takes the fun out of it."

She felt trapped, as if a cable had suddenly snapped and wound around her. Memories of the miserable loft in Fortune and all the other shoddy makeshifts ignited anger so hot that she dared not speak till she thought it was under control. "Are you saying that we'll never stay in one place? That as soon as we prove we've got a field, we'll move on?"

"What's wrong with that? I found you in an oil camp, Katie, and you sure didn't kick about going to Mexico."

And she had known when they married, hadn't she, that Ranger work had grown too tame for him? That he loved danger, loved to gamble? Dismayed more than angry now, she cast about for words to make him understand. "Oil people sometimes have to move a lot when they're getting started, and have to take some chances. That's all right when you're young, all right before there are children. But I always supposed that if we were lucky enough to get to where we are now that Lone Star would have a headquarters and you'd operate out of there."

He shook his head. "I don't know where you got the notion I could hang around an office. If I misled you, I'm damned sorry." His tone and smile were tenderly rueful. "Believe me, honey, you wouldn't like what I'd be if I got glued to a desk."

He was right. This was something they should have settled before the wedding. Only she couldn't have known then how a baby would change everything. What Hardy wanted would be devastating for Johnny. She couldn't keep her voice from trembling.

"Hardy, have you stopped to think what it's like for me in those awful little towns? Not knowing anyone, hating those tacky rooms, trying to keep Johnny well and happy?" She stopped for breath. Furious disappointment brought tears she couldn't suppress. "Maybe I can't expect you to change, Hardy. But I can't go on like this, either."

"When Johnny's older—"

"Hardy! I—I think I'm going to have a baby."

She felt a pang at the quick joy in his eyes. He moved to take her in his arms but something in her expression stopped him. "When, honey? Are you sure? You've skipped before."

"Yes, but this is two months and I— Well, you leave so early that you probably haven't noticed, but all I can eat at breakfast is dry toast." At this matter-of-fact physical detail, constraint between them dropped. He stepped close and drew her to him, laughing, kissing her hair and forehead. "Maybe we'll have a Fourth of July baby. Katie, I'm tickled to death! Look, it's almost Thanksgiving. Why don't I take you home for the holidays while I go lease-hunting? I'll come when I can, Christmas for sure, and then after New Year's we can move. I'll find you something decent if I have to build it!"

"It's not just a nice house, Hardy. It's a *home*, a place to stay and have neighbors and plant flowers—a place to live, not just stop at, a place where Johnny can make friends and go to school."

Hardy's face clouded but he must have reminded himself of her condition because he spoke gently. "Katie, you wouldn't like what would happen to me if I had to stay in one town. But we'll work something out. When Lone Star gets really solid, maybe we can set up headquarters in a place you like, and I'll be there as much as I can." He touched her protesting lips with his fingers and smiled. "Sweetheart, Johnny's not quite three. Anyway, I drifted around with my dad and I can't say I ever minded."

"You were with him and his friends in your own little Ranger world," she said bitterly. "Children can't play around a derrick or swim in a slush pond."

"Listen, I'll do the best I can to satisfy you—short of rusting away in an office. Let's give the whole thing a rest till after the baby comes."

"If you think I feel this way just because of the baby . . ."

He shook his head, pulling a droll face. "Lord forbid! Brought up the way you were at Old Orchard, no wonder that's your idea of a home. But I'd go crazy there after a week unless . . ." He gave a devilish chuckle. "Unless your folks leased the place for drilling. Be mighty interesting to see what's under that oil seep." He laughed at her appalled speechlessness and kissed her long and hard and wooingly. "We'll figure it out, sweetheart. Hell, when we have that baby, I'll probably get home more than you'll want me!"

As you haven't done for Johnny. Wounded, but knowing Hardy hadn't meant to hurt her, Katie received him; but part of her stayed aloof, would never be able to quite trust him again.

It was wonderful to be again at Old Orchard, though Mark was visibly frailer and, for the first time, his shoulders stooped a little. Johnny was with him most of the time, even napping on the divan in the judge's study. The curly black head bobbed along at the judge's knee during a daily stroll around the place, and a tame pony was bought so the boy could accompany his grandfather when he rode. Johnny loved to cuddle in Vinnie's lap for stories or sit on the piano bench while she played, but the judge was Johnny's idol and, in a strange sad way, in those weeks between Thanksgiving and Christmas, the boy probably gave the man

more delight than either of his own sons had—Fayte taken away
early to return spoiled, Talt never known about till he was grown.

Mark should have had a son. To watch hers with him was to
Katie both beautiful and frightening. How much time could they
have left? The judge was eighty-four and, though he never mentioned it, Vinnie said he had chest pains now and then and shortness of breath. Katie treasured this time with her father,
understanding him for the first time as a person who had survived
the maiming of his body in a poisonous war that brought a shameful death to his father and betrayal by a wife and son, and had
achieved serenity and wisdom.

He gave Vinnie all the credit, but Katie, seeing her mother
anew as well, realized that to an orphaned waif, he had become
father, friend, and lover, one she could repay in some measure by
serving as the right hand he had lost. Their lives had grown together like trees so close they merged into one trunk. Katie hated
to think how it would be for Vinnie without Mark, but Vinnie was
rooted deep at Old Orchard, which she had reclaimed when almost a child. She would endure.

Christmas was the fullest, most blessed one Katie could remember. Thos brought his Eulalia down to meet the family, and
Talt came, too. Hardy drove up Christmas Eve in a new black
Cadillac muddy from back roads and piled high with gifts for
everyone, including a red tricycle for Johnny. An important deal
was pending and he'd have to leave the day after Christmas, but
he'd driven three hundred miles to be there and Katie was
touched.

Next morning, the judge took presents from the tree and sent
each to its recipient by way of Johnny, who was so absorbed in
this responsibility that he seemed disappointed—almost—when
his grandfather laughed and said, "Well done, laddie. The rest are
yours. Why don't you see what's under that sheet?" Lacking
paper large enough, that was how they'd draped the tricycle.

Shrieking with glee, Johnny climbed on and pedaled around
the room before he anticipated Katie's command and said, "Outside! I go outside!"

But first he ran to the judge and hugged him ferociously.
"Thank you, Grampa, thank you!"

The judge looked embarrassed. "Thank your daddy, boy. He
stopped in Fort Worth especially to get your tricycle."

"Daddy?" The child's hazel eyes widened with amazement as he stared at Hardy. He seemed to be searching for something. He didn't find it. The eagerness faded from his face. Crossing to Hardy, he gravely extended a hand. "Thank you, Daddy."

Hardy flushed. "You're welcome, Johnny. Now take it outside." When they were alone together, Katie said, "You never called him 'son.' When he was little, you held him sometimes and even kissed him but now you never do."

"He's not a baby. My dad never hugged and slobbered over me."

"Maybe not. But you knew he loved you."

Hardy turned. "What do you want, Katie?"

"For you to do what you said you would—father him!"

"You want me to put on a big show? The kid's smart. He'd see through it in a second." At her stricken silence, Hardy caught her hands. "Listen, honey, I just don't know how to act with boys his age. When he's older—well, then, I can take him with me, teach him the business."

"And till then you'll just be a stranger who sleeps over now and then?"

"Katie!"

She drew her hands away and went to stand at the window. "I hope this child's a girl. Otherwise, I don't think I could stand to see the difference in the way you'd treat your son and Johnny."

"You won't believe that maybe there wouldn't be a difference?"

"No."

He came closer, not touching. Together, they looked out at the winter orchard, serpentine branches tortured without their summer disguise of leaves and fruit or blossoms. The ugly, gnarled tree that weathered all the seasons. She was only thirty but in her inner being she felt like the trees. This was her winter but spring would come again.

She put her hand in Hardy's, sad for him now, but sadder for Darcy who would never again feel and smell and hear the starting of a summer. Oh, granted that somehow he did see through Johnny's candid eyes, that somehow he was present in that new sweet flesh! Her grieving love overflowed to Hardy. He did his best. That neither of them was the person the other had thought they were marrying was no more his fault than hers.

XIII _____

Except for Johnny, who was sleeping, the family stayed up to drink to the New Year, 1916. Katie, on the sofa between Hardy and Talt, looked slowly at each of those faces reflecting the light of the fiery logs that darkened and flamed with the drafts. The judge and Vinnie held hands like young lovers, his silver head bent to her still mostly golden one. Thos and Eulalia shared the loveseat. Eulalia was only a few years younger than Vinnie. They had become good friends and Vinnie had told Katie how glad she was that her brother and Talt seemed settled at last. This was all the close family except for that grandson the judge didn't know about, B.S. Fayette, who was probably also ignorant of Mark's existence.

Katie thought of another boy who would never know his real father. She wished she could tell Talt, but the wiry old man seemed to sense a kinship closer than the one through Katie herself and had complicated Johnny's life by making it necessary to decide which high knee to scramble up on. Johnny had solved that quandary by sitting first on the lap of one grandfather, then moving to the other.

"May we all be together next year," said the judge, in a last toast. They drank, and kissed each other. That night the judge slept his way peacefully out of the world.

Thos, Talt, Hardy, and Esau were pallbearers. Mark Sevier was buried on the other side of the white stone, so close to Hester that if dead hands could reach, they might have touched each other. There was room for Vinnie beside him; but though this resting place beneath the roses was beautiful, Katie thought her mother might rather make ashes to mix part in the cave dust, part in the orchard earth.

Vinnie knelt when the grave was filled, touched her face to the rich soil for a long time. When she rose her cheeks were wet but she was calm. "He told me last night he was happy, that the only thing he regretted was that he wouldn't see Johnny grow up. I want to thank you all for coming, for giving him this end."

Then her face crumpled. Thos patted her head against his shoulder, comforting her as, almost a lifetime ago, she had heartened him at this very stone where they'd hoped to find refuge and met with more death. Katie took the hand of her own brother, Talt, and they knelt down together.

Hardy was already late getting back to his new leases up in the Panhandle, but he urged Katie to stay with her mother for a while. Vinnie, however, insisted they leave together. "There's time to get settled before you grow unwieldy," she said in that common-sensical way that was always steadying though sometimes annoy-ing. "I'll be fine. I've got Esau and Corinth and Thaley and many kind friends." She kissed her daughter on both cheeks and smoothed her hair as she had when Katie was small. "Go with your husband, dear. But, remember, I want to come about a month before the baby and stay till you're on your feet."

Nothing would shake her, so a few days after the funeral, Johnny said a tearful good-bye to his pony and the dogs, not much appeased by the tricycle in the backseat with him, and they started out, Katie and Johnny waving back at Vinnie till she passed out of sight.

Hardy had rented a nice house in Amarillo with a fenced yard where Johnny could play, but they were there less than a month. A promising anticline yielded two dry holes, losses the small company could ill afford. "I've got some leases around Burkbur-nett that I won in a poker game," Hardy said the night he decided to abandon the second hole. "Maybe they'll be lucky."

She was beginning to hate that word. "Why don't you hire a geologist?"

"A doodlebug's cheaper. Hell, honey, the most any of these theories do is give a man encouragement to drill. First we had creekology, looking along water courses; then there were salt domes; now it's anticlines. Sure, oil's been found in these places but not consistently, and it's also been found where geologists swore there couldn't be any. Oil's still a great big gamble."

"You like it that way."

"Might as well, since that's the way it is." She was doing dishes. He came up behind to put his arms around her, nuzzle the side of her cheek. His hands met above where their baby had stirred just the day before. "Katie, there's no use dragging you and the boy over to Burkburnett. If we don't hit oil there, I think East Texas is worth a good try. If that doesn't do it, unless Rance finds some good producers, Lone Star will just have to do contract drilling till we get enough cash together to operate."

The profit from Texerenla and their earlier finds had evaporated so quickly? If they'd invested that money in almost *any*thing else . . . Hardy read her thoughts.

"You can make it fast and lose it faster," he said. "Banks won't lend small independents money. They've heard of too many wells that blew in at five thousand barrels a day and real quick simmered down to a hundred. Which is why independents sell producers to big companies. We don't have the capital to build refineries and pipelines and set up our own marketing outlets. But someday Lone Star will." He kissed her; it was like a pledge. "And then we'll base the company near whatever field of ours you like best and you can have exactly the kind of house you want."

"But you won't be there much."

"When I am, we'll have a brand-new honeymoon! Come on, honey, given what we both are, let's do the best we can."

"If you're leaving, I don't want to stay in Amarillo."

He looked hurt. "I thought you liked the house."

"I do. But *damn,* Hardy! You're the only reason we're here. I'd be miserable stuck here alone."

"I don't know what we'll find at Burkburnett. May have to live in a hotel."

She glanced around the kitchen, curtains she'd made, cupboards she'd painted, the new linoleum. Her caring, time, and energy, as abandoned as Hardy's dry hole. Everything Vinnie had ever done at Old Orchard was there to see and enjoy; living acquired a richer texture because of the years the home had been shaped by Vinnie and the judge. Now that she was a mother, this rootless life made Katie feel as if bits and parts of her peeled from the walls of ugly boardinghouses, were walked on by uncaring feet, died in the plants no one else cared enough about to water. Wasted. She felt wasted. Yet that night she started packing.

In summer, the dirt roads raised suffocating clouds of dust. In this time between winter and spring, they were quagmires. Three times that day, the Cadillac had to be pulled out of boggy ditches by tractors. Katie's back ached from the jarring. They ate the lunch she had packed sitting in the car while rain poured down. Johnny whimpered for a toilet but couldn't go when Hardy, tight-faced with irritation, took him off the side of the road and shielded him with a poncho. They started on. Within half an hour, Johnny, in his sleep, soaked himself and the crib mattress they'd put in the back for him.

Hardy swore. Katie cleaned up the mess as best she could, comforting Johnny, who sobbed with shame. She held him on her lap the rest of the way to Burkburnett, though sharp little fingers were beginning to press inside her. By the time Hardy had found rooms, she was cramping so hard that she had to ask him to get a doctor, but it was too late. She miscarried a few hours later. Vinnie came to stay with her and take care of Johnny.

"I want to go home," Katie whispered when she saw her mother. Grasping the small, capable hand, she sobbed like a child. "Oh, Mama, I want to go home!"

When Katie was able to travel, Hardy drove them to Old Orchard. "You just rest and get strong," he said as they parted. "I promise, honey, you're going to have a home."

One where he'd be a visitor? In some bleak oil town where she'd have to struggle alone to make a place where their children could have a sense of belonging?

Drained of more than blood and strength, she kissed Hardy good-bye and wished him luck. He turned to the car, then swung back and caught her to him savagely. It was as if, in the depths of his heart, he shared the knowledge that welled up in her as Johnny ran to Esau, asking about his pony.

This was the only home she would ever have. And it was not his.

No well at Burkburnett, but Rance brought in some hundred-barrel wells in the Panhandle; selling these to a hard-driving independent, Harry Sinclair, gave Lone Star the money to accept a plea from drought-stricken farmers near Ranger. In return for leases on 20,000 acres, Lone Star would drill a test well at least 3,000 feet deep. The farmers were sure there was oil beneath their parched acres; there had to be or they'd lose everything they had.

Much had happened in the year and a half since Hardy brought his family to Old Orchard. The long-feared spill of Mexico's Revolution across the border came in March 1916, when Villa's band raided Columbus, New Mexico, and killed seventeen. Pershing was ordered to pursue Villa into Mexico. It was only in January of 1917 that he was ordered back after nearly a year of futile chasing through the mountains and several clashes with President Carranza's army.

At the end of that same month, Germany warned that its submarine attacks would resume and a U.S. liner was sunk the day the country severed relations with Germany. War was declared in April, conscription imposed in May for men between eighteen and thirty. Hardy was three years older than that, and oil workers were exempted anyway because production was vital to winning what was the first war of planes, tanks, trucks, ambulances, subs, and destroyers. Verdun had been saved in 1916 by troops and munitions brought in 40,000 trucks and tractors; oil-fueled equipment had won the Battle of the Somme. And in the United States, since 1914, the number of cars had increased by four million, tractors by 27,000, trucks from 85,000 to over 500,000.

Once the war was over, Hardy said, airplanes were bound to become an important means of transport. All the world's ships would soon be powered by the fuel that had rested so quietly in its underground strata till sixty years ago, and only found its major uses after the turn of the century.

"I almost feel historical," Katie told her mother with a rueful smile. "I *am*," Vinnie said with a chuckle.

Hardy's well blew in wild at Ranger a few days after the

McCleskey discovery well showered oil from its 1,700 barrels a day. In March 1918, Lone Star brought in two gushers. The Ranger boom was on, frenzied drilling in all directions. But Hardy put Rance in charge of operations. When he came to Old Orchard, he was already in uniform.

Four months later, Second Lieutenant Hardy Alastair led his men in the second battle of the Marne, the decisive three-week conflict that turned the tide of the war. He was at Ypres, pursued the enemy east of the Meuse, and was badly wounded by machine-gun fire only a few days before the armistice, November 11, 1918.

Katie, of necessity, had learned to drive. With Vinnie and Johnny, she met Hardy's train in Pleasanton. She didn't recognize the gaunt man on crutches until, after hopping down the steps, he looked up. His gray eyes were the same color but they were blank shields now instead of openings. As they embraced awkwardly, she was aghast at the thrust of his bones, like a skeleton bound together by skin. Decorations marched across his chest and he wore the bars of a captain.

He kissed Vinnie. Then he and Johnny, who would be six on Christmas just a few days from now, gazed at each other, Johnny's eyes full of awed joy, Hardy's winter gray. Johnny reached up for a hug. Hardy put out his hand.

The war took 112,432 U.S. soldiers' lives, over half through influenza and pneumonia that swept the camps and then killed nearly half a million people in forty-six states. Christmas was somber in many American homes, despite relief that the World War was over, and pride that the courage and spirit of scarcely trained U.S. fighting men had carried their exhausted Allies through the last battles.

Mechanization accelerated by the war had pushed the country into a new era. Old Orchard had been equipped with a telephone several years before so that Katie could stay in closer touch; now they were commonplace, and Katie wondered what Hester would have thought of the Frigidaire that replaced the old icebox. Vinnie had reluctantly sold her buggy, though the team reveled in green meadows. It was impossible to drive horses without having them frightened off the road or choked with dust by trucks or cars. Vinnie kept her skirts long, saying she'd been brought up to think that showing an ankle was immodest and she was too old to change, though she thought Katie looked nice "just as long as you don't show your knees." The surprising thing was that though Katie continued to loop her thick honey-brown hair in a French knot, Vinnie had a bob and marcel wave.

"Much cooler and a sight easier to keep," she said briskly to some remark of Hardy's. "I couldn't have done it if the judge were here, but I'm glad to throw away those hairpins."

Hardy's grin flashed some of his old mischief. "Well, Lavinia"—he always called her that—"I guess it's okay as long as you don't go to France. Someone might take you for one of the daughters of joy who started that fashion."

As wickedly, Vinnie glinted back at him. "At my age, I'd consider it a compliment."

Katie broke the law for the first time by placing a standing order with a Pleasanton bootlegger for the bourbon that eased Hardy's pain and helped him sleep. Prohibition had been ratified that January of 1919; the only difference it made, according to Thos, was that people would now not only drink but break a law to do it, and the suppliers would profit.

In March, U.S. veterans met in Paris and formed the American Legion, but Hardy had mothballed his uniform and ribbons. Still thin, still limping, though he had discarded the crutches, he announced one morning at breakfast that he was going to make the rounds of Lone Star's holdings.

"We're making a million a month off our Ranger wells," he said. "Might be the time and place to put in our own pipeline and refineries." A smile touched his lips as he looked at Katie. "Why don't you come along, honey? A guy named Conrad Hilton's put in a hotel at Cisco—calls it a cross between a gold mine and a flophouse. We could stay there while we get your house built."

Katie's heart sank. The boom at Ranger and Hogtown, or Desdemona, where the main street had been torn up to make room for derricks, had brought a flood of lawlessness that made the old-time booms look innocent. Mobs had run lawmen out of town three times and hijacking and daily collection of bodies was routine until, with Rotary Club leadership, the citizens smashed gambling halls and dumped whiskey into the gutters. Things were quieter now, but she shrank from the idea of living where everyone was fevered with the search for fabulous wealth.

That was when Katie faced the inevitable: Lone Star's head-quarters, hence their home, would have to be at an oil center. Smelly, raw, probably on the wind-scoured plains she found so stark and depressing. But that was how it would have to be if she and Hardy were to weld their divided lives back into one again.

Blessedly, Vinnie said, "Why don't you leave Johnny here while you get located?" He was in first grade and walked to the one-room school at the crossroads. "It's hard on kiddies to change teachers and classmates in the middle of a term."

"Good idea, Lavinia." The hint of a plea mixed with challenge in the gaze Hardy fixed on Katie. "Can you be ready tomorrow?"

By August, Lone Star's pipeline ran from wells to refinery, and a mansion was going up on a wooded knoll above a creek fifteen miles from Ranger, the nearest attractive site available because of inflated land prices. Katie was glad she wouldn't have to live in town and that Johnny could walk to the small school two miles away. He could have his pony too and one of the Old Orchard dogs. The time was past when most children finished school in the place where they'd begun, and that had never been the case for children whose fathers followed the booms.

Now that her long-promised home was taking shape, Katie threw herself into designing windowseats looking out over where she'd plant flowers, a kitchen with all the conveniences, Johnny's room with its own door opening on the veranda, and a guest suite with its own small kitchen where she hoped Vinnie would often stay.

Hardy was tanned and fit again, the limp almost imperceptible, though purplish-white pits in his leg and thigh would mark him till death. Katie's scar was invisible, but something had happened when she miscarried. All the doctors she had seen said she could probably not conceive, or, if she did, she would not carry a child to birth. She proposed to Hardy that they adopt a child.

"We can, if you really want a baby around, honey. But as far as I'm concerned, if it's not mine, why bother?" As she gasped, he went red to his thick, dun-colored hair. "Katie, that's not what I meant! Johnny's different."

She thought bitterly, *Yes, he's different—Darcy's, not yours. You give him your name and home and everything he wants—except you.*

Hardy limped over and kissed her, pressing her face between his big hands. "Let's face it, sweetheart, I'm not cut out to be much of a father. But I still think when the boy's older..."

"Of course. The day he leaves home you'll decide to get to know him."

Hardy stiffened, then laughed ruefully. "Katie, I think that's the way it usually is. Mothers are for growing up. Fathers, well, maybe they're for later."

Or not at all. Love couldn't be commanded, but it hurt her to see Johnny's worship of his father, his eagerness to win a nod or word of approval. Hardy never rebuked the child or did anything Katie could specifically complain about. He just didn't love him.

Katie was planting tulip bulbs by the sundial that September, happy that the house would soon be finished. After Christmas, they could bring Johnny to a house they had a good chance of making into a home. She wasn't expecting Hardy till late, so at the sound of a motor, she got up and took off her canvas gloves, hurrying around to the drive. Hardy got out of his sleek new Cadillac, his limp so heavy, his face so drained of color, that she ran to him.

"What's wrong, darling? Do you feel bad?"

His grin twisted his face. "About as bad as I can, honey. It—it looks like this field's going dry."

Katie's head spun. She peered at him, hoping it was a joke, but the lines in his face had deepened as if faint cracks had been enlarged with a chisel. "What—are you sure?"

"The flow's dropped a little, but it looked like the field would go on producing for years." He shook his head and rubbed his hand across his eyes. "What was a seven-thousand-barrel-a-day gusher five months ago went dry today. The oil's gone. Sucked out."

It took time to realize the enormity. Not only Lone Star's best wells gone but most of the company's money invested in a now useless pipeline and a refinery with nothing to refine.

The house...Katie looked at the completed outside, the graceful veranda, the stained-glass panels in the doors, the alcoves where she had planned to sit and read with Johnny. "We can sell this."

After a moment, he nodded. "Guess it's the only thing that

makes sense. Can't headquarter at a busted boom town." He kissed her. When he stepped back, he looked better. "Well, I'll get back and see what I can salvage. Shall I drop you at the hotel?"

"Let me plant these last few bulbs," she said, kneeling, steadying herself against the earth. "Maybe—maybe they'll come up next spring."

Book Three

HARDY

I _____

By selling leases, the house, and his interest in Lone Star, Hardy paid his debts. He refused personal loans from Rance and Thos, contrived to give the men he had to lay off a week's pay to tide them over to the next job. After taking Katie to Old Orchard, he sold the Cadillac for enough to buy Katie a Packard and pay his way to Colombia, where the International Petroleum Company had taken over the vast field discovered in the jungles by Transcontinental.

That Christmas of 1919, Johnny's seventh birthday, was the last Hardy would spend with the family till 1923, when he came back with enough money to do contract drilling in the Permian Basin of southwest central Texas. Johnny was finishing eighth grade. Hardy didn't even suggest that Katie bring the boy to the oil fields. It was as if he had vowed to live alone until he could offer his family everything that had been snatched away that disastrous September when Ranger went dry.

When Johnny was fourteen, he begged to work for Hardy as a roustabout, but Hardy, his eyes on Katie, said it was too dangerous. They both knew he was thinking that if her son were killed or maimed, she would blame Hardy. Johnny ran off, though under evident compulsion he sent a card from Seminole, Oklahoma, where Lone Star, now headed by Rance, was drilling in an exciting new field, discovered when everyone thought there would be no new discoveries in Oklahoma.

"I'm digging ditches and laying pipe, digging cellars for new wells, and filling water coolers and pumping and doing just about everything except working on the derrick," he wrote. Katie smiled to imagine his disgust. *"But I'm learning to mix the soup. Don't worry, Mama, I just help the shooter and watch. But someday I'm going to be the shooter."*

He ended with a promise to be back for school, but a giant hand pushed on Katie's heart. Johnny was the image of Darcy at that age except for more green in his eyes. He moved with the same sure grace, had the same laugh. Would she lose him young, as she had lost his father?

He came home just before school started that autumn of 1926, more man now than boy though his six-foot frame needed a lot of filling out. After months of doing a man's work for good pay, it must have been as hard for him to fit a classroom as it was to fit the desk, but he dutifully brought home his books and studied, part of his bargain with his parents to finish high school if he could go to the oil fields in the summer.

Hardy was drilling at Borger, northeast of Amarillo, a mile-long main street of gambling and dance halls, notorious for pimps, prostitutes, gambling, robbery, murder, and people disabled by jake leg, caused by drinking a brew of Jamaica ginger made popular by Prohibition. In spite of periodic raids by Texas Rangers, it was the wildest boom in years.

When Hardy, on shares, brought in a five-thousand-barrel-a-day well, Katie was thrilled for him, though they hadn't lived together in so long that she felt as nervous as a bride-to-be. She awaited him with mingled feelings, glad he had recouped his fortunes but reluctant to leave Old Orchard and Vinnie, who was becoming blinded by cataracts. After his first jubilant phone calls, when he said he'd come for her as soon as he had a place for her to live, Hardy's communications dropped to hasty postcards. And then, without warning, he drove up one night in a new Rolls-Royce.

He hugged Vinnie, shook hands with the son who was now as tall as he was, hesitated, then caught Katie against him, kissing her with a kind of desperation, whispering, "I love you, honey. I'll always love you."

Foreboding gripped her, but she made him sit on the veranda while she fixed bourbon over ice. When she took it to him, he was saying to Johnny, "I'd like to have you working with me, sure, son. But Borger's the toughest place I've seen, worse than the early days because of bootlegging."

"Seminole's not exactly a Sunday school, Dad. I—" Johnny glanced at his mother and bit back whatever he'd started to say. "We'll see.'"

It dropped there. After supper, Hardy asked Katie to come for a drive in the moonlight. "Why don't we walk down by the river?" she countered.

They passed the oil seep above the bluff and took the old path that ran beneath the cave. Sitting on a ledge, Katie searched Hardy's face in the silvery light. The lines of age didn't show, but beneath his cheekbones there were shadows like gashes. "You're not eating well enough," she said, an echo of what she'd told him for sixteen years.

"Katie." He sat down at her knee, turning to grip her hands. "Katie, I hope you can forgive me."

A girl was pregnant with his child, a beautiful girl of eighteen, young enough to be his daughter. There were no jails in Borger, but a heavy chain fastened between two trees. Prisoners in leg irons were secured by this chain. That was how Hardy had found Rosalie Krantz, chained between two blowsy old whores, drunk on jake, her silk scarlet dress hiked up over her knees, black hair trailing in the dust, her skin fair and soft as a baby's. He'd known she was a whore, but she was so young, so lovely, a flower doomed to be crushed. He paid the sheriff to unchain her and carried her to his hotel, bathed her, and put her to bed.

"She stayed with me." Hardy stared at the ground. "I swear, Katie, I never meant to do anything but start her in a decent life. She was so pretty, so sweet—it just seemed like such a waste."

"I suppose she's a orphan."

"How did you know?"

Katie shrugged. "And I suppose she fell in love with some man who got her into the life."

She didn't intend the mocking note in her tone. Hardy stiffened. "No. She lived with an aunt and uncle. The uncle was always trying to crawl in her bed and the aunt worked her like a slave. She ran away. For a while she waited on tables but no one cared what she did, so after a while she started taking the easy money. She's a nice kid, but she's sort of like a wild well—lots of energy that has to blow off somehow."

"And you think you can tame her?"

"I don't want to tame her. Just take care of her." He raised his head, and even in the dim light, she saw his pain. "Katie, I love you. I never meant for this to happen. But the baby. . . ."

Katie took the blade, turned it toward her vitals, and drove it home herself. "You ought to marry her. Since we're not Moslems, we have to get a divorce."

"Katie—"

"There isn't any other way—if you love her."

After a silence, he said, "I do. But my God, Katie, I love you, too."

"But she's the one carrying your baby, Hardy. You gave my son your name. It would be poor thanks if I kept you from fathering your blood child."

"What will the boy think?"

"Johnny? I'll tell him I didn't want to move to Borger or follow the oil strikes. And that's true enough."

He said gratefully, "You always loved Old Orchard. I guess it's more your home than anything I could give you." He raised her hands to his lips. "You won't want for anything, Katie. I'll invest enough in stocks and bonds to provide for you and send the boy through any college he chooses."

She couldn't keep a tinge of bitterness from her laugh. "The only school Johnny wants is the derrick. God help us, he wants to be a shooter."

"Then he'd better learn it from the best. Let him work for me next summer, Katie, and I'll get Tex Thornton to show him the ropes—and put the fear of nitro in him."

It would be strange—but wonderful—if by depriving Johnny of a legal father, the divorce freed Hardy to finally love the boy who had always worshipped him.

"Why don't you ask Johnny?" she suggested. "And now I'd like to just sit here a while." She felt blood draining from her; when it was all gone, she would crumble like dried ash.

Hardy got to his feet. The streaks of white in his hair gleamed in the moonlight and she realized he was forty-two, old by oil field standards. She had grown middle-aged waiting for him to hit another gusher. Now he would have a young wife, a sweet new baby, while she lost her husband and was losing her son.

When Hardy was gone, she groped her way into the cave, all the way to the spring. She hurt. No matter how brave a face she put on it, she would be seen as a woman discarded for a younger, fresher one. She buried her face on the stone and sobbed as she had when she was young. Slowly, her spirit was quieted by the ripple of the spring and the ancient calm of a place where many before her had taken refuge.

Melissa was born the seventh of May of 1928, in the first green warmth of summer when the roses by the family gravestone bloomed so prodigally it seemed they were giving their sweet smell and color to the dead. Hardy phoned the news. He couldn't keep the proud excitement from his voice.

"You don't seem disappointed that you didn't get a son," Katie said.

"How could I be? Melissa—she's absolutely perfect, Katie." His tone changed. "I wish you could see her."

"Maybe someday. Send me a picture."

He did, and had the tact to send one of the baby alone. But Katie searched that tiny face for the image of the girl who was Hardy's love, and her fingers shook. Black hair pointing into the forehead in a widow's peak; arched black eyebrows, dimpled cheeks, pointed chin. A dainty cat face. Nothing there of Hardy.

Staring at the photo, Johnny closed his fists. "Mama. I—I won't go to Borger next month if—well, if it'll make you feel bad."

Katie smoothed his cheek. He had the longest dark eyelashes, and though his green-gold eyes seemed too large for his thin face, when his facial contours matured, he would be so much like Darcy that a tide of longing swept over Katie, made bearable only by seeing how her dear love lived in their son. No, no matter what it had cost, no matter that it had rived a fatal break between her and her husband that was now inevitable and legal, she couldn't regret that she'd been Darcy's, that Johnny was his child. She kissed the boy and smiled.

"If you've got to be at a rig, dear, I'd rather it was with your father. He'll try to keep you from taking crazy chances. Just remember, you promised to finish school."

He looked pained. But then he grinned. "Sure, Mama. I'll be back this fall. But this summer—golly! Dad's told me Tex Thornton's going to show me how to shoot wells. And Mr. Thornton, he's the best there is."

"He gets in the papers most," Katie agreed. Of all the jobs in the oil fields, why had Johnny picked the most dangerous? All she could do was hope that the thrill would be replaced by fear before he lost his life or was maimed in some part of that body she had cherished and tended when he was small enough to lie in her arms.

He worked with Thornton that summer, sending photos of the two of them beside a car fitted with padded clips to hold the shells of nitroglycerine. Driving such a vehicle was even riskier than lowering the torpedoes down a well to blast a formation into fracturing and releasing oil. Hardy refused to let Johnny drive, but by the end of that summer Thornton trusted the young man, clad in asbestos, to help him enter a raging fire and put it out with explosives. When Johnny came home for his senior year at Pleasanton High, he was like a young lion that soon would have to hunt its own meat.

Along with his photos of Tex and Hardy and his oil-rotted clothes, he had a tinted picture of Melissa that he set up on his dresser. "She's the sweetest thing, Mama," he said, with an almost pleading glance at Katie. "And she sure likes me. Even when she had colic, if I picked her up and walked her, she'd stop crying. Lots of times she went to sleep sort of curled up on my chest with her rear sticking up in the air."

"Did you like Rosalie?"

He flushed and glanced away. "Well, sure. I didn't want to, but she just sort of bubbles. She's a little crazy, maybe, everything's either just wonderful or so awful that she cries, but things can't get dull around her."

It was more than that. Steeling herself against the piercing hurt, Katie knew her son and husband loved the same woman. For the first time, hatred for Rosalie flamed from the ashes of resignation. Wasn't it enough that the little whore had Hardy and a baby? If she made trouble for Johnny . . .

Barring her arms across her breast, Katie kept her back to her son, staring out at the white gravestone above the river till she could speak normally. Bitterness ate at her like acid. She must not reproach Johnny, but she feared for him. Next summer, even if it meant telling Hardy why, she would try to see that Johnny didn't live under the same roof as Rosalie.

The damage of the divorce was internal; it hadn't really changed the routine of Katie's outward life. Every morning, she worked in her father's study, now her retreat, until noon. His publisher had asked her to revise his works for new editions, and she was editing his later journals while making a coherent book of her Mexican oil experiences out of letters and her diaries. Her father's editor had seen the first part of the account and had offered a contract, but she preferred to finish first since it gave her a sense of control.

On pleasant afternoons, she walked with Vinnie or took her driving or to call on friends. On cold or rainy days, they sat in the parlor and sewed or did duets on the piano, or Vinnie reminisced about the old days while Katie made notes. Her mother's life deserved a book even if it was printed only for the family. Most Sundays they were invited to dinner or had friends at Old Orchard for one of Corinth's feasts.

It was a tranquil life though there was a kind of unreality about it, a sort of being frozen in time, neither young nor old. Katie was sealed from physical love though sometimes she dreamed, sometimes felt that deep secret throbbing as she wakened. When she undressed, she studied her body, still beautiful and firm, and wondered if hers would be the only eyes ever to see her like this until she was dressed for the grave. A few widowers paid suit but she discouraged them. She could never love anyone as she had Darcy; she couldn't knit her life into anyone's as she had with Hardy. There had to be some fire in a new attachment or else she'd rather live alone.

For a few weeks after the shock of knowing that Johnny's first love was Hardy's wife, Katie had to fight self-pity and bitterness with every fiber of her will. She would not steep her soul in poison or turn a necessary shield into an impenetrable wall. In a perverse way, it was heartening to find that she still had so much feeling; her emotions hadn't leveled as much as she had thought. If she could feel such desolate anger, might she be capable of equal joy? So she wrestled with her devil until November, when Vinnie broke her hip and worry for her mother crowded everything else out of Katie's mind.

In spite of faithful nursing, Vinnie got pneumonia. Thos, Talt, and Hardy were at her deathbed and, with Johnny, served as pallbearers when she was buried beside Mark.

Hardy was thin and brown. He looked tired, but he said every well he'd drilled at Borger was a producer. Katie couldn't bring herself to ask after Rosalie, but when she inquired after Melissa, he beamed. With some diffidence at first, then with irrepressible pride, he talked of the six-month-old's accomplishments. She could almost crawl. She had the softest cooing language and noticed everything. Her hair was so long she already wore ribbons. The colic that had plagued her at first had vanished. Yes, she was perfect. Altogether lovely.

He had to hurry back to Borger, but Thos and Eulalia stayed for a week, helping sort Vinnie's things. They left the day Hardy returned with a basket in the backseat of his Rolls. When Katie heard a motor and looked out, he was reaching down, and when he straightened he was holding a baby.

Katie's head spun. She clamped her jaws against the scalding rush of outrage. Had he taken her polite interest as a wish to see this—this almost-bastard? But when she met him on the veranda, his eyes were bleak in a face so haggard that she cried out.

"Katie," he said as if each word were being drawn from his entrails with red-hot tongs. "Rosalie—she's left me. Can you— will you—take care of Melissa?"

II _____

How could anyone leave such a baby? When Katie held the
small sweet body, her breasts ached as if trying to create milk.
She took the child because there was nothing else to do. Within a
week, in spite of the physical demands of caring for an infant,
Katie could not keep from hoping that Melissa would grow up at
Old Orchard, that Hardy would never take her away.

Johnny heard of Rosalie's desertion in silence but with a flash
of shocked pain in his eyes. He ignored Melissa for several days,
but one night when he was studying on the rug by the fire, the
baby crawled next to him, curled up between his knees and chest,
and went to sleep. Johnny scowled. But when he got up to get a
drink, he put a cushion in his place and, when he returned, eased
himself protectively down beside her.

That night, he carried her to her crib in the small room next to
Katie's. From then on, her femininity enchanted him while she
responded to his deep, male voice, his strength and bigness now
hers to command. She was happy with Katie and lavished charm
on Corinth, Esau, and Thaley, but when Johnny came home, her
little bottom twitched comically as she crawled to him and
reached up, patting his face and hair, shrieking ecstatically as he
nuzzled his cold nose in her soft neck. Her first steps were made
to Johnny. After that, she followed him like a puppy, crawling

when her legs gave out; usually she ended up borne high on his shoulders.

Hardy never wrote but phoned sporadically, sometimes from East Texas, sometimes from the Permian Basin fields, to ask how Melissa was. He said little about his business, but Katie gathered that he had sold his wells at Borger and was looking for new leases. He called one night in May, voice so slurred that Katie was sure he'd been drinking. Pity overwhelmed her, and anger at the girl who had used and left him. If Rosalie had half of Melissa's appeal, it was easy to understand Hardy's enslavement.

"Melissa's first birthday's this Sunday," Katie said carefully. "Why don't you come for a few days? She's growing till you'd hardly know her, and of course she's walking everywhere."

He didn't answer for so long that, alarmed, she called his name. "Sorry," he muttered. "I've got to wind up a deal in the Panhandle. Melissa's too little to know the difference."

"You aren't."

"Hell, Katie, you can't want *me* hanging around!"

Her heart lurched. Did she? She wouldn't follow his oil quests again; the wife part of her had suffered and died with the divorce. But she was still a woman. At forty-four, she was still beautiful but her skin was drying; there was in her body the instinct to flower a last time in Indian summer before winter came. Yes, she would sleep with Hardy if he wished it, but she could not marry him again. That was over.

Steadying her voice, she said, "Don't be a fool, Hardy. I'll always care what happens to you. Johnny adores you. And Melissa ought to have one parent, at least. If you can't come for her birthday, come as soon as you finish that business. Nothing else you do is as important as knowing your child."

He laughed. "Same Katie. Straight to the core. Do you always have to be so goddamn right?"

She thought of Darcy with a rush of passion and regret. "You know I'm not. But Hardy, do come."

"All right. Next week." He hesitated. "Katie. Thanks."

She swallowed what felt like a bruising obtrusion in her throat. "Melissa's a love. I don't know what I did without her. We'll save you a piece of her cake."

* * *

Why not hold the celebration after Hardy arrived? Johnny enthusiastically agreed. Melissa wouldn't know or care. Corinth started mixing the burnt-sugar cake as soon as Hardy pulled into the drive, and after supper that evening, she proudly carried it to the table, its single candle ablaze. Johnny showed Melissa how to blow it out, and her blue eyes sparkled as everyone applauded.

They drank her health in cider made from Old Orchard apples. Afterward, dressed in the ruffled blue dress Katie had made for her, blue ribbons in her curls, she sat in the little chair Johnny and Esau had crafted and hugged an immense teddy bear Hardy had brought her. As her eyes grew heavy, she dragged the bear over to Johnny and tried to crawl into his lap, but he picked her up, along with the bear, and put them in Hardy's arms.

"Stay with your daddy," Johnny said, "and Esau and I'll sing you your favorite song."

He got the guitar he'd learned to play the first summer he was in the oil fields. After his skillful slim fingers tuned up, he grinned at Esau and they blended their voices in "All the Pretty Little Horses."

> Black and bay, dapple and gray,
> Coach-and-six, and all the horses . . .

The baby kept jerking upright to keep awake, but by the last hypnotic chorus of "Hushaby, don't you cry," her grasp relaxed on the teddy and she slept against her father's heart. Katie's eyes misted with tears, so grateful that Hardy was home that she felt only a small stab of wishing that Melissa could have been hers, too.

After Katie got Melissa into her thin nightie, Hardy carried her to the crib and smoothed her hair as she murmured. Katie tucked in the bear. To her amazement, as she and Hardy entered the main room, he reached for his wide-brimmed Stetson, like those he'd worn in his Ranger days, and said, "Thanks for inviting me, Katie."

"You—you're not leaving?"

"Got business at Burkburnett."

Anger heated her. "And you've got a daughter—who won't remember you if you leave before you get acquainted again."

His mouth quirked. "Acquainted? That's a hell of a way to be a father. She wanted in Johnny's lap tonight. She doesn't know me or need me." He shrugged but there was pain in his eyes. "That's all to the good, since I can't raise her."

Johnny set down the guitar, rising, much thinner than the man he called father but just as tall. "Dad, please. Please stay a couple of days—"

"Can't, boy." Hardy trailed a hand over Johnny's shoulder. "Take care of your mother and sister, hear?"

"Why don't *you?*" Johnny cried.

Gray eyes clashed with hazel. It may have seemed to Hardy that he was staring at his long dead rival, the man who had gotten a son on Katie when Hardy himself could not.

He raised his hand. Johnny whitened but didn't flinch. Katie seized Hardy's arm. "What's the matter with you?"

"I don't belong here," Hardy said. "Don't ask me again."

He lunged out of the room. Katie watched her son, wanting to take him in her arms, comfort him, but his face closed and he turned away. Esau and the women left with sorrowful looks and muttered good-nights.

Katie went out to sit in the warm, scented darkness by her parents' graves. Should she tell Johnny the truth about his fathering? Would it hurt less than wondering at Hardy's behavior? She didn't know, but she was willing to sacrifice Johnny's opinion of her if it would armor him against Hardy's rejection. No answer came from the rose-shaded graves. After a long time, she went to her room. She had slept alone there as a child and now seemed fated to sleep alone all the rest of her life.

Johnny worked for Hardy that summer. When he returned to Old Orchard for his last year of high school, he seemed worried. When Katie pressed for the reason, he said reluctantly, "Dad's drinking."

"He always has."

"Not like this, Mama. He doesn't eat. Sobers up on black coffee and cigarettes. Sometimes he's fogged up for four or five days. His old hands carry on the best they can but things are going to hell and he doesn't seem to know it—or care." The boy gulped and his eyes pleaded. "Mama, could you—?"

"I'm not his wife, Johnny." She smiled wryly in spite of the oppressive tightness in her chest. "He never listened real well anyhow."

"You are too his wife, Mama. Rosalie was his sweetheart, but she was too wild to stay with anyone, even her baby."

"He divorced me," said Katie angrily. "I'm not his keeper."

Johnny just looked at her; with Darcy's eyes. She was flooded with memories, a great wave of pity for Hardy, a tide of defeated helplessness.

She cared. God knew she would always care. But beyond taking care of Melissa, what could she do?

A few weeks after Johnny came home that autumn of 1929, the stock market plummeted and grew steadily worse. Panic led to mass dumping till, during a frenzied three weeks, the market and credit structure of the whole country was in ruins. The securities Hardy had bought for Katie were worthless, the companies bankrupt. It happened so quickly and so far away that she couldn't comprehend it beyond the fact that no money was paid into her bank account. For her, it was no real disaster. She had saved over the years and had a modest inheritance, beyond Old Orchard, from her parents. Then Rance called.

"Katie, I know you and Hardy aren't together, but I thought you ought to know. He's in bad shape. That girl he married, she got too much morphine in a Baton Rouge whorehouse. The madam found Hardy's address and wrote him. He went to bury her and he's been drunk ever since."

One part of Katie said, If that's what he wants to do, no one can stop him. But in the extremity, she just had to try, as she'd tried to pull Darcy back from the boiling pit of Dos Bocas. "Keep an eye on him, Rance. I'll be up as soon as I can."

Johnny wanted to go with her, but she said, "If you want to help, son, stay here and take care of Melissa. I don't know when I'll be back. I'm taking Hardy out to West Texas where he can't find a bottle and I'll keep him there till he's dried out or dead."

Johnny stared. "Good Lord, Mama! He'll go into fits, maybe hurt you!"

"No, he won't. I'm going to lock him up in a shack or doghouse at one of his played-out wells and he's not getting anything but fresh air and water till all that booze flushes out of his system."

"At least take Esau. Or Uncle Thos."

"I can do better alone." She straightened her shoulders. "Kill or cure. Will you take care of the baby?"

"You know I will. But Dad—"

"You wanted me to do something. Stay clear while I try."

Rance met her on the steps of a run-down boardinghouse and tossed a greasy old satchel in the trunk. "Don't come in, Katie. I'll bring him out."

Rance half dragged, half carried Hardy to the car and heaved him on the backseat where he mumbled and collapsed in the pillows Katie had heaped there. Panting, Rance banged the door. His hair had turned almost white in the years since she'd known him at Baygall.

"Best thing would be to keep him liquored up till you get him home, Katie. I'll get his bottle. Hope to God you can pull him out of it."

"Can you look after his business till he gets back?"

"Katie, there ain't no business. Before he went to Baton Rouge, he paid off his crews and shut down the rigs. Creditors came down like buzzards and sold off the equipment. He not only ain't got nothing, he's in hock up to the eyebrows."

She felt as if the ground moved beneath her. Shaking Rance's hand, she said, "Thanks, Rance. Wish me luck."

He nodded. "Katie, Lone Star's having it tough too, but if you need some money, I can—"

"I have some. Thanks again, Rance."

"Well, let me know if I can help." He came back with a nearly full bottle of whiskey and stood in the street, waving, as Katie steered out of town, not worrying much about Hardy's blurred curses whenever she hit a rut. She had groceries in the trunk, a big water jug, bedding, necessities, and some cotton cord.

Once they found shelter and isolation, they weren't leaving till Hardy was sober or one or both of them were dead, and right then she was mad enough at him not to much care how it went.

They spent the night parked at the side of the road outside San Angelo. Katie bought tamales from a street vendor and some pumpkin *empanadas*, little fried pies. On the kerosene camp stove, she brewed strong black coffee with the slightly bitter tang of chicory that Hardy liked. He groaned, probably with headache, as he began to rouse from his stupor. Katie gave him coffee.

He sipped it gingerly, looking around, and when she refilled his cup, he said, "Where the hell have you brought me, Katie? And why the hell are you doing it? Why aren't you home with Melissa?"

"Melissa's fine. I'm just trying to see that she's not left an orphan—or worse, has a drunk for a father." Katie marched to the stove, filled a plate with tamales, and set it on the running board. "Get some decent food in your stomach and you'll feel better."

"I'm not hungry."

"Of course you're not. You're so soaked with booze that your guts must be damn near pickled. But you're going to sweat it out or vomit it out or whatever it takes till you're dried out."

"Who asked you to butt in?"

"I'm taking care of your little girl. And a young man who worships you and calls you father deserves better than what you're becoming."

"So let me go to hell—the sooner, the better. I'm not worth this, Katie. Pile in your car and go home. You've never wanted to be with me. Why bother now?"

She slapped him hard. His head snapped up and his eyes blazed. For the first time, he was recognizable, though his eyes were bloodshot.

"Listen, Hardy Alastair! There's been things on both sides that are hard to forgive, much less forget, but I still care what happens to you! Now, I could say I'm only here because of Melissa and Johnny, and that's a lot of it, but not all. *I* care. I want you to straighten up and be a man. Will you?" The brand of her palm showed pale beneath his tan. He stepped awkwardly over the food and stood shaking, gripping the door of the car, and pain shot across his face.

"Katie, I—I've lost everything. There's nothing I can give you. Even if you'd have me again, I can't marry you or what you have would be forfeited to pay my debts."

"All right. We won't marry. But we'll scrape together enough for you to get back in contract drilling, or you can take a job with Thos or Rance. You *can* start again, Hardy. You've got friends. You know the business. Anyhow, haven't you always said the real thrill was in digging a well and hitting oil, not in spending the money?"

"I said that when I was one hell of a lot younger." He was trembling, and as if his legs would hold him no longer, he sank down, leaning against the car. His mouth twisted. "All right, Katie. I'll give it a go. But I don't know if I can do it."

He tried to eat but vomited, retching so violently that Katie didn't urge him to try again. His shaking became palsy. Would it be better if he had a little to drink? Katie had heard of drunkards who died when suddenly deprived of alcohol. This was no place to deal with delirium tremens.

Hoping that she was doing the right thing, she poured a little whiskey in a glass of water and gave it to him. Next morning, he had coffee but couldn't eat, and he was shaking so hard he spilled the weak drink she mixed him. The drink steadied him enough that he could sit in the front seat with her as they drove through mesquite and greasewood flats. Some faded leaves clung to the stunted mesquite but it was nearly winter; a norther might howl over the plains any time now. Katie hoped they would be at Old Orchard before a bad storm came.

In McCamey, a small town surrounded by derricks and red storage tanks, Katie got the gas tank and water jugs filled and bought more groceries. There was no store near Castle Gap, the canyon to the west cutting through distance-blued mountains. Hardy had leased hundreds of acres on the flat land for next to nothing and nothing was what they had yielded, but there'd be some kind of place where they could stay now.

"I was drilling over by Castle Gap when the first well blew in here at McCamey in the fall of 1925," he said, gazing around the streets with their frame businesses. "Next morning, a grader cut in streets right behind the surveyors. The day after that, someone started building a filling station and café. Ten thousand people roared in before you could spit. One Texas Ranger, a friend of mine, was all the law there was." He sighed wistfully. "Sure has quieted down."

"A good thing," said Katie starchily. She gave him another much-diluted ration of whiskey and they headed for the plain below the mountains.

* * *

A gnarled old mesquite befriended the one-room adobe with its corrugated tin roof. The house and tree stood on an embankment above a dry stream bed, survivors of debris left from the dry holes Hardy had drilled. The wounds in the earth had been filled in with rocks and probably old two-by-fours. There was nothing in the shack but a rusted oil barrel with part of the front cut away to make a stove, a couple of shelves pegged to the wall, and a lot of empty cans and rubbish.

Hardy helped clear the mess and set up the cots, but he was trembling and his skin looked clammy. He collapsed on a cot, head in his hands. Katie looked from him to the bottle. He shuddered and pushed himself to his feet.

He moved to the shelf. Katie held her breath. He took the bottle, fingers tightening around the neck. He stumbled to the door and hurled the bottle against a boulder. It shattered. He turned to Katie, swaying, gripping the door frame.

"Okay, honey. Root, hog, or die. If I start having fits, keep out of the way." He crossed to her, wavering like an old man or an infant. "I love you, Katie. Always have, always will. Whatever happens, thanks."

She fought back tears. "You'll feel better when you have some coffee. Maybe some soup—"

He reeled. His head snapped back and his whole body convulsed. She tried to get him to a cot but he fell on the dirt floor, thrashing till he stiffened as if with a surge of electricity, then went limp.

Horrified, she called to him, then bent over him and listened for a heartbeat. She finally detected a sluggish, reluctant pulse. Had he had an epileptic seizure? If there'd been any whiskey, she'd have given him some. Should she drive to McCamey for a bottle? A doctor? What if he died, what if she'd challenged him to do something his wrecked body couldn't endure?

Only the memory of his throwing away the whiskey nerved her for the battle. Much better than she did, he knew the consequences of abruptly giving up what was in fact a powerful drug, but he'd chosen to do it. Maybe he knew he couldn't taper off.

She couldn't get him on a cot so she made a pallet on the earth and managed to drag him onto it. Then she pillowed his head in her lap, smoothing his hair, curly brown shot with white. All she could do was watch with him and pray that he would win.

It was harder than she could have imagined. She had drowsed off, still holding him, to be roused in dim twilight by movement. She looked down into baleful eyes that flamed as he sat up and reached for her throat.

"Rosalie! You little whore! Rosalie, why'd you leave us?"

Katie gripped his wrists. "Hardy! I'm Katie!"

"No you're not." He laughed wildly. "Katie wouldn't be here. She's at Old Orchard with her boy who looks just like his daddy, and that's not me!" He lapsed into mumbling but lay back down.

Devastated to know that her infidelity still gnawed in the cellars of Darcy's mind, Katie made coffee and heated canned soup. She got the brew down Hardy and a few spoonfuls of broth. Then she rolled a blanket around him and tied it with the heavy cord she'd brought. She didn't want to die yet and there was too much chance of his hurting himself or her to leave him unrestrained.

Exhausted, she lay on a cot and went to sleep, fully clothed except for her shoes. Sometimes, Hardy's struggling and cries pierced her slumber but these were only twists in the nightmares that filled her night.

Sitting up as dawn woke her, she gazed, terrified, at the motionless bundle. "Hardy?"

No answer. For a terrible moment, she thought he was dead. Then his eyelids fluttered. She put coffee on and unloosed the upper cord, freeing his hands. He'd feel less helpless that way and, at least while she was awake, he couldn't do much damage without the use of his legs.

His pupils were dilated when she brought him coffee. She propped him against the wall and he drank as she held the cup. Suddenly he spewed the hot fluid over her. "Trying to poison me?" he gasped. Staring at the floor, he screamed. "Give me my gun! See that rattler?"

"Hardy, there isn't anything bad here. Look." She reached down to where he was gazing and touched the floor. His shout vibrated in her ears and he dived forward, pounding at the hard dirt. Sobbing, he clawed at the ground and writhed. His head fell back.

Oh, God, help him. Help him get well. Katie washed his face and then made some oatmeal and forced herself to eat. She was going to need strength.

It was the most hellish three days she had lived through, but on the fourth morning, Hardy was in his right mind, though shivering and too weak to stand. She scrambled eggs for him, made toast, and put evaporated milk in his coffee for the extra nourishment.

All the time her heart was expanding, little by little, like a flower curled tight against a storm sensing that it could allow itself to open. She was so grateful that it seemed the desolate place was rimmed with golden light, washed clean in chill bright air. That night she and Hardy slept in each other's arms, passionless, warrior comrades embracing after a deadly battle. Next morning, they started home.

III _____

They had a real Thanksgiving, joined by Thos and Eulalia. Thos's eyes still had a youthful sparkle, though they saddened beneath his laughter when he played bear with Melissa, growling on his knees while she shrieked and pummeled him before she fled to Hardy or Johnny.

"Can't get my daughter to come visit and bring little Rachel," he said ruefully. "I guess if I want to see them, I'll have to go to New Orleans. I reckon I better before Rachel grows up." He pulled a tinted photo from his wallet. Big dark eyes looked out of a thin oval face softened by wispy black tendrils escaped from a headband of rosebuds. "Wish I could get Tamara and her man to come spend Christmas with us sometime, but I guess Tam's grandparents brought her up to think Texas is still full of wild Indians." He sighed. "They never forgave me for taking Judith away. They think it killed her, following the oil camps."

"We'll go see them," Eulalia said, smiling at him fondly. "Maybe if we prove we're not heathens, they'll let Rachel spend a week or two with us in the summer now that she's ten years old."

"Bring her here if you can," urged Katie. "She'd have fun playing with Melissa and there aren't many young branches on our family tree." As she said it, she saw Hardy's face and realized that Melissa was no relation to her family; no, not even to Johnny. Yet the child was as dear to her as if she'd borne her. Katie had come near to hating Rosalie; for the first time, she felt sorrow for Hardy's young love, all that life and energy wasted like the exploding of a wild well that brought only havoc, then cratered. But at least something of Rosalie survived in Melissa, just as Johnny, who had never seen Darcy, moved like him and turned his head in that same alert, graceful way.

So there was death but there was life too, and Hardy had pulled himself up from what was worse than dying. His eyes held Katie's across the room. Her body warmed, eager for him, for the comfort and delight they found in each other's arms.

Yes. This was the best Thanksgiving she had ever known; she even felt that her mother and father and Hester, who had lived in this house for so long, were there in spirit and felt their joy.

As he had done after the Ranger disaster twenty years before, Hardy settled his debts though it stripped him. At least that made his credit good. He wouldn't take a loan from Katie. Bad enough, he said, that the stocks and bonds he'd bought for her had crashed. Nor would he take a drilling superintendent's job with Lone Star, though Rance Gorman swore up and down that the offer was legitimate. After Christmas, Hardy traded his diamond ring for an old Fort Worth spudder and truck and took off for West Texas.

Pinched by drought and the worsening depression, a farmer's organization had raised enough money to finance a shallow well of the kind the spudder could dig, and Hardy agreed to put down exploratory wells on their leases for a share of any production.

Johnny, just turned seventeen, wanted to go along, but Hardy narrowed his eyes and growled, "You talking like that when you'll get your diploma in five months? Don't let such a crazy notion roost overnight in whatever you're using for brains."

Johnny flushed but said stubbornly, "You need a tool pusher, Dad."

"Couple of those farmers have worked on wells some. They'll do—till you get out of school." He grinned, dropping a hand on

Johnny's shoulder. "As soon as you crawl out of that cap and gown, I'll be expecting you. But I hope to hell there won't be any wells for you to shoot."

"I don't care about that as long as I can make you a hand."

Hardy slapped the boy's shoulder. "You can sure do that."

Katie had been thinking. With Johnny out of school and Melissa four years from starting, there was no reason not to join the men. Hardy needed her as much as Melissa did, and even if they had to live in a tent or shack, Melissa would be happier with her father and beloved Johnny.

Lifting her face for Hardy's kiss, Katie hugged him and said, "Look around for a place big enough for all of us."

"But you hate oil camps."

"This is different. We're starting in again." She kissed him again and whispered in his ear. "Hardy, if—if you'd like to, you could find us a preacher."

She heard his breath catch. He kissed her with the passionate tenderness of their honeymoon and swept her around in a waltz step. "All right, honey. Guess we are a shade too old to be living in sin. I'll find a house and a preacher and we'll start digging wells!"

The first well was a producer, modest but enough to let Hardy get a cable-tool rig. After two more wells, he hired another crew, and by the time the family joined him that June, Johnny with his diploma hidden at the bottom of his suitcase, Hardy had five crews pounding the sands. He also had a spacious old farmhouse with a shaded breezeway rented from an elderly couple who had moved to town on the proceeds from the oil he'd found under their rocky soil. And he had a justice of the peace in the person of Jacob Kreutzer, who ran the little crossroads grocery and feed store.

Katie had expected a quiet wedding. In a way, she felt they were reaffirming what had never ceased to be, and was at first dismayed to see farmers and drilling crews assemble in the shade of the trees surrounding the store. Introducing her, Melissa, and Johnny, Hardy glowed with pride that brought cheers from the well-wishers.

Flustered but touched, Katie decided it was the nicest wedding anyone could want. Plank tables overflowed with food, there were jugs of lemonade and pots of coffee, and after the feast Johnny got out his guitar and those who weren't too sated danced until dark. For once, farmers allowed their daughters to whirl with oil workers usually considered too tough and ornery to be let within a mile of a decent woman. Melissa danced too, spinning at the edge of the party till she fell down beside Johnny with a laughing gasp. She clapped while Katie, close in her husband's arms, smiled past his shoulder at her. Katie knew she had never been so happy.

All that summer and fall, Hardy and Johnny worked close enough to come home for supper and sleep at the farmhouse. They hung a swing for Melissa on the big oak by the porch and built her a playhouse beneath the grape arbor where she played for hours with the black kitten a neighbor gave her. The house was old-fashioned but comfortable. Katie enjoyed cooking for her men but was relieved that they had enough clothes to take the greasy ones to a laundry in the nearest town. She felt useful and needed but not burdened. Only Hardy's physical condition troubled her, and his growing urgency to bring in a gusher.

He had chest pains and shortness of breath but refused to see a doctor. "Just not as young as I was," he said, waving her off impatiently. He sat down as if his legs had melted, and his lips were ashen. "I'll be fine this fall when it cools off."

No pleading could induce him to rest more or seek medical help. He only pushed harder. The wells he'd drilled for the Mustang Creek Landowners' Association were bringing in a respectable sum but none of them produced more than a hundred barrels a day.

"Maybe it'll be like this from now on," Katie ventured. "Maybe all the best sands have been discovered."

Hardy snorted. "There's plenty of oil. It's just hiding down there in the rocks." He waved a disdainful hand at the derricks scattered among the scrub mesquite and greasewood. "When you hit a little field like this, hell, it's almost the same as farming."

"Yes." Katie nodded. "Farming's a gamble, too. Will it rain? Will blight or bugs get the crops? If you get the stuff to market, can you sell it?" For the nation's financial ills had gotten no better and it seemed no day passed without news of another bank or business failure.

"That's not what I mean, and you damn well know it, Katie. Remember that gusher at Tupan? Those wells blowing in wild at Baygall, just knocking the crown-block through the top of the derrick, all that power boiling out of the hole like it'd never stop? I want to get one more like that! And it won't be here."

Katie felt a tide of the old weariness but reminded herself that things were different now. Johnny was grown up and Melissa was happy as long as her men came home. In an emotional equation, Rosalie had balanced Darcy, removing the guilt that had tainted those difficult years after Mexico. It was not in Katie to thwart or belittle this dream of Hardy's.

"Have you picked a place to drill?"

"I want to try again at Castle Gap. I've always figured there was oil there if the bit dug deep enough." He grinned and took her in his arms, thanking her not in words but with the fervor of his kiss. "That's where I got another shot at life, Katie, thanks to you. It ought to be a lucky place. I'll put every dime I've got in the game—but not your share of what we've made off these little wells. That's for you and the kids and it's in cash, not in those skittery stocks and bonds."

Hardy tried to get Katie to stay at the shady farmhouse, but she said, "Melissa and I came to be with you. And I can cook for the crews." She didn't add that she wanted to be there if he had to abandon the well.

He hired workers from McCamey to build a bunkhouse close to the old adobe and add a floor, another room, and a ramada to it. Other men built the derrick on a spot selected after consultations with a geologist and an old McCamey tool pusher who had a reputation for locating oil by "feeling" it as he walked over productive sands. The site was near the dry stream bed half a mile from the house. Hardy had arranged for his best two crews to follow him in ten days; everything was ready when they drove up, and Hardy spudded in the well himself with his lucky old Fort Worth machine.

"I ought to smash a bottle of champagne against the derrick," Katie teased.

"Make it a case," said Hardy, moving with the quick grace that had distinguished him before that tired breathlessness drained his vigor. "We'll have it on ice the day we bring in the Katie Melissa Number One."

The men worked around the clock, so Katie reverted to her Baygall schedule, breakfast at midnight for the graveyard tour and supper for the day crew now ready to go to bed; at noon, breakfast for them and supper for the ones who'd worked through the night. She made bucket lunches for the men to eat at the derrick, and every few days drove to McCamey for fresh food and, until cool weather set in, ice.

If Johnny missed the excitement of handling nitro, no one could have guessed it from the way he hammered out the bits or helped devise a fishing tool when the string was lost at two thousand feet. Sometimes, watching him help Hardy screw a newly dressed bit on the drill stem or swing pipe into position, she forgot they weren't truly father and son, so smoothly did they coordinate their motions, rarely needing words.

She was relieved to see that Johnny kept watch on Hardy and tried to spare him exertion. Hardy's enthusiasm had put some of the old spring in his step but he was gasping by the time he walked from the derrick to the house, and he cut down on the highly spiced foods he'd always loved, claiming they caused what he called indigestion but what Katie feared was something worse. Still, his spirits were high even though the hole was nearing four thousand feet with no oil in the cuttings.

That was early in October of 1930. The stock market was sliding and, by the end of the month, shares were dumped for anything they would bring. Ruined financiers committed suicide as panic swept the country, and hopes of better times after last year's market disasters were drowned in the overwhelming flood of the Great Depression.

The world still needed oil, though, and farmers forced off their land or men thrown out of their regular work flocked to the oil fields to vie for wages that, though lowered, were princely compared to those paid in other occupations—if a place could be found at all. No time, Katie thought, for Hardy to keep the bit pounding at a hole already twice as deep as many producers; but he seemed determined to keep on, as if his conviction that the sands held oil could make the oil be there, as if Fortune must reward this defiant gamble.

Five thousand feet. He let one crew go, working a full tour himself with Johnny as his tool-dresser.

Six thousand. He paid off the other crew though, eyes wet, the driller offered to stay on for shares. Shares of what he surely suspected would be nothing.

With Johnny, Hardy drilled deeper. He wouldn't take a loan from Katie. "Not a cent of yours goes into this hole, sweetheart." He could still smile and she realized all over again that for him, as for many, it had always been the search that mattered, just as gold fever was more than hunger for the gold itself.

"I'm sinking every cent I have," he told her, "and if I'm bust —well, we sure dug us one hell of a hole."

He did let her do what he had once so fiercely opposed, spell him at the drilling for an hour or so several times a day while he stretched out to rest beside a napping Melissa. At first Johnny was afraid his mother would get hurt, but when he saw she enjoyed the vibration of the bit hitting, pleasured in the creak of the walking beam, occupied the lazy bench as if it were a throne, he quit worrying and a new bond was added to all of those that joined them. He was so perfectly made and beautiful, so like Darcy, and the resemblance warmed her now instead of hurting. These would have been happy days if she hadn't feared for Hardy.

At seven thousand feet, they lost the whole drilling string up to the rope socket. They lowered several fishing tools without success. At last Hardy sent down an impression block, pounding it to make it take on the imprint of the top of the lost tools. "Damn string's under the side of the casing shoe," Hardy muttered, studying the mold. "Come on, son, let's see if we can hammer something out to grab on to this."

They spent two more weeks lowering grabs, spears, and specially made tools, but nothing could get hold of the embedded swivel. On New Year's Day, Hardy cut the engine.

"That flanges me up. Plug the hole and that's it."

Nothing Katie could say changed his mind. When the well was plugged, he sold his drilling outfit in McCamey and gave the truck to Johnny, who was going to work for Rance at Lone Star. For the first time in a long while, Hardy was willing to let Katie drive him, and by mid-January they were at Old Orchard.

Hardy never complained or voiced regrets. He was tender with

Katie and Melissa, always gentle, increasingly tired. On fine days, he sat on the porch, gazing off across the river. He died in his sleep a few days after Melissa's third birthday in May. The doctor said it was his heart. Some whispered that drink had ruined him. Katie thought he died of broken dreams.

Johnny came for the funeral, helped carry his father's coffin to its place beside Vinnie, who had always had a special love for Hardy. Afterward, head lowered, Johnny said, "If I hadn't gone to work for Rance, maybe Dad would have kept the drilling outfit and we could have poor-boyed till we got some money."

"No. Johnny, he wanted a gusher. You helped him try. He really died the day he gave up on the well. And his health was gone. There wasn't anything left that he wanted to do that he could do."

Johnny picked up Melissa, who was a little shy of his stiff dark suit. "He loved Melissa—and you too, Mom."

"Yes. But he thought we'd be better off without him. Hardy *had* to be successful, dear, and he needed excitement." She blinked tears and swallowed. "He was happy those last months while we drilled. He dug deeper than any cable-tool rig ever had. He gambled all he had. There was . . . magnificence in his losing."

Johnny's young face twisted. "But, Mom! Dad—well, he never seemed to like me much. It was just this last year that we started to know each other."

Katie hesitated. Was it time? At some point, she had decided to tell Johnny about his true father, mostly because she couldn't bear to think that after she was dead, Darcy would be only a dim memory. Even if it made Johnny angry with her, she wanted him to know. But she had thought to explain when he was older.

It was watching Melissa bury her face against his brown throat that decided Katie, for her thoughts flashed back to another boy and girl who had grown up here at Old Orchard, she and Darcy. Johnny was sixteen years older than Melissa, but if one day their love changed, wouldn't it be best for them to know they were no blood kin? She felt she owed it to Hardy too, so Johnny could understand why the man he called his father had seldom behaved like one.

She began with telling how Talt had brought Vinnie his

motherless son—and here Katie reminded Johnny that Talt had been Mark's son, her own half brother. She told Johnny the story of her and Darcy through the mounded grave in San Roque de Ransom, and how Hardy had assumed the baby's parentage.

Johnny listened as if she were pulling veins and arteries out of him, leaving him bloodless flesh. One of the hardest things Katie had ever done was hold his dilating eyes with hers and continue on to the end. He set Melissa down and got to his feet.

"Is that all?"

Her throat constricted. She nodded, accepting as deserved her son's shocked outrage but begging for mercy.

He stood there, tall and strange in the new black suit. "No wonder Dad—Hardy—no wonder he didn't want to see any more of me than he had to!" His jaw ridged. "I guess I don't see why you waited till now to tell me if you had to tell me at all."

Each word lashed her. She bent away, clenched her hands in her lap. "I loved your father, Johnny. You look just like him. He—part of him lives on in you. I thought you ought to know it."

"All right. I know." He sucked in a ragged breath, turned, and left.

At the roar of the truck, Melissa's face puckered. She gripped Katie's skirt. "Johnny gone?"

"I don't know, honey." Katie took the child on her lap and hid her face in the soft dark hair.

It was close to midnight when Johnny came home. Katie put down her book and asked if he wanted something to eat. "No, thanks." He sat down on the edge of her footstool as he had done when he was little, though now he had to bend his knees. "Mother, I'm sorry I got mad. It—it felt like you were trying to take away the little I had of Dad." At her stricken protest, he smiled indulgently as if he were the older one. "Oh, I know you weren't. I'm sorry the man you loved so much got killed that way, that things never worked out for you. But it doesn't make any difference for me to know I'm Darcy Ransom's son. My father was Hardy Alastair."

Katie bowed her head with swift, hot tears, unutterably grateful that she hadn't forfeited her son. "I think he felt that way too,

Johnny, especially when you stayed with him to the end on the last well."

"You were with him too, Mom." Johnny smiled a little. "Even Melissa was."

Katie nodded. She reached out blindly. Johnny's arms closed around her as she clasped him and then they were weeping, comforting each other, comforting themselves.

Book Four ——————————————

MELISSA

I _____

Much as Melissa loved Gran, there had never been a time when Johnny hadn't been the sun of her life. She was light and happy when she was with him, dark and heavy when he was away. Tall, laughing, with hair black as her own and wavier, his green eyes held the warmth of sunlight. She thought if you could hear sunlight, it would be his voice. His strength had been her delight from the time he carried her on his shoulders. But he wasn't her brother; Melissa didn't exactly understand why. Nor was he an uncle, or her father, either.

She remembered her father, just a little. There were two enlarged pictures of him in her room, one as a Ranger, hat pulled low and a rifle in his hand as he sat on a big gray horse. The other showed him at a derrick, soaked from the gusher he had just brought in. There wasn't any picture of him at Castle Gap, out on the lonely plains of West Texas where he'd made his last gamble.

Melissa remembered her mother not at all but she had a little ivory box that held Rosalie's wedding ring, and a silver frame engraved with vines and roses held a snapshot from Hardy's wallet, faded and worn, but showing a face that Melissa was beginning to recognize as the one in the mirror, a triangle face turned heart-shaped by a widow's peak, with a long nose, and eyebrows that winged upward. Rosalie's mouth was thin, though, while

Melissa's was shaped in the generous curves of her grandmother's.

Of course, Katie wasn't really her grandmother, but that was just another of the mysteries grown-ups had, like why Rosalie wasn't buried with Hardy out by the great white stone carved with the names of the family who had planted an orchard here and raised the first cabin. Melissa knew about Vinnie and her judge and she knew that Hester was the mother of Talt Ransom who was Johnny's grandfather. She could remember the old man whose muscles were like corded rawhide and whose tawny eyes glowed from a leathery mask that cracked when he laughed.

Talt had lived at Old Orchard after deciding, at seventy-eight, that he could no longer do a twelve-hour tour on a well. He and Johnny often played chess of an evening while Gran played the piano or sewed and they listened to the radio. Melissa knew how, long ago, Vinnie had saved Talt by hiding him in the cave. It was fitting that these people whose lives had interwoven now slept beneath the roses, but there were breaks in the pattern. The judge's first wife, Regina, wasn't here, or Johnny's father, or Melissa's mother. Not that Melissa worried much about those puzzlements. She couldn't miss her mother when Gran was like one. And Johnny—he was everything, father and brother and something more.

Even when she understood the danger of his job, it never entered her mind to coax him to do anything else. She was proudly worshipful of his power to quench an inferno with explosives or fracture rocks far underground to send the oil flowing.

His office was in Pleasanton. When Melissa was twelve, instead of taking the school bus home, she started going to the brick building that had a cubbyhole office and big shed for storing and mixing explosives. She answered the phone, sitting behind the scarred old desk, and rode home with Johnny in his truck in time for supper.

If Johnny was out on a call, she'd catch a ride with Jim, Thaley's son. Thaley kept house and helped Gran cook. Her husband, Otis, took care of the orchard and yard. Johnny had a helper, Soup Morton, a heavy, balding man with twinkling blue eyes, who'd had the fingers of his right hand sheared off by the drilling cable as it wound around the bull wheel. He could still work on a rig with his thumb and stump of forefinger, but he felt he'd had a warning.

"Treat nitro with respect and it's safe as singin' hymns in church," he told Melissa as he carefully mixed the liquid explosive. "But on the derrick, there's a hunnerd things can go wrong that you can't do nothin' about—cable breakin', boiler exploding, well blowing in wild, gas knocking you out or catchin' fire." He stroked the torpedo almost affectionately. "At least this stuff has rules."

There were no rules to Johnny's bookkeeping and billing. From the number of people who came in to pay without being billed, Melissa guessed there were others not so honest. She was not disposed toward records or arithmetic, but since these were what Johnny needed, she got Katie's permission to take a business course that summer, and after that, she kept the books, sent the bills, and made sure the bank account was in order.

She was glad to help Johnny any way she could but what she really wanted was to go with him on his jobs, be there in case anything happened. On weekends he sometimes did take her on production shots.

"How do you know how much soup to use?" she asked after he had considered a while and then sent down a charge that brought in a good well. "How do you know what it's like down there at five thousand feet or more?"

"Well, there's the driller's log. Tells what they've hit and what they're drilling in, and if the hole's in a proven field, I'll know its history."

"Johnny! There's more than that."

He chuckled as he steered the truck deftly through some chuckholes and cast her an amused glance. "All right. It may sound crazy but I *think* myself down in the bottom. I can feel and smell and touch what's there. It's like I'm the charge myself and have to figure out if I can do what it takes or if I need more power or could do the job with less. And don't you go telling that to anybody."

She laughed, glowing at sharing his secret. "I won't." She sobered. "But Johnny, aren't you scared down there?"

"No. It's after I send down the charge that I start sweating. I've had torpedoes pushed right back up by a surge of gas or oil—and no matter what yarns you've heard, nobody catches a torpedo. Even if they weren't spewed up by tremendous pressure, they're slippery with oil, maybe eight feet long or more, and they weigh ninety pounds for a thirty-quart charge. I *have* put my foot over the hole and managed to stop the torpedo that way."

"You could have been killed!"

He shrugged. "Not much choice, honey. This well was so close to three others that you could jump from one derrick to the other. The torpedo would have hit the crown-block and exploded all over the place before the men could get clear."

Melissa shivered, but, if it were possible, adored him even more. A few days later, Soup was laid up with flu and Melissa persuaded Johnny to let her help him mix the explosives. "You would if I were a boy," she argued. "Soup says the mixing really isn't very dangerous."

"Mother would have my hide."

"What if she said I could?"

"I'd say you'd ganged up on me."

"Please! You did it when you were younger than I am."

"You already keep the books and send out bills."

She made a face. "Yes, because you and Soup don't. But I want to be able to do everything but set the charges—and I may learn that someday."

He gave her a strange look. It was as if he were seeing somebody else in her, someone he remembered with pain. "Melissa, this isn't the way you ought to be spending your time, holding down the office while you miss out on things your friends are doing."

"I go to parties and ball games. I'm in the Glee Club and Debating Society."

"Maybe, but—" His jaw hardened. "I'm going to hire a bookkeeper. I've been a pig, keeping you from enjoying yourself."

"But I *want* to help," she cried. At his scowl, she pleaded, "Can't you remember how you felt when you were my age? You went to school but hadn't you already decided what you wanted to do with your life?"

His face softened. He said, "I guess I knew since I was five and the folks took me to see the Fourth of July fireworks. I wanted to learn how to use whatever made those rockets and shooting stars and drifts of colored flame."

"Well, then?"

"We'll ask Katie."

The white in Katie's yellow-brown hair had lightened the waving mass that started as a neatly pinned knot each morning and was, by evening, a cluster of vagrant tendrils. At fifty-eight, Katie was straight-backed and slender. Her cheeks were hollowed and there were lines at the corners of her wonderful green eyes, but her smile was a blessing and her laughter came quick and warm after her first shock at Johnny's question.

Brow furrowing, she looked from one of them to the other. "You know explosives are just that, child?"

"Yes. But, Gran, I will be careful!" Melissa pressed her lips tight on further pleas.

Katie studied her son, having to look up at him for he was almost a foot taller. "You wouldn't argue, would you, if Melissa were a boy?"

"But she's not."

"Neither was I but I could have made a pretty good driller— and enjoyed it—if Hardy hadn't thrown a fit. That was thirty years ago. Now that so many men are off at war, look how many women are doing their old jobs, riveting and welding in defense plants. I think Melissa should have a shot at any job she wants, provided she can do it." Katie grinned. She still had all her white, strong teeth. "But you're the boss, Johnny."

"Hell I am!" He groaned. "With both of you after me! All right, Melissa. You can start helping with the soup. But one bit of foolishness and it's back to the front office."

"When," asked Katie sweetly, "are you going to pay her a salary?"

Johnny's eyes widened. "Why I . . ." He swallowed, coloring. "I'm sorry, Melissa. I just never thought. Of course you earn a salary. I'm collecting twice what I did before you started sending bills and keeping track of things."

"I don't want a salary."

"Of course you do," said Katie in the brisk way that meant no arguing. "Money is independence, girl, and it's a good thing for a woman to have a skill that'll let her earn her own way. You aren't really free if someone else pays your bills."

"I don't want my wife to work," growled Johnny.

"Neither did my husbands, but it was a good thing I could." Katie squeezed Melissa's hand. "I'm proud of you, dear. It's about time this family produced a woman who can work in the oil patch, and you've picked a line that'll get you respect."

"If it doesn't get her killed," Johnny muttered. But the next day he told Melissa to apply for a Social Security number and wrote her a check for back wages that made her head swim. When she protested, he said grimly, "You just go put that in savings, Missy, and by the time you're married, you can tell your husband you're independently wealthy and you don't have to wash his socks or cook his breakfast."

She didn't remind him that she did these things for him, or say it was her joy.

Johnny was attractive to women and sporadically took them dancing, dining, or to a movie. At thirty-one, he had been engaged only once, to a Dallas girl who had broken it off because he refused to give up explosives and take a post in her father's oil company. When the Japanese bombed Pearl Harbor two years ago, Johnny had rushed to enlist, but the local draft board refused to accept him. Oil was vital to the war effort and few men could fill his specialty.

No matter how he felt about it, he served the country better where he was. That didn't altogether ease his conscience, especially when thousands of young men died storming beaches in the Pacific, but after several appeals, he went on with his business, which, if it was any comfort, held more risks than those encountered by most servicemen. He drove himself as if he didn't deserve to enjoy the invitations women breathed over the phone, and often he didn't go home between jobs but caught a few hours sleep at the office and ate whatever Melissa or Soup fixed for him on the hot plate, before he loaded torpedoes in their special fittings at the back of the truck and headed off to bring in a well, rejuvenate an old one, or put out a fire.

There was no longer a problem about getting Melissa home. She'd gotten her driver's license at fourteen like many other rural youngsters, and drove Katie's battered pickup to Pleasanton and back except for Wednesdays, Katie's shopping day. When she was younger, Melissa had feared that each new woman Johnny went with would be the one he'd love, that he'd marry before she, Melissa, was old enough for him to see her as something besides his kid sister, which was the way he introduced her to customers.

She wanted to scream at him that she wasn't, but didn't since that would remind him of the painful fact that Hardy, whom he'd loved and considered his father, was not. Last year, Katie had finally drawn up a family chart for Melissa, including Hester and Talt and the judge's lost son, Fayette, who'd died in Mexico as Morgan Fayette.

"And his son bought Belleforest, Gran? Have you ever met him?"

"No. He became one of the richest men in the country by drilling slanted holes in the East Texas boom of the thirties. That is, he stole oil from other leases and ignored prorationing that had been set up to give all producers a share of what was a weak market. He piped illegal oil over into Louisiana and made millions." Katie looked back at something she didn't like and her mouth hardened. "He must have someone keeping an eye on Old Orchard though, because every time I've had money worries, his attorneys have written to ask if I'd sell."

Melissa thought of the graves by the white stone, the cave hiding the spring. "Oh, Gran, you never would!"

Katie hugged her. "No, love, I never would. I hope that either you or Johnny will live here and your children will grow up in this house just as I did and you have."

"I want that, too," murmured Melissa. She didn't voice the wish so deep that it amounted to a constant prayer, that the next children playing Vinnie's cherished piano and reading by the fireplace where they could glance up at Great-grandfather McCready's hunting knife or Great-grandmother's Bible, both carried by twelve-year-old Vinnie all the way from West Virginia, would be Johnny's *and* hers. If they weren't... well, if she couldn't have Johnny, she'd have no one at all. Sometime, surely, he'd have to see she was growing up. He already loved her, she knew that, but the way he did had to change.

He had been called out on a production shot the May day of 1943 when she turned fifteen, expecting to be home that evening for a chunk of fudge-frosted devil's food cake and home-churned ice cream. Melissa came home a little early to soak in lavender bubble bath, put on hose and high heels and a white piqué dress with a swirly skirt and low-cut sweetheart neckline. With a trembling hand, she applied mascara she had bought that day at the drugstore, and shadowed her eyelids with a pearly turquoise that the salesclerk had assured her would set off her blue-gray eyes. A hint of rouge, lipstick just a shade darker than natural, a white piqué headband that held the curls behind it in what Melissa thought was a sort of Madame Récamier disarray. She looked in the mirror with surprise and a mingling of delicious fear and joy. *I am beautiful—prettier than Mama, even. If Daddy left Gran for her, won't Johnny have to love me?*

She felt guilty for the thought. After all, it was Gran, not Rosalie, who had baked the cake for this birthday, for all of them. So as Melissa danced into the kitchen, she gave Katie a special hug and kissed her with fervor.

Katie kissed her back, noted the eye makeup, laughed as she said, "If you lick the frosting spoon, mind you don't get it on your dress."

"I'm too old to lick spoons now. I'll save it for Johnny."

"Who's twice your age, my darling!"

Melissa circled Katie's waist and swung her in a circle. "Oh, Gran, don't you see? That makes him young enough again!"

They smiled at each other with great love before Melissa got out the best china and began to set the polished old table.

II _____

Johnny had told them not to hold dinner since the well where he was working was many miles away and over a bumpy dirt road. They did wait, though, till the corn muffins were hard, the succulent peas creamed with tiny new potatoes turned mushy, and the salad wilted. "We'd better go ahead," Katie said as night spread from river and orchard to enfold the house. "Since it's so late, he'll surely eat on the way home."

Melissa nodded reluctantly. "But let's save the cake and ice cream."

So many things could happen to a shooter. She tried not to think about the truck hitting a bump and exploding as so many had over the years, pushed away those awful stories about a face peeled off like a mask, a body so obliterated that nothing identifiable could be found. Many a nitro hauler's remains had been scraped off the road into a bucket. Melissa compelled herself to eat these favorite foods Katie had prepared, but they stuck in her throat.

She and Katie were doing dishes when the phone pealed. Katie picked it up. After a moment, she handed it to Melissa. "You'll understand what's needed better than I do."

It was the driller of the well. Johnny had successfully sent down a charge that made the oil flow, but gas had erupted too and

281

the well caught fire. Though everyone in the field had rushed to fight the blaze and dig trenches to keep it from spreading, neither steam nor water could smother it. Johnny had asked the driller to call Soup and have him bring three or four thirty-quart torpedoes. When Soup didn't answer, Johnny told the driller to phone Melissa and ask her to find a driver who'd transport the load.

"Yes. Yes, I can do that." Melissa's mind whirred as she hung up. It was Saturday. Soup had said he'd be leaving right after work to drive down to Houston to visit his daughter, who had just presented him with his first grandchild. He was probably just about getting to Houston now; asking him to come back would add at least four more hours to the time it would take to deliver the explosives—and they'd be driven by an aging man who'd already spent eight hours on the road after a full day's work.

Every minute the fire raged was that much more danger for Johnny and all the men at the field. Melissa didn't want to waste time calling around till she found a good driver who'd take on the chore. The fastest thing, the best for Johnny, was to go herself.

Not wanting an argument with Katie, she spoke as she un-zipped the white dress and pulled it over her head, "I've got to go in and help whoever I get to drive to load the torpedoes. And I'd better ride along to make sure he doesn't go too fast and blow everything to smithereens."

Katie gave her a long look. "You know, I think *I'd* better go with the driver to make sure *she* doesn't hit those bumps too hard." Melissa's jaw dropped. "How did you . . . ?"

"I watched you." Katie smiled serenely. "Let me dump this coffee into a thermos and let's get on our pants."

The eight-foot-long cylinders weighed ninety pounds each, and Melissa and Katie were panting by the time they had clamped them firmly in padded compartments in the back of an old truck Johnny kept in case he ran out of explosives and Soup had to bring more. Katie winced as Melissa climbed under the wheel and shut the door with the force necessary to hold it.

"Be careful, Missy. We don't want your fifteenth birthday to be your last."

"Don't worry." Melissa shifted into gear "We aren't out to set speed records—just to get there."

Paving ran out at the Pleasanton city limits. Lights shone from an occasional farmhouse, but as it got later, there were not even these for company. Melissa was grateful for Katie's comforting presence, though it made her even more cautious. That, of course, was why Katie had come. Melissa consciously relaxed the tautness making her neck ache, and eased the truck gently into dips and smoothly up slopes, alert for anything that might cause her to brake. "Tell me about Dos Bocas, Gran."

Katie gave a startled laugh. "Gracious, child, I'd think you'd want a happier tale than that!"

"It was happy. You and Johnny's father came out of it alive. But tell me how the oil brine seethed and how scared you were—how you held to that root and to Darcy so he could climb up."

Katie did and the ice in Melissa's veins warmed a little as she gripped the wheel and prayed and thought, *Maybe someday I'll tell our children—Johnny's and mine—how we brought these torpedoes—how every mile lasts forever and the dark's so thick the headlights barely move it and then only for just a second till it closes in behind us again. It's as if there's nothing but this road and it's waiting to kill us. I'll be glad, even, to see that fire.*

She wasn't. At first a peachy glow on the horizon, then baleful redness that towered into inverted cascades of flame outlining derricks, tanks, and shadows that were men, the fire seemed to engulf the world. Melissa stopped among a mass of trucks, fire engines, and other vehicles, some occupied by people who had apparently driven out to watch. She directed a deadly wish at them before she jumped out of the truck and hurried toward the man striding her way in an asbestos suit, pushed-back helmet, gloves, and boots.

He gripped her arms. "Missy! For God's sake!"

"Gran's with me." Her legs felt as if they were dissolving. "We brought the soup."

His eyes blazed like the inferno behind him. "I'll see to you later!" He shouted to another man who brought an asbestos covering that they wrapped around one of the torpedoes. Then, alone, Johnny walked through the flames.

He lowered the torpedo into the hole, a priest intent on a rite that might appease his fiery god if the deity accepted it. Johnny moved back; there was a roar from the earth, a belching, gurgling rumble. And the terror died.

* * *

It was dawn when they sat down to birthday cake and ice cream. Less than a day had passed, but Melissa felt years older. Now that the drive through the night was over, she chilled to think what could have happened if she'd veered off the road or jarred the torpedoes.

That was nothing to the awe and dread of watching Johnny enter the fire. She knew it would haunt her dreams. But he had won; she had helped. And though he'd made her swear never to drive nitro again, he looked at her in a different way.

Maybe, she told herself, trembling as their hands brushed when she poured his coffee, maybe he was starting to see her as a woman. "Dad would be mighty proud of you," he said, smiling up at her.

Her joy was smothered by the way he claimed her father as his, making himself her brother. That wasn't what she wanted—and it wasn't even true!

After school was out that summer, Johnny often took Melissa with him on routine production shots. When these were far out in the country, she packed a picnic lunch and made thermoses of iced tea or lemonade as well as one of the strong black coffee Johnny liked. She set out their meal in the best shade they could find; often the only shade was a tarp rigged from the truck to a fence post, but sometimes, blessedly, a stand of live oak in a pasture or huge old cottonwoods or walnuts spread cooling green branches over a creek or riverbank. She so pleasured in his company that once he smiled at her in puzzlement, shaking his head.

"You shine, Missy. As if you had a light inside."

She didn't tell him that the light was love, that a man's touch from him would ignite it into flame that no explosive could quench. Surely, before too much longer, he must see that for himself? Surely by her next birthday.

They didn't have that long.

The last week in a humid, sweltering August, they were up near Borger and stopped there for lunch. They drove slowly, having two torpedoes clamped in the back. As they were passing through town, Melissa looked at the biggest trees and wondered if any of them could have been the one her mother had been chained to when Hardy paid her fine and took her home to love. As if reading her thought, Johnny said, "I never knew anyone as alive as your mother, Missy. She was only a few years older than I was, though she never saw me as more than a kid."

Melissa quailed at a quick stabbing certainty. "You loved her."

"How could I help it? I tried to hate her because Hardy left Mother for her, but the first time I saw her—she was a wild well, Missy. All that energy, that beauty. She tried to control it, she *wanted* more than anything to be a good wife to Dad, a good mother to you. But her own force blew her away."

Melissa shivered. She felt that force in herself when she longed for Johnny, but softening it was Hardy's steadier spirit and determination. And while Katie wasn't blood kin, Melissa had grown up safe in the strength of her loving kindness and must surely have absorbed at least some of that.

"I'm going to be a good wife," she said defiantly, and Johnny grinned at her vehemence.

"Sure you will, once you grow up and pick your man. That may be the tough part. I've noticed how the guys flock around when you're with me. I had to tell that young driller today that you're barely fifteen and it'll be two years at least before I let you go out with anyone from the oil patch. You need some practice first with high school boys."

Boys! Clenching her hands, she said fiercely, "When I go out, it'll be with a man, not a boy! And I think it's up to Gran, not you, to approve or disapprove."

Johnny whistled. He shot her a green-gold glance that made her feel as if she'd swallowed sun-warmed wine. "Mother's got good judgment. But sometimes a man, being one of the varmints, can pick up things a woman doesn't. You can like or lump it, honey, but till you're eighteen, I'm damn well meeting anyone you want to date. If you go off with a fellow I haven't okayed, just count on my turning up at the show or dance or wherever you are and getting to know him then."

"And what," she demanded frostily, "will you do if you don't like him?"

"I'll take you home myself."

"If—if you had the nerve to humiliate me like that, I'd run away!"

His face went stony. "And break Katie's heart?"

Melissa simmered but had to say, "Well, no, I couldn't do that."

Relaxing, Johnny gave her hand a swift pat. "Look, Missy, it's simple. Let me meet your beaux ahead of time and there'll be no fuss."

It sprang to her lips to tell him that he needn't worry, he could meet the only man she'd ever want by looking in the mirror, but the waking femininity in her wanted *him* to court her, to speak his love first. Yet how could he do that while he persisted in thinking of her as a sister?

She sighed, resigning herself to wait for a while longer, and at that moment, Johnny swerved off the road, veering along the soft earthen shoulder as a blurred, hurtling mass sideswiped their fender and careened into the opposite ditch, burrowing into the reddish embankment.

Melissa crouched forward, remembering the two torpedoes. The explosion, miraculously, didn't happen—not from the nitro, anyhow.

Johnny, white to the lips, braked to a stop as if trying not to break eggshells. He sprang out of the truck and sprinted to the ice-blue Cadillac convertible. Its elegant nose was jammed into the dirt, crumpling it and the bumper.

All that could be seen of the driver was a sheen of long red hair and tanned bare shoulders slumped over the wheel. Melissa, cold with fear, got out and reached the wreck almost as Johnny did. Melissa thought the strong smell meant there was a leak in the car, but then she saw the silver flask, its contents spilled across the soft gray suede upholstery.

Johnny's hands were careful as he lifted the driver's head and eased her back against the seat.

"Are you all right?" he asked.

Dark lashes opened to reveal russet eyes set off by high-arching feathered eyebrows. The long face was not beautiful, nose blunted at the end, chin overprominent, mouth too large, but as the light turned dark red hair into a crown of glory and the woman smiled up at Johnny, she was enchanting. Wiggling her wrists, flexing sandaled toes, she moved her head from side to side experimentally.

"I seem to be fine. Devil's luck, Dad would say." She glanced at the truck and her eyes widened. "My God! You're hauling nitro!"

"Yes." Johnny measured out some of his anger though he held back more. "It's a fluke that we weren't all blown sky-high." He reached over her, picked up the silver flask, and slung it as far as he could into the brush. "If you want to drink, do it at home."

"My drinking habits are none of your business."

"When you damn near killed me and Missy?" Johnny's eyes glowed. "You're old enough to know better, ma'am, but since you don't, I want your father's name and phone number—or your husband's."

Her slender throat tilted back; laughter came in rich, swelling waves. "Will you ask Dad to spank me? Sit me in a corner?"

"It's late for that," said Johnny tightly. "But he could lock up your car keys till you get some sense."

"He won't." She reached for an expensive lizard purse. "What'll it cost to fix your fender?"

"It's not that easy, ma'am."

She shrugged. "Well, if you're going to be tiresome about it, I'll give you an extra thousand."

"What you'll give me is your promise not to drive while you're drinking."

Amazement heightened her color. Unlike the skin of most redheads, hers was smooth and unfreckled, its tawny cream accented by her low-necked, sleeveless dress of white cotton figured with tiny apricot roses. Her legs were long and brown and her fingernails and toenails were tinted mauve. She was all careless style and, though she hadn't the hint of a wrinkle, Melissa judged her to be at least in her mid-twenties—grown-up, not waiting to be. Feeling the current between the woman and Johnny, Melissa's heart sank.

Studying Johnny, the stranger said, "What's to keep me from promising and then calling my bootlegger at the next filling station?"

"Not a thing. Except your word."

The amber stare probed him, challenged, and though a smile hovered on curving lips, the deep-pitched voice hesitated. "You mean that." She was puzzled.

Johnny straightened. "How about it, miss? Do I drive you to a garage or to the judge?"

She gave him a graceful lift of her shoulders. "All right. I promise. No more Jack Daniels in the car. Shall I sign my name in blood?"

"You're goddamn lucky that yours—and ours—is still where it belongs." He opened the door. "Come on. I'll drop you off at a garage that does good work." Her tapering fingers closed on his arm as she got out; she didn't let him go till he had helped her into the truck.

In between them, Melissa felt as if they were still touching and she was an awkward, inert barrier, one that ached and, wounded, curled into itself.

Katie stood very still before she picked up another apple and began to pare it. She and Melissa were making applesauce and jelly from the windfalls. "You want to bring Madge Fayette here?"

"I'd like to, Mother." Johnny didn't plead.

He didn't need to. After all, thought Melissa through a tumult of fear and pain and outrage, hadn't his mother, and she herself, for that matter, always wanted him to have what he wanted? But who could have dreamed he'd want Bernard Silks Fayette's daughter?

Dropping slices in the kettle, Katie sighed. "Does this mean—does it mean you're getting serious?"

Johnny chuckled. "Hey, Mom, haven't you been telling me for the last five years that I should do just that before I dry up into an old curmudgeonly bachelor?"

"But you haven't known each other very long. Not quite two months."

"Mother, if it weren't for the way you feel about her family, I'd have asked her to marry me weeks ago."

Melissa set down her bowl and fled. As she refuged in her room, closing the door, she heard Katie saying, "Of course, son, if you feel that way, it's time we met each other."

Madge was completely charming, deferential to Katie, admiring the house, standing in silence at Mark's grave before she slipped her hand in Johnny's and said huskily, "I'm his great-granddaughter. I hope he knows I'm here. We must be some sort of cousins, Johnny. Isn't that strange?"

"He's my grandfather," Johnny said with a grin. "But I'm not going to try to figure it out."

Melissa had. Madge's father was Johnny's cousin so presumably that made her a sort of second cousin. Of the four of them standing by the weathered white headstone, she, Melissa, was the only one not related to the judge, though she was also the only one blood-related to Hardy Alastair. She went to stand protectively beside his mound.

Madge gave her a half-smile and said to the man whose rapt face brushed her hair, "Now, darling, it's time you met my father, and Mrs. Alastair, I hope you'll come, too. We're giving a little party at the Petroleum Club now that Daddy's decided to build a house at Belleforest."

"He is?" asked Katie.

Madge nodded. "He'll still be in Houston most of the time, but he's always thought of having a house that would be as much like the original mansion as possible."

Katie was seldom flustered but it seemed the breath had been emptied from her before she recovered. "That'll be interesting," she said warmly. "It was a beautiful place, from what my mother said. And yes, of course I'd like to meet your father. We've had some business correspondence. I suppose you know, Madge, that he wanted to acquire this place because its history's intertwined with Belleforest's."

"Daddy's tenacious about some things," Madge said. "But if Johnny and I—oh, you know what I mean, Mrs. Alastair! It's wildly romantic, the mansion raised again, the old rifts healed." She gave Melissa the edge of her glowing smile. "Do you have a long dress, Missy? You'd be the youngest person there, but if you don't mind that, I'd love to have you at the party."

"I don't have a dress." It came out sounding normal though Melissa felt she was strangling. Before she could choke them back, scathing words tumbled out. "It—it's almost funny that your father's going to build back the house *his* father burned down!"

Katie gasped. Johnny barked, "Melissa!" But whirling blindly, she was gone.

III _____

Johnny and Madge were married early in December at Old Orchard with just the family, including Uncle Thos, still spry at eighty-six, Aunt Eulalia, and Rance Gorman, who had given Johnny his first job. The aging driller wasn't actual kin, but had been a customer of Katie's at her Baygall restaurant, a partner of Hardy's, and a good friend through the years. From the way the wiry driller, whose pockmarks had almost disappeared in his leathery face, hung around Katie, Melissa decided he was in love with her. This struck Melissa as both unseemly and ludicrous. Katie—well, she must be fifty-eight, at least, and Rance was older than that. Thank goodness Gran didn't seem afflicted with foolish notions and treated him only with direct and honest affection.

That was about Melissa's only satisfaction in those awful upside-down days that buried her hopes, nourished till the ring was slipped on Madge's finger, that Johnny would wake up, that he'd realize Madge was selfish and spoiled and probably wouldn't want him once she got him. But he hadn't. There was a rich luminance in the possessive pride with which he watched his bride, and when he kissed her to seal their vows, his brown hands held her as if she were the most precious thing on earth.

Melissa watched through a haze, suffering as if her chest had been flayed open to her naked, quivering heart. She would have given anything to have escaped sitting there while the minister's words buried her dreams, but there was no way to avoid it. She had refused, however, to accompany Katie down to Houston tomorrow for the huge reception Bernard Silks Fayette was hosting. His wife, Madge's mother, had died several years before, so he'd asked Katie to serve as hostess and she had agreed.

Bernard, with his pink cherubic face and thinning red hair, was a disappointment to Melissa. Katie had said little about her half brother, Fayte Sevier, who became Morgan Fayette after fleeing the fire he'd helped set at Belleforest. But Melissa sensed that there had been much more to Katie's troubles with him than that final encounter at Dos Bocas when he'd tried to kill Darcy and had slipped into the caldron. Melissa sent a glance toward Katie.

She must, as their son was married, remember Darcy, dead for thirty-two years. Did it still hurt? How could people live through such things? *Maybe the way I'm sitting through this wedding,* Melissa thought bitterly. Part of the worst of it was that she couldn't tell anyone, not even Gran, how she really felt. They'd say it was puppy love, that she hero-worshipped Johnny as a big brother. She couldn't bear that.

Everyone was standing. Swallowing breath that seared her lungs, so did Melissa. Oh, if only she could go through the floor or roof or wall—be anywhere but here! Then, as if by a lance thrust, she was transfixed by Madge's amused stare.

"You look like the end of the world, Melissa. Heavens, I'm not taking Johnny off to the South Pole. Aren't you going to wish us happy?"

Flushing, Melissa looked past the woman who contrived, in her ivory satin and lace-medallioned gown, to look both regal and virginal. Eyes on Johnny's perplexed face, Melissa gulped and said, "I wish you happy." She endured Madge's fleeting kiss.

"Thank you, dear," said Madge.

Mockery edged her smile, and Melissa determinedly kept her head high though she felt her pride draining away. She hadn't told her secret to Katie or to anyone who might have helped her bear it, but Madge knew, and she drew pleasure from Melissa's pain.

"As you know," Bernard was saying to Katie in what was meant to be an ingratiating manner but which came off overbear-

ing. "I've always hoped to unite Belleforest and Old Orchard."
He winked pudgily. "You mustn't think, though, that Madge staged
this marriage out of concern for her poor old dad's wishes. I was
beginning to think she'd never meet a man she'd marry who'd have
the stuff to take her on." His pale gray eyes appraised Johnny as if
examining a racehorse. "When they have their first son, I'll sign
Belleforest over to him. If he's named for my father."

Katie tensed. "That's up to them," she said amiably, turning to
answer some question of Rance's, and Melissa knew with startled
shame that Katie too was tormented by this marriage, and for
reasons older than Melissa or even Johnny, though she'd said
nothing about it, and had been only gracious and welcoming to
Madge.

Could it be the vibrant, living face brought back memories of
that mysterious half brother who must have been, in some terrible
way, something more than that?

Before Johnny and Madge had been a year married the new
Belleforest rose white and majestic among huge dark oaks. Bernard gave a Christmas ball, his daughter acting as his hostess. She
had asked Katie and Melissa to serve eggnog and hot buttered
rum. Though Melissa took it for a taunt that the Fayettes now
possessed the homeplace of Katie's father, she accepted in order
to keep Katie company, to avoid offending Johnny, and out of a
desire to see what Bernard's expensive Houston architects had
produced from the old plans and drawings of the original Belleforest that had been safe in the judge's Pleasanton office when the
house burned.

At Bernard's urging, they arrived early so that he could show
them around. Melissa searched for ostentation or false notes, but
she searched in vain. From the brick-paved ground floor with the
breezeway running through it, through the drawing room,
ballroom, and great hall on the main floor, the bedchambers and
dining room on the upper story, the bannisters, wainscoting, and
mellow oak floors were waxed to reflect soft light from chandeliers and sconces. Draperies and rugs in muted tones comple-
mented tasteful wallpapers and antique furniture that had cost a
fortune. Madge joined the tour, and as they returned to the drawing room, she touched the rosewood piano that much resembled
Vinnie's at Old Orchard.

"Can you see why I'd love to live here?" she demanded of them. "Daddy wouldn't care. He won't get up here more than a weekend or so a month. Don't you think it's wicked, Katie, for this to just be here with nobody living in it?"

"It's your father's home, dear," said Katie diplomatically. "And it might get dull for you out here in the country."

"It's dull in Pleasanton." Madge's velvet dress was a deep garnet that should have warred with her hair but instead matched lights from it. She examined her wedding ring as if it hurt her finger, moving it up and down. "If we have to be buried in the hinterlands, Belleforest at least has style."

"You're welcome to it, pet," said Bernard indulgently. "Face it, though. You'd throw some famous parties but you'd still be bored." He spread appealing hands to Katie. "Can you talk your hardheaded son into moving to Houston and being my partner? When I bring it up, he goes all cold and formal and insulted, but there's really more in Houston than I can handle."

Katie's erect back stiffened. "I've never talked Johnny into— or out of—anything, Bernard. He's worked hard for his business and it's what he loves to do."

"Yes," agreed Madge viciously. "He gets his fun from wrestling torpedoes, shooting wells, and dousing fires. So when and if he comes home nights, he's too tired to go out or even—even—" Madge bit off whatever she'd been going to say and gave a tight, jeering little laugh. "His idea of a perfect evening is a hot shower, slouchy old clothes, a shot of whiskey, a great meal that I'm supposed to miraculously know when to start fixing, and then the paper, radio, and beddy-bye."

Katie's voice was dry. "That sounds like what most men want who've put in a physically hard day. As I recall, Madge, you had some problems with this before you married. You must have known he can't do his job and dance and go to parties."

"I didn't think he'd be so damned stubborn. If he'd work for Daddy—"

"My dear," said Katie in a firm but courteous way, "this is nobody's business but yours and Johnny's. You'll have to work it out. But think about this: would you want a man who would, in effect, draw a salary from your father for being at your disposal?"

Madge's jaw dropped. Her eyes glinted but before she could speak, Bernard hugged her and chuckled. "It's true, you know, sugar. Playboys bore you. Have a baby, why don't you? That'd fill your time."

"I don't want a baby!" Madge whirled on Katie. "Johnny's told me all about how you followed your husband around to ratty places and let him sink every dime he had in that dry hole out at Castle Gap. *He* thinks that's great. *I* call it stupid!"

"Madge!" rebuked Bernard.

Katie shrugged, gave her daughter-in-law a straight look, and smiled reflectively. "Maybe it was. But Hardy gave me a lot, too. Looking back, the only thing I'm sorry for is that I didn't give him more."

More? More than to raise the child he'd had by the woman for whom he'd divorced her? Again, Melissa was humbled by Katie.

Katie's declaration brought furious color to Madge's cheeks, but before she could speak, Bernard caught her wrist.

"Cars coming up the drive, sugar."

"Oh, God! The local gentry!" Madge picked up a crystal decanter and poured herself a stiff drink. "Johnny swore he'd try to be here—but is he? Has he called? Of course not. If he makes it at all, it'll be just in time to drive me home."

With a frown at the glass she had half emptied in two swallows, her father said, "Put down that drink and go greet your guests."

"*Your* guests, Daddy," she snapped. "I don't *have* any friends in this lousy little burg." She tossed down the rest of the whiskey, smoothed her hands along her hips, and moved down the hall as the bell sounded.

Johnny, wearing the slate-gray suit he put on for funerals, arrived in time to dance several numbers with his wife. Gracefully following the music, his dark head bent to her bright one, they were the handsomest couple in the great ballroom, but neither was smiling, and Johnny's eyes were so hollowed that Melissa suspected he'd had no sleep the night before. Bernard proffered his cup to Katie for more eggnog and said, "Their kid should be good-looking with smarts to match."

"You're speaking theoretically, of course."

"They haven't told you? Madge's dancing days are about over for a while. They're expecting in May."

If Katie was upset because she hadn't been told, she didn't

betray it. "May's a good time to have a baby. Texas summers are endless when you're heavy and uncomfortable."

"Madge won't be uncomfortable alone, you can bet." Bernard touched the rim of his cup to Katie's. "Here's to our grandchild! What would our folks think about this? Would they be glad? Or horrified?"

Katie drank the toast. "I think it's as you say, Bernard. Our children will have a wonderful baby. That's all that counts."

Melissa felt sicker by the minute. One part of her had hurt for Johnny when he looked strained and unhappy, but another part had guiltily rejoiced that he was learning Madge wasn't right for him—or for any man who wasn't content to devote all his energies to her. They'd both be better off apart. But a child . . . Johnny couldn't leave a baby to Madge's caprices, especially since she drank a lot more these days, or perhaps just bothered less to hide it.

He was properly caught; he'd never get away. Blurting an excuse, Melissa fled to an upstairs bathroom. She cried and washed her eyes, thought she had control of herself, then imagined a child that looked like Johnny, one she could never have, and sobbed even harder.

The baby came May 23, 1945, two weeks after Melissa's seventeenth birthday, while the Allies, after storming the beaches at Normandy, battled for France. Named Katharine Marguerite after both grandmothers, the tiny, perfect girl had a soft fluff of gold-red hair and, as the newborn mistiness disappeared, eyes of gold-mottled green. Prepared to loathe this bond that manacled Johnny to Madge, Melissa fell captive the first time she stayed with Kitty while Johnny took Madge to dinner and a movie.

"I'd never want to leave her," she told Katie next morning. "She's so warm and soft and *new*—those teensy fingers! There's a dimple in her cheek that moves while she's having her bottle and she works so hard at that bottle, even pushing from her toes."

"She's a darling," agreed Katie, who stayed with the baby several afternoons a week so Madge could go shopping and have her hair done. "Isn't it funny about Bernard? He took one look at her, forgot about wanting a boy, and deeded Belleforest to her."

"Reserving the drilling rights," Melissa said dryly. "Well, she may have Madge's hair, but she has your eyes, Gran, and your face. She'll be more Alastair than Fayette."

The moment she said it, she wished she hadn't. Johnny was Alastair only in name. Katie looked stricken, but only for a second. "Kitty's Sevier on both sides. To be honest, Missy, she looks a good deal like her Great-grandmother Regina, to judge from portraits. She's got lots of people in her, but she'll shape all of it into somebody absolutely herself. That's the wonderful part."

"She's still *our* baby, Gran."

Katie looked a little sad. "Yes. I think she is."

That gave Melissa the push to ask something that had been worrying her. "Gran. Do you—well, do you think Madge doesn't like babies?"

"She's never been around them, dear."

"And she's not around Kitty more than she can help."

"It's a big change for her."

Melissa snorted. "She hasn't quit drinking and she smokes more than ever. She got furious when Johnny wanted her to nurse the baby."

"Lots of women are afraid nursing will ruin their breasts."

"That's what they're *for!*"

Katie's lips twitched. "Not entirely. Anyway, I don't think mother's milk, given unwillingly, helps a child much. I doubt if Madge dislikes Kitty as much as she finds her a nuisance and not very interesting." At Melissa's hot protest, Katie raised a hand. "Wait till Kitty's about two, able to walk and talk and look adorable. Madge'll change her clothes six times a day and keep her hair all curled and ribboned."

"Kitty's not a doll," Melissa retorted.

"No, and she won't let Madge forget that, believe me. Give them time."

Johnny's business paid well enough to afford a motherly woman, Mrs. Bartlett, who came in daily to clean, do laundry, and help with the baby. By the time she got back her figure, Madge was spending most of her day at the country club, swimming, playing bridge and tennis, just as she had before Kitty.

Katie knew this, but she still stayed with her granddaughter two afternoons a week, much to Mrs. Bartlett's relief, since it gave the woman some uninterrupted hours to get her work done. Johnny, however fatigued he was, made a point of taking Madge out several times a week. Melissa delighted in those evenings with the baby, but she couldn't stifle scornful resentment at

Madge for making everyone else put themselves out to keep her in a reasonable humor. You'd think having a baby was a sentence to which she'd been unjustly condemned; and she expected compensation from the world in general and Johnny in particular.

On the occasional day when Mrs. Bartlett couldn't be there, Madge would come by the office and ask Melissa to take care of Kitty. This was no big problem since the baby still slept much of the time, and usually Melissa could put aside her accounts long enough to enjoy cuddling her while she had her bottle, or carry her around the room so that Kitty could gaze at the calendars and pots of geraniums and begonias. One day, however, Madge walked in while Soup and Melissa were cleaning the shed.

"What a mess," said Madge, wrinkling her nose. "Well, I'll just leave Kitty here in her basket. She'll want her bottle in a little while."

Melissa straightened. It was so obvious that she was and would be busy. "I'm sorry, Madge, but I'm too dirty to touch the baby, and we want to get through with this today."

"It shouldn't take both of you. Surely you can clean yourself up, Melissa, and do some bills or something while you watch Kitty."

Melissa was hot and tired and knew Madge was off to play bridge and sip iced drinks. Brushing back a strand of hair that had glued itself across her forehead, she clipped her words. "I'm not your hired help, Madge. I work for Johnny."

"And that's not all you'd like to do for him, is it?" Madge's white teeth showed between thinned lips. "I bet you rub against him every chance you get."

The attack was so sudden and preposterous that Melissa stared in disbelief before her wrath exploded. "You would think that, you lazy bitch! You've got the best man in the world and the sweetest baby but you don't want to do a thing for them. You're mean and nasty and—and—"

"At least my mother wasn't a whore chained out on a boom-town street," said Madge with a poisonous smile. "If Katie hadn't been soft and given Hardy Alastair a divorce, *you'd* be a bastard —and it won't surprise me when you turn up with a few of your own." Madge's eyes glittered. "They'd just better not be my husband's!"

Furious as she was, Melissa realized that she wasn't dealing with a responsible person. She'd smelled the whiskey on Madge's breath. Her anger froze, allowing her to put it aside for the moment. "You're drunk, Madge, or out of your head. You shouldn't be driving. Let Soup take you home. I'll keep the baby and send her home with Johnny."

Soup was right there, but Madge didn't lower her voice. "Morton gives me the creeps—those pink nubs instead of fingers. If that happened to Johnny, I couldn't stand for him to touch me. I've already told him that!"

She began to cry, and then Madge's insults were nothing to the horror that gripped Melissa. Johnny was married to a woman like this! Sick at heart, she said, "Soup can watch the baby. I'll drive you home."

Madge began giggling through her tears. "I guess you'd better. I'm seeing three of everything."

When they reached the pleasant brick house on the edge of town, Melissa had to shake Madge to rouse her enough to get her into the house. Slipping off Madge's shoes, Melissa left her on the bed and slipped out of the house with a miserable sense of having intruded on Johnny's private life, of having seen what she shouldn't have. How would Johnny manage unless Madge changed?

When Johnny, in from a field near Dallas, asked why his wife's car was in front of the office, Melissa said she had suddenly not felt well and had to be driven home.

Johnny stared at her, jaw hardening. Melissa couldn't meet his eyes. Without even a cup of coffee, he picked up the baby and went to his truck.

"What'll he do, Gran?" Melissa wept. "If she takes Kitty in the car with her when she's like that—"

"She won't. Johnny'll do something."

His first remedy was to impress on Mrs. Bartlett that when she couldn't come, she must send a reliable substitute. This was simple, since her niece, sister, and eldest daughter all needed work. Johnny's surprising feat was in getting Madge to go to a "health resort." This was done with Bernard's help, for apparently Bernard's ready acceptance of Johnny as a son-in-law was rooted in mounting despair over his daughter's drinking.

While she was gone, Johnny and Kitty stayed at Old Orchard,

and wrong though it was, Melissa would have rejoiced at having them there except for Johnny's pain. He spoke briefly and matter-of-factly about Madge, but he lost weight, drove himself even harder, and the only time he smiled was when he played with Kitty.

He looked stunned, though, when, holding his daughter, news came that the United States had destroyed the city and people of Hiroshima with the atom bomb. Katie took the baby from him and sheltered her protectingly. They were all thinking that babies sweet and fresh as Kitty had died in Japan. The war would have to end now but the world would never be the same.

At the end of August, Madge came home. "It seems strange without Kitty and Johnny, Gran," Melissa said as she prepared, without enthusiasm, for her senior year of high school.

"It was stranger for them to be here, Missy." Katie watched her in a way that brought hot blood to Melissa's face.

So Katie knew. Did everyone know except Johnny himself? Compressing her lips, Melissa started ironing a batch of fall cottons. Her classes seemed to have nothing to do with her, and her plan to study geology in order to form a partnership with Johnny was impossible now, at least the partnership aspect of it.

She couldn't stop loving him, but she had to stop letting him fill up her heart. If she could endure it, she'd work for him till school was out, but then she had to go away, begin a life of her own because she could not share his. Oh, but she would miss him! Him and Kitty and Gran. It would tear her heart out by the roots but what else could she do?

IV _____

Madge seemed to have no memory of the day she'd called Melissa's mother a whore. She was pleasant enough when they met, which was seldom. She had stopped drinking and, in one of those tacit bargains struck by married people, Johnny had agreed to move to Belleforest. Bernard employed a staff though he was seldom there, but Johnny continued to pay Mrs. Bartlett and her niece to look after his family.

Even so, it must have gone much against the grain to live under his father-in-law's roof in a style far beyond Johnny's means. But if that was the price he had to pay for Madge's sobriety, he was evidently resolved to do it. He took on more distant jobs and was gone much of the time, but they seemed to have struck a livable compromise.

Compromise! What did that have to do with loving? To Melissa, who would gladly have traded a long life without Johnny for a short one with him, the situation was grotesque and continually mocked her feelings. She dated a few classmates but they were so callow that she gave up on that. Her work at the office had kept her from making girl friends and she felt isolated from both her contemporaries and Johnny.

Gran—well, Gran was there, the rock foundation she'd always been. But Melissa could no longer be sure what she herself might do. Her rebellious rage was like one of Johnny's charges; it wouldn't take much to explode it.

This must be how Rosalie had felt when she took the first step to that shameful chaining, and perhaps what had driven her to leave her baby and the man who loved her. Melissa was terrified by her own desperation, the recklessness that whispered Madge wasn't the only person who could drink, that there were many ways to go to hell and maybe then Johnny would be sorry. . .

She pulled herself up harshly. Gran deserved better than that. Yes, and the dead father Melissa could barely remember for all his love and sacrifice and shame, he deserved that his daughter in some measure justify his choice. She told herself to keep busy and get through the crawl of time till graduation.

All plain enough, though cruelly hard to do. Since she couldn't live with Johnny, she must find a way to live without him. In her present mood, she'd like to be a shooter herself.

Perhaps Madge felt that way too, but her way of setting charges was to speed, racing police till her license was suspended despite Bernard's influence, and to give elaborate parties at Belleforest. That diversion coincided with Bernard's political ambitions, the most urgent of which was to be appointed to the Railroad Commission, the powerful agency that regulated the oil and gas industry and decided how much a producer could pump. Bernard had a lot of enemies, going back to the last big boom, East Texas in the thirties, when he'd had his drillers slant crooked holes, and compounded his felonies by secretly piping hot oil into Louisiana. Though some of his drillers went to jail, Bernard hadn't. Now, with his beautiful daughter as hostess, he was intent on making friends who could help him into the position he craved.

Johnny disliked the kind of party Madge gave and he detested those filled with political figures. As Madge complained, he appeared just often enough to show that they were still married.

That Christmas she gave a dinner dance the governor had promised to attend, as had a senator, several representatives, and a passel of state legislators. There would be house guests from Houston, Dallas, Midland, and West Texas. It was the most ambitious entertainment Madge had attempted and her arrangements had the precision and aura of a battle plan.

A week before, when she and Johnny came to dinner at Old Orchard, she invited Katie and Melissa. "I'd appreciate your help so much," she said. "With that many people, I can't look after them all myself." There was an edge to the smile she gave her husband. "Johnny's not much good at moving around and doing introductions. He gets in a corner with some friend of Mr. Alastair's or a former driller and that's it—when he condescends to be there at all. I especially set this party for his birthday *and* Christmas when he surely wouldn't be going out on some stupid well."

"I go when I'm called." Johnny's tone was expressionless. "You never asked me when you fixed the date, Madge. I'd put off anything but an emergency to spend Christmas with you and Kitty, but my last idea of celebrating a holiday is to fill up the house with politicians and wheeler-dealers."

Madge's thinly tweezed eyebrows climbed and it wasn't rouge that colored her cheeks. "Are you saying you'll go to *work?*"

"I will if I'm needed."

Their eyes dueled. She set down her coffee cup very carefully. "This means a lot to me, Johnny. If you're going to humiliate me—"

"I think we'd better go home. Excuse us, Mother, Melissa. The food was wonderful." He got to his feet and picked up Kitty who, at almost seven months, liked to rock on her knees and was starting to crawl. "Kiss Gran and Missy good night, baby."

She laughed and tangled her fingers in their hair while they kissed her. "Thanks for dinner," said Madge. She snatched up her coat and rushed out ahead of Johnny, who kissed his mother before he followed.

Katie shook her head. "I hope they learn to get along before Kitty's old enough to get caught in the middle."

"She wanted Johnny because he stood up to her," Melissa said with bitterness. "Now she wants him to act like a gigolo."

"Not really, child."

"How do you keep from telling her off?"

"I've got a well-bitten tongue," Katie said, smiling. "Anything I said would just cause more trouble, anyway. Sit down, honey, and let's have our chocolate mousse. At least they'd finished except for dessert."

* * *

Christmas Eve, Johnny and his family came to Old Orchard for dinner and exchanging gifts. Capacious red wool stockings that Katie had knitted and embroidered with each name hung from the mantel. Enchanted by the lights and tree ornaments, Kitty looked like an elf in her crimson stockings and hooded sweater. One of her presents was a rocking swing horse and she sat in it among a heap of stuffed animals, cloth books, pull toys, and dolls. Bernard's present, given by Madge in his absence, was a savings account in Kitty's own name, funded with ten thousand dollars. He'd been invited that night but was entertaining the governor and several Houston friends.

Watching the baby was the only joy of the evening for Melissa, though Katie had made gingerbread men and hot mulled cider to enjoy while she played carols on the piano. Johnny and Melissa stood behind her and blended their voices with hers as they had since childhood in the dear, familiar songs, but Madge was restive and finally said, "Look, darling, this is lovely, but we need to take Kitty home and put in an appearance at three open houses."

Katie's fingers drooped for a second on the keys but she rose immediately and smiled. She took her daughter-in-law's hands. "Thanks for coming, dear. Merry Christmas."

She and Melissa sang on for a while, but it wasn't the same—and it never would be if Madge had her way. Katie got up from the piano and began salvaging the best paper and ribbons. "Wasn't Kitty a sight? Next year, she'll really have a time."

Melissa gave a laugh. "So that's how you do it, Gran."

"Do what?"

Sinking on her knees, Melissa gave Katie a hug. "You find the good thing and concentrate on that."

"What's the alternative?" said Katie, grinning. She had on a green dress that matched her eyes, and the soft light was kind to her face and hair. She still was beautiful, though it was more a beauty of the spirit. She said, suddenly wistful, "Anyway, the baby is a love. I'd like to think my parents saw her tonight. But most of all . . . Darcy died so young, Missy, so far from home. I hope he knows he has a granddaughter."

Melissa hugged Katie again. "I'll bet he does." Her throat was tight. Parents didn't always love their children, at least not enough. She hadn't been much older than Kitty when Rosalie ran off.

That night, for the first time in her life, Melissa dreamed of her mother. She knew it was Rosalie though the woman ran from her down a long tunnel with a bottom so slippery that Melissa kept falling down, calling, "Mother! Mother!" as she struggled to get up.

The dream left Melissa depressed and restless, so even though it was Christmas Day, she went to the office to catch up on accounts, made a grilled cheese sandwich for lunch, and worked till time to go home and dress for Madge's party.

How that woman blackmailed them! Katie would never choose to go to that sort of affair, which Melissa also loathed, yet when Madge asked them, they went for the sake of peace in the family.

It was a troubled peace. Madge had asked them to come early and she met them at the door, brushing aside Katie's admiring comment on the white Grecian gown that bared one shoulder.

"Do you know where Johnny is?" she demanded of Melissa, ignoring Katie.

As was her habit, Melissa had glanced at the log that morning. "I haven't seen him, but the log said Dutch Humphrey needs to prove to his backers that he's got oil before they'll give him another dime. So Johnny's gone to try to shoot the well. It's not far, maybe fifteen miles. He ought to be back before the party."

He should, in fact, have been back long ago, unless something had gone wrong. As always when Johnny was on a job longer than he should be, dread gripped Katie, made it a conscious effort to breathe. But Madge wasn't frightened. She was infuriated.

Grinding out her cigarette, she said in a shaking voice, "He's not going to get away with this! I'm going out there and he'll come straight home or he needn't come at all!"

"Madge, dear," began Katie, but her daughter-in-law ran to the front closet, hurled on a coat, and snatched her car keys off a hook. "We should be back before people start arriving, Katie, but if we're not, you and Melissa can do the greeting."

"I think I'd better drive you," said Melissa. Oh Lord, had something happened? "The road to Humphrey's lease is mucky; we'll need a truck. You'd better change that dress if you don't want to ruin it."

"Goddamn him! Working in all that stinking mud and oil when he doesn't have to!"

"Don't bad-mouth oil, sugar," advised Bernard, suddenly appearing, as if he'd been keeping out of the way till someone was there to act as a lightning rod for his daughter's rage. "Why don't you stay here? The party'll go ahead just fine without your hubby but it does need you."

"We'll be back."

He sighed, but he picked up the intercom and told one of the gardeners to bring a truck around in front. "Remember, Madge, you'll get further with a man like Johnny using kisses and 'pretty pleases' than you will with vinegar."

She ignored him and sent a maid for two pairs of rain boots. "You'll need a pair, too," she said to Melissa. "I don't want you looking scuzzy at the party. We can kilt up our skirts under our coats."

Katie, of course, knew Melissa was worried. They had both expected Johnny to be home. The oil fields were much safer than they'd been at the turn of the century when Katie's first husband died at Spindletop, but no one knew better than she how deadly the work could be. Not for the first time, it occurred to Melissa that it took immense self-control for Katie not to plead with her only child to give up his dangerous calling. All Katie said, though, was, "Drive carefully, Melissa."

The road to the lease was a quagmire; Melissa stayed in second gear, fighting the wheel, trying to keep from lurching off the road. It was entirely possible that Johnny was stuck someplace—and with all her heart, she hoped it was nothing worse than that. "Can't you go faster?" Madge demanded. "At this rate, it'll take us an hour to get there."

"Look at the road," invited Melissa. "We try gunning down it and we'll be in the ditch."

"We'll be late for the party!"

"Damn your party."

"I knew you didn't care about it! Or care how I feel, you little bitch! I'll bet you only offered to drive in order to make me turn up late and look silly!"

"It doesn't take me to make you look silly. You are!" The truck skidded. Melissa set her teeth so tight they ached and got the vehicle back in the ruts. "What doesn't enter your mind, I guess, is that Johnny might not be *able* to come home."

Madge started to scoff, caught the meaning. "You—you mean—"

"I don't know. I hope not. But that's why I came. Otherwise you could have taken off in your Caddy and been mired to the hubs by now for all the difference it'd make to me."

Madge chewed on that. Melissa could only hope that being jarred into considering her husband's danger would soften Madge's anger even if they found him safe—and God grant they did.

Pump jacks were working on both sides of the road, dipping up and down like those mechanical birds that rhythmically dip their beaks to water and lift them out. Madge stared at the lettering on the containers in a big tank farm. "FAYOIL—why, that's one of Daddy's subsidiaries. I didn't know it operated outside of East Texas."

"The Humphrey lease is just ahead. Look, there's the derrick." Melissa relaxed slightly when she saw no sign of fire. "And there's Johnny's truck." Now that it appeared he was all right, she shrank from invading the field. "Madge, he's been held up by something. Why don't we turn around and get you back for the party?"

"Are you crazy? I didn't come out here because I love churning around in mud. Johnny's got to get it through his head that he can't do me this way!"

"Well, at least let me go tell him you want to see him, you can say whatever you have to here at the truck. If you put on a show for all the men, you may just wreck any chance your marriage has."

Madge gave a fleeting laugh. "I should think that's exactly what you'd like."

"I don't give a damn about you," Melissa said flatly. "But I do about Johnny. And you're what he wants—God only knows why."

"Well, aren't you noble!"

Melissa said nothing. Maneuvering through the ruts, she pulled up beside Johnny's truck. Several torpedoes were still in their clamps. Madge eyed the ankle-deep muck with disgust and turned, grimacing, to Melissa. "All right. Wade through that mess if you want to, but get him over here damn fast!"

"He's just sending down a charge," Melissa told her. "See? They've lowered the torpedo with that cable. I can't bother him right now."

"Scared?"

"Not especially. Johnny knows what he's doing. But he won't budge till he knows if the charge worked."

"Sweet Jesus!" cried Madge, wrenching open the door and tucking up her skirts beneath her coat. "You'll always have some stupid excuse!"

She pelted through the slime, which glistened with the shows of oil that had kept Humphrey drilling deeper. Melissa, swearing under her breath, jumped out too, though she could scarcely haul Madge forcibly back to the truck. The woman hadn't a dog's hair of common sense. Sloshing toward the derrick, Melissa groaned as Madge yelled up at her husband who gave her one disbelieving look before all his attention riveted on the hole again and he turned his back.

That sent Madge into fury that even she must have known she had to control. She fumbled in her purse and brought out a cigarette and lighter.

"Don't!" Melissa cried and lunged for Madge even as she heard a sound like a giant whisper coming from the hole and saw the line go slack.

She knew what that meant even before Johnny shouted, "It's coming back up! Run! Madge, get out of here!"

Gas or oil or both were welling up, driven by tremendous pressure, thrusting the torpedo upward. If it hit the crown-block, it would explode the whole derrick. But Madge, angry, ignorant of the true situation, perhaps thinking Johnny was trying to bluff her, flicked open the lighter in the same instant Johnny set his heavy boot over the head of the torpedo, forcing it to stay beneath the rim, taming its impetus so that, straining, with infinite care, he allowed it to come up easily. He clasped the oil-slick container, setting it down gingerly on the derrick floor.

A fountain of black oil gushed up simultaneously, and before it could be capped, the spark of Madge's lighter exploded the world. Melissa had seized Madge's wrist a second too late. They hurtled together against the engine house. Melissa struggled to see Johnny, glimpsed him running for his truck, and then something was falling on her. Melissa threw up a shielding arm, tried to drag Madge out of the way, but there was no time. Crushing weight on her ribs, a sweep of flame above, and then impact on her head that snapped out her consciousness.

Rousing slowly through layers of aching confusion, she thought she was pinned beneath parts of the exploded derrick. But she found that she could move, and there wasn't any smell of oil or fire.

"Johnny!" She tried to rise but a sledge drove into her skull.

Hands soothed her. "Johnny's alive, dear—hurt, but he'll be all right."

Melissa opened her eyes and looked at Katie; beyond her was what could only be a hospital room. She touched the bandage on her head, winced at the pain in her chest. "Madge?" she whispered, and Katie's face gave the answer.

"Madge died instantly. Part of the crown-block hit her. It was a miracle no one else was killed."

"But the fire—?"

"Johnny put it out. But wind had swept sparks to the FAYOIL tank farm and pumping wells. All in all, it destroyed over a million dollars worth of oil and equipment. Let's not talk about that now, honey. You had a concussion and got about half your ribs smashed."

"But I'm not dead." Suddenly, because Madge was, Melissa began to cry, not so much because of what that would do to Johnny, but simply because, though Melissa had often hated her, Madge had been so vital, so alive; it was monstrous that she could cease, in just a twinkling, to exist.

Crying hurt both ribs and head and Melissa stifled her sobs as soon as she could. Grasping Katie's hand, she said, "Johnny? Where is he?"

"He was burned putting out the fire. Because you and Madge were so close to the derrick, he didn't take time to put on his asbestos clothes."

Melissa cringed, and felt flames searing her own body. "But you said he'll be all right?"

"He'll live. But he'll need a lot of skin grafts. And his right hand, Missy, it's burned to a sort of stump."

A shocked silence. Then Melissa asked, "Can I see him?"

"He's all bandaged and doped up."

"I—I still want to see him." Tears coursed down Melissa's face again, salty in her mouth. "Oh, Katie! If I hadn't taken Madge out there!"

"If she hadn't been set on going—if she hadn't opened that lighter," Katie said bitterly. "The lighter was still in her hand and Humphrey saw her start to light a cigarette." She stroked Melissa's hand. "She'd have gone out there, hell or high water. Don't blame yourself."

"Please. I have to see Johnny. Just for a minute."

Katie grunted. "Well, let me see if I can talk the nurse into it. I reckon you could be wheeled right down the hall in your bed and look in the door."

When Melissa peered in, her breath caught. The form on the bed was swathed in gauze, and tubes dripped solution into the body. It didn't seem possible that mass could be alive. But in her horror, she gave thanks that under those bandages, under the charred flesh, Johnny *was* there.

As they wheeled her back to her room, she had a flashing memory of what Madge had said; that she couldn't stand for Johnny to touch her if ever he were maimed. Well, he was maimed; and he would never touch her.

V _____

Bernard's secretary called Katie and said Bernard did not want her to attend his daughter's funeral. The day after he buried Madge in the family vault in Beaumont, his lawyers filed suit against Johnny, or his estate, for negligence, manslaughter, and damages for the huge losses at FAYOIL. "But Madge was to blame!" Melissa cried, trying to sit up and collapsing at the knives in her ribs. "Johnny did everything he could to put out the fire. Bernard must know that!"

"I'm afraid he doesn't care," said Katie wearily. "His only child is dead. All he wants is to ruin Johnny."

"I wasn't the only one who saw her use that lighter."

Katie shook her head. "Missy, they're gone. All of them."

"What? But Humphrey got his well."

"Yes. But now he and his backers have sold out to Bernard and the whole crew's disappeared. My guess is that Bernard paid them plenty to get them out of the state and leave no addresses."

"And a court would think I'd lie for Johnny."

"Wouldn't you?"

Melissa didn't answer that. Katie rose, looking old. "I'm going to talk to Bernard in a few weeks when he may be thinking

310

straighter. Among other things, I want him to feel free to visit Kitty."

"That'll be awkward, with him suing Johnny."

"He's still Kitty's grandfather."

A terrible thing flashed into Melissa's mind. "Do you think he'd try to get her away from us?"

"No doubt he'd give half his fortune to do just that, but I don't see how a jury could send Johnny to prison, though they may fine him everything he's got and a lot more."

"Let me go with you, Gran."

"I'd like to have you, Missy." Katie gave a shudder that was only part acting. "When Bernard and I are together, it feels as if we're all kinds of people besides ourselves. Regina's in him—and his father, who gave me plenty of grief. On my side there's Vinnie, and we both share the judge—just as we now share Kitty." Katie sighed. "I'm glad this will be settled before she's old enough to know what's going on. I wonder if I should take her with me when I go to see Bernard."

"You should take *me*. *I* can tell him how it happened."

"Missy, he doesn't care. All he sees is that his daughter's dead. If you're there with me, looking not too much the worse for the explosion, it would just grind in deeper what happened to Madge."

Melissa supposed that was true. But how awful it would be for Johnny, when he emerged from the drugs that dulled his agony, to learn that his wife was dead and his father-in-law wished that he were. Compared to that, losing his company and all his money wouldn't seem like much.

On the tenth day after the accident, Melissa was sent home in an ambulance with orders to lie down most of the time. She still had blinding headaches but her ribs were knitting well. She would have been delighted at being out of the hospital if she hadn't felt she was deserting Johnny just as he was undergoing skin grafts.

He had attained consciousness enough to insist on knowing about Madge and Melissa. When Katie broke it to him, he went so still she was afraid he'd died. He had surely wanted to.

When Katie took his bandaged hand and fearfully called his name, he whispered, "If I'd gone to her party..."

"And then," said Katie, brokenly relating it to Melissa, "he cried for the first time since he was a baby, so far as I know, and nothing I could say helped the least bit."

"He doesn't know yet about the lawsuit?"

"I hope he won't have to." Katie pulled at her handkerchief. "I'll talk to Bernard first."

That was wasted endeavor. Returning home, Katie did something Melissa had never before seen her do except after a company dinner. She poured herself a jigger of brandy that she took in one swallow before she sank down on the ottoman beside the couch where Melissa spent most waking hours. Kitty, who'd been playing on the rug by the fireplace, laughed and streaked to her grandmother, pulling up on her skirt to clamber on her knees. In her oblivion to all but her baby wants and pleasures, she was a blessing. But her likeness to Madge was increasing as her face lost some of its infant roundness and the red-gold curls grew longer and darker.

Melissa sat up too quickly but scarcely felt the twinge. "What did Bernard say, Gran?"

"He said——he said that he'd always thought I had something to do with his father's death in Mexico, and now my son had killed his daughter. He said he'd have Johnny killed except that he'll suffer more the way it is."

"Oh, Gran!"

Katie went on tonelessly, "I offered him the Old Orchard. He's always wanted it, you know. I'm already planning, if the suit goes against Johnny, to sell the place to help pay the judgment. Bernard just laughed."

Sell Old Orchard? It was as easy to envision the end of the world as a time when Gran wouldn't live at her home place. "You can't do that, Gran! Johnny won't let you."

Katie shrugged. "I'd do it gladly if Bernard would drop the suit. But there's only one way he'll do that."

Melissa's heart leaped. "What's that?" she asked eagerly.

"He wants Kitty."

Melissa froze. "Johnny would never give her up."

"Of course he won't. But that's Bernard's price."

"It's the cruelest thing he could think of!"

"To be fair about it, he adores the baby. And she is all he has left."

"Except for his millions."

"They can't buy a life that's gone." Cradling Kitty in one arm, Katie took Melissa's hand and held it strongly. "Listen, honey, Johnny's alive. He won't ever be the same but he'll work again, he'll breathe sweet air and laugh and feel the sun warm him. Whatever else is lost, he'll have that—and we'll have him. We're richer than Bernard, whatever he does. I can't blame him for wanting Kitty. And of course he has rights we'll respect, but even he, when he's rational, must know she's better off with us."

"He may not think so if you sell Old Orchard and we move into some ratty apartment."

Katie laughed; color came back into her cheeks. "Don't get melodramatic, Missy. I'm not all that dedicated to paying Bernard money he doesn't need. Johnny wouldn't let me live in a hovel. We'd buy a decent, comfortable little house with at least one big tree."

A single tree? When she had scores of woodland giants here, oak, hickory, maple, and walnut, as well as the orchard she had watched bloom and fruit most of the years of her life? Melissa gripped Katie's hand so hard Katie flinched.

"Gran! You can't sell this place, you just can't. If Bernard wins, it won't pay him off entirely anyway, so why do it?"

"I know," Katie agreed, "but I've been offered pretty fancy sums by oil companies who'd like to investigate that old seep. The house is quite a landmark."

"And the graves?"

Katie paled. "I'm sorry," Melissa cried. "But oh, Gran, Gran!"

"We'd have to move the graves. Or build a fence around them and reserve that place."

"If anyone drills the seep, they'd ruin the cave and spring."

"Do you think I don't know that?" Katie's tone was the coldest she had ever used to Melissa. "But as I've said before, the main consideration is that Johnny's alive. He'll need to go on with his work—if his hand permits. His credit and reputation will be a lot better if it's clear he's done everything he can to pay the judgment." She freed her hand and rose, still holding the baby. "Please, let's not talk about it now." Tears glittered in her eyes.

Stabbed to the heart, feeling like an ingrate, Melissa swallowed and said, "Gran, whatever you decide, I'll help."

Katie dropped a kiss on her forehead and called to Thaley to warm the baby's bottle. Something nibbled at Melissa, something about oil and Old Orchard, though she pushed it away. Vinnie and Katie had always rejected any offers to drill there. But if it were sold and the new owners drilled anyway...

That was it! Johnny had always thought there was considerable oil on both sides of the river, especially in the bottoms where the river made a curve behind the orchard and there were shaly banks and outcroppings. If he could bring in some wells, if he could get some good producers, he might possibly satisfy the judgment. It would be months before the case came up. Surely he'd be working before then.

If only the oil was there, enough of it! Heedless of aching ribs and bursting head, Melissa sprang up and hurried to find Katie.

Johnny was home for Kitty's first birthday. The surgeons had been skillful. There was a tightness to the skin from nose to hairline and faint seams along his jaw, but it was mostly his right hand, its stubbed fingers like the hacked bole of a tree, that testified physically to his ordeal. In his manner and spirit he was marked worse. His movements had none of their old grace; he moved heavily, awkwardly as if weighted with invisible irons. He stayed in his room most of the time, and when he came to meals or sat for a while under the trees, he was possessed by reveries so bleak that it seemed insulting to talk of daily matters.

"He doesn't even play much with Kitty," Melissa despaired to Katie. "Gran, he's—he's like a shell with nothing left inside."

"I'm sure that's how he feels. It takes time, honey."

"But the trial's set for September and he doesn't show the slightest interest in drilling down behind the orchard."

The papers had been served on Johnny while he was still in the hospital. Bernard hadn't softened, nor had he come to see his granddaughter. "I think," said Katie slowly, "that Johnny feels so guilty that he doesn't care if he loses all he has. But he'll surely start coming out of that."

"Have you told him you'd sell this place?"

"Not yet. Right now it would just sink in, become part of his nightmare. But as he gets stronger, as his will fixes on life again, then it'll matter."

Melissa groaned. "What if the trial comes and he's still in this haze?"

"Maybe it'll take the trial to snap him out of it. Johnny's always been a fighter, Missy. He could have died from those burns but something in him struggled to live. It'll take hold. Just wait."

The hardest thing to do.

Melissa graduated. Johnny attended the ceremony, doubtless at Katie's behest. "So you'll be off to college this fall," he said at breakfast next morning. "I'll have to find a new office manager. If I have an office."

Katie had been urging Melissa to apply to the University of Texas but Melissa couldn't imagine going away while the family was in such trouble. "I can see you through till January," she said. "I'd like a little break from school. The spring semester's soon enough." She and Katie exchanged hopeful glances. This was the first time Johnny had spoken of going back to work. The business was closed down, of course, though Soup hung around the office from habit.

A few days later, driving for the first time, Johnny went to the office. Melissa came along and plugged in the coffeepot while Johnny, with his left hand, sorted through messages Soup had scribbled down. "Most of these folks will have called in other shooters," he said, handing the sheaf to Melissa. "But you could check and see if there are a few who still need me. I'll have to start back slow. Not sure how this hand's going to work."

A crushing load slipped off Melissa with a sensation more gratefully freeing than when the tape had come off her ribs. She started calling while Johnny, with Soup, checked over supplies. Johnny's old customers were interested in his recovery even when they had no current job for him, so it took a while to work through the memos.

After passing on his clients' good wishes, Melissa said, "I've scheduled you for just one production charge a day the rest of this week, all within seventy miles of here. You'd better let Soup or me drive."

"Yeah," said Soup, blue eyes solicitous. "No use rushing."

"All right," said Johnny. "In the morning, then."

"Right," said Soup, dropping a hand on Johnny's shoulder. "Hail and thunderation, boss, it's great to have you back!"

"Good to be back." Johnny's face seemed a trifle less taut. "That coffee smells good, Missy. Reckon we could have a cup before we go home?"

They sat and talked a while, Soup bringing Johnny up to date on the latest producers and dry holes. Melissa's blood hummed as if a clogging thickness had turned swiftly fluid. It would be all right: Johnny had taken his first step back.

As they drove home, there was a glory to the early summer greens, wildflowers, and blossoming fruit trees, as if a heavy veil had been swept away. Katie's determined cheerfulness at dinnertime changed that evening into real laughter as Melissa reported some of the day's phone conversations. Kitty, always sunny, responded to the lightheartedness by taking a turn on each grownup's lap and inviting a mock tussle.

How good it was to hear Johnny laugh without immediately clamping it off. For the first time since the explosion, Melissa went to sleep smiling, eager for the morning.

She drove Johnny in next day to spare his strength. Soup had the torpedoes ready, and as soon as they were loaded, the men drove off, Soup at the wheel.

Let it be fine, Melissa prayed. *Let Johnny have back his work.* She reviewed the files, wrote reminders to several overdue accounts, and began sending notices to former clients that the business was again in operation. She was debating whether to make a peanut butter sandwich or lunch at the small café across the road, when the truck pulled up the drive and stopped by the shed. Melissa hurried to the rear door. The smile withered on her lips as Johnny climbed out, face dead, eyes looking at her without recognition.

"Call those other people. Tell them I can't come."

Soup made a warning shake of his head, and Melissa said, "You mean put them off till next week?"

"I mean cancel."

Dread gripped Melissa. "Johnny, have you—have you hurt yourself?"

"You might say that. I put myself in a spot where someone

could ask, just as I was sending down the charge, who I intended to kill today."

"Oh, Johnny, no!" Who would say a thing like that? The answer came at once. "Whoever said it, that was really Bernard talking." She caught Johnny's arm. "He paid them—or blackmailed them."

Roughly, Johnny pulled loose. "Doesn't much matter." His face looked as haggard as when he'd first left the hospital. "I've shot that kind of well a hundred times. If the first torpedo wasn't enough, I was set to lower another. But—all of a sudden, I didn't know anything. I wasn't sure. I didn't know what was going on at the bottom, couldn't even guess." His jaw was fixed tight and rigid, the grafted places showing white like old brands. His words were a dry whisper. "I didn't *know*. I went shaky as a newborn calf and pulled that charge up out of there." Sweat stood out on his forehead. "Come on, Soup. Let's unload these torpedoes."

Melissa planted herself in his way. "Are you going to let Bernard run you off?" She was desperate enough to use scorn as a whip.

"I sure am if I can get that rattled by a cheap crack from some guy who didn't show his face. He wasn't even one of the crew. Just turned up to watch, the way some people do when they hear a well's going to be shot. The driller ran him off."

"Well then, Johnny—"

"Look! What matters is that I went to pieces. I'm not fit to be on a rig, risk other people's lives."

"It must just be too soon."

"Maybe. In a month or two, one year, five years, God knows when, I'll trust what I'm doing. Till then, I'm not shooting any wells. I'm not sure if I can ever put out a fire again. Clear enough, Missy? Think I'm a coward?"

She couldn't speak, so full of hurt and fear for him that she silently cursed Madge and Bernard as she stepped out of Johnny's way and opened the shed door.

Johnny explained his early return to Katie in the fewest possible words. She moved toward him with her arms outstretched. He turned away. Katie's hands dropped to her sides.

"It was too soon, dear," she said after a moment.

"Forever may be too soon. Don't worry, Mother, I'm not going to mope around the house. Maybe I can get a job on a pumpline."

Tending the pumps was a necessary and perfectly respectable job, but one usually taken by aging men who could no longer do the heavy labor of a roughneck. To go to that from being a premier shooter was like an ace pilot becoming a grease monkey. Behind Johnny, Melissa and Katie's eyes met.

Then Katie said, "Son, how would you like to find a driller and make some wells in the bottom field?"

VI _____

When Johnny saw that Katie was determined to sell the home place if the judgment went against him, he agreed that drilling was a better alternative. Rance Gorman was looking for a lease and accepted an offer to drill on shares with an alacrity that confirmed Melissa's suspicion that he cherished more than friendship for Katie.

Rance had made and lost several fortunes, been married four times, and was presently reduced to poor-boy wells and bachelordom. He hauled his outfit down from the Panhandle, accompanied by his sister's sons who roughnecked for him. Pete and Frank had their uncle's lanky build but were blue-eyed and towheaded with freckled skin that reddened and peeled instead of tanning. The three set their trailer in the shade of some big oaks near the curve of the river, but they were mightily pleased at Katie's invitation to eat at the house. Johnny completed the crew with Soup and Melissa to run errands.

By late June, the site was picked, a road cut from the blacktop to the location, the derrick raised; the day the well was spudded in, Katie served champagne at supper. Rance had warned his nephews to be closemouthed about where they were working when they went for their weekly fling in Pleasanton, but a few days after the location was abandoned as a dry hole and a new well begun, a derrick sprouted across the river on the land Bernard had bought up to extend Belleforest's boundaries to the river.

"Be damned!" Rance snorted. "Old B.S. aims to dig him some offset wells." B.S., in addition to its taurine connotation, meant bottom sediment, the settlings in an oil tank.

Offset wells could be drilled near a property line in order to capture oil tapped from the same sands by a well on another lease. Another derrick went up on Bernard's side, and a third and a fourth, ranged at quarter-mile intervals.

"If there's oil around here, that bastard almost has to hit it before we do," Rance growled that night at supper. "Want we should keep drilling, Katie?"

"It's the only chance to raise the kind of money we may need." Katie's eyes reflected the light of the candles she liked to have on the table even when feeding a drilling crew. "I'm ready to put my savings into it." Her smile swept from him to Pete and Frank. "We'll pay you for drilling, Rance, if we don't get oil to go shares on. If you're willing, I say let's keep going as long as there's a chance."

Johnny nodded. Two weeks of outdoor work had browned him and put increasing spring back in his step. "I'll put in everything I've got."

Rance's tobacco-stained teeth showed as he chuckled and reached for another chunk of corn bread. "If you feel that way, by gob, we'll make hole till we run out of locations or bring in our twenty-thousand-barrels-a-day well!"

"Let's have champagne on that," suggested Katie, rising.

Her friend smiled at her, admiration softening his sharp hazel eyes. "If it's all the same to you, Katie, could we make it Jim Beam?"

That Bernard was drilling two to three dry holes for each of the Katie Company's was small comfort as Rance and Johnny plugged their fourth dry hole two days before Johnny had to be in court.

"B.S., he's just writing it off his taxes," grumbled Soup. "Makes him no never mind."

Johnny took off his hard hat, running his hand through damp hair that, waving down, hid the scar seared across his forehead. He was still gaunt but could put in his twelve hours right along with young Frank and Pete. "Well, it shouldn't be long till we know if we need the oil."

Rance gazed at him, whites of his eyes made even larger by his tanned face. "If Hardy could hear you say that! Listen, son, ain't never a time when an oil man don't need it—and for a sight more than the money!"

How good it was to hear Johnny laugh! Surely his spirit must be healing. Whatever happened with the lawsuit, he should get back his confidence, the controlled daring that had made him at an early age one of the best shooters in the business. He leaned against the derrick and peered across the bottoms.

"Well, Rance, where do we try next?"

Without warning, Bernard drove up the night before the trial while the Katie Company was finishing off a second cherry pie. Startled though she had to be, Katie invited Bernard in and asked if he'd had supper.

He didn't seem to hear. His pale eyes slid over the men till they fixed on Johnny with the flash of a hawk's talons. "John. If you'd come outside, I'd like to talk to you."

The quick hope with which Johnny glanced up died as he saw the implacable set of his father-in-law's face. Bernard looked now more like a bloodhound than a cherub. Johnny excused himself and followed.

Melissa poured coffee and brought extra cream for Rance, feeling chilled. Straining to hear if voices raised, she filled Katie's cup and pressed her hand to give and take comfort. Kitty was in bed, but how strange that Bernard hadn't even asked to see her.

It wasn't long, though it seemed forever, before a car door slammed and a powerful motor roared. Johnny didn't come in, though. Could he have gone somewhere with Bernard? Wild fears jumbled through Melissa. Unable to wait, she was starting for the door when Johnny came in.

His face was corpselike beneath its weathering. He sat down and drank the coffee Melissa poured before he said a word. "Can you believe he had the nerve to ask for the baby?"

"Why, the old sonuvabitch!" Rance choked.

After what Bernard had said to Katie months ago, neither she nor Melissa were completely surprised. But it had been clever of him to wait . . . while the trial neared; while the Katie Company exhausted its capital in one dry hole after another.

"He said he'd drop the action." Johnny's voice was numb. "And he'd quit drilling offsets if we still think there's oil down yonder."

"Hell, boy!" spluttered Rance. "Of course you told him where he could shove it!"

"That was easy." Johnny lowered his eyes. Melissa longed to hold the dark head against her and smooth his hair. His tone was scarcely audible. "What was hard was when he said I'd taken his daughter, so I owed him mine."

"Don't believe that, Johnny." Katie's voice gleamed like a sword. *"His* daughter caused that whole awful thing. Bernard doesn't know how to raise a child, either. He just indulges and spoils. The worst thing that could happen to Kitty would be for him to get custody."

Johnny nodded. "I know. But—" He suddenly rose and left the table. The others looked at one another, and Rance swore vigorously, bit off the flow in mid-imprecation. "Sorry, ladies. But can you beat that?"

"We'll beat it." Katie tilted her head back. From somewhere in her hard-bought grace, she found the power to smile. "One way or another. Even if Bernard takes every *thing* we've got, we have each other—and we've got Kitty."

Rance raised his coffee cup. "I'll drink to that—and to you, Katie. I always knew you were one hell of a woman. You're more so now than when you stood off that mob in Baygall, or when you took Hardy out to Castle Gap."

She blushed like a girl. "God bless you, Rance."

He scowled. "More like it if He'd bless the well we're goin' to start diggin' soon as this one's plugged."

Soup filled in for Johnny, and Thaley cooked and fed the crew while Johnny went to court each day, accompanied by Katie and Melissa. Johnny's lawyer, Malcolm Ballou, was an old high school friend of Johnny's and had lined up dozens of character witnesses who would testify to Johnny's record, but from the way several women jurors wept and the grim expressions of the men, Bernard's renowned lawyer from Houston, Joe Bob Rutherford, had assured the verdict from the first day.

"It was Christmas," he intoned sadly, shaking back his shaggy chestnut hair, reproaching Johnny with melancholy dark eyes. "The most family day of the year—and your own birthday, Mr. Alastair. The Humphrey well was no emergency. There was no threatened loss of life or property. Yet instead of taking part in the celebration your wife had planned for weeks, in spite of her pleas and humiliation, you went out on a day when any man of normal feelings would have been home with his dear ones. Small wonder, then, that Madge went after you, begged you to honor the basic responsibilities of a married man."

The corpulent, white-haired judge had political ambitions. He never called Rutherford on excess of language or implication, but when short, sandy-moustached Malcolm tried to make the point that the party, far from being a warm family affair, was an extravaganza to further Bernard's ends, the judge ruled him out of order.

Since Melissa was the only eyewitness, the jurors listened to her with special intentness. Malcolm asked her simply to give an account of what happened from her arrival at Belleforest till the explosion. She tried to do this straightforwardly, but Rutherford was constantly on his feet with objections.

"The witness says Madge Alastair was 'past being reasoned with,'" he blasted. "This is an unwarranted accusation of mental instability from the accused's foster sister, who, so far as I know, has no training in psychology. I insist that she confine her statements to fact."

"Objection sustained," said the judge.

When, under cross-examination, Melissa said that Madge had gotten out her cigarettes and lighter, Rutherford said gently, "But did you see the lighter flare? Actually *see* it?"

"Madge flicked the lighter as the oil spewed up."

"But you had your eye on the hole and what your brother was doing with the torpedo he had mistakenly lowered, the charge that clearly wasn't needed since oil came gushing up—"

"Objection!" called Malcolm. "Mr. Rutherford has no professional expertise from which to judge my client's decision to set a charge."

"Objection overruled," rapped the judge. "Proceed, Mr. Rutherford."

"Now, Miss Alastair," droned the patronizing voice, "it was a

moment when you might well have assumed something had occurred when in fact it had not. Can you positively swear that the
explosion was not caused by metal striking against metal?"

"Of course I can't swear that! Nobody could. But I saw flame
in the lighter."

"Eyes play tricks, as does memory. That was a moment of
great tension and drama."

"I saw the flash! I called to Madge and was running toward
her, reaching for the lighter, when—when—"

"You sustained a concussion in the blast," he remarked sympa-
thetically. "It's entirely understandable that you might have a
blurred impression of that day's tragic events. Small wonder,
then, if you had a confused or blank memory of what happened
before your injury."

Except for Mrs. Bartlett and her niece, the Belleforest staff
stated that Johnny, to his wife's distress, rarely attended her parties, often worked on Sundays and holidays, and had threatened
to divorce her and sue for custody of their child if she wouldn't
seek treatment for her drinking problem—which she had done.
The picture Rutherford artfully sketched was of a high-strung,
spirited young woman in love with a husband who preferred work
to family and constantly left her in the embarrassing position of
entertaining without him. No wonder, when he'd flouted her on
Christmas Day, that she'd gone out to reason with him...

Johnny's witnesses were mostly roughnecks and drillers, the
kind of men, as Rutherford implied, who would side with a
shooter no matter what, and who lacked the delicacy to understand how Johnny's behavior had tormented his wife.

On the stand, when Rutherford grilled him about the explosion, Johnny said, "I didn't see my wife get out her lighter. I was
busy holding down that torpedo. I've heard a lighter was found in
her hand—"

"*Heard*, Mr. Alastair?" Rutherford echoed reproachfully. "So
you're willing, sir, to blame this disaster on your dead wife who
is no longer here to defend herself?"

"I haven't blamed her."

"Your foster sister has."

"Melissa told what she saw."

"And you want to believe her. Isn't that true, Mr. Alastair?

You want to believe her in order to avoid taking responsibility for your wife's death?"

"I've wished a thousand times I'd gone to her party. But what I did at the well—I used the best judgment I had, based on years of experience. Given the same set of circumstances, it's what I'd do again."

"Is it?" Rutherford leaned forward, his voice soft but carrying. "If you're so sure you were right, sir, how is it that you've been out on only one call since your recovery—one on which you panicked and quit?"

"Objection!" shouted Malcolm.

"Overruled," snapped the judge.

After ten days of testimony, the jury took six hours to return a verdict: guilty of criminal negligence and manslaughter. A two-year prison sentence was suspended but FAYOIL was awarded three million dollars.

"At least it's over," said Katie on the way home. "If there's any oil in the bottoms, it'd better show up fast."

"Mother, I won't let you sell Old Orchard." Johnny gazed out at the trees, the fruit almost ready for picking. "Bernard can have my best truck and the little I have in the bank. I'll pay him every dime I earn above expenses till I'm so old I can't work."

What Bernard had done was make sure Johnny would carry the full burden of Madge's death all the rest of his life. With everything he earned forfeit to Bernard, Johnny would be almost a serf.

Katie didn't murmur soothing words or hopes that Bernard might relent.

"What we're going to do is find some oil," she said. "If it's not at Old Orchard, we'll find it someplace else."

"Drilling takes money."

"We'll get it."

"Not by selling the place!"

Katie shrugged. "We'll do whatever it takes. I had planned to sell to help pay Bernard, but it makes better sense to stake you and Rance and have a shot at satisfying the entire judgment. Then you can get on with your life."

"I won't let you do it, Mother."

She looked down her straight nose at him. "Look, young man, if I've decided to become a wildcatter in my old age, there's not much you can do about it. Anyhow, we can drill a few more wells before our cash drip gets serious."

A week later, the Katie Company had to abandon another dry hole. Katie always set a good table, but when she knew spirits were low, she got into the kitchen with Thaley and produced an especially lavish meal with one of her mouth-watering desserts. Tonight it was strawberry-rhubarb pie topped with homemade vanilla ice cream.

When the aura of disappointment was somewhat alleviated by the physical glow that follows good food, Katie tipped her fingers beneath her chin and looked around the table. "Listen, boys, I went down to the cave this afternoon, and while I was sitting by the spring, almost drowsing off, I thought I heard my mother speak. She said that what we want is on a slope with a big hollow tree. There's a place like that a quarter mile from where we got this last duster. Why don't we try it?"

Rance and Johnny looked at each other. After a moment, Rance said, "Why not? Dreams've found oil before this."

Slender as the portent was, it lifted everyone's mood. Katie played the piano that night, and tired as the men surely were, they sang a while before trooping off to bed.

When they were gone, Melissa surveyed Katie with a little frown. "Gran, did you really dream that?"

Katie grinned at her. "Honey, don't you know the reason they needed geologists even back before geologists knew much about what they were doing was that it helps to have someone give you the courage to start drilling?"

They were plugging the duster when Bernard appeared one afternoon and asked Johnny to talk with him. Melissa was there, having brought the men chilled cider and cookies. She watched Johnny go over to Bernard's car and stand by the window. Bernard couldn't have said more than a few words before Johnny stepped back, tight-drawn as a bowstring.

Raising a hand, Bernard went on talking. Johnny shook his head. Bernard was still urging something on him when Johnny walked away, heading for the river, where he stood staring at Bernard's offset wells.

Bernard finally veered his Lincoln around in the truck ruts, churning up a fog of dust as he drove away. Johnny stayed where he was, a solidified shadow. Melissa hurried to him, taking a glass of cider. "What was that about?" she asked while he drank mechanically.

Johnny exhaled a breath as if it had poisoned him. "He wants me to go to work for him."

"*What?*"

Absently massaging the stumps of his burned fingers, Johnny spoke as if to himself. "The man's crazy. He hates my guts. But if I'd be his 'special assistant,' he'd pay me a generous salary and commute the judgment so that it would be considered paid if I work for him till the end of his life."

"He wants you under his hand—where he can grind you down anytime he feels like it."

"I'd still do it before I'd let Mother sell Old Orchard."

"Johnny, no!"

A faint smile curved his mouth. "Maybe he won't rivet a chain around my neck. But if the dream well doesn't produce, Missy, I can't let Mother sink her last savings to drill dry holes. I won't let this turn into something like that Castle Gap well Hardy went broke on. I'll take Bernard's offer first."

He went back to help with the plugging. For every producing well, how many ended like this, how many marked the loss of everything a small operator had, or of a desperate farm family's hope that underground riches would save the barren surface?

Johnny called the new prospect "the dream well." Didn't all wells begin that way? But some ended in a ruinous nightmare made crueler by the vision. As for Johnny going to work for Bernard—Melissa went cold at the thought. He wouldn't wear a slave's brand, but the brand would be on his spirit; Bernard would fetter him hand and foot. It was an unspeakable vengeance, and there was more in it than punishing Johnny, for, through him, Bernard could avenge himself on Katie for whatever had happened to his father at Dos Bocas, exact a final toll for the account begun between their families when Belleforest burned.

When Melissa got back to the house, she went out to clear leaves from the graves and trim hips off the rosebushes to encourage new blooms. The air was sweet with yellow petals drifting upon the soft green mounds, the later ones with simple brass markers. Melissa polished these to bring up the names.

Hester and Talt, Johnny's grandfather and great-grandmother;

Vinnie and Mark Sevier beside the aunt, uncle, and infant cousin that Vinnie had found buried beneath the great white stone; Hardy and the baby he and Katie had lost. Caleb and his wife were there, and Esau, who had died of a heart attack ten years ago.

All of them had dreamed. What mattered now was the love they'd shared, the love that had made children and brought those children up. In all that company, Hardy was the only one joined to Melissa by blood, yet she felt that she belonged to them all because of Katie's love, and because she herself loved Johnny.

She touched Vinnie's grave, the ground warmed by the autumn sunshine. Unthinkable to sell this place. But it was unthinkable too that Johnny should serve Bernard.

It might be pagan, but with all her might, Melissa invoked her beloved dead. *Let there be oil in the dream well! Let there be oil you saved for us till now.* A childish rite, she knew, one that could change nothing if the oil wasn't there. Still, she felt better as she went into the kitchen and asked Thaley if she'd like her to make a spice cake for supper.

VII ────────────────────────

When they spudded in what could have no other name but the Katie's Dream, Bernard's crews started four wells across the river and worked around the clock. Rotary wells weren't actually begun with a spudder as a cable-tool well was, but the term had carried over.

"If you can swing it, Katie, we'd better hire a graveyard shift," said Rance, neatly blotting up the last of his gravy with a biscuit. "Otherwise, if B.S.'s sand shares oil we might hit, his wells will hog it off before we even get a show."

"Get the extra men," said Katie, not hesitating. Her brow furrowed. "What do you mean, if Bernard's sand shares our oil?"

"We're drilling an anticline. The river's carved its channel through the rocks down below, and from the way the layers run, I'd reckon there could be oil on one side and not on the other. If it's all in our sands, B.S. can drill clear to hell and get nothin' but brimstone. Hope he does. But if the pool spreads under both properties, then we better get there first."

Katie went to the phone. "You keep drilling, boys. I'll hire a crew—Bailey Scott, if he's not busy."

"He's the best," said Rance. "But he's like me, women and cards keep him broke."

Bailey, yellow hair whitening but eyes still cornflower-blue in his broad, freckled face, took over that night when Rance's crew stopped. On both sides of the river, rotaries swiveled down, and the deeper Katie's Dream grew, the closer the bit ground to the truth that would either free Johnny or make him Bernard's zombie.

Melissa could scarcely sleep, knowing that Bailey's crew and Bernard's four were out there drilling. The third night, still wakeful in the small hours, she got up and dressed, left the house as stealthily as a married woman meeting a lover.

A tattered moon was rising in the east, a remnant of its full glory, but enough to show her way. The late September days were warm but the night wind blew cool. Melissa lifted her face to it, drawing in the moist, rich smell of leaves crumbling beneath her feet, the acrid tang of the river, a hint of roses.

She loved spring but autumn more, winy golden air, the blaze of scarlet, orange, and yellow. Passing through the orchard and the scent of apples, she soon reached the road to the dream well. She stopped among some oaks on a knoll where she could see Bailey's men working in the glow of rigged lights.

Across the river, Bernard's four crews labored. Bailey Scott knew one of Bernard's drillers. The man had told him that Bernard had offered the crew that struck oil first a bonus of two thousand dollars per roughneck and a custom Caddy or equivalent cash to the driller. That added more fuel to the race, though Bailey's friend had confided that while the expert crews Bernard had hired would, of course, use their best skills, they really hoped Johnny and Rance would win.

Lights jolted across Bernard's land and stopped, a big sleek car glinting in the illumination from the first derrick. It was too far to recognize the man who got out but he shambled like Bernard and he wasn't dressed in work clothes. Melissa's heart speeded till blood pounded in her ears.

That dreadful man! Did he come there every night? She hated him, yet felt unwilling pity. He had no one left but Kitty. Of course, that must be part of his plan; if Johnny worked for him, he could demand access to his granddaughter. Demand, when it would have been gladly given if he asked.

Melissa didn't like being this close to him, even at night when he couldn't know she was there. Turning to go, she heard the wheeze of Johnny's old truck, still fitted for torpedoes, still with his asbestos suit in a locker box. She faded out of range of the truck lights, staying off the road until the truck had jounced on to Katie's Dream. Johnny had worked twelve hours and must be exhausted, but with so much riding on this well, it obsessed him.

Shivering, Melissa started home. Win or lose, it should be over soon.

At five thousand feet, oil began to show in the mud and cuttings forced out of the hole. But the bit struck a formation that resisted, so instead of the thousand feet a day they'd been averaging, they were making only a few feet. Melissa, who'd taken the crew's lunch down, was there when Rance looked hard at Johnny.

"If them rocks was fractured good, cracked apart to let loose whatever's down there, I bet we'd have us a well."

Johnny didn't speak. His arms were behind him, hidden from the other men, though Melissa could see the tendons of his good hand ridge as it grasped the burned one. She remembered all too clearly what he'd said after he'd walked off that only shooting job he'd attempted since the accident: *"I didn't know what was going on at the bottom—couldn't even guess . . . I'm not fit to be on a rig, risk other people's lives."*

He said now, "I don't have my business anymore. We'd have to get the nitro from another outfit. Might as well hire a shooter along with it."

"Why do that when you're the best?" the old driller asked.

Pete and Frank nodded, and Soup looked at Johnny eagerly. "C'mon, boss. Let's get that stuff and bring in Katie's Dream!"

"Let's," said Melissa. Resting her hand on Johnny's, she willed him to see in her face not only her love but whatever could strengthen him of those whose blood she carried; the worshiped man who had fathered his spirit if not his body, the woman who had been his first boy's love. "Johnny, let's go."

They had made their offering of trust. Johnny looked at the rotary, laboring at that barrier almost a mile below. His shoulders straightened. Some of the old spark gleamed in his eyes.

"I'll be back soon as I can get some nitro."

Rance grinned. Soup gave a wild yell. "We're gonna get a well! You boys have the valves and everything ready to pipe it off!"

Soup made for the truck with Johnny, but before he could climb in, Melissa got in the middle. This was more than bringing in the well, vital as that was. It was a trial for Johnny, one that might bring back his old power or bury it forever: she had to be with him.

Four torpedoes were clamped on the truck and Johnny was writing a check when Bernard walked into the supply shop. He had shrunk except for his paunch and there was a twitch at the corner of his left eye.

"You must be getting desperate if you've worked up the nerve to try shooting." His unpleasant grin showed tobacco-stained teeth and pale gums. He winked at the owner of the shop, a gangly former driller named Slim Hoskins. "I hope you're getting cash for anything you sell Alastair. His mama had a dream there was oil out by an old tree and damned if they haven't drilled there!" He chortled.

"Plenty of oil dreams turned out true, Mr. Fayette," said Hoskins quietly. "Up in Illinois where I come from, a widow, Mrs. Weger, was having a mighty hard time. She dreamed she saw a rig out by her henhouse, and mind you, she didn't even know what the thing was. But when an operator leased her farm, that was where they got a discovery well for a good field. And I was roughnecking over at Ranger in 1917 when we drilled a ten-thousand-barrel-a-day well right at the big live oak tree where Mary Rust dreamed it was. And there was—"

"Sure," Bernard cut him off, "they've found oil with hazel branches and magnetic doodlebugs and by asking fortune-tellers and folks who claimed they could feel oil flowing under their feet. We all know that until seismographs, finding oil was mostly luck, and it's still a gamble. You can't blame people for trying stuff like that back in the early times, but to drill a dream *nowa*days..." He stared at Johnny with eyes the color of frozen pond scum. "To me that sounds like a loser who'll grab at anything because he's going under."

Melissa whirled on him. "You—you awful man! Can't you find something better to do than hound Johnny?"

Bernard looked her up and down, vented an obscene laugh. "Why, you'd like to snuggle up to him, wouldn't you? Take

Madge's place? Or were you doing that while she was still alive, whoring like your mother?"

Melissa struck him. Johnny caught her arm. "Come on, Melissa. He's crazy."

"You bastard!" Bernard howled after them. "I hope you blow up that well and yourselves with it! God damn you Alastairs! I'll see you all in hell!"

Thrust in between Johnny and Soup, Melissa was shaking, trying not to cry. Johnny had heard what Bernard said about her. Did it shock him, make him disgusted with her? Patting her shoulder, Soup muttered, "Pay that old devil no never mind, Missy. He's spittin' out the meanest trash he can think of."

Melissa sucked in a long breath. All of a sudden, she knew how, if a bit could feel, it would feel like to grind through barriers, unconcerned with pride, intent only on the truth that waited at the bottom. Defeat or treasure, she ground through.

"Bernard wasn't all wrong. Johnny, I love you. I always have." At his astonished side-glance, she winced but managed to keep her voice level. *"Please* don't say we're like brother and sister. That's not how it is for me. And please don't say I'm too young. Don't say anything. Just think about it."

"But Missy—"

She raised her hand. "I know you're not over Madge. That may take a good while. Fine. I can go to school next semester. You can have as long as you need. I'm just asking you to give us a chance."

He groaned. "Damn it, Missy, pay attention. I'm sixteen hard years older than you. Even if we pay Bernard, I won't be clear of what's happened. It's used me up." He held his maimed hand in front of her. "How can I hold you with *this?"*

She took his hand and kissed the scarred stump of each finger. Tears blurred her eyes. When he jerked away from her, gripping the wheel, she thought he was angry. But why was he accelerating?

"Sonuvabitch!" Soup gasped. "He's trying to run us off the road! And he don't care if he rams us!"

The dark green Lincoln was hurtling toward them. If it hit the truck, the torpedoes would blow both vehicles sky-high. Bernard had gone crazy, whether permanently or for the moment wouldn't matter if he crashed into them or made them flip.

A dirt road turned off sharply to the right. Johnny maintained speed till the last possible second, then braked and swung onto it. A bump could set off the nitro: Melissa held her breath. At least she'd die with Johnny, and at least he knew she loved him.

Peering back, she saw the Lincoln rocket past, brake too abruptly, spin into a bank, ricochet against the other bank, and burst into flames.

Johnny stopped the truck. Snatching his asbestos coat and gauntlets from the back, he yanked them on as he ran for the blazing wreck. Melissa ran after him. Soup dragged her back.

"Stay clear! Johnny'll get the old buzzard out if 'n it can be done."

Soup got a shovel and pick out of the truck, pulled on cowhide gauntlets, and loped as close as he dared to where Johnny was wrenching at a jammed door. Yelling, Soup thrust the shovel at him.

Johnny smashed the windshield, leaned in and dragged Bernard out, slapping fire from his hair and clothing. Soup helped carry Bernard to the truck and rode in back while Melissa held the unconscious man. The burning Lincoln couldn't set fire to anything. They left it burning and drove for the hospital.

Bernard would live. He had a fractured pelvis but instinctive sheltering of his face had kept the worst burns to his arms. Johnny's hair and eyebrows were scorched but he was all right otherwise.

"That old suit sure came in handy," Soup said after they had reported the "accident" to the police. To Melissa's outrage, Johnny hadn't said Bernard was trying to wreck them, only that he'd tried to make a turn while going too fast.

"You're going to let him get away with that?" Melissa cried as they got into the truck, Soup at the wheel this time. "Soup and I can swear that he was trying to kill us! And Slim Hoskins heard him talking in the shop! Don't be a fool, Johnny, he needs to be locked up."

"He can't do any damage for a while." Johnny sounded so exhausted that Melissa's heart smote her and she choked back further reproach. She doubted that Bernard would show any gratitude, but at least, having risked dying in order to give Bernard back his life, Johnny shouldn't feel so bad.

"You sure knew what to do, boss," Soup drawled. "Didn't have to think it over while he sizzled—though that might not have been a bad idea."

"Didn't have time to think." Johnny brushed off some of his scorched hair, wrinkling his nose. "But shooting the well, that's something else."

"You'll do it," said Melissa.

Their eyes caught. Johnny looked at her as if she were someone he was just meeting, someone he wanted to know. Turning her face toward him, he laughed and brushed her cheek with his lips. He had done that many times: this was different.

"You know something?" Johnny said to her, "I think I will."

It was four in the afternoon when he sent down the first charge, moving with the sure grace that Melissa had feared gone forever. Without hesitation, he lowered the second torpedo, and a third. Rance was with him on the derrick but the rest of them waited below. Katie was there and Bailey Scott's crew had gotten out of bed to see if there was oil.

Across the river, Bernard's four crews stopped drilling and gathered across the bank. They didn't know yet that their employer had been hurt.

There was a rumble in the earth, that familiar sound, like a monster stirring. Johnny and Rance gave a shout and Rance turned the valve that would hold the oil back till it could be connected to a pipeline.

Rance jumped down and hugged Katie. "It's there! All we need is to find out how much and decide whether to produce it ourselves or sell it to a big company."

Cheers floated from across the river. Rance went down to the bank and shouted, "Hey, boys, I'll stand you drinks next time we all hit town. Now don't you reckon you better make hole and see it there's oil on your side?"

Melissa got up on the derrick. She meant to throw her arms around Johnny, something she could have done before that moment of revelation in the truck. Now, she halted, confused. He came toward her and gave her a real kiss, full on the mouth, a man's kiss, not a brother's. Her truth had reached the depths of him and found an answer there.

* * *

The Katie's Dream could flow ten thousand barrels a day.
Rance had already started another well. There was no trouble now
in getting backing and they decided to merge with a leading independent that would lay the pipeline and do the marketing. After
expenses, the Alastairs' three-quarters share could start paying
Bernard.

He was out of the hospital, though still under nurses' care at
Belleforest. He hadn't sent thanks or apologies so Melissa supposed he cherished his grudge. It was a surprise, then, to answer
the phone and hear his voice.

"Melissa? I'd like to see my granddaughter. Will you bring her
over for a little while?"

Alarm shot through her, but though she examined his request
with great care, she couldn't believe he'd harm her now—though
he'd been ready enough to kill her and Soup to get revenge on
Johnny.

"I'll come," she said after a moment. She didn't want to but
Kitty was his only flesh. "The baby's sleeping but should wake up
in about an hour. Shall I bring her then?"

"That'll be fine. Thank you." He didn't even choke on saying
it!

She dressed and put out a light green corduroy overall and top
for the little girl. "I wonder what he wants," she worried to Katie
who picked up the waking child and cuddled her till she squirmed
and asked for milk.

"I don't know." Katie began brushing the gold-red curls while
Melissa brought milk and a graham cracker. "Shall I go with you?
I can wait in the car."

"You don't need to do that, Gran."

Katie laughed. "I want to, Missy. I'm curious as the dickens!"
She sobered quickly. "I'd like to hope Bernard's ready to behave
like a human being but that's asking too much. Most likely he just
wants to see Kitty and hasn't the nerve to ask me to bring her
after the things he said when I went to him about Johnny. So he
asked you."

"Then come along." Melissa washed the small face, screwed
up in protest, kissed the nose, and pushed on a shoe. "I never
could understand why he's ignored her all these months."

"Maybe he was too set on breaking Johnny to care about much

else. Since he didn't succeed, let's hope he's decided to be reasonable."

Remembering the cruelties Bernard had flung at her, Melissa doubted that. She tied Kitty's hair back with a green ribbon and smiled at her as proudly as if the baby were her own. Katie smiled, caressing Melissa's cheek. "I know how you feel, honey. That's just how I felt when you were her age."

Each holding a tiny hand, they walked out to the car.

Bernard was in a reclining chair, a blanket over his legs, his arms thick with gauze. Kitty stared at him, keeping a firm grip on Melissa's skirt.

"Hi, Katharine Marguerite," he said gently. "Got a kiss for your grandpa?"

She held on to Melissa who said, "Let her get used to you, Mr. Fayette. Are you feeling better?"

"Better than what?" His lips curled back from those pallid gums. "Sit down, young lady. Would you like some coffee? Tea? What would the baby go for?"

"She loves grape juice. Orange, if there isn't any grape. I'll have the same."

He picked up the intercom and gave the order, then leaned back to regard them both with pale blue eyes. "So you made a producer. And my men drilled four dry holes—right across the river." He gave a rusty laugh. "Well, it's the old saying, isn't it? Oil is where you find it."

Unsure how to respond to his affability and certainly not trusting him, Melissa said cautiously, "I guess everyone's always thought there was oil on the place but it was never needed before."

He raised frizzy red eyebrows. "You mean that Vinnie, and Katie after her, preferred having the place beautiful to being millionaires?"

"When you have enough, what can you do with more?"

His laughter creaked again. "I don't know whether you Alastairs are stupid or smart. Doesn't matter." A maid brought a silver tray. He frowned at the orange juice served to Kitty in a punch cup, to Melissa in a crystal goblet. "Tell cook to keep grape juice on hand from now on," he instructed the maid.

"Yes, Mr. Fayette." The handsome black woman offered petits

fours and chilled grapes before setting down the tray and leaving at Bernard's nod.

Kitty adored grapes. She clutched all she could in her hand. When these were devoured, she ventured toward the tray, which was on a table near Bernard. Considering him gravely, she inquired, "Gwanpa like gwape?"

"Will you bring me some?"

Wresting them from the main stem, she collected a handful and fed squashed specimens one at a time into his mouth. "Poor Gwanpa," she said, lightly patting the bandaged arm. "Hurted."

She selected a petit four and offered it, then occupied a footstool beside him and alternated feeding him and herself till Melissa said, "That's enough for you, Kitty."

Kitty grabbed the last chocolate cake. Bernard laughed. "That's it, honey, they can't get it back once it's in your mouth. Grandpa will send some cakes and grapes home with you." He called the maid, who took the tray away but returned quickly with a basket she placed on a stand by the door.

Kitty toddled over to examine a bronze lion doorstop, declaring it a doggy. Bernard's face softened as he watched her; she must be very like Madge at that age, Melissa thought. In spite of his power, he hadn't been a lucky man—or a nice one, either; and Melissa watched him as she would a dangerous, if injured, wild animal.

His gaze swung to her. His mouth tightened. It was clear he liked her not a whit better than she liked him. That was good. It kept things honest. "If you're wondering about the judgment," she said, "we'll have a sizable check any day now, and that'll go directly to your business manager."

"Don't bother."

"What?"

He gave her a crooked grin. "The judgment only meant something when Johnny couldn't pay it."

Melissa pondered. "You mean you hoped it'd give you control of him? Give you the baby?"

"It might have if I hadn't been facing the whole bunch of you. Johnny was in a bad way after the fire. I could have gotten him if it hadn't been for you and Katie. But he'll do fine now and it's not in my best interest to be on bad terms with my granddaughter's father—or family."

"What does that mean?"

He looked at the child who was crooning over the lion-doggy. "Hell, that baby's all I've got. I want to have her visit—get her a pony, take her on trips when she's older. I want to be her grandpa."

"If things had gone the other way—if you'd gotten her some-how—would you have let us see her? Would you have let Katie be her grandma?"

He seemed to shrivel but there was dignity in the way he answered. "No. No, I wouldn't."

Melissa sighed. "Neither Johnny nor Katie would ever keep you from seeing Kitty as long as you didn't do anything that would be bad for her." Anger brimmed over and she gave him a furious stare. "You're lucky it's not me that has the say about it. I wouldn't be so generous."

He laughed outright. "Ah, Melissa! Why do you think I asked you to come today?"

"I guess even you didn't have the gall to ask Katie or Johnny."

Bernard shook his head. "Wrong, my indignant young friend. I haven't an ounce of shame. I know they're decent, kindly peo-ple." His tone made the praise a mockery. "I wasn't sure about you."

"And now you are?"

"You came, didn't you? You encouraged the child to treat me nicely."

"You're her grandfather. Whether I like it or not—and I don't."

"But you won't interfere with my plans to see her."

"I don't see what *I* have to do with it."

Bernard shook his head. "Let's not pretend. I don't suppose you've discussed it yet, and it may even be a year or two, but you'll marry Johnny."

Dumbstruck, Melissa blushed. She said, "I wish I were as sure of that as you seem to be."

"It'll happen." Bernard made a dismissing gesture. "You'll be Kitty's stepmother. It all comes down to your having control over what I plan with Kitty." His voice dropped and he watched her shrewdly. "I'm not worried now. You were raised by Katie and that raising took."

"Luckily for you."

He smiled.

Melissa got to her feet. "You're a wicked old shark and I'll never trust you. If you try to give Johnny any grief, I'll give you all I can. But if you behave, then of course you can have your fair time with Kitty."

Bernard eyed her with cynical amusement. "I guess I'll just have to behave, then, won't I? Don't forget the basket. Oh, I've instructed my lawyers to draw up a document forgiving the judgment."

"I won't say thank you. It should never have been awarded."

"You don't have to thank me. Just bring Kitty over when you have time. Or let me know when I can send someone for her."

"We'll do that." Melissa paused. She fought against saying it. She detested this man, yet oddly it was the truth. "I hope you're better soon."

Taking the basket in one hand and Kitty's hand in the other, she went down the hall of the mansion built on the foundations of that first Belleforest where Katie's mother had been her judge's right hand so many years ago.

"Isn't that wild?" Johnny said that evening when Melissa related everything, leaving out what Bernard had said about her and Johnny. "Of course, three million's nothing to Bernard, but I'm glad he finally has the sense to see he's got only one granddaughter. And a dandy one she is!"

He raised Kitty over his head and nuzzled her soft throat. She gurgled with delight. He put her in Katie's arms. "Would you read her a story and put her to bed? I want to take Melissa for a walk along the river."

Joy flooded Melissa like living light. She enfolded both Katie and the baby in her arms, kissed them both, and slipped her hand in Johnny's.

FROM THE NATIONAL BESTSELLING AUTHOR

LAURIE McBAIN

All the passions, adventure and romance of 18th century
England are woven into this bestselling trilogy that
captured the hearts of over 4 million readers.

MOONSTRUCK MADNESS, Book One
75994-2/$3.95US/$4.95Can
CHANCE THE WINDS OF FORTUNE, Book Two
79756-9/$3.95US/$4.95Can
DARK BEFORE THE RISING SUN, Book Three
78848-4/$3.95US

More spellbinding stories

WILD BELLS TO THE WILD SKY
87387-7/$3.95US/$4.75Can
DEVIL'S DESIRE 00295-7/$3.95US
TEARS OF GOLD 41475-9/$3.95US

And her newest bestseller

WHEN THE SPLENDOR FALLS
89826-8/$3.95US/$4.95Can

A powerful novel of unquenchable passions, of two mighty
families swept by the raging winds of war to a destiny
where only love can triumph!